PRAISE FOR CAROLE NELSON DOUGLAS and the MIDNIGHT LOUIE series

"If it's murder, it must be Midnight Louie time . . . CAT ON A BLUE MONDAY is a veritable feast for connoisseurs of sparkling wit, engaging characterizations and imaginative invention. It's no mystery at all why this remarkable author's audience grows by leaps and bounds with every new book."
—*R*A*V*E Reviews*

"Douglas is on a roll! CATNAP features two of the most lovable characters you'd ever want to meet: public relations expert Temple Barr, a petite redhead with a high heel shoe fetish, and the irrepressible Midnight Louie."
—Mostly Murder

"Carole Nelson Douglas is a genuine mystery star."
—*Mystery Scene*

"Carole Nelson Douglas is one of the first ladies of the mystery scene."
—*Romantic Times*

"Midnight Louie captured my imagination from the first page."
—Sandra Brown, *The New York Times* bestselling author of FRENCH SILK

"Carole Nelson Douglas is a master!"
—Jennifer Roberson, author of LADY OF THE FOREST

"Douglas has a fertile imagination."
es

"Carole Nelson Do S
—Amanda Quick

"Douglas is a maste t

Tor books by Carole Nelson Douglas

MYSTERY

IRENE ADLER ADVENTURES:

I. *Good Night, Mr. Holmes*
II. *Good Morning, Irene*
III. *Irene at Large*
IV. *Irene's Last Waltz*

MIDNIGHT LOUIE MYSTERIES:

I. *Catnap*
II. *Pussyfoot*
III. *Cat on a Blue Monday*

HISTORICAL ROMANCE

*Amberleigh**
*Lady Rogue**
Fair Wind, Fiery Star

SCIENCE FICTION

I. *Probe**
II. *Counterprobe**

FANTASY

TALISWOMAN:

I. *Cup of Clay*
II. *Seed Upon the Wind*

SWORD AND CIRCLET:

I. *Keepers of Edanvant*
II. *Heir of Rengarth*
III. *Seven of Swords*

*also mystery

CAT ON A BLUE MONDAY

CAROLE NELSON DOUGLAS

FORGE®

A TOM DOHERTY ASSOCIATES BOOK
NEW YORK

CAT ON A BLUE MONDAY

Cover art by Joe DeVito

A Tor Book
Published by Tom Doherty Associates, Inc.
175 Fifth Avenue
New York, N.Y. 10010

TOR® is a registered trademark of Tom Doherty Associates, Inc.

ISBN: 0-812-53441-7
Library of Congress Catalog Card Number: 94-2342

First edition: May 1994
First mass market edition: December 1994

Printed in the United States of America

0 9 8 7 6 5 4 3

For the real and original Midnight Louie:
nine lives were not enough

Contents

CAT ON A BLUE MONDAY

Chapter 1

Louie's Dog-day Afternoon

I like nothing better than playing the role of Sage in the Shade.

I am well suited to the part, particularly when I tuck my four limbs underneath me—I am the agile type, and double-jointed to boot. Then I let my limeade-green eyes narrow to inscrutable and attractively tilted slits. Just give me a Number One Son and a sackful of fortune-cookie sayings and on a clear day I'll find Judge Crater, or maybe even Jersey Joe Jackson.

So here I am, on a dog-day afternoon in August, lounging in the shade of the calla lily stand behind the Circle Ritz condominiums, doing what comes naturally: watching others work while I snooze.

My delightful roommate, Miss Temple Barr, is occupied by the pool with Mr. Matt Devine. For once, these two are sensible enough to stand in the shadow of the lone palm tree that dusts the ocean-blue Las Vegas sky while clouds swirl above like schools of succulent albino carp.

In fact, this pair is sensibly attired in what look like dust sheets you put on unwanted furniture in abandoned houses, possibly haunted. Normally my little doll takes care of her innate stature problem by balancing on three-inch heels, but today she is—for the first time in my acquaintance with her—out of doors and barefoot.

She does not act happy about this fact, moving her weight from one narrow tootsie to the other until she reminds me of those shilly-shallying hot-pink neon birds perched atop the front of the Flamingo Hilton like an avian chorus line. I must admit that I prefer a short woman. She has less far to stoop to extend affectionate greetings and thus does it more frequently. Also, being petite, she is less inclined to try to do what I abhor: pick me up. I am not your run-of-the-mill pickup. As for Miss Temple Barr, she finds her own lack of stature a shortcoming, so to speak. Me, I say you see a lot more interesting things closer to the ground and can smell out a rat—human or literal—in no time flat. Why do you think Sherlock Holmes was always scrabbling around on his hands and knees looking for clues? Trying to overcome his height handicap, of course, not to mention a genetic predisposition to insufficiency of the sniffer.

Right now the ground at Miss Temple and Mr. Matt's end of the pool is not good clue territory, being covered by thick mats, which in turn are covered in an irritatingly bright blue vinyl. I can smell the chemical perfume of pure plastic from here.

Obviously, Mr. Matt Devine is about to give Miss Temple Barr a lesson in the ancient and oriental arts of self-defense.

This I cannot object to, despite the sloppy dress code and the vinyl mattresses defacing my view and foiling my olfactory skills. My little doll could use some beefing up in the self-confidence concession.

Because of the intimate relationship I share with Miss

Temple Barr, I have seen her sit bold upright in the night, ever since two dudes with ball bearings for knuckles did a number on her in the Goliath Hotel parking ramp a couple of weeks ago.

As I say, I will be snoozing with my usual concentration when she will lift up from the bed linens like a corpse about to take an unauthorized stroll in a horror movie. I awake at the slightest disturbance of the sheets, and cannot recline on wrinkles, being as sensitive in this regard as a princess to a pea.

At such times, I smell the slight tang of human sweat, which overpowers even the English lavender-scented dusting powder Miss Temple uses after her bath. (Unlike superior species, she must actually immerse herself in large quantities of water to keep clean; hence the need for powder afterward, so her clothes do not stick to her skin. I am a practicing nudist myself, and have never heard any complaints, especially from discriminating ladies of my kind—and others.)

"Oh, Louie," Miss Temple Barr will say a moment after jerking out of her slumber. She sounds glad to see me there, which she should be. When it comes to protection, I am nothing to sneeze at.

She curls her lacquered claws into the roll of muscle at the back of my neck, which has me positively purring. Unlike a lot of ladies these benighted days, Miss Temple Barr has long, strong nails that she does not hesitate to paint in a carnivorous red color. This is not the least of her attractions for me, although her equal propensity for being up to her matching lipstick in crime and punishment is also encouraging. I love a mystery almost as much as I do a massage.

In fact, my own set of claws came in handy in apprehending the Stripper Killer at the Goliath Hotel Rhinestone G-string Contest—incidentally saving my little doll from a dreaded death-by-Spandex.

A small *Las Vegas Scoop* item in Crawford Buchanan's Broadside column described my latest foray into criminal apprehension—the criminal being the one who was apprehensive, not me. As usual, Buchanan put my feat in the most degrading light:

"An alley cat around Las Vegas leaped into literal action last Friday when the Goliath Hotel serial Stripper Strangler went after local PR flack Temple Barr. The cat, an overweight, solid-black layabout named Midnight Louie, fell from atop a costume cabinet where it was sleeping just as the Strangler was about to tie the luscious Miss Barr's neck into a double-Windsor knot. The sleeping puss proved unlucky for the killer when its claws, extended during the plunge, accidentally raked the perp. Talk about a timely pussy foot. Must have been Friday the Thirteenth somewhere."

Crawford Buchanan can mangle the truth faster than the Goliath killer could strangle a stripper. My plunging to the rescue of my delightful roommate was no accident: I was buying time until Lieutenant C.R. Molina could rush in with the cavalry from down the hall.

Of course, I am used to feats of derring-do, thanks to my back-alley days, now long behind me. Miss Temple Barr, on the other hand, is a tiny thing, though spirited. I fear that the shock of a severe beating followed by the Attack of the Stripper Strangler would make even the heroine of a Roger Corman movie a trifle overwrought.

She now keeps a flashlight beside her bed. This is a sinister implement, sheathed in a black, rubbery material, that would serve well as a weapon in addition to lighting up the darkness. It also stinks. If only human attackers were as sensitive to smell as I am, they would be knocked out.

Every time my little doll has one of these midnight misadventures, she performs the same routine. First she sinks her fingers into my warm fur, if I am there, which I usually am these days—or nights, rather. I do have an escape clause: the open bathroom window. Miss Temple Barr's rooms are on the third floor and the window is small, so no felon larger than a midget is able to enter, although I can both enter and exit with the ease of a garter snake. Nowadays the domestic life suits my more laid-back style. I rarely take a nighttime stroll unless I have business of a crime-fighting or personal nature abroad.

Anyway, Miss Temple takes up her high-tech flashlight and I see the back of her Garfield T-shirt as she makes a tour of the premises, particularly of the French doors leading to the patio.

She returns, often with a granola cookie. This I keep strictly between herself and me: a lady's nighttime habits are no one's business but her own. I must admit that I do not relish crumbs in the bed, especially when they are the sort I do not personally find consumable, but I understand my little doll's need for comfort after her attack, and at least she has not yet imported any crumbs of another sort entirely to her—and my—queen-size bed. There is only one King of the Hill here and the name is Midnight Louie.

Of course, it is because of a dude before my time that Miss Temple was so rudely interrogated by the pair of hoods in the Goliath garage. His name at least I approve of: the Mystifying Max. His game was okay also: magician. What was wrong with him was that he vanished—permanently, and without bothering to tell Miss Temple. I would not do such a thing to a little doll like her unless I was roadkill, which I fear is one of the theories that is bothering my lovely roommate about her missing ex-significant other.

To tell the truth and speaking from my own experience around here, I cannot understand why any dude in his right mind would walk out on Miss Temple Barr, who has hardly any faults except for her addiction to certain health foods, including a preparation called Free-to-be-Feline. That is her only lapse in taste, and the Mystifying Max could have put up with it. After all, he did not have to eat anything worse than granola. I have managed to ignore the Free-to-be-Feline for nearly a month now, with the result that I am getting a superb class of delicacies ladled over the top as a temptation: smoked oysters, baby shrimp in creole sauce and other appetizers that add up to a full-meal deal, as they say on the television.

Perhaps there is one tiny incident I am not fond of, although it is understandable. After the attack on Miss Temple, her helpful neighbor, Mr. Matt Devine, stayed the night. I hung around long enough to see him ensconced on the living-room hideabed; then I comforted my little doll in the bedroom until she drifted off to a Tylenol-3 sleep before I skedaddled on errands of an investigative nature. All right, in this particular case I had a personal interest—my lost ladylove, the Divine Yvette, had witnessed the first stripper murder.

All that is history as I sit here drowsing, humming along with the bees circling the calla lilies. The Goliath killer is in an institution for the criminally insane; and I am the victim of a criminally frustrated romantic entanglement. The Divine Yvette has returned to Malibu with her mistress, a so-called actress named Savannah Ashleigh.

The future holds nothing more for me than bittersweet memories and the sour breath of the lonely alleyways I tread. Speaking of which, I should cruise by the Crystal Phoenix Hotel and see if they have replaced the carp in the decorative pond. Last time I went by there, a sudden population drop occurred, and Chef Song, who keeps the pond stocked, could be heard hurling Chinese curses to high heaven.

But he is an optimist, and almost as fond of carp as I am. I am sure that a new batch is frisking in the sunlight and bobbing near the surface, looking for tidbits from tourists. At the least, I will be able to snatch what looks like some fallen Tender Vittles, which is what these fat fish eat.

Sufficiently stimulated by my imagination to move, I do a slick fade into the calla lilies before you can say "Charlie Chan."

Chapter 2

Nancy Ninja Strikes Again

"Where's Louie?" Temple stared toward the calla lilies' red-and-yellow blooms bright against large green leaves. "He was there just a minute ago."

"Probably got bored by how long it was taking us to get going," Matt said pointedly. "I thought you didn't want any witnesses."

"Right. I'm still not sure I'm cut out for this." Temple savagely jerked her waistline sash tight. "I feel like Dopey the Dwarf in this outfit."

She stared down at herself drowning in loose, white cotton pajamas she wouldn't have worn to a junior-high slumber party.

The most disconcerting sight was her bare feet, flour-white against the blindingly blue-vinyl mat they both stood on. Matt's feet were lightly tanned, at least, and therefore interesting instead of pasty. Of course, Temple found everything about tall, blond and handsome Matt Devine interesting, darn it. Matt remained oblivious to all but his lesson.

"This outfit is called a 'gi'," he said, pronouncing the word with a hard "g."

Gee, Temple thought. Okay. She plucked unhappily at a gigantic sleeve.

"You'll get used to it," Matt said, "and it shouldn't feel too big. I got a child's size, after all."

Temple watched his warm brown eyes grow dismayed as he realized that his intended reassurance had gone right for a sore spot with Temple: her height, or—more precisely—the lack thereof.

She shrugged fabric-swaddled arms, not used to making a hissing rustle with her every move. "Great. Teach *Shirley* Temple to do this, then; not me. She'd probably even sing something."

"This won't be so bad. I'm not going to give you chapter and verse of any particular discipline, just some tricks that you can use if anyone attacks you again. Jack Ree showed me the short-form women's defense stuff. Anyone can do it."

Temple eyed Matt, who looked as right in his gi as Robert Redford would, if ever RR would descend to doing a martial-arts movie. Maybe Matt's light tan and sun-gilded hair made his gi look less like a flour sack with a rubber band in the middle.

"I still don't know if I want to do it," she said. "I've never been good at athletic things. Balls always went over my head and team captains always picked me last."

"That's the beauty of the martial arts," Matt insisted with an enthusiast's seriousness. "They all grew out of the peasants' need to defend themselves without the weapons the nobility took for granted. And Asians are a small people; any martial art is based on discipline and skill, not on size and brute force."

The last two words made Temple wince in memory. "Those two guys were brute force, all right, up close and personal."

Matt stepped nearer and lowered his voice. "Are you going to group?"

"Going to group! That's so California, Matthew." Temple looked up at Matt in the shade. This was definitely one way to get closer to Matt Devine, and she certainly wanted to do that, didn't she?

"Group therapy is not exclusive to California, and my name isn't short for Matthew." He sounded a little stiff, even a little miffed. Temple's surprised silence forced a further revelation. "My name is . . . Matthias."

"Oh." Matthias was an odd name; was that why it bothered him? Temple decided to move past the issue. "It still shortens to 'Matt.' And couldn't I see a counselor solo?"

"Sure." Matt relaxed into his usual good humor once back on neutral ground. "But then you wouldn't hear the stories of people who've been through the same thing as you have."

"Most of them haven't." Matt's smooth face roughened as he began to object. "I know they've been attacked," Temple said quickly, "but by muggers or husbands and significant others, however nasty. How many other people in 'group' are going to have to confess to getting creamed by a couple of professional thugs intent on beating information out of them? They won't believe me. In fact, I have a hard time believing me."

Matt's smile was rueful. "I've never known anyone who was so outright embarrassed at being the target of a crime, but I'll bet there are a couple just like you in that group-therapy session. That's why you need to put your own experience in perspective. And this is an all-women's group."

"I'll look like a crybaby compared to people who've been really abused. Rape victims—"

"Survivors," Matt corrected. "We're trying to get away from reinforcing the victim feeling. You're a survivor."

"Survivor. I guess if I can survive interrogations by Lieutenant Molina, I can survive playing Teenage Mutant Ninja Turtle with you. Okay, Counselor. I'm ready. Let the games begin."

Matt's manner became all business, as if a screw at the top of his head had tightened. Temple, still sheepish about what she was trying to do and the costume she had to wear to do it, realized that the martial arts were serious stuff to him.

"First," he said, "are you pretty much recovered physically? No sore spots?"

Temple nodded. "Amazingly recovered. I can see how abused women keep hoping the abuse will stop."

"You don't have any old injuries, say, from high school? A broken wrist or anything?"

Temple shook out her arms in the long sleeves. "Not yet."

"You won't break anything here. That's why the pads. You said you weren't athletic in school. What about at home, in your family? Did you have any brothers and sisters to tussle with?"

"Not in the physical way." Temple let her head wag from side to side in resignation. "You sound like Molina during an interrogation. Yes, Officer, I had brothers and sisters; two each. And, no, we didn't go at it much, for fun or for fury, because I was—naturally—the youngest. And the littlest. With eight years between me and the next youngest, obviously my siblings were too grown-up to have much to do with me—other than providing endless icky clothes to hand down."

"So you were almost an only child; that's interesting."

"To a counselor, maybe. To me, no. You know how they say parents overcontrol the first child and loosen up for the later ones? Well, I was such a tail on the dragon that my parents got neurotic all over again. In fact, my brothers and sisters all joined in, when they weren't bequeathing me clothing in lousy taste. Everybody knew what was best for me, except me."

"Sounds like you were the apple of the whole family's eye."

"Yup. My father called me 'Ladybug' till I left home. And when I flew away *from* home and left Minneapolis with Max—they went ballistic."

"They sound a little smothering. Try to direct your frustration with your family into what we're doing here. Redirect the irritation into action. And remember, I'm not going into the 'Kung Fu' mystical stuff. These are just some moves you can use to get an attacker off balance."

"Will I be able to throw you over my shoulder?"

"Eventually," he promised with a smile.

She sighed, looked around again for witnesses, found none, then grimaced. "Just don't call me 'Grasshopper.' "

Temple padded barefoot into the Circle Ritz and up to her apartment. She hated to "pad." It made her feel like a child who'd gotten out of bed to ask for a glass of water, like she had to ask permission of someone for whatever she wanted.

Matt had been right. She was more deeply irritated by her family's overprotectiveness than she knew. When she drew on that ancient annoyance, pretending to be Nancy Ninja didn't feel so weird. Not that she'd get to the stage of tossing him that quickly.

In her bedroom she fought the fabric knot and won. Round One for the little lady in bare feet. When she shrugged off the—what was it, a uniform, a costume?—gi, the unfurling fabric released the scent of her own sweat, faint and pleasantly pungent rather than reeking.

Temple changed into aqua knit shorts and top, then slid her bare feet into cork-soled wedgies two-and-a-half-inches high at the heel. Did she feel more self-confident—any more vindicated, or vindictive? Had she made a breakthrough in her slo-mo relationship with her attractive but elusive neighbor? Maybe.

She walked to the bedroom/office at the unit's other end, detouring through the kitchen to snag a glass of Ruby Red grapefruit juice. Visions of chopping a thug in the bridge of his nose with the hardened edge of one hand, then jamming the heel of the other hand under his nostrils so the presumably broken bridge bone would drive, splintering, into his brain, burned as gory-red in her head as the grapefruit juice in her hand.

Matt wasn't teaching her that maneuver, but she'd heard

of it. Maybe going through the motions now, learning the moves that she hadn't known when the two men had attacked her, would restore something they had taken. Maybe. At her desk, a pale-pink Post-it note with the group-therapy phone number stuck out from the top of her computer screen like an anemic tongue.

She ripped it off, then lifted the phone receiver and dialed. Maybe going through the motions of anything—even survival—wasn't enough.

Chapter 3

A Hiss in the Night

Midnight Louie was waiting for Matt Devine at the corner of the Strip and Charleston when he walked to work that evening.

Matt always walked to work. First and foremost, he didn't own a car; second, his job was to sit still and listen to whatever misery poured out over the phone lines from seven at night to three in the morning. Those were the hours that Las Vegas glistened at its most garish, when the most angst overflowed lowball glasses and lonely hotel rooms and human psyches.

Matt sometimes considered himself a silent butler, sweeping up the ashes of other people's lives.

"Hey, Louie," he said in greeting.

Not many black cats hung out in Las Vegas, which was a risky venue for a bad-luck symbol as old as superstition itself. Only one acted like he owned the place—any place he happened to be.

Of course Midnight Louie wasn't waiting for him. The cat was a roamer by nature and their paths had happened to cross this one time. Still, Louie must have recognized Matt, for he began trotting along behind him as if in search of a treat.

Matt glanced up at the cliffside of massive hotel facades set well back from the rush-hour Strip flowing with eight lanes of hot, semi-stalled metal. He spotted the relatively modest outline of the Crystal Phoenix, its neon spray of the legendary bird glowing faint against a still-sunwashed sky.

Matt turned down a street, appropriately named Shadow, into thinning crowds. Louie kept pace with a businesslike trot more common to dogs than to cats, but then, Louie was an uncommon cat. At least he seemed to think so.

"Temple will be worried to hear you were so far from home," Matt found himself telling the cat, as if it were a dog, as if people could really communicate with either species.

Matt was used to living alone. Having even a silent partner to talk to was a nice change.

Down the block, a modest shopping center crouched only blocks behind the Strip's high-profile glitz. Matt sometimes thought the Las Vegas Strip was a gigantic Hollywood set, that all the hotel fronts were hollow behind, propped up by long aluminum poles, and that the people streaming into the lavish facades disappeared into a Twilight Zone where everything that happened was one long Technicolor, computer-enhanced hallucination.

Where he was heading was no hallucination. A homemade sign reading "ConTact" covered what had been a dry cleaner's until eight months before.

Louie was still running with him. Behind them, the sun burned Matt's shoulders even as it slipped beneath the rocky eleven-thousand-foot facade of Charleston Peak and its neighboring mountains. Maybe they were delusions, too. The desert was famous for mirages.

Matt opened the door, felt the air-conditioned coolness hush out at him. Midnight Louie bent to sniff the threshold.

"Coming in?"

The cat stepped back, shook its foot, and remained outside.

"Got company?" Sheila glanced up from her phone niche.

"Just a cat." Matt let the vaguely smudged glass door close behind him on its slow automatic swing so like a sigh. Louie regarded him gravely through the glass, then turned and trotted away. "It belongs to one of my neighbors."

"He lets it roam this far?" Sheila sounded surprised.

"Temple doesn't have much to say about it. The cat adopted *her* and apparently is used to keeping his own hours."

Sheila slid him a glance at the mention of "her." Matt had seen that look a thousand times before, the quick speculation whenever he mentioned a woman. And how did Sheila know how far away he lived?

Sheila Pulanski. She had a master's in social work and a bland manner that did nothing to overcome a personality as dishwater-dull as her hair, her slightly pocked skin, her resigned, rain-puddle-gray eyes. Yet she still wanted to know what women Matt Devine knew, and how, and how many, and what "she"—or they—were to him.

Those assessing glances always disappointed him, made him tense in some ancient form of defense. Defense from what? Speculative glances? Women? Or just the damn predictability of it? He couldn't help what he looked like.

He went quickly to his own phone niche. Like all nonprofit hotlines, ConTact was an ever-needy organization. When a local high school donated part of an outmoded language-lab setup, the board of directors had jumped at it. So the office didn't look like much, no more than a boiler-room telephone sales operation, with each counselor drawing a chair up to a table sheltered by a three-sided barrier covered in white, sound-absorbent tiles drilled with ranks of small, dark holes.

Matt pulled his chair close to the table and lifted his headset off the aluminum hook jammed into one of the convenient holes. The soft, gray-foam pads settled on his ears like a comforting muffler. He was connected to the night again, to the anonymous callers, to the surge and fall of need all around him, all around everyone if they would only listen for the constant, surflike hiss of agony pulling back and hurling forward in endless conflict: *Help me. No, stay away! Just talk to me, please. No, don't tell me to leave, let go, escape, grow up, go to group. Help me.*

Matt found his lips quirked into the smile that he least liked, a resigned smile that tasted of spoiled milk. Temple, for all her spirit, had shown the same push-pull indecision this very afternoon: afraid to admit that she could be hurt; needing assurance that it wouldn't happen again. He tried to help—here, and there this afternoon—but he couldn't even help himself. Helping is another form of addiction, he reminded himself, only more socially acceptable than most. He ought to know; he'd made a career of it.

Sheila's silver-salted, wren-brown permanent bristled around the edge of the barrier. "We're it tonight. Two of the volunteers have some kind of flu."

He nodded. Six booths. Three employees. Three volunteers. Even the employees weren't paid much. Those in the helping professions aren't supposed to help themselves to much profit, unless they're slick society shrinks or corporate consultants.

Still, it was a lot more than he'd made at his last . . . job.

The phone rang. It, too, was donated, a humped, old-fashioned model in Crayola flesh-color that felt stickier than Silly Putty. As soon as Matt picked it up, he set the receiver on the makeshift rest of a horizontal Rolodex file. All the calls here went through the earphones, misery in stereo.

"Hel-hello?" The voice was elderly, anxious and female.

"ConTact," Matt said. "Can I help you?" His voice, he knew, was Bing Crosby smooth and reassuringly male. He was used to reassuring everyone except himself.

"I'm so worried."

"About what, Ma'am?" He hated using the hackneyed address, but there was either Miss or Ma'am for women.

"I finally had to do something."

He waited. Usually people who reached the brink and

actually dialed ConTact were like dam waters ready to overflow the concrete bunkers of convention that contained them. This woman still sounded uncertain, even regretful now.

"I . . . I don't mean to bother anybody. I just mind my business and live alone. But—"

"What's wrong?" he asked.

"They're walking around my house, trying to get in."

"Who?" Sharper.

"I don't know. They come a lot lately. I know they're there, though I don't keep a dog. I'm . . . afraid."

"Ma'am, if it's intruders you're worried about, you'd better call nine-eleven. Or I can do it for you. What's your address?"

"Not . . . really intruders. Someone. Something. Maybe the doctor is wrong, and I need a hearing aid. Maybe if I heard better, I'd know it was just the meter man."

He listened hard, to her and to the background, trying to gauge if anything might be truly wrong, if her voice would suddenly sharpen into a shriek as the call became a human drama in action and he still didn't have the address. . . .

"You can hear me just fine. Where do you live, Ma'am?"

A pause. "I'm not used to telling strangers that on the phone. Security, you know—"

"If someone is intruding, I need to know your address to send help."

"Yes, I know you do. But maybe no one is there. It's just that it's happened before. In the evening. I hear noises."

"What kind of noises?"

She was silent again, her obviously elderly voice stilled with fear and shame. Being old, being alone, made for a lot of fear, and then shame at the fact of that fear, Matt knew.

Still, he wasn't ready for her answer when it came.

"Hisses," she said at last, reluctantly. "Angry, seething hisses."

Chapter 4

Cat Burglar

It is a terrible thing to be laid off, even if it is only from a self-appointed position.

While everyone else is relieved that the stripper competition at the Goliath Hotel—and its murderous complications—is over, I find myself with mixed feelings. Perhaps my uncharacteristic malaise is caused by the Divine Yvette's departure, though it is unlike me to get down in the whiskers over a dame, no matter how heavenly.

Speaking of Devine, I am more than somewhat worried about our neighbor of that nomenclature. The Bard of Avon is almost as famous as Nostradamus for his rhyming couplets, and I recall something about "By the pricking of my thumbs, something wicked this way comes."

Now, I do not have these opposable appendages, although I understand that they are highly regarded in some circles. However, I have a most versatile appendage of my own, plus a full set of fairly agile digits at the end of all my limbs. I do okay. But if anything pricks when something wicked comes this way, it is the hair at the base of my tail, just where I cannot reach with anything, no matter how acrobatic I am, and I am a natural contortionist, among other things.

The base of my tail has been atwitter for two days, and something tells me that Mr. Matt Devine will need my services in not too long a time.

After seeing him to his place of employment, I decide it is not much to look at, although from Miss Temple Barr's reaction, Mr. Matt Devine definitely is. I will have to take her word on this, because folks of her kind all look alike to me, or at least fall into certain readily recognizable types.

This is a little game I play. Miss Temple Barr, for instance, strikes me as a sprightly Somali named Cinnamon. (Somalis are long-haired Abyssinians; besides a red-haired coat, they have a luxuriant foxy tail and are pretty foxy in other respects.) Mr. Matt Devine would be your cream Persian, pet rather than show quality. There is something effacing about Mr. Matt Devine that puzzles me. The Mystifying Max is not in the least effacing, though I have never met the dude except via the poster Miss Temple Barr used to keep on the inside of her closet door. He is without doubt a Burmese. (This is a most mysterious breed, with sleek, dark chocolate-brown hair and a hypnotic green gaze not dissimilar to my own.)

As for me, I am bits and pieces of the best of everything; the only proof positive of my superior—and haphazard—breeding is my divinely developed sense of curiosity. Right now that itch in arrears is running rampant. By the morning of the next day, my brain has gone full circle. I sit on the hot cement by the Circle Ritz pool—a momentary shock for certain unmentionable parts—and stare up at the pleasing, curved shape of this landmark so dear to my heart, or rather to my stomach. I can see Miss Temple Barr's third-floor terrace, its potted oleanders undulating leafy green fingers over the black wrought-iron railing rather like landlady Miss Electra Lark waving "toodle-oo."

Speaking of which, I stare farther up. Two floors above my not-so-humble abode is Miss Electra Lark's penthouse, with a similar, though larger, terrace. Certain mysterious noises have emanated from the landlady's premises since I consented to become Miss Temple's roommate two months ago. One can imagine how loud these bumps in the daytime—for I seldom hear them at night, which eliminates at least one theory, to Miss Electra Lark's credit—how loud these bumps must be to penetrate even my sensitive ears two floors below.

At least there is one mystery I can poke my nose into, and I intend to do it right now quite literally.

I bound to the ancient palm tree, whose curving trunk makes a long, gentle, beneficent arc over the Circle Ritz. Forward motion, as the football commentators call it, carries me up a bridge of super-tough bark, but these claws were made for climbing and that is what they are going to do. . . .

Momentum swings me down on a delicate palm frond. For a moment I sway perilously, so far aboveground than even my fabled four-point landing style will not save me. Then I leap into thin air and plummet safely onto the Circle Ritz roof, five stories above the Big Splat.

I perch for a while, and preen while catching my breath, then loft idly down to Miss Electra Lark's patio. This is the most dangerous part of the venture. Her patio is crammed with bushes snipped into familiar-looking silhouettes, no doubt by an obsessive-compulsive with a large collection of manicure scissors. I land revoltingly near one silhouette teased into the shape of a poodle fresh from the groomer.

Yet I have no time to waste in critiquing the topiary. I brush against the French doors, testing for an unlocked door. A low rattle as the portal bows to my superior force, not to mention my nineteen pounds, tells me that I have a prayer. I stretch up—far up. I am a long dude, as well as a bit long in the tooth, and my forepaw curls around the lever. Then I jerk, hard. The door springs ajar to my expert touch. I drop down to nose it open, sticking my puss into a room shrouded in shade, every miniblind drawn tighter than a miser's line of credit.

I push into the soft, cool dark, lulled by the hum of the air conditioner that reminds me of my dear, departed mama. The open door admits a bar of hot, bright light behind me. It slants across an array of funky furniture that would do a garage sale proud. It reveals dust motes and sofa legs and vases so ugly they should be put in jail. It bounces off the lurid green glow of a watching eye from under the opposite sofa.

Before I can do anything, my sharp ears flick at the sound of another door being opened, deep in the apartment's interior, by a key.

Chapter 5

Calling All Cats

"Wait here in the entry, dear. I'll find that paper in a minute."

"Won't you need light?" Temple called after Electra's vanishing figure, her forefinger poised on the light switch to the right of the double entry doors.

Around her, in the fun-house glimmer of Mylar vertical blinds that lined the semicircular space and shimmied in the slow turn of a lazy ceiling fan, icicle-slices of her own image vibrated in the dim light.

"No," came Electra's fruity voice from the shadowed depths of the penthouse. "It's right here."

Temple was seriously tempted anyway. Electra's rooms were always kept dim, and darn few people saw them. One flick of her forefinger and she would satisfy a portion of her curiosity—at least about everything within range.

She could always pretend she hadn't heard. Temple took the plunge.

Nothing happened. Whatever light the switch had once controlled was gone, perhaps replaced by the ceiling fan, whose control box was on the other side of the door. Temple looked up. No light attachment, either. Double darn.

So she stood politely waiting, trying to look innocent and wondering if her flick of the switch had turned on something else in the place—maybe a coffee maker, or an iron. Wouldn't it be her luck? And the minute she and Electra left, the accidentally turned-on item would start to burn down the whole Circle Ritz. Guilt was a terrible thing. Poor Raskolnikov. Maybe when Electra returned, she should just cave in and confess.

Temple edged back to the wall and flicked the switch to its up position just as Electra's sandal-shod feet shuffled over the parquet floors.

Dazzling light flooded the entry area, as narrow and glaring as a sky-sweeping spotlight.

"Oops! Sorry," Temple said. How did a light switch that was off in the up position go on after being turned off again?

"Argh!" Electra complained, bustling over to the switch in a muumuu almost as brilliant as the light. She switched the lever down and the glare vanished as obediently as one of the Mystifying Max's magical objects. "That's for dramatic effect, at night."

"Where is it coming from?" Temple squinted against the sudden darkness. Her eyes finally followed Electra's pointing finger to an up-light sitting on the floor.

In the room beyond the break in the blinds, something glimmered, marble-round and as lurid green as a laser beam. Temple heard a muffled thump as Electra took her firm upper arm in hand and ushered her from the penthouse.

Although the halls in the forty-year-old Circle Ritz building were not alleyways of illumination, the glow of wall sconces seemed daylight-bright compared to the secretive shadows in Electra's digs.

"I thought I saw—" Temple began.

"Oh, people are always thinking they see something in my place. It's all the junk I collect."

"I thought I heard—"

"This is an old building, dear, and the palm leaves scrape on the roof. Now here's the flyer. I bet you can do something with this."

"I bet not." Temple took the popsicle-pink sheet over to a wall sconce's pale light. First she had to dig her glasses out of the bronze tote bag over her shoulder before she could read the too-fine print. "Cat shows are as common as fleas, Electra. Every Civic Center in the country has 'em in alternating months. All the advance publicity you can get is a photo of a funny-looking cat in the paper, and any amateur could manage that. Besides, what can they pay me in? Cat litter? Louie almost never sullies his box at home."

"Not this show; it's not common," Electra insisted, coming over to point a pudgy finger at various blocks of information, which gave Temple a chance to admire her Black Grape nail polish with silver stars arranged in various arcane constellations.

"Look," Electra insisted, "this is the mother of all cat shows. Every recognized breed will be represented, even curly coated Rexes. And there's a costume show; that ought to be newsworthy."

"Cats in clothes? That's silly, Electra, and probably the Humane Society would have a thing or two to say about it."

"Not a meow. These breeders are fanatics about cat care. They wouldn't do anything harmful. In fact, it's quite the other way around."

"What do you mean?"

"Oh—" Electra reclaimed the flyer to stare at the obligatory facts of date, time and place. "My friend Cleo Kilpatrick, who raises Manx, says the Fancy Feline Club that's sponsoring this show has gotten some odd phone calls."

"Odd catcalls? Sounds like an ill-tempered audience. What kind of odd calls can a cat club get?"

"People calling up and . . . hissing. Or maybe it's real snakes. They can't tell."

"Someone is calling up a cat club and putting agitated snakes on the line?"

"Fascinating, isn't it? I thought you'd be intrigued."

"Intrigued! Why on earth would you want to involve me with these loonies?"

"Several of my friends are Fancy Feliners and they don't take these calls lightly. Lots of folks hate cats, for some reason, and these purebred cats are worth mucho money. The cat people are real worried."

For answer, Temple dug again in her tote bag. She finally pulled out a slim case, from which she deftly extracted a pale mauve card with her medium-long fingernails, which today were varnished a tasteful seashell pink.

"Read my card. It says 'Temple Barr, *P.R.*'—not '*P.I.*' "

Electra shrugged generous shoulders even more generously shrouded in a howling Hawaiian jungle print. "Maybe it's not a bad idea to broaden your job description, the way you keep running into murders."

"You sound like Matt."

"Speaking of Mr. Devine, I saw you two playing out by the pool—"

"Working out. Matt's teaching me the fundamentals of self-defense."

"How are you two getting along?"

"You're the one who should be the P.I., Electra. Just fine. Me student, he teacher. He taught me how to turn my wrist to break a handgrip and tried to talk me into thinking about how to push an attacker's eyes out."

"Yuck!" Electra's gray eyes, the only neutral thing about her, narrowed to revulsed slits. "That nice man knows ugly things like that?"

"Apparently we nice women should, too, if we're going to be safe on city streets. How about it? I promised Lindy I'd go over to Paradise and see the revamped Kitty City Club. Wanta go with me?"

Electra waved the pink sheet. "Trade-sies?"

Temple groaned. "Oh, all right. I'll contact the cat people; I feel like I'm in a forties' horror movie already. Call me an old-fashioned girl, but I hate going to a stripper joint alone."

"Whatsa matter?" Electra chuckled as she locked her double doors and stuffed the pink flyer into Temple's tote. "Afraid you'll get mistaken for one of the acts?"

Temple rolled her eyes. "Not likely. I'm afraid I'll get taken for having unnatural inclinations."

By then they had reached the elevator. Electra pushed the mother-of-pearl button. With a weary wheeze, the elderly car came creaking upward. Both women faced forward, contemplating the noises.

"I think making crank calls to a cat club is weirder than women going to a strip club," Electra said finally.

"Nowadays," Temple said, sashaying into the wood-paneled car first, "probably."

Broad daylight made no bones about the purpose of the building at Paradise and Twain: "Strip joint" was written all over it in the rude graffiti that covered the boxy, windowless, stucco exterior. An unlit neon sign loomed over the flat roof like scaffolding abandoned by da Vinci and ceded to Peter Maxx.

"New name," Electra noted, impressed.

"New female management," Temple said. " 'Les Girls.' I like it. Much classier than 'Kitty City.' "

"I can't imagine why that greasy Ike Wetzel agreed to sell after all his shenanigans to blackmail his old dancers and control the strippers' contest."

Temple glanced at Electra. In broad daylight there was no overlooking the silver hair worn in a modified Mohawk and streaked with stripes of royal blue to match the surreal palm leaves in her muumuu pattern.

"I doubt that Ike had much to say about it," Temple admitted. "The stripper murders brought up so much bad old business in his personal and professional life that Lindy was finally able to buy him out before someone drove him out. Let's go see what wonders worker-ownership can do for a strip club."

"Whatever," Electra said, "it takes major money to run a

place like this, however humble-looking. I don't see how a bunch of strippers managed it."

"Consortium, Electra, consortium of ecdysiasts," Temple corrected her in airy tones as they strolled into this showcase of female flesh. "You'll never make a P.R. person without the politically correct spin."

Dark as Hades. Still. Cold as an archangel's breath. Still. Loud as a den of drummers. Still.

Temple and Electra stopped at the chill dark inside the door, waiting for their eyes and their body temperature to adjust. Their ears were another matter. Rock music blared at concert pitch.

Temple leaned close to Electra. "Do you think it's a tad less loud?" she shrieked.

Electra nodded her two-toned head, her silver streaks painted a glowing lavender by the ultraviolet lights above the stage.

A cocktail waitress—pert, blond and attired in something unbelievably brief and interesting, even to other women, merely from a technical point of view, like "How does she get into it without dislocating anything essential?" and "Can you wash it in a teacup, really?"—ankled near enough to be perceived in the perpetual twilight.

According to the movement of her mouth, she was asking, "Drinks?"

"Lindy," Temple both mouthed and screamed back, hoping that was not the name of something new and trendy and alcoholic, like a Lindy Hop. Or a Lite beer, maybe?

A pert blond nod, and the two women were following a mostly unveiled rear to the front of the establishment.

Men, alone and in twos and threes, sat scattered at the tables. Now was the prenoon hour, a predictable dead zone in the stripper business. Lethargic girls gyrated at poles distributed atop the bar, fanning themselves with their ghostly Seven-Year-Itch skirts (literal knockoffs of Marilyn Monroe's white, circle-skirted, halter-top dress immortalized in the hot updraft of a sidewalk grating and the camera's icy, ogling eye). They left less to the imagination than Monroe had managed to do.

At a side table, Lindy Lukas was waiting, wrapped in a cigarette fog. Strip palaces and their habitués were not worried about such wimpish concerns as secondhand smoke.

"Sit down," Lindy pantomimed with proprietary gestures of both hand and mouth. She lifted a glass afloat with urine-colored liquid. Both Temple and Electra shook their heads.

Lindy stood, smiled, and beckoned them across the floor, past the raised stage where a woman wearing a scant collection of glitter-dusted rubber bands was writhing to the shrill promise of "She Works Hard For The Money."

In moments they had ducked through a curtained doorway—not the one used by performers to enter—and were able to shut a door behind it and find themselves in the plain-Jane women's john: two cubicles and a sink.

"Ooh," Electra said, now that conversation was possible despite the bass *thump-thump-thump* beyond the graffiti-decorated door. "That costume on stage looks as if it would *hurt!*"

"It doesn't if you're in shape," Lindy said cheerfully.

She herself was retired from stripping and had gone happily to overweight and jogging suits adorned with outrageous sayings. Today's was "Get It Up Before It Gets Up and Leaves."

Her dyed hair was as matte-black as the drugstore eyeliner choking her eyes into smoky slits. The cigarette rode her fingers like a favorite ring, fogging her voice with world-weary harshness. But her hazel eyes brimmed with excitement.

"Wait'll you see what we've done in the dressing room," she told them. "Don't ask any questions; just look."

She flourished another door open. Temple prepared herself for the long, dispirited alley of facing mirrors, furnitureless space, concrete floor studded with cigarette butts, and battered lockers at one end.

"Oh. This is nice." Electra edged over the green indoor-outdoor carpet like a pleasantly surprised realtor. "Very cozy."

"Look." Lindy waved her cigarette-bearing hand at one wall, a magician drawing smoke away from an illusion.

A sign-in board had blanks for each performer's name and hours. Another board held an array of combination locks for the lockers, unheard of in the stripping business, where privacy was a bad joke from beginning to end. A third board, labeled "Miscellany," held tacked-up plastic baggies filled with safety pins, Band-Aids, tampons, sample perfume vials, dark makeup for tan marks, light makeup for bruises, nail files, run-stop—everything the improperly attired stripper might need in a pinch.

"Neat." Temple studied the array, hunting ideas for her own travel kit-cum-tote bag. Then she looked down the once-naked facing countertops flanked by mirrors. Lightweight metal folding chairs painted in rainbow colors lined up along both sides, like would-be perches for Walt Disney butterflies.

"It could be any chorus girls' dressing room," Temple said in amazement, remembering the bus-station rest-room air that had haunted this dressing room the last time she'd seen it, when it was as if the women who used it were not worth a moment's convenience. Now no food stamps littered the floor like unused bus transfers. No dreary, gray functional pall draped everything like a spiderweb.

Lindy's beaming smile could only be called maternal. "You're right. Classy. Ike would have—" She glanced nervously at Electra's venerable silver hair.

"You remember 'Moll Philanders' from the Over-Sexty Division of the contest," Temple said. "Black leather and the silver Hesketh Vampire."

"—shit a brick." Lindy, though shocked, suddenly relaxed, studying the now-demure Electra. "Hey, that was some bitchin' number you did with that motorcycle."

"Thank you, dear," Electra said modestly. "Not everybody has to go undercover by uncovering, but I managed. This is very homey."

"Yeah, thanks." Lindy whirled back to Temple. "Oh, and did you notice the Midnight Louie shrine?"

"Louie? A shrine? He *would* be pleased. What do you mean?"

"Well, he nabbed the strangler, didn't he, with his own personal claws? We have only one unlocked locker, and it's all his."

She pointed. One of the repainted lockers—royal blue—stood ajar, its bottom lined in turquoise crushed velvet, the kind usually found on overstuffed sofas in seedy furniture stores near downtown bus stations.

Lindy bent to pull out two bowls from under the locker, then gesture with a nicotine pointer to the locker's top shelf. "A variety of food in case he shows up."

Temple trotted over on her high heels to eye the stacked cans with suspicion. "He really should be eating Free-to-be-Feline exclusively."

Lindy shrugged and straightened up with an impressive joint creak. "Let the poor dude live a little."

"But I don't understand. Why the royal treatment for Louie?"

"How do you think he nailed the Goliath killer? He was here that day; he must have spotted the perp then."

"What day?"

"The day you, that prissy protester and I came over here to see what a real club looked like. Afterward, one of the girls said she found a black cat slammed into one of the lockers. She let him out. He must have been stalking his suspect."

"I *thought* I saw a big black cat skedaddling as we left that day, but I figured Louie couldn't be way over here . . . though he does like chorus girls' dressing rooms, I hear."

"Anyway, we figured giving a locker to you would be kind of silly, and you wouldn't much care for the association, so we decided on the cat instead. And we like the company."

"He comes to visit?"

"Sure." Lindy tapped the top shelf. "This is primo cat crap; Doris got it with her food stamps."

Temple let her eyes roll. She could see the headline now: "Destitute Stripper Lives on Cat Food." Thus do tabloid rumors begin. And meanwhile, Louie was living it up in every dressing room in town. She turned to Electra.

"You should have seen this room before."

"Not nice, huh?"

Temple and Lindy nodded in grim tandem.

"Well, it's real cheery now," Electra pronounced. "Makes me want to roll the old Hesketh Vampire out of the shed and tune up 'Wild Thing.' "

"Hey," said Lindy, "you can do your act in my place anytime."

Electra managed a polite simper of demur, but she looked more pleased with herself than a woman of well over sixty should in a strip joint.

"So it's all your place now?" Temple asked.

"Me and the other girls—and our silent partners."

"Silent partners? They're not—"

"Nothing shady," Lindy said quickly. "Think we'd screw it up now after finally getting a club to run by ourselves? No way, Mae West! We found some guys with a little money and a lot of time to invest. They should be here by now. Come on, I want you to meet them."

Temple dragged the Plexiglas high heels of her black patent-leather Stuart Weitzman's as she followed Lindy and Electra back into the boom-box atmosphere beyond the ladies' john. She didn't want to meet the sort of men who back strip clubs, and certainly not while she was wearing patent leather shoes! Much as she supported these women taking some control over their lives—and livelihoods—she still suffered qualms of political correctness at the whole idea of strippers. She had glimpsed too much of the life's ugly underbelly of use and abuse during the stripper contest and the preceding murders to like it. Love the stripper, hate the strip.

Oh, joy. The piped-in music was momentarily mute. Quiet was an assault of another sort, that made the stripped-down, functional architecture of raised horseshoe stage and bar, tables and chairs, seem perverse, especially the brass firemen's poles shining here and there like something Faye Wray should be chained to.

A group of men sat at one of the big tables up front, right by the stage lip and overhead lights and sunken fans aimed to blow up hair and skirts—what there was of them.

Temple was shocked to recognize one of the men.

"Eightball?" She was even more shocked by how her voice rang out in the uncommon stillness.

"Eightball!" Electra roared with affection, descending on the slight old guy like a Hesketh Vampire, all silver and blue and raucous and revved up.

"How you been?" Electra asked, embracing him heartily. "Hey, Wild Blue, how goes the cloud chase?"

Another old gent nodded, and from where she hung back, Temple could still see how he got his nickname. Somehow he'd stolen Paul Newman's eyes, and maybe even Paul wasn't the gritty youngster he used to be in old movies.

The introductions were a flurry that left Temple aware of tan, seamed faces, of thin or absent-without-leave hair, of ears even bigger than Ross Perot's, of shy smiles and gnarled hands that gripped hers with surprising strength.

The names rolled by like a vaudeville cast: Eightball O'Rourke. Wild Blue Pike. Spuds Lonnigan—really! Pitchblende O'Hara, Cranky Ferguson. Another name came up. The Glory Hole Gang.

"Yeah," said Wild Blue, sitting, as they all did, after dragging chairs over for Temple, Electra and Lindy. Gentlemen of the Old School. "We run that ghost town out on Ninety-five. Glory Hole. We're the Glory Hole Gang."

"You *were* a private detective," Temple accused Eightball O'Rourke.

"Still am," he said. "And we still are a Glory Hole Gang. See, we accidentally made off with some old silver dollars after W.W. Two, and then we lost 'em—it's a long story. Someone found 'em a couple years ago. We ended up exonerated—a big word for a bunch of old guys—and our ghost town turned out to be a lucrative tourist attraction.

We had a little jingle in our pockets to invest, and Lord knows, we spent enough lonely decades in the desert to appreciate an oh-ay-sis of civilization like this."

Here they all chuckled in concert, while Temple tried to figure out what a "consortium" of battered and fiercely independent strippers had in common with a band of outlaws elderly enough to be their grandfathers. Maybe it was no earthly use for each other, and in that absence of malice lay safety and a well of regrets lost beyond retrieving.

"You," Temple said suddenly. "I've seen you before."

She was not addressing private-eye Eightball O'Rourke, whom she certainly had met—and employed—during the ABA murder and cat-snatching escapade.

The small man of fifty-something slid his straw fedora with the snappy madras-plaid hatband across the tabletop as if it were a shell in a street game before 'fessing up. "It wasn't here at Kitty City, where all these old guys play Walter Mitty."

"I know where it wasn't," Temple said, "but where was it? The Circle Ritz! You were feeding Midnight Louie pastrami!"

"Sure, I've been known to feed the kitty, at poker tables all over this city."

"Don't play coy with me. You're the one who brought news of Crawford Buchanan's heart attack. He's not one of the silent partners, is he?"

"What's with silence? Crawford wanted in. I just told him conflict of interest's a sin."

Temple eased back in her chair. "I'm glad somebody's willing to point out the straight and narrow to Buchanan. The club columnist for the *Las Vegas Scoop* has no business having a financial interest in any club." She eyed the man with a last suspicion. "Aren't you Crawford's bookie, and isn't your name Cosanostra or something?"

"Bookie I am, and that's no slam. But pardon me, Ma'am, it's Nostradamus," he answered with a small bow. "Glad to meet again the famous Circle Ritz's unsung shamus."

"You mean Midnight Louie, no doubt. After all, he's already got one 'shrine' in his honor."

"To the contrary, my dear Miss Barr. Louie's not half the sleuth you are."

"Charming." Electra directed a high-beam smile at the courtly bookie.

A motion behind the glass walls of the dj's booth indicated that the blessed silence was about to be cursed with cacophony again. Temple slapped her hands on the table.

"Nice meeting you all, but I must head back to the famous Circle Ritz." She eyed Electra. "I've got to call a woman about a cat show. Coming?"

"You toddle on without me, dear." Electra's silver-starred nails made like comets as they waved her away. "I'll, uh, stick around with the guys for a while."

"But I'm taking the car."

"That's okay. I'll hitch a ride with the boys. You must have some sort of wheels, right?" Her glance interrogated the circle of oldsters, who nodded as if they'd never heard of restricted licenses.

"I can always take you for a spin in my biplane," Wild Blue offered with a grin. "Out to Lost Camel rock."

This last reference caused everyone to laugh, leaving Temple in the dark. Must be a notorious Lover's Lane for the over-sixty set she thought. Probably they all parked out there and played Lawrence Welk tapes on their car audio systems and picked their false teeth in four-four time. On the other hand, given the way age stereotypes were collapsing nowadays, who could say what the zesty set was up to? Probably a lot more than she was these days.

The sound system kicked in with brass, spit and no polish. Temple backed away from the companionable table—folks looking at each other instead of the stage, imagine that—waved good-bye to Lindy, and made fast tracks for the door. This was one time she couldn't hear the committed clip of her high heels.

Outside, in the glaring sunshine, a prickly wave of loneliness flooded her. Nothing to do but go back to an empty apartment and call a woman she didn't know about something she didn't want to know about: a rinky-dink cat show and callers that hiss in the night. No rendezvous with the long-gone Max to contemplate, no one she loved waiting in the apartment she loved. Even Midnight Louie had vanished for the day on some feline mission or other.

Was Matt right? she wondered as she clicked toward the Storm's sleek metallic aqua sides, though not even that jaunty sight could lift her sudden malaise. Was she getting hooked on the odd nearby murder now that Max was out of her life? Did she crave the excitement of a crime fix? Did she *like* being the target of crazed murderers and homicide Lieutenant Molina's unending skepticism?

Or did she just have an uncanny talent for landing dead center of the scene of the crime?

She unlocked the Storm and gingerly pulled open the hot metal latch. Inside, the car was a shell of sweltering plastic surfaces and a genuine-fabric hot seat.

Temple stared at the collapsible cardboard shading her windshield: the Pink Panther in full feline stalk on both sides, coming and going. Somehow, a cat show couldn't compete with the five-course exhilaration of the American Booksellers Convention and a stripper's competition, both with a generous helping of murder on the side.

Who'd want to kill a cat other than some deranged pit bull?

Chapter 6

Bad Karma

I cannot say that I am relieved when Miss Temple Barr and Miss Electra Lark exit arguing into the hall, leaving me in the penthouse, in the dark.

For one thing, my legendary skills at seeing in the dark are more than somewhat exaggerated. I am not one to pooh-pooh the notion that I possess heroic powers, but I must admit that there is enough wall-to-wall whatsitz in these rooms to make me long for my look-alike, the black cat with the Eveready flashlight batteries. I could use some technological assistance.

Not having any at the moment, I opt for the next best thing: a bright idea. I jump up on a table studded with knickknacks, managing to land—by some miracle—straddling two scorpion paperweights and a lava lamp cord. Once at window height, I paw among the miniblinds until I have bent a couple out of shape. A boomerang-shaped sliver of daylight slices the dimness like a machete.

I turn and regard all that I can see: the room I occupy, which appears to be accoutered for dining, and portions of adjacent spaces. Opposite me is the familiar dead gaze of a television screen on empty—only this one is inset into a blond box I have never seen the likes of before. And atop the television case sits a large green glass ball, held aloft by a sculpture that resembles a conga line of cockroaches.

I breath a sigh of relief. Yes, even Midnight Louie has his anxieties. I was worried about meeting some megasize dude on his own territory, without a clue, in the dark. But now I spy the faint reflection off other glass balls here and there and realize that Miss Electra Lark is merely partial to shiny globelike objects, rather than keeping a secret menagerie of dogs—or, worse, demons.

I arch athletically down to the floor. Actually, it would have been an athletic arch had the lava lamp cord not snagged in my foot. I resemble an arch myself—just call my maneuver the St. Louie Arch—as I twist in midair to extricate myself. Naturally, I do, barely pulling the lamp along the table more than three inches, and pounce lightly to tepid parquet.

Now that I am safely ensconced and at my leisure, and have a windowslit to see by, I decide to take a peek around. Obviously, Miss Electra Lark is a collector of sorts, and I am always interested in what people stock up on. Miss Electra Lark seems to have a taste for furniture styles that I have not seen since visiting the Ghost Suite at the Crystal Phoenix, which dates—untouched—from the 1940s. I writhe in and out among various overstuffed pieces attired in fabric patterns so loud they sing the "Hallelujah Chorus."

Ceramic ashtrays almost as noisy squat on every tabletop, some with rhinestones embedded in their free-form shapes. Bauhaus this is not. A pole lamp upholds a corner of the room, its various light bulbs wearing shades of maroon, forest green and chartreuse. This last chartreuse is an attractive color when it is on little green apples and in the eyes of a lovely lady of the feline persuasion, but on lamps it is a disaster.

I settle down in the middle of the room under a chrome dinette set whose chairs are upholstered in pearlized gray *plastic* while I mop my fevered brow. Actually, my brow cannot get fevered, since dudes of my ilk do not sweat, even under the most extreme pressure. But I am certain that I can get brain fever, at least, from exposure to such assertive furnishings. No wonder Miss Electra Lark does not want anybody to see her place; I would not either, if I lived in a vintage junkyard . . . come to think of it, at times (bad times), I have.

At least that baleful slime-green eye is not upon me anymore. It must have been a reflection of the lava lamp in a chrome chair leg or one of the dozens of crystal balls scattered around the joint.

I tidy my whiskers, which look best when they are a snappy pure white against my best black suitcoat, and make sure my tail has not snagged any dust that I may have inadvertently picked up on my unexpected slide across the tabletop. Midnight Louie does not descend to domestic duties, even by accident. The word "house," when attached to the word "work" or "cat," is not in my vocabulary, no more than that most obscene of terms, "pet."

I am gazing about the premises, wondering where to wander next, when I spot another orb of green, this one near floor level. No doubt this is the eternal gleam of some common household machine, such as a VCR, to show that it is on and ready to perform at the flick of a button, unlike myself.

On the other hand, it could be the eye of some uncommon household familiar, and given Miss Electra Lark's apparent fondness for the trappings of the occult, my speculations could run riot.

In fact, the more I think of it, *I* could run riot. There are more things on heaven and earth, Horatio, than I care to meet in either place, or even dream of.

I pinch myself to make sure I am not in La-La-Bye Land. Sure enough, I draw blood. I have no alternative but to face off this unknown entity. I do not know the layout well enough to run, and would have to turn my back to the room while working on the French door lever. I do not intend to die with one paw jammed on a piece of foreign hardware.

What is up? I growl in a low, surly tone. I do not care to ask "Who is there?" just in case the eye I spy does not belong to a Who, but a What. No point in irritating a genuine What by miscalling it a Who, I figure.

My agile mind casts back on all the one-eyed beings of my acquaintance, either first- or secondhand, including a few nasty deities from times gone by I have heard of. I mutter a plea for protection to Bast and shimmy forward on my belly over the smooth parquet floor.

I am as soft and slow-flowing as licorice syrup. Before you know it, I am up against a sofa covered in cocoa-colored nubs interwoven with gold fibers. A cocoa-satin fringe undulates at my eye level, playing peekaboo with the one-eyed Jack, Jill or jinn lurking beneath the terminally ugly sofa. Could this be Veronica Lake's ghost I see? I am open to any possibility.

Now is the time to make my move. I thrust my puss past the fringe, my whiskers twitching at this unpleasant contact. I repeat my interrogatory growl in a deeper tone of voice. I lash my tail back and forth behind me. I sneeze at the myasthma of dust that rises both fore and aft, thanks to my own efforts.

In the instant my vigilant eyes squeeze shut during my involuntary spasm of reaction, something shifts. I am now staring into *two* hellish green gleams about an inch apart. Either Miss Electra Lark's VCR likes to hide under the couch and comes with dual warning lights, or something living is facing me.

"House security," I growl in my most Dobermanish voice. "Come out of there with your ears down and your mouth shut."

I hear no accommodating slither. Instead, I hear a low, soft "No."

This is not a literal "no," of course, but the message is unmistakable. I do not waste time arguing. I withdraw, then approach the sofa end. Taking a power stance, I dash at the arm with all of my nineteen pounds of macho might. The sofa lurches a few inches over the smooth wooden floor. Your average dude would not be able to do this, and I do not recommend trying this in your own home. It tends to aggravate the owners.

But this is an emergency. Consider it a form of pest removal, even if the so-called pest could be a demonic being. I am not deterred. I rear back and launch my unbridled weight again. A screech of wood sofa legs on wood floor, an indignant and unearthly echoing yowl from beneath the sofa and—mission accomplished.

The lurker has ceased and desisted. I am now confronted by a spectral aura of bristling gold and silver. From the center of a dark face mask, two brilliant, perfectly round green eyes glare at me like twin earths if I were seeing double on the moon.

I have faced down many an evil eye in my day—feline, canine, human, even reptilian. I am not intimidated by the bigger, the meaner, the smarter or the sneakier. But now I have met my match. Never before have I encountered a stare of this magnitude, like indigo ice. I gulp and gather myself, not sure whether my best bet is to offer attack—or apology.

Even as I dither, which is most unlike me, an unseen wind lifts the aura that surrounds the surreal peepers. Something pushes me in the chest, hard. The next thing I know, I am head over tail by the pole lamp, which has kicked on at the impact. Six pools of relentless light pour down on my groggy form like interrogation-room lights from a Cagney gangster movie.

The eyes and the aura are stalking over to me on unnervingly noiseless feet. Four of them, I am alert enough to notice. That eliminates vegetable and mineral. But what kind of animal is this?

"How did you do that?" I gasp, untangling my various extremities.

"Karma," says the creature, stopping a whisker's breadth away.

I still cannot tear my gaze from the awful indigo eyes, though I notice that for all their unnatural roundness, they have a slight tilt. Could this bozo be a bozette?

"Karma," I repeat, wondering if it is some exotic form of martial art. I will have to observe Mr. Matt Devine's lessons with a more studious eye from now on. "You did not lay a glove on me," I add with a growl.

The low trill that comes from under the dark mask around the eyes is mocking. If I did not know better, I would describe it as a laugh, but demons do not laugh.

"I do wear gloves," my assailant points out in a deep, throaty voice that is oddly Tallulah. It waves two white fore extremities.

The silver-and-gold aura is settling down into a glimmering robe of soft fur. Flattened dark ears perk above the unblinking eyes. I realize, amazed, that I am staring at one of my own ilk, though I have never seen the like before.

"Karma," I repeat, for lack of any stimulating repartee. I am not often off balance, but at the moment, my brain is screaming "Tilt!" like a broken pinball machine.

"That is my name," the creature says. "Yours is Midnight Louie." And it looks me over with a familiar stare.

"I cannot claim the honor of *your* acquaintance."

"To my honor and your loss. I am . . . aware of your doings."

I do not like the superior tone that is drenching me, so I struggle to a dignified seated position while I secretly check my physique for damage. "Just who—or what—are you?"

"I am a resident of these rooms."

"So you say you live here." I am getting my bearings

now and use my best Lieutenant Molina snarl. "How come I never heard of you?"

"You have *heard* me," it answers with a hoity-toity smirk.

I narrow my eyes to their most laserlike green slits. "*You* are responsible for those strange noises I hear two floors down in Miss Temple Barr's unit now and again."

"You have good . . . ears," it concedes, and in that moment I recognize it for a she rather than a he. A He would have been trying to pin back my ears by now, with me at such a disadvantage. A She would stroll around and rub in the indignity.

"Just what kind of critter are you?" I ask.

"You mean my breed, or my nature?"

"They are the same thing."

"Only to the uninquiring."

"Listen, lady, I got as much curiosity as the next dude. Are you going to keep on making like a sphinx, or what?"

The brilliant baby-blues blink. Slowly, like the shutter on a very expensive camera. I can almost hear the mechanical snick as they slide apart and the motionless, blue-marble eyes fix on me.

"I was born a Birman," she says, as if she has transfigured into something else since then. Yeah, sure.

"Birman," I repeat, playing for time. I have heard of a Burmese, one of those many oriental breeds, but what is a Birman? I am never one to admit ignorance when I can play tight-lipped and get informed for free.

I examine her in the down-lights of the pole lamp, which cast unfortunate maroon, chartreuse and forest-green shadows on her pale fur. This is one big babe. I do not know yet how she swatted me without seeming to lay a white glove on me, but I can see she is big-boned, with a broad head as round as her intimidating eyes. Come to think of it, she reminds me of Lieutenant Molina in that department. Even her whiskers are thick. Not Lieutenant Molina's—this character Karma's.

She has a long, massive body and sturdy legs with

strong claws under those polite white gloves. The rest of her is a creamy golden color shading to silver in the light, but her ears, bushy tail and facial mask are as dusky as a delta twilight. That mask is creepy; all the better to see her big, bright, wolfish indigo eyes. I decide that it is no indignity to get sideswiped by this limousine of a lady.

"Listen," I say, licking my own gloveless paw apologetically. "I did not know you were a legitimate resident. I am sorry if I messed up your furniture arrangement. I will replace it."

"Do not bother," she says, even as I look toward the sofa to figure how far I have to shove it back into place.

It *is* in place. I look to Karma, who is sitting there while her fur slowly settles. She does not look half as fierce without her battle halo, but she is still one mysterious lady.

"I suppose you managed that the same way you knocked me into pole-lamp heaven?"

"Things are not always what they seem, especially when the primal brain has brought out the beast in one."

"You calling me intemperate?"

"Only . . . primitive." Karma brushes a long, spidery hair above her right eye. "You have many lives to traverse, Midnight Louie," she says sadly, "before you can commune with the higher self."

"I would rather reach the higher shelf than the higher self. That is where all the goodies are invariably kept."

Karma shakes her head as if dislodging an unpleasant flea from her left ear. "Life—and death—are more than the temporal attainment of physical possessions or pleasures, Louie."

"Temporary attainment and physical pleasure have been just fine with me so far."

"So far," she repeats in a vague tone. "So far. . . ."

"I will leave now," I say firmly, rising with my usual grace and dignity.

"You may leave, but you will not outrun your fate. You do not have that many lives left, Louie, and you are not an advanced enough soul to be assured of returning in a higher form. Be careful."

"I *am* a higher form! And I do not worry about returning when I have no intention of leaving. As for advanced souls, the only good thing I ever heard of that was advanced was a paycheck."

"I see death," Karma says so calmly she might be posing as the Dark Dude himself in the flesh.

"In . . . person?"

"I see death in a collective mode. Death is collecting soon. Reaping. It bends close to you, close to those near to you."

"That is nothing new," I answer with as much swagger as I can muster; after being wrapped around a pole lamp, that is not a great deal. "Danger is my middle name."

The blue eyes widen and deepen into lapis-lazuli pits. I swallow, seeing into them as Miss Electra Lark might gaze into her many crystal balls. They are more bottomless than the house drinks on the Strip and as honeyed and cloying as ocean-blue Curaçao, straight up.

"I see death in two places, on two levels. I see danger for those around you. I see you, Midnight Louie. I see Libra in the ascendancy. Beware Libra! I see many of our kind in danger."

"Libra?" I reply without a blink. "I do not believe in these horrorscopes. Besides, I am a Pisces myself. And how many individuals of the feline sort are in danger?"

"Many," comes the answer as a shudder shakes Karma's pale, silky form.

That is the difficulty with these purebreds: too neurotic, especially the reçlusive kind. Even the Divine Yvette is a tad . . . skittish, no doubt the result of being kept too often in a pink-canvas carry-bag. I understand that a certain shade of pink is calming to the human psychopath, but I believe that this same tint does nothing for felines except encourage them to become color-blind.

I yawn and ask again, "How many?"

If I am going to sit still for predictions of disaster, I want a precise body count.

"Dozens," Karma replies in a faint, keening voice.

"Dozens, huh? Sounds like a normal day at the animal pound."

Karma shudders again. Perhaps the air conditioning is kept too high, because I do not feel the urge to shake so much as a whisker.

"Do not mention that place of sighs and slaughter," Karma warns me in a doom-filled voice. "Why do you suppose I must sequester myself in silence and shadow? To keep the anguish radiating daily from that Place of Infamy from interfering with my sensitive apprehension of more specific and less common crimes against our species. I tell you that there will be chaos soon, that it will decimate our kind, an utter catastrophe."

"Dozens threatened with death, you say, but not at the pound?"

"Perhaps . . . a hundred or more."

"Where can sitting ducks of the feline stripe be found if not in the cages at the animal pound?" I muse aloud, inadvertently striking a rhyme just like my bookie pal Nostradamus.

"That is your job to find out," Karma growls softly. "I am a mere conduit, a receiver."

I tell her that I do not know why I should believe a word of this hokum. "Who made you Psychic Central?" I ask.

Karma sighs and settles into her haunches, forelegs tucked in so she resembles a mandarin on a rice-paper scroll.

"I am Birman-born," she announces at length.

"So I heard."

Another sigh, no doubt of exasperation with my ignorance—or more likely, with my failure to be impressed by pedigree. "We are temple cats."

"You mean like my pal Moshe the Mouser at Beth Israel?"

"A more Eastern temple than that," Karma answers

with the usual disdain. These know-it-alls-in-advance are always disdainful. "We are the Sacred Cat of Burma and companions to the priests of the Temple of Lao-Tsun, who worship a golden goddess with blue eyes named Tsun-Kyan-Kse."

"Recently?" I cannot help inquiring snappily. All these foreign words sound like the menu at a chop-suey establishment.

"Time is a dream in the windowless eyes of an ancient house," Karma replies in a dismissive singsong.

Just what this means, I cannot say. Perhaps it is one of those pithy oriental poems called a haiku, which are not supposed to make sense.

Karma goes on to chant. "One day"—presumably in this Never-Never Land of Unaccountable Time—"evil men attacked the temple and killed the head priest as he meditated before the goddess."

I'd spend a lot of time meditating before a golden goddess with blue eyes myself.

"The priest's pure white cat, Sinh, put his paws on his dead master's body, defying the enemy raiders to defile the dead."

I recall a saying among veterinarians of my acquaintance: "If it is white, it will bite," and I must admit that my own experience bears out this aphorism, especially in the case of pit bulls.

Karma's voice continues, a growing purr rising under her voice like the three-hankie sound track on a Benji movie. "As he did this, his body fur grew as golden as the goddess, while his paws remained as white as snow, for purity. His legs, face, ears and tail became the color of earth, and his yellow eyes turned celestial blue. For seven days and nights, Sinh remained before the goddess, refusing all food until he died."

Oops. Sounds like this cross-dressing dude had a death wish, which would not be surprising.

Karma, however, cannot read my mind. Perhaps it is too close at hand, or perhaps she does not deign to do so. She continues, much taken with the story of her supernatural ancestry.

"Sinh took the old priest's soul to paradise with him. And when the other priests met to choose a successor for the head priest, the one hundred white temple cats marched into the main hall, assuming the image of changed Sinh as they came. They circled a young priest to replace the old one fallen. And since then, the Birman wears the golden coat of the goddess, has her sapphire-blue eyes, bears the earthy marks of death and the pure-white paws of triumph over evil and death."

Karma lifts one of these prissy-gloved extremities for my inspection.

"Well," say I. "A touching story. My own forebears have a certain supernatural caché dating back to medieval times. We were persecuted for our color and suspected association with humans of a parapsychological persuasion. You Birmans had it soft in comparison. Purrsonally, I cannot see myself as the pampered companion of some priest. The contemplative life is not for me."

Karma shrugs. "That is obvious," she says in the Royal We tone of a Sacred Cat of Burma.

This chick is definitely living in the past, which does not speak well to her skill in foretelling the future. Still, she is a cool old doll in her own ditsy, self-important way, and I decide it would not hurt to sniff out the Las Vegas scene and see if there is someplace besides the dreaded pound where a plentitude of cats abides, ripe for the mass catastrophe this Karma doll is so fond of predicting.

Chapter 7

Sister Act

With just three of them there, it was inevitable that ConTact's phone lines would jingle like the nickel slots in the Sahara Hotel all night long. Sitting in the overhead fluorescent glare, watching the dots dance on the dingy acoustic tile and waiting for the luck of the draw in terms of incoming calls, was a lot like gambling, Matt often thought.

At least he found himself half-hypnotized by the unpredictable rhythm of it, the dullness of silence and murmuring voices around him interrupted by a shrill ring; then he was off to the races—thinking, talking, judging, guessing, persuading.

ConTact, being a generic hotline, took all comers.

At eight-fifteen, he convinced a rape victim—survivor, Matt grimly revised—to seek emergency-room attention after he reassured her by giving her some idea of what to expect. At nine, the Shoe Freak called. This well-educated-sounding woman fretted in precise, academic tones about the worldwide conspiracy to ruin women's feet with high-heeled shoes. Her exhaustive personal surveys of podiatrists and fashion columnists proved her point, and she cited these experts monotonously.

Matt smiled when he recognized her voice. She was a "regular," and harmless, except for monopolizing phone time that could help someone who was out of control. The Shoe Freak was never out of control, which was both her problem and her salvation, in an odd way. She had found her obsessive hobbyhorse and could ride it to death without doing drugs or committing kleptomania or turning to any of another half-dozen pressure-releasing habits that are so destructive. Matt tried to shepherd her off the line as quickly as possible without refusing her a few moments' outlet. He smiled again as he thought of what would happen if he could put Temple on the line in his place some night.

"Brother John," the Shoe Freak was saying in her even, automaton voice, "you know that the reason men rule the world is because they don't destroy their arches in killer shoes."

"Do men rule the world?" he asked, the smile still in his voice.

"It's nothing to smirk about. Certainly men rule the world," she began in a tone that promised a new and more predictable ax to grind.

"I'm sorry—another line is blinking like crazy. We're down on staff tonight."

"The only men senseless enough to cram their feet into these contemporary torture machines are transvestites, and my studies show that even they have shockingly high occurrences of bunions, hammer toes and fallen arches, despite the part-time nature of their high-heel wearing—"

"I really must hang up," he interrupted, worried now that someone at the end of his rope might be hanging figuratively from an unanswered telephone line.

"Of course," she said in haughty tones, as if he had been

the crank caller, not she. "I'll send you a copy of my full thesis when it's written."

On that threat, he punched another button to an open line and braced for the next caller. "ConTact."

"Hello," began a doubtful, elderly female voice.

Matt tried to balance the usual preconceptions with the need to get an instant fix on the sex, age and emotional state of his caller. This one sounded like she was dialing a local pizza place and wasn't too sure of what she had reached. For a moment he wondered if this was a redial from the hesitant woman with the hissing problem.

"I don't suppose this is the ordinary call you get," the voice went on, gaining strength and purpose.

"None of our calls are ordinary," he put in gently as a bit of disarming humor, "and I can't tell yet about yours."

"But I imagine the rules of your vocation are pretty strict."

Something about the phrase rankled. His fingers reached for the pad on which he often doodled during his long hours on the phone with the naked and the damned. A psychiatrist would have had a field day with his free-form inkings in black, blue and red ballpoint, he thought as he made the first stroke.

"We're supposed to talk about you," he reminded her, again gently. Unlike many his age—thirty-three—he had eternal patience with the elderly. He'd had experience.

"I'm not the problem."

By now, the voice, though no younger, had grown wry and rueful. It had a personality. Matt found himself beginning to relax. Whatever she wanted, she wasn't on the brink of a pressing personal crisis. He began to grow curious.

"Your situation doesn't sound critical. Maybe you should try Ann Landers."

She sighed. "I'm trying to find someone."

"Or the police."

"Someone I haven't seen in . . . oh, eighteen years."

Matt was momentarily stumped. "How about a private detective?"

"I know where this person is."

"Oh. Is it a relative?"

"Not at all."

"And if you know where he—she—"

"He."

"If you know where he is, why can't you approach him yourself?"

"I don't know where he lives. And where he works, he isn't reachable in the normal sense."

"Surely someone where he works can take a message?"

"I don't know. Will you?"

"Me?"

"I imagine that in your line of work there are rules about not identifying yourself."

"Quite true. We use pseudonyms, just like the people you phone at the classified department of the newspaper. It protects our privacy, and the focus shouldn't really be on us, so we all have nicknames, if you will."

"What is yours, young man?"

For the first time, Matt felt naked about giving his working name, as if even this false barrier was about to be breached. The ballpoint pen's smooth plastic barrel clung to a palm suddenly slightly damp.

"Brother John," he said.

A silence.

"Is that you, Matthias?" the woman's voice demanded with a note of suspicion and satisfaction that tensed his mind and body with an ancient anxiety. And momentary paralysis.

He had to answer. You don't elude a voice like that, the imperious tone of an old and old-fashioned teacher wrapping the innocuous question with invisible barbed wire.

"Ye-es," he admitted, against all the rules, against his inclination. He'd been so relentlessly trained not to lie that even the polite—or protective—social falsehood froze on his lips and then the truth came stuttering through.

Matthias. No one had called him that in . . . years.

His pen was still, the intersecting red and blue spirals on

his notepad bleeding color in a crazy-quilt pattern. The pen, as if on its own, began writing the block letters in a deep, paper-biting childish fashion: M-a-t-t-h-i-a-s A-n-d-r-e-w D-e-v-i-n-e. M.A.D.

"Who are you?" he asked.

That wasn't against the rules. Callers were the ones who were supposed to reveal themselves in this counseling game, not him. Not Matthias, whom he hadn't thought about in a long time. Once he'd turned fourteen, he had made everybody call him Matt.

"Sister Seraphina O'Donnell," came the answer, one that made him both sigh in relief and clench the pen so tightly that he accidentally retracted the point with a snap.

The barrel end pressed the pad and left a tiny "o," like an invisible bullet hole.

"Sister Superfine!" he said in amazement before he could stop himself. It was what all the kids had called her, and it was a kind of compliment.

"So they tell me," she said with a chuckle. "I'm sorry I made you break the rules, but I'm glad you answered my call. I'm too old to feel like a fool on the telephone."

"How did you know . . . I was here?" Surprise was giving way to other emotions: anxiety, even anger.

"You did get a recommendation from the Monsignor at Saint Stanislaus to get the job."

"Oh, that. I'd forgotten. What can I do for you, Sister?" There he was, back; back in respectful, grade-school mode, but with a hard-earned adult confidence giving an edge to his question.

"I need a . . . personal consultation."

"Are you in Las Vegas?"

"Don't sound so incredulous, Matthias." A laugh in her voice modified the arbitrary tone.

Sister Superfine, for all her popularity at St. Stanislaus Catholic grade school, had been a disciplinarian as unshakable as a drill sergeant. That's why the boys had all secretly loved her and the girls had feared her.

"Las Vegas," she was continuing in a schoolhouse voice,

"has more churches per capita than gambling casinos. I've been transferred to a long-established Hispanic church here, Our Lady of Guadalupe."

"That's a long way from a Chicago inner-city Polish neighborhood, Sister."

"Well—" Now *she* sounded pushed, cornered. "I'm retired, Matthias." *Forgive me, Father, for I have grown old* . . . an unpardonable but inevitable sin, even in the church.

"Your kind never retires, Sister Seraphina," he said quickly. "That's why you called me. What's this private consultation?"

She laughed again, apologetically. "We have a little problem at OLG. I was hoping you could come out to see us on your off-hours."

"Yeah, I could . . ."

"It wouldn't take much time, and I don't know where to turn."

Now, coming from super-competent Sister Seraphina, that was a startling confession.

"What about the pastor at our Lady of Guadalupe?"

A long pause, the kind Matt was used to getting on the ConTact phone. The closer the questions cut to the bone, the longer it took to get an answer.

"He's . . . part of the problem. Please, Matthias. I'll tell you when you come. I just thank God I thought of you, and found you."

He would go, of course. He would go even though the idea gave him the heebie-jeebies, and he didn't want to see this sad parish, Our Lady of Guadalupe, with its freight of eternally poor parishioners, with its idle, retired nuns put out to pastures not heavenly but all too human, with its mysterious pastor who was a problem. He had been there, and it wasn't his problem anymore. Or was it? But you don't say no to an old nun, to an old, favorite-teacher nun, to an old, never-forgotten nun who knows how to track you down. Do you? Matthias didn't.

The ballpoint drew a series of thin red lines through the

name so painfully yet carefully printed amid the much-inked squibbles.

"I'm not what I was," he said. Even he could hear the strangled tension in his voice.

"I know," she said, sudden, warm, sad compassion in hers. "I know," she repeated, without using the old name again. "None of us are."

Chapter 8

A Close Shave

Temple had never seen so many cats. Temple had never seen so many cats in cages. Temple had never seen so many different kinds of cats.

She stood north of downtown in the middle of one of the Cashman Convention and Sport Complex's loftiest, sparest exhibition halls, a vast concrete-floored vault echoing with excited human and feline voices in ear-splitting counterpoint.

Rows and rows of tables bore rows and rows of steel-mesh cathouses, so to speak. These were not the pastel canvas carriers allotted to the likes of Savannah Ashleigh's pampered Persian, Yvette. These were outright cages of metal mesh, but the proud owners and breeders had added homey touches.

Blue-gingham curtains swagged the first cage front that Temple paused before. Within, a matching gingham-covered pillow harmonized with a powder-blue plastic litter tray in the cage's opposite corner.

Amid this gingham glory reclined a huge, snub-nosed, vanilla-haired cat with chocolate-brown fur frosting the tips of its muzzle, legs and tail. The creature lay in slit-eyed feline repose on the bare space between the pillow and the litter box, its plumy tail lashing the water dish now and then like a languid, fur-bearing metronome.

Temple pulled her glasses from her ever present tote bag to read a card affixed atop the cage: LAZY H Farms, Home of Champion Himalayans. Stud Service Available.

The comatose cat opened eyes as breathtakingly azure as . . . oh, Lake Mead, or maybe even Paul Newman's electric baby-blues. Then it yawned hugely with slow and practiced expertise. Presumably this was a recumbent stud from the appropriately named Lazy H. It certainly resembled a sultan of the cat world. Even Midnight Louie had not mastered such studiedly sublime hauteur.

Temple cringed interiorly. One look at these purebred pussycats and Louie's mongrel origins were too obvious to overlook. These cats had class, had pedigrees, had price tags high enough to require life insurance.

Temple left the unruffled tomcat and strolled down the aisle, peering into cages and studying cards. Some cages were shimmers of royal purple lamé draperies; a few favored organza in the color orange. Pink tulle dusted the harsh grid of many a steel cage, while the pussums within displayed a blasé feline resignation to captivity and competition that Temple couldn't imagine Louie adopting for one moment.

Cleo Kilpatrick, Electra's cat-breeding friend who had obtained Temple's visitor's pass, rushed over after attending to her row of cages. "What do you think?"

Temple gazed around and shrugged. "Impressive. But I haven't seen one . . . human-looking cat, if you'll pardon the expression, since that little black one in the cage at the entry."

Cleo, a fortyish woman smartly attired in a T-shirt with a spangled leopard rampant across her substantial chest, shook her carefully frosted head. "That's the Humane Society stand. They try to place their more attractive homeless cats at the shows. We give them free space."

"Terrific. Uh. What kind of . . . cat? . . . is this?"

Cleo leaned inward to study the animal in question. "Oh, that's a very rare cat, but it's not a recognized breed."

"It does look ready to be sauteed or something. I've never seen a cat look so much like a plucked chicken."

"It's supposed to. That's a Sphinx."

"It looks more like a naked lunch." Temple shivered in sympathy. "Isn't it cold without any fur?" she asked sensibly.

"No . . . a Sphinx's body temperature is four degrees higher than the ordinary cat's. Most owners keep them in sweaters when they're not on show."

Temple gingerly bent to study the creature's hanging creases of greige skin at flanks and chest. "That furrowed forehead is so sad. Seeing a naked cat is awfully shocking. And the ears are so big. I keep thinking of Dumbo."

"Have you ever seen your own cat wet? He might look as spindly as this one."

"Not Louie," Temple swore with conviction.

"Anyway, the Sphinxes are here just as a curiosity. They don't breed true."

"So they're a genetic freak?"

"An anomaly," Cleo said quickly. No negatives to anything feline were permitted anywhere near a Fancy Feline fancier. "That's how some of today's most prized breeds began, with one oddball kitten in a litter who was carefully bred and cultivated."

"I certainly can cultivate some print exposure for this poor, overexposed kitty," Temple said. "Where is the woman Electra told me about, the one who got the threatening phone calls before the show opened?"

"Threatening?"

"Hisses sound pretty sinister. Absolutely viperish."

Cleo just laughed. "You haven't been around cats much, have you? Cats hiss plenty if provoked. I think Peggy is imagining things, or else someone she irritated recorded a cat fight and is playing it over her phone."

"This Peggy irritate a lot of people?" Temple asked, dutifully following Cleo as she wove between rows to the big central aisle.

Cleo stopped, allowing Temple to stare pupil to pupil with a huge, long-haired white cat that resembled a snowy owl with great gold eyes. She expected it to cry "Who?" at any moment.

"Everest Sweet Snowball Heavenly Hash," Cleo rattled off automatically as she gazed fondly on the gigantic feline. "Champion Persian male. Two years old. Great doming. They call him 'Hash' for short."

A cartwheel of stiffened lace circled the animal's neck like an Elizabethan collar, no doubt to keep it from licking its lavish ruff. Temple examined this mound of powdered and blue-rinsed fur and found a face that was short on nose but big on eyes. "It looks like a white Pekinese."

"They breed Persians for that flattened nose, but frankly, that makes the animals prone to breathing difficulties. A more natural nose may now be permissible with some judges."

"Hooray for Hollywood," Temple said sardonically. Cat breeders were beginning to get on her nerves almost as much as unearthly purebred cats did. "Have they resorted to giving these cats collagen to ensure the proper profile?"

Cleo eyed Temple as if she were crazy, or worse, a heretic. "That would be strictly forbidden. The point is to breed for the look. Any breeder who physically tampered with a cat would be barred from competition."

"What would that mean?"

Cleo grew even more incredulous. "That person's cats would be as dead as dodoes. No one would buy them, no one would covet a mating with that source, the kittens would be worthless and the breeder would go out of business."

"These shows are *that* important?"

"They are if you aren't just running a kitten mill. Listen, Temple, our breed standards are serious and are rigorously applied. We may not get rich selling purebred cats, but we certainly take it seriously. It's an achievement similar to nursing along a bonsai tree. Years go into forming the proper line to produce a champion.

"We slave over these cats, we primp and pamper them. If we're very, very lucky, sometimes we get a kitten that can go all the way in its class. It's like owning the winner of the Kentucky Derby, only there are no roses and not much money in it, unless you count all we spend on our animals."

"But it's not a hobby—a pursuit—worth intimidating anybody for?"

Cleo considered that while running her admiring eyes over Hash's immaculately indifferent body and soul. "I suppose people can get wrought up over lesser things. This isn't just what you call a hobby, you know. Cat people are passionate on the subject."

"Then a rival might want to unnerve Peggy Wilhelm to get her to withdraw her cats from competition?"

Cleo puckered her lips and seemed to consult the Oracle of the magnificent Everest Sweet Snowball Heavenly Hash. The great yellow eyes blinked, and Cleo shook herself out of her reverie, turning her full attention on Temple.

"Might," she said, nodding. "Might go to any length. I tell you, people get crazy about these cats. Sometimes you'd think they were their children. You ever hear about the Texas cheerleader mom's murder attempt? It made time on 'A Current Affair.' "

"The only current affairs I know about are my own, I'm afraid," Temple said with a grimace, "and sadly lacking."

Cleo shook her particolored, fine-coated head. "Some people get too competitive for their own good—and anybody else's. In that Texas case, a stage mother tried to hire a killer to ice the mother of her daughter's cheerleading rival, figuring the rival would be too broken up to try out for the squad. Over cheerleading! Anybody who fixates on any kind of competition can go over the edge. I'm afraid your friend who's worried about Peggy's cats has good reason."

"Then let's go find Peggy and talk to her," Temple suggested.

They moved into the main aisle, a perpetual-motion melee of people carrying cats. Temple eyed perfectly groomed Persians dangling limp-legged from the hands of their breeders, who held them at arms' length on the way to the judging area to avoid ruffling a single hair.

She tried to picture herself carrying Midnight Louie that way. All she could see was four flailing black legs and a sprained, if not broken, wrist for her.

Temple gawked at lean, short-haired oriental breeds being whisked to and fro in the same fashion. The Siamese, in particular, were so attenuated from narrow head to hindquarters that they looked like something from an El Greco nightmare.

She and Cleo paused to watch a judge rate a cat—a fluffy white one with gorgeous blue eyes—that looked half-normal.

"Oh," Temple said, instantly enamored.

"Turkish Angora," Cleo explained. "They're long-haired but much rangier than the Persians, which are a cobby kind of cat."

While they watched, the judge sprayed the tabletop with disinfectant, then fetched a snowy beauty from its cage. Temple tensed at the no-nonsense way the man handled it—like an inanimate object. He posed it on the table, examined its head, legs and tail, all the while making loud and personal pronouncements for the benefit of the people occupying the folding chairs arrayed before the table.

"No cat I know would put up with that," Temple remarked, although she knew only one cat, which maybe was the point.

"These are show cats. They're used to it, and they're ranked on how well they respond to handling."

"Sounds like white slavery to me."

Cleo Kilpatrick stared at Temple. "You could be right. That attitude could be the problem."

"Huh?"

"Peggy Wilhelm could be hearing from animal-rights activists. Some are such fanatics that they don't even feed their dogs and cats meat, fish or dairy products. Some local types could have decided that cat shows are cruel."

Temple nodded. That made sense. "Where is Peggy's stand?"

Cleo paged through a sheaf of papers. The locations of the various breeders were indicated by microscopic numbers on a layout sheet that had to be checked against a separate list.

An exasperated Cleo hissed like a cat—or a snake—and pulled her half-glasses, dangling on a pearl cord around her neck, up to her nose. "Looks like . . . row L, numbers sixty-six to sixty-eight, or eighty-six to eighty-eight."

The two women hurried in the direction Cleo indicated, Temple's purple Liz Claiborne high heels on concrete drawing frowns from breeders intent on calming their animals.

Temple's eternal curiosity kept slowing her to a crawl. In covering two rows, she made the acquaintance of Japanese Bobtails, which sported the kind of tails they were named for; Manx, which had no tails; and American Curls.

"Those ears are far-out." Temple paused to study the crimped appendages on an otherwise normal feline head. "Mr. Spock, I presume? Any relationship to Scottish Folds?"

"Oh, you know about Scottish Folds," Cleo commented with some surprise.

"Know *about* 'em? I personally *know* the two most famous Scottish Folds in the country—Baker and Taylor, the corporate kitties. Bookish types."

Cleo shrugged, a gesture that made the leopard emblazoned on her chest seem to snarl. "That's right. The cats that were kidnapped at the booksellers' convention were Folds, weren't they? American Curls are a newer breed, but they're being developed in the same way."

Temple took in this particular American Curl's name, which reflected paternal and maternal forebears—Earesistible Curly-Q-Tip of Cuticurl—then moved on. A moment later she was pausing to examine the paperback book splayed open atop a cage. The cover was tracked with little red catpaw prints and titled "The Cat Who—" something.

Then a cat of another color caught Temple's attention: a short-haired calico animal with calm hazel eyes. "Cleo, this cat doesn't look any more special than my own Midnight Louie."

Cleo perched her dangling glasses on her nose and leaned near to examine the feline. "Ordinary housecat," she pronounced.

"What's it doing here?"

"There's a housecat category."

"Really? Just for ordinary cats?"

Cleo smiled. "But only the extraordinary ordinary cats win. They're judged like the rest, though not against breed standards."

"Hmmm." Temple strolled along a row of seemingly common cats. None had Everest Sweet Snowball Heavenly Hash's air of aristocratic disengagement. "This one's almost as big as Louie. How come he merits the red-satin hangings?"

"That, my dear, is not just any ordinary house cat. Don't you recognize him?"

Temple eyed the outsized tiger-striped animal. It was big enough, and blasé enough, to be a male used to cat competitions, but why should she recognize some cat-show regular?

Cleo burst into sudden, and vapid, song. " 'If it's whisker-lickin' yummy, it's Yummy Tum-tum-tummy.' "

Temple looked at her as if she had momentarily succumbed to cat-scratch fever.

"You know, the TV cat-food ads. For the Yummy Tum-tum-tummy brand. Maurice is the spokescat. We're lucky to have him here in person."

"Right." Temple eyed the dignified animal again. The only thing she could picture him doing with a bowl of Yummy Tum-tum-tummy was burying it. She bent down, bringing her fuchsia-framed glasses right up to the cage. "He looks almost as big as Louie," she observed.

Maurice blinked and twitched his large pink nose.

Temple had never cared for tiger-striped cats, but this one had a tiger-sized nose. Louie's nose, on the other hand—or head—vanished into the unremitting black of his expression, against which the tracery of his snow-white whiskers was as delicate as the strokes of Chinese lettering.

"Hey, my cat's cuter than this one," Temple concluded, unbending.

Cleo smiled with weary recognition. "That's why we have a household-pet category; everyone says that. This fellow was a stray under a death sentence at the animal pound when his trainer picked him up. Temperament's the thing when it comes to on-camera cats. Would your cat do well under lights?"

"I don't know. He's pretty laid-back when he wants to be, especially on my best silk dresses." Temple eyed the catatonic Maurice again. "Do they give them tranquilizers?"

"Strictly forbidden," Cleo said, shocked. "At least at cat shows. I don't know what they do on camera."

"Probably coax this fellow to perform for pellets of Free-to-be-Feline," Temple speculated glumly. "That's probably what Maurice, the Tummy Tum-tum-tummy cat, does cartwheels over. My cat won't touch the stuff."

"Free-to-be-Feline is a lot better for him," Cleo said sternly, moving on down the row.

A shriek of alarm halted both women in their tracks. Cats' ears flattened all around them. A second shriek—this one more a horrific wailing—echoed through the concrete vault.

Cleo was running toward it.

"What's happening?" Temple asked breathlessly, her tote bag banging against her ribs and hip and her high heels as brittle on the concrete as sleet.

Cleo turned as she ran, her half-glasses pummeling the glitzy leopard face on her chest. "I hope it's not— Golly, that's the direction of Peggy Wilhelm's setup!"

Other people were rushing toward the screams. Cleo and Temple were at the head of a pack. Temple glimpsed cats milling in their ruffle-draped cages, cats crouched in cage corners, giving low, eerie growls. Cats . . . hissing.

It wasn't hard to tell who Peggy Wilhelm was. She was the buxom, brown-haired woman clutching a seminaked cat, pacing like a tiger in front of her cages with a face frozen in shock and outrage.

"What happened?" Cleo demanded as soon as she and Temple made an abrupt halt.

The distraught woman thrust the animal toward her and Temple as mute evidence, then just shook her head.

"Oh, my . . ." Cleo's face wrinkled in consternation and denial.

"What's wrong with her Sphinx?" Temple asked in a low tone.

"That's the problem," Cleo said. "Her cat isn't—wasn't—a Sphinx. It's been—"

"Shaved!" Peggy Wilhelm wailed, pacing like a bereaved mother cradling her lost child.

Temple studied the strange form. Along the hairless backbone and midsection, the cat resembled the Sphinx she had seen earlier, but it also reminded her of a Siamese with blanched paws that had been given a one-two pass with a U.S. Army hair clipper.

"What . . . was it?" she asked Cleo discreetly.

Not discreetly enough to escape Peggy Wilhelm's outraged ears. "A Birman," she wailed. "She was perfect. She could have been a contender. Grand champion."

Crooning cat people gathered around, their faces studies in helpless sympathy.

"Has she been hurt otherwise?"

Peggy hadn't thought to look. She had only seized her violated cat and clutched it as close as possible. She examined the narrow legs, the stomach, the face. The shaving job was not impeccable, leaving ridges here and there reminiscent of what Temple had been told was a curly-coated Rex. A two-inch-wide swath denuded the top of the head to the tail tip; another crude slash narrowed the cat's middle like a cinch belt.

"No cuts, thank God . . . but she's out of competition for at least a year."

"Sounds like spite," Cleo said reluctantly. "Or rivalry."

"When did it happen?" Temple asked.

Peggy slowly replaced the cat in its cage, latched the door, then regarded the cluster of people. Temple's interrogation seemed to have a calming effect.

"I don't know," she answered. "I set up at seven this morning, then brought Minuet and the others in. After that, I had to leave to help my aunt with her morning feeding—"

"Your aunt has a baby?" Temple couldn't help interrupting. Peggy Wilhelm herself looked well past fifty.

"Feeding of the cats, of course," Peggy explained irritably. "She's too old to handle it herself. Anyway, I just got back and . . . that's what I found."

"What are they supposed to look like?" Temple wondered.

Peggy stepped away from the cage behind her to reveal a blue-eyed beauty with long, cream-colored fur, pristine-white feet and the soft, lavender-gray markings of a lilac-point Siamese on muzzle, tail and legs.

"Oh." Temple was in love again. It was a good thing she was already committed to Midnight Louie, unpedigreed nobody that he was, or she'd go home with a cat breeder's ransom in exotic purebreds, at least the long-haired variety. "Such a shame," she said with new understanding.

Peggy Wilhelm just shook her head. "I had that coat brushed and powdered to sheer magic."

"Then the . . . assault had to have happened after you left at—"

"Eight or so."

"—and now." Temple consulted her wristwatch, then the onlookers. "How many people were here between eight and ten-twenty this morning?"

Scattered answers came.

"A couple dozen, but we were all involved at our cages."

"Most of us were coming and going."

"Who was closest to Peggy's cages?" Temple asked.

An awkward silence held while folks figured this out, and also figured out if saying anything would incriminate themselves or a neighbor.

"I was grooming my Smoke Persians at the end of the

row," a large woman in an orange-velour sweatsuit volunteered.

The vast majority of breeders were women, but not all of them.

"Are the cats' cages arranged according to breed?" Temple wondered next.

"No," Cleo said. "It's more interesting for visitors if the cats are intermixed."

"And probably more diplomatic to keep direct competitors from seeing each other's animals," Temple added. "Would anyone notice someone who shouldn't be here messing with the cats?"

Heads shook in concert. Cleo took it on herself to explain again. "Everybody's focused on their own cats, their own cages, on getting everything ready. An astronaut in full gear could walk in here and dewhisker every untended cat in sight. We'd never notice."

Temple sighed. "Wouldn't the cat cry if it was being suddenly shaved by a stranger?"

Peggy Wilhelm shook her grizzled, tight-curled head. "These animals are trained to be groomed and handled—both by owners and strange judges."

"What can we do?" a tall, thin, young woman in a red knit sweater asked.

"Nothing," said Peggy. "Now. Just watch each other's stands so it doesn't happen again."

"Great." A tall man in a plaid sports shirt grimaced. "We don't even open until five P.M. tonight. Maybe we should start a crime-watch patrol. Any volunteers?"

"Good idea!" Cleo seconded.

Cat people moved away in an animated clump, discussing self-defense plans.

Temple eyed the skinny, shaved cat in the cage. "Somebody must really hate cats to do this."

"Or me," Peggy Wilhelm put in bitterly.

"It does look like a rival, doesn't it?" Cleo asked.

Peggy nodded. "Those phone calls were a warning. Maybe I should have stayed out of the show. Now I'll have to be here all the time the cats are present. I don't know who will take care of Aunt Blandina's cats."

All three shook their heads in downcast contemplation of the quandary, and its cause.

The abused Birman lifted a pale, unshaven forepaw and began to lick it.

"Maybe I could do it," Temple was horrified to find herself saying. She abhorred a vacuum in volunteering. "Just twice a day all right?"

Peggy Wilhelm was less than ecstatic. "Who are you? What do you know about cats?"

Cleo made a hasty introduction, then added, "One reason I specifically wanted Temple to handle the cat show publicity is that she's been involved in crime at similar events before. She found the corporate cats that were kidnapped at the American Booksellers Convention last Memorial Day, not to mention a dead editor, and several dead strippers at the Goliath competition last month—"

"Look," Temple interrupted in the interests of not sounding like the Typhoid Mary of murder, "I didn't 'find' the strippers' bodies; just the editor's, and that was enough."

"But can you feed cats?" Peggy Wilhelm wanted to know with the severe face of a wet nurse handing over a charge.

"I've got only one, but he's nineteen pounds, so I guess I do all right."

"What kind is he?"

"Alley."

"Oh." So much for Louie. "I guess you could do it. I'll call Aunt Blandina and tell her you'll be over this afternoon. She lives only a few doors from me, on Sequaro."

Temple pulled her fat organizer clutch out of her tote bag and wrote down the aunt's address and phone number, as well as Peggy's.

"Maybe we can talk later about the phone calls," she said, putting away her arsenal of information.

Peggy Wilhelm nodded while eyeing the new, punk-look

Minuet at her pathetic grooming ritual. "I've got to find a sweater for the poor dear before she catches her death." Her eyes narrowed with fervor. "If I ever find out who did this to her, I'll shave them where it hurts!"

Chapter 9

Nunsense Call

Our Lady of Guadalupe was what its name implied: an aging parish in a mostly Hispanic neighborhood. Matt watched skin tones on the street deepen as he neared the pale adobe tower he had steered by for the past few blocks.

Oleanders and rose bushes bordered the fronts of little old houses not much bigger than shotgun shacks. He hadn't heard that term until he had left Chicago for sunnier regions. It specified homes so small that a shotgun fired from the front door wouldn't expand its pattern enough to scratch so much as a sill before it exited the back door.

These sleazy, peeling constructions of slatboard, along with the occasional stucco, wouldn't have survived a Chicago winter, nor would their residents. But warm climates allowed substandard housing to stand longer than it should; heat couldn't kill as easily and obviously as cold could.

Black wrought iron underlined a house here and there,

usually in the form of burglar bars, though it was often for looks rather than for security. One enterprising homeowner had upended a claw-footed porcelain bathtub in his front yard, painted its inside the saccharine shade of bright blue that can never be found in nature and represents the Virgin Mary for some reason, and installed a plaster statue of her, head and eyes downcast modestly to the left, hands folded prayerfully over her flat breast. Despite the cheapness of the plaster icon, the sun carved graceful shadows into the folds of her long, gathered gown.

Yard ornaments—pots and vases and birdbaths and donkeys burdened with baskets of geraniums—scattered over the gravel and dirt like a pecking flock of gaudy, migrating terra cotta. Huddled under the dubious shade of ramshackle carports or a stand of scraggly trees stood hulks of Detroit's best—past tense. Twenty-year-old red Monte Carlos bleached rust-pink rubbed fenders with jazzed-up brown or yellow Firebirds. Some newer-model cars tricked out with fuzzy dice hanging from the rearview mirror had been restyled into bad-looking low-riders.

Matt heard the distant squeal of kids—lots of them. This grade-school playground would not be the vast, open area of asphalt he remembered from his Chicago school days, but a shaded, dusty patch with kids in clusters under the tree-bordered edges, where the worn swing sets and jungle gyms creaked and shook to lazy users in the becalmed desert heat.

His walk had worked up a light sweat that evaporated as soon as it appeared. He paused before he came to the church, a low, cream-painted structure with a rusty tile roof, its single, square bell tower rising three stories on one side.

The church was planted deep in the neighborhood. Houses stretched away from it with hardly a demarcation line. The school and playground must sit on the other side, Matt decided as a harsh bell clanged. The screeching voices softened into giggles that cooled to faint laughter, then silence.

The houses nearest the church were obviously the oldest and largest in the neighborhood. Matt studied them, trying to pick out the convent and failing. In Chicago, churches were as obvious as dump trucks: large, lumbering edifices that called attention to themselves, established red brick or gray stone behemoths with naves that aspired to cathedral heights. Rectory and convent were built to match, impressive structures that parish children passed with hushed giggles.

Here there was no institutional signal, just a lot of vaguely mission-style little houses, and then, the Big House. Matt nodded as he stared at Our Lady of Guadalupe, a low box with a pointed roof and that one plain tower. More churches should be built in such proper proportion to the people they serve.

Sister Seraphina had given him the address, but he headed to the two-story adobe building that he figured was the convent, then looked for a number. It would be interesting to see if his Catholic grade-school instincts were intact after all these years.

When the address numbers got large enough to read, he saw he had been right. Matt smiled to himself. Maybe the lack of yard bric-a-brac had given the place away. It was too neat, too stripped down to the essentials. No matter the architectural style, every convent had that in common, that bare, clean, dustless feel. Rectories, on the other hand, no matter how modern, always broadcast an air of fusty, bachelor disorder on the brink of becoming unmanageable.

He entered a small courtyard edged in sun-loving, white-and-magenta periwinkles and rang a doorbell.

Despite its modest exterior, the place was large enough to swallow all sound of the bell. Waiting at a convent door always felt like waiting for the Wicked Witch to open the Halloween portal: which nun would come? Grade-schoolers at St. Stanislaus all had their favorites—and their mortally feared.

The broad wooden door swung open with an energetic *swoosh* that sucked hot air past Matt. A figure was framed in shadow.

"Matthias!" Sister Seraphina greeted him with robust delight. "Come in."

Just before he stepped over the threshold, an unseen lurker darted past, a dusty yellow cat big enough to tap his knee with the tip of its tail.

"Peter!" Seraphina admonished in a fond tone no thirteen-year-old hardened case would heed. "You're a pretty pushy gatekeeper. Did he get hair all over you?" she asked Matt.

She turned to conduct him to the visitors' parlor, and Matt found himself expecting something: the billiard-ball click of oversized rosary beads. But that memory came from his earliest grade-school days. Nuns no longer wore robe and rosary and wimple. Still, Sister Seraphina had been in uniform—a black habit with white touches at the headdress—when he had made her acquaintance in the fourth grade. He secretly dreaded seeing her without her charismatic costume. He had more than twenty years to bridge; seeing her aged would be bad enough.

The dim hall was paved with quarry tile. She led him to a small room floored in the same dull red color, with interior wooden shutters drawn against the heat.

"Sit down. Would you like some lemonade? Iced tea?"

"The tea would be great."

She was gone before he'd had a good chance to look at her. Perhaps she felt the need of intervening props as much as he did. Her voice's sprightly tone had been familiar, but forced.

He looked around, then sat down in a carved wooden chair of mismatched Queen Anne-Hispanic style, upholstered in a maroon velvet. Convent furniture was never new. If a convent had been constructed in the fifties or sixties, its furnishings had once been new: blond, uncompromising lines that hinted at the Scandinavian but were too plain to pretend to a style that required a capital letter. If the convent was older than thirty or forty years, it was filled with hand-me-downs from the wealthier parishioners or some ecclesiastical rectory.

This chair appeared to be an escapee from the latter, but in one factor it was the quintessential convent chair, whatever its age: it was bare-armed and -legged, and hard-seated to sit on.

Still, it suited this warm climate and this Spanish atmosphere. Sister Seraphina did not.

She returned quickly with a tray bearing a pitcher of iced tea, two glasses, a saucer of fresh-cut lemons and a sugar bowl with spoon. Matt rose to help her install it on a desktop, then captured a lemon slice for his tea. The small wooden table next to his chair had no such frippery as a coaster, but it did have a doily with a solid center and an elaborate, airy edging that stood up like a clown's ruff. On this he placed his sweating glass, which now echoed his own condition, and confronted the past in the person of Sister Seraphina O'Donnell.

She was summing him up as well, he saw, so they simply sat and did so until her mouth folded tight to avoid a laugh, and he sipped his tea. Strong as shellac. He squeezed more lemon into it.

"You haven't changed," he began.

"All my ex-students say that," she noted complacently. "They assume I must be ninety by now."

"You look great," he said.

"How do you know? How could you tell what I looked like before with the habit?"

"Do you miss it?"

She paused, then shook her head. At least she still wore glasses, the frames as effacing as ever. Her hair was white with accents of gray, permed and cut into the modest Social Security, old-ladies' style that is easy and inexpensive to maintain.

She wore a silver crucifix inset into a largish wooden cross on a thin chain around her neck. Other than that, her dress was ordinary, though Matt thought he detected a thrift-shop look: A-line khaki cotton skirt; short-sleeved, blue-striped polyester blouse; low-heeled, sensible shoes that might not be real leather; no rings, no earrings.

For a moment, the outfit seemed oddly familiar. He puzzled to place it, then smiled: a dead ringer for Lieutenant C.R. Molina's low-key, workaday garb. Trust a nun to find another uniform when her order did away with the dramatic medieval habit she was used to.

He took two more sips from his sweaty glass, then set it down on the circle of doily for good. "So. Our Lady of Guadalupe isn't as tranquil as it looks. How did you get here?"

"Retirement," she said with a curl of her mouth.

Matt was startled to note the faint, pale sheen of lip gloss. As happened to many older women, white hair brought out the color of her eyes, hazel-green. The deep-rose lip gloss complemented the new color scheme. It wasn't vanity, merely a desire to look reasonably healthy at an age when everyone wrote you off.

"So many parochial schools in Chicago have closed," she went on. "The convents have become old-nuns' homes. At least here I can do 'community organization' work. But I'm out of the teaching game, and high time."

"Is Saint Stan's school closed?" Matt asked.

"Not yet. But there aren't nuns enough to staff it. All lay teachers nowadays, and even though they still accept substandard wages, it costs so much to keep it going . . ." She shifted on her chair, a hard-seated side chair with faded brocade upholstery. "Our Lady of Guadalupe is in the midst of a major fund drive to underwrite some renovation, and the grade school. It's vital to the parish, to the neighborhood."

He nodded. His thigh muscles were beginning to feel the strain of the demanding chair. Catholic churches depended on their parishioners to underwrite everything—if the parish were poor, it was endangered. St. Stan's served a large, working-class neighborhood, but everybody who was Polish was Catholic back then, and the widows' mites poured in until the statue of the Virgin loomed above a mass of shining candles.

"What's the problem?" he asked.

She fidgeted again on her chair. "I know you work nights and getting you out in the afternoon is an imposition, Mathias—"

"It's no trouble," he assured her, adding, "and I go by just 'Matt' now."

Her face froze. The ex-teacher was about to insist that the student would be called by his full and formal name. But those days were gone with the habit and the wimple.

"Matt," she repeated meekly. He wasn't fooled. "Well, Matt—" she enunciated the terminal t's like a machine gun spitting bullets "—some very odd things are happening since our fund drive began."

"Odd?"

"Disturbing," she corrected herself. She folded her hands on her lap—khaki-colored hands, plain, the nails virtually unnoticeable. "There have been noises outside the convent at all hours, even lights in the neighborhood, flashlights, all of it bright enough or loud enough to awake us, and alarm us."

"Kids," he diagnosed quickly. "Probably just hanging out, but it could be gang activity, or drug deals."

"Right next to the church?"

"Sorry, Sister Seraphina, but kids these days would do drugs in the sanctuary if they thought it was a safe place."

"It used to be," she commented sadly. "All those adorable little altar boys, growing up to be lookouts or drug runners."

"Not all," he said.

She smiled at him, then sobered. "That's not the worst. We've been getting strange telephone calls. At night."

"You mean the harassment may be specific?"

"It is now." She paused for emphasis, for dramatic effect, a teacher making sure her most sluggish student was getting this. "Sister Mary Monica has been receiving obscene phone calls for five days."

Matt winced. Nuns, especially old nuns, really were elderly innocents. Reared in a day when proper young girls were spared even the mildest oath, much less four-letter words, they had lived in a world that kept modern crudities at bay. That did not mean they were completely naive, for most of them were wise and worldly enough to survive change, even to their ancient orders. But obscenity and its effects were not dulled by modern usage. It was a weapon among them, it amounted to attack. That made Matt wonder who would be sick enough to bedevil—and that was the right word—these old women in this particularly savage way.

"A random caller," he suggested.

Sister Seraphina shook her curly, poodle-like head. "Again and again, often several times a night?"

"Sometimes these people like the reaction they're getting. The first call is random, then they have your number."

"Sister Mary Monica is . . . somewhat deaf," Sister Seraphina conceded. "She doesn't have her hearing aids in at night, so she was slow to realize the nature of the calls. That might have . . . encouraged the caller. She hung up as soon as she realized that she didn't understand the conversation, of course, but he still calls back," Seraphina went on.

"Is anyone else at the convent getting these calls?"

Seraphina shook her head as she rose. "I'll get her so you can ask her any questions you might think of." She hesitated on the threshold. "It will take a while. Mary Monica isn't as fast on her feet as she used to be."

Seraphina was. She whisked away, leaving Matt to inspect the mostly bare walls. A crucifix was impaled to the plaster above the desk, on which the pitcher—not opaque green plastic, but real glass—sweated profusely. He heard the distant drone of an air-conditioning plant and reflected that it must have been installed after the place became a convent, for surely it had begun as a private house, a large private house, almost hacienda size.

Hard to imagine the raucous shriek of a perverted phone call disturbing this place of prayers and domestic calm, this last oasis for lives of long service. Yet Matt smiled at the notion of a misguided obscene phone-caller fixating on a deaf, elderly nun. It revealed the act for what it was: so unsexual, so pathetic.

Rustles and shards of sentences down the hall announced the stately arrival of Seraphina with the elderly nun. He really didn't want to meet Sister Mary Monica; he had nothing to ask her. Apparently Sister Seraphina had thought he should see her, and what Sister Seraphina thought—now as then—was what was done.

He stood and went to the threshold to assist her.

The first thing across it was the faded red-rubber tip of a wooden cane as plain and solid as a church pew. Black, lace-up shoes followed with a floor-hugging shuffle. He wondered for the hundredth time where on earth old nuns got those ancient oxfords nowadays; there must be a Perpetual Supply House of Sisterly Shoes, similar to salvage stores that stock an eternal supply of military mufti.

Swollen ankles and shapeless calves were encased in the elastic pumpkin-tan of support hose, the opaque kind that looked like a mask used by a burn-victim burglar with an I.Q. of twelve.

Matt suddenly realized that he had never paid such close attention to a nun's legs before—no matter her age—and quickly brought his eyes to her face, blurring past an expanse of tiny navy and yellow flowers, a cotton duster with a snap front.

Her face was even more seamed than he had expected, though unrealistically flesh-tinted plastic was affixed to her ears like Silly Putty. The hearing aids. She was stooped, one gnarled and liver-spotted hand curled around the sturdy curve of the cane's handle. A large but flat wart rested near one eyebrow, whose thin, rakish gray hairs sprang every which way. Her eyes were the pale, gray-blue of great age, as tremulous as moonstones underwater, a late-life shadow of baby blue.

The anger that rocked him nearly blasted him back a step. He was used to voices on the phone, long-distance victims, never viewed, only heard. He never had to face them.

Afraid to say anything lest his voice shake with fury, Matt bent to take the old woman's elbow and lightly guide her along the uneven tiled floor. She arrived safe at his former chair and settled gingerly on the edge of the velvet seat, as if afraid that she might stick and never rise if she settled more fully into anything at her age. Which was—? He glanced at Sister Seraphina, who smiled.

"Sister Mary Monica is ninety-three," she said without his asking. "She can't understand when we speak in normal tones, which is just as well. She's vain about her age and would be in quite a pet if she knew I'd revealed such personal information."

"This man—it is a man?"

Sister Seraphina shrugged. "One would think so, yet Sister can't really hear well enough to tell."

"How does he call only her?"

"We don't number enough to have a convent switchboard; there are only six of us here. Each nun has her own number on the phone in her room. We'd run ourselves ragged otherwise, and it seemed a modest luxury."

"Of course." Matt stared perplexedly at the tiny old woman. He bent down to make sure she could see his face, his mouth when it moved.

Sister Seraphina introduced him, her tones bellowing deep from the diaphragm with the ease of a teacher who had been able to call an entire hollering playground to silence after a recess.

"This is Matthias, Mary Monica, my former student."

Sister Mary Monica tilted a hearing aid toward her friend, but kept her watery eyes on Matt. "A darling lad," she pronounced at the top of her lungs with the merest lilt of Irish brogue. "Are you a detective?" she asked him with great interest.

Matt almost laughed. Her deafness was an invisible cloak of defense the caller could not penetrate. His "victim" was pleased by the attention the incidents brought her way.

"No. I'm a counselor," he said, producing his own loud but deepest voice.

He watched her eyes read his mouth and her own mouth pantomime the right word. Coun-sell-or. She paused for a moment. "Like Perry Mason? I like Perry Mason. But I don't like Hamilton Burger."

Good old Ham Burger, the guy you always loved to hate on the oldest Perry Mason reruns. Matt smiled.

"Not that kind of counselor," he said slowly. "I work over the phone."

Her eyes were blank.

"Telephone." He pantomimed a rotary movement, then realized that most phones nowadays were push-button.

Still, she was old enough to get the idea. Her head nodded in long, slow swoops and rises. "Telephone." She pointed to Matt. "You call?"

"No! People call *me* for help."

She nodded and smiled again. "Maybe I should give your number to the one who calls me. Seraphina says he is a bad man, but he has never hung up on me."

Matt realized another thing. Her poor hearing had made telephone conversation difficult. Only family or close friends would have the stamina to try it, and she would have few of either left. Here was a caller who refused to go away, no matter how much of the conversation she missed. In a way, Sister Mary Monica and her obscene phone-caller were a match made in heaven.

He straightened and turned to Sister Seraphina. "How did you figure out the nature of the calls?"

In answer, she bent down to the old nun. "Tell Matthias about what the man says, Sister."

"Such a nice name, Matthias." Sister Mary Monica beamed at Matt. "The disciple who replaced Judas. A very fortunate and redemptive name, young man. Man. Oh, yes. Well, he must be very fond of philosophers."

"Philosophers?" Matt didn't have to think to raise his voice; shock did it for him.

She nodded and gazed at her cane handle. "Always talking about philosophers. Mainly, Immanuel Kant. Kant this and Kant that. A learned young man."

Matt, puzzled, gazed at Sister Seraphina, who met him

with a limpid look. He was about to repeat the philosopher's name—Kant—when . . .

"I see," said Matt. "And how do you know that he is a young man, Sister?"

Her head reared away as she gave him a don't-kid-me look. "All of them are young men to me now, Matthias." Her laugh was high and thin, but much relished.

"What else does this caller talk about?"

"Oh . . . animals."

"Animals?"

She nodded. "He is a great animal lover, which is fine, because we have Peter and Paul here, you know. And many cats next door as well. He is always speaking of the pussies." She paused. "And I believe—it is too bad you are not a detective, young man, because I think this is a clue! Like on Perry Mason." She invoked the name of Perry Mason as another nun would St. Peter's. She leaned forward and fixed him in the glare of her watered-down eyes, now fierce with conviction. "I think that he is a breeder of dogs by trade, because he is always talking of bitches."

The last word, loudly uttered, hung in the quiet convent air. Matt, appalled with himself, choked the desire to laugh. Then he turned sober. True innocence was a weapon that could confound the sickest evil.

Sister Seraphina smiled as she had used to when a pupil performed with stunning excellence. "That was splendid testimony, Sister. Worthy of a witness for Perry Mason. Now you must rest."

Sister Mary Monica looked at Matt. He knew he made an excellent audience. She pursed her lips, reluctant to leave the witness box, this fine, carved chair so judicial-looking.

"Come along." No one resisted Sister Superfine at her most persuasive—and her most commanding.

Once again the snail-slow progress was made; once again Matt cooled his heels. While Sister Seraphina escorted her charge back to her room, he mused on the silence and respected it, respected a place whose clock kept the time of its oldest and most frail resident. Outside, in the distance, the

Strip was heating up for the four-o'clock traffic jam, when it turned into a slow-moving river of hot metal and hotter tempers, while neon by the mile and the million-candlewatt was warming up in the wings.

Here . . . here was a million miles away. He sipped his ice-cold, strong tea.

When Sister Seraphina returned, he almost started.

"She's lucky," he said.

"No," she returned, "saintly, I think, in the old sense of true innocence. I wish I had it; I wouldn't know what you asked, or that these calls are indeed obscene."

"I'm surprised you do," he admitted.

She was too old to flush, but he sensed the impulse. "Oh, Matthias, you would be surprised at what old nuns know nowadays. At least the very oldest are spared. We are a dying breed, you know. An extinct species. I wonder that anyone would bother to harass us."

He frowned. "Perhaps another of a dying breed. What about changing the number?"

"We did. Three days ago."

"And—"

"The calls continue. And they're from someone who knows our routine. They invariably come after final prayer."

"Maybe someone in the neighborhood can see your lights go out."

"Not the way these old houses are constructed, to keep out the day's heat. They tend to be shadowed inside."

He glanced to the heavy wooden shutters at the window and nodded. Just then, a thump sounded outside the window. Seraphina leaped up from her chair, a grim look of teacherly discipline on her face. She had never resorted to the ruler, but her voice could be equally as sharp a weapon.

He moved quickly to the window and jerked the shutters wide. A pale yellow cat sat on the wide adobe sill, blinking sagely.

"Oh . . . Paul!" Seraphina bustled over to crank the window ajar enough to admit a fairly fat cat. "He is such a roamer, you know. Off on ecclesiastical missions, no doubt, to the mice and lizards instead of to the Romans and the Ephesians."

"Peter and Paul," Matt noted. "I don't suppose you allow Peter to go by 'Pete'."

She quashed a smile. They watched the cat loft to the floor with a soundless grace, then stalk over to the desk where the beverages reposed.

Matt saw Sister Seraphina crank the window tight again, and draw the shutters. Non-Catholics often envisioned convents as mysterious, cloistered, closed-up places. The reverse was true, but not here at Our Lady of Guadalupe lately. Sister Seraphina O'Donnell, that formidable teacher and now community organizer, was scared.

"I'm not the police," he said suddenly.

"We don't need the police," she said with swift repudiation. "We dare not have the police," she added more softly.

They stood by the sealed window like coconspirators, their voices softer than shadow.

"Is there a reason?"

She nodded, her face utterly grim, all business. "A good reason, Matthias." He didn't challenge her unconscious reversion to the old form. Besides, she was invoking the boy he used to be, or perhaps the man he had become, and had ceased to be.

"A very good reason," she repeated, real grief in her sharp eyes. "Father Hernandez, our pastor. There is nothing he can do."

"Of course the parish priest must be upset by this sort of thing, but surely—"

"Nothing. He is not . . . fully competent."

"What do you mean?"

"He does nothing lately but sit in his office at the rectory."

"How old is he?"

She laughed, a bit bitterly. "Oh, not so old. Not like us in the convent. Perhaps forty-seven. And he was fine, and functional, until two weeks ago."

"How could a man decline so completely in such a short space?"

"You ought to know, Matthias."

Her eyes probed deep, spoke volumes, chapter and verse, more than her mouth said. He felt as if he reared back from her words, but he had moved only mentally. Into the past.

"I see," Matt said in a flat, nonjudgmental voice. "He drinks. A whiskey priest."

Black humor lit Sister Seraphina's pale green eyes. "Tequila," she corrected primly. "He is, after all, a proper Hispanic."

Chapter 10

Cat Heaven

Temple sat in the Storm at the curb, gazing past its sleek aqua nose at the neighborhood.

This was one of the oldest parts of Las Vegas, so old that it had slowly ceded to becoming a Hispanic enclave. Most of the homes here didn't even have central air conditioning. Ancient, wheezing, window models hung askew along the sides of the battered old houses, looking as abandoned as the cars stripped down to bare metal that lay marooned with empty fender sockets.

Temple sighed and gritted her teeth. Perhaps her Girl Scout tendency to volunteer had taken her too far this time. "P.R." was not short for "Pet Reliever." What had she gotten herself into? The sun would soon be slinking behind the Spectre Mountains, and this neighborhood probably wasn't even safe for stray cats.

She studied the house again: a sprawling, distinctive, two-story Spanish place with a Hollywood twenties air, its pale stucco walls etched with the shadows of ancient bushes and pines planted when the only neighboring structures likely had been the church down the block and scattered houses on half-acre plots. The home had been expensive before all the ticky-tacky, ramshackle post-war housing had sprouted up just as Bugsy Siegel was doing gross things to the Strip, like opening a hotel as flashy as its name, the Flamingo.

A promise is nonreturnable goods, Temple reminded herself, fanning her Pink Panther sunscreen over the dashboard, gathering her tote bag from the passenger seat and springing open the driver's-side lock.

She emerged into still, searing heat, locked the door and slammed it. The street was quiet, almost too quiet. She began the long stroll up the flagstone walk outlined by a fringe of weeds that scratched her bare ankles.

"Merow."

The demanding voice belonged to a beige cat with a ringtail, who materialized beside her and began soothing her weed-whipped ankles with its furry sides as it wound past her calves.

"You must be one of my hungry customers," Temple speculated. "Come on down!"

It followed her, whether by invitation or inclination, one could never tell with a cat.

An overgrown courtyard—desert scrub—led to a shaded, coffered front door. No doorbell. Only a cracked wood sign warning: "No Solicitors."

Reluctant, she lifted the heavy black-iron knocker of vaguely Spanish design and let it fall on the metal backplate. She never knew how hard or how soft to bang a knocker, or if she could trust it to be heard, especially in these large, rambling houses. Now she had to decide how long she could wait in good conscience before trying again.

Waiting, something she was never good at, she changed her weight from foot to foot. At her ankles, the cat purred, drooling intermittently on her instep; luckily, the Claibornes had an indecently low vamp. At least Louie, no matter how hungry, didn't drool.

She finally gripped the knocker's smooth, warm metal—it was that hot on a Las Vegas September afternoon—again and had just lifted it when the door cracked preparatory to opening.

Clunk! A feeble, interrupted knock. So she was announced to the suspicious face revealed by a sliver of open door.

"Hi. I'm Temple Barr. Your niece, Peggy Wilhelm, asked me to come over and help you feed your cats."

"Why isn't Peggy here?" an elderly, suspicious voice asked.

"She had a . . . problem with one of her cats at the show and can't leave."

"Those dratted show cats. Not worth the powder they put on 'em. A shame to pamper those creatures when there are plenty of homeless cats to go around. Do you have a cat?"

"Sort of. He comes and goes."

"What's the name of Peggy's sick cat?" the old woman asked suddenly.

"Minuet!" Temple answered with alacrity, as if she were standing by a blackboard and someone like a teacher had demanded a right answer and she had better give it as if her life depended on it.

Open, Minuet. The door yawned almost wide enough to admit her. The yellow cat slithered through.

"Well, come in, then. Paul, too. No, Peter! We've got an extra mouth to feed, I see, so I can use help. I guess you're not a scam artist trying to bilk an old woman."

"No, I'm a P.R. woman."

"P.R., huh?" In the dim entry hall, the old lady turned to regard her and lifted an incredibly carved cane from the floor. It almost seemed that a long, thin totem was admonishing Temple. "Let's hope that stands for 'Pretty Reliable.' "

Humbled, Temple followed her guide deep into the bowels of the house. She had an impression of massive, old-fashioned furniture jousting the walls and each other, of magazines in table-high piles. Area rugs scattered hither and yon raised wrinkles to trip Temple's high heels, but not her hostess, who clumped through the clutter like a safari guide in darkest Africa.

Another impression took Temple by the shoulders and shook her. Pet odor: a thick, heavy aura composed of cat, litter box, shed fur, dander and sour milk—and a whole ozone layer somewhere near the ceiling of Tuna Breath, big time.

Temple struggled to breathe through her mouth and talk at the same time without sounding asthmatic. "How mandy cats do you have? I mean—" breath "—many."

"Oh, I don't know." A switch clicked. Overhead fluorescent lights flickered like heat lightning, then burst into artificial brightness.

They stood in an ancient kitchen that had battered wooden cupboards and a dangerously heaving quarry-tile floor. Newspaper clippings and notes covered every cupboard, and all of them fluttered from their Scotch-tape anchors like tattered sails under the lazy rake of an ancient ceiling fan. No expensive, computerized Casablanca models here. No Humphrey Bogart in a sweat-stained ice-cream suit, either.

Just countertops cluttered with bags and boxes of cat food, and cats. Just cats on the floor. Cats atop the cupboards. Cats in the sink. Cats on the old olive-green refrigerator. Cats probably *inside* the old olive-green refrigerator.

Temple sneezed. "Oh, excuse me."

"You're not allergic to cats?" the old lady asked with even more suspicion.

"Not that I know of," Temple said, taking advantage of the light to study Peggy's aunt, Blandina Tyler. Never married, never sorry. Now eighty-four and still upright except for the aid of her cane. Canvas open-toed shoes over fish-belly-pale white feet—oops! She was doing it again. Conducting a look-see from the feet up instead of vice versa. Bad habit.

Okay. White hair that had been that way for so long that it was tinged yellow as well as gray, gathered into a loose braid down her back. One of those shapeless plaid cotton zipper-front housedresses old ladies who are not too svelte always wear. Comfortable and suitable for the mailbox out front or the nearest convenience store. Miss Tyler's hands were ridged with veins, but capable looking. Right now she had the cane hooked over one sinewy wrist and was tearing open a Yummy Tum-tum-tummy box.

"Stupid manufacturers. Always make these boxes harder than Capone's vault to break into. And this is nothing compared to an ordinary aspirin bottle. I swear, it's a conspiracy to get old people off Social Security by having them get heart attacks trying to open these child-safe bottles. You can see who everybody cares about, and it isn't the 'aging population.' "

Temple hurried over to help, tripping on an assortment of rag rugs and lazy cats, but not fatally. She could tell that Blandina Tyler wasn't big on home safety.

"Say, kid, you can't do a thing with those fancy nails."

"You'd be surprised." Temple punctured the box's dotted line with a lacquered crimson thumbnail and ripped the top off, much to the amazement of Blandina Tyler, and perhaps to the round-eyed litter of Siamese kittens pictured in full yowl on the box cover.

"Put 'em in the foil pie tins you see around," Miss Tyler ordered gruffly.

To fulfill this simple instruction took about half an hour and many trips back to the kitchen to wrestle open other boxes. Miss Tyler took to leaning against a counter and watching Temple trot back and forth while eluding outstretched cats. For all the old lady's grumpy refusal of assistance, Temple guessed that she needed it.

Certainly a twice-daily run around the Tyler house—upstairs, downstairs, in my lady's chamber, bending and stooping, carrying and pouring—would match any aerobics routine in the city. Then came litter detail; in a word, box-dredging. Miss Tyler used the clumping kind of litter, from which waste was removed with a slotted spoon. Carrying an empty plastic garbage bag like an out-of-stock Santa, Temple then made her obeisances at the foil roaster pans scattered as lavishly through the house as the feeding stations. By now, her nose was numb to all scents, and she was sneezing liberally from litter dust.

"Are you sure you haven't got a cold?" Miss Tyler asked narrowly on one of Temple's many unhappy returns to the kitchen. "I don't want my cats catching anything."

Temple studied the assembled felines, ranging from milling, meowing gangs to complacently dormant layabouts. She blew out a stream of warm air to lift her short curls from her damp forehead, then took another clattering run through the house. At least the rooms were air-conditioned. She spotted ventilation grilles in the old plaster walls and figured that Blandina Tyler, who apparently had lived here forever, had gone to the expense of having the house cooled.

"That's a good girl," Miss Tyler said in the tone a person uses to a docile animal when Temple returned to the kitchen, food box empty and all pie tins filled. "Sit down and have a ginger cookie." She indicated a table piled with magazines, and cats, that was draped in a yellow-checkered piece of vintage oilcloth.

Temple pulled a fifties' dinette chair over a rag rug as wrinkled as brain coral and three inconvenient cats' tails, then sat down gratefully. These shoes weren't made for walking, and especially not for running in the Feline Feeding Marathon.

Miss Tyler came over, limping a bit now that her cane was still swinging from her wrist, and offered an open cellophane package of those oblong store cookies with a lush layer of white icing. Temple hadn't had one since she was . . . well, knee-high to a kitchen stool.

"Thanks," she said, trying not to think of how many cats had been slobbering over the open bag.

Yet, as far as she could see, the house had been cleaned and dusted, if cluttered.

"Have you always had cats?" she asked.

Blandina Tyler leaned a weary hip against a chrome kitchen stool. With the weight off her feet, her hands were free to roam the braille of the hand-carving on her cane, which they did with absent familiarity. Temple could tell that she loved that cane, that carving, almost as much as she must love her cats.

"No," the old woman startled her by saying. "I never intended to have a single one. I'd lived alone in this house for many years and was content to do so forever. Then some boys down the street came by one night making a racket to wake the dead, and they . . . threw a litter of kittens on my doorstep. Kittens they'd gotten drunk on beer."

Temple winced. She didn't want to hear what boys could do to cats—and kittens—because she'd always suspected it.

"A couple of them died," Miss Tyler said, her gnarled hands strangling the cane where it curved around to the head. "But four lived. After a while, the girls would come with their rescued strays. 'Please keep it, Miss Tyler.' Or with whole litters. 'They will go to the pound, Miss Tyler.' 'My brother is giving them marijuana, Miss Tyler.' 'She was hit by a car on the Big Street, Miss Tyler.' "

Temple looked around in awe. "All these cats were foundlings? Just by opening your door, you got so many?"

Miss Tyler nodded. "I was lucky. There were no relatives on my father's side, so I inherited this house and some substance. I could afford to take mangled cats to the vet. I could afford to have them neutered. I could afford to feed them. Motel cats that live on room-service trays; half-wild cats dumped in the desert scrub. Abused cats with cigarette burns on their bodies, with cut-off tails and ears and put-out eyes."

Temple winced again. She didn't think she could stand to hear what this old woman knew about boys' inhumanity to cats. Man's inhumanity to man, woman and child was bad enough.

"I took in a stray," she said, as if to prove she was doing her part. "He's a big bruiser—over nineteen pounds. I can't keep him in, though. Sometimes I worry . . ."

"You should. Eat your cookie."

Both comments were stern. Both were to be obeyed. Temple nibbled on the cookie and her conscience. "I guess I should have him fixed."

"You should keep him in," Miss Tyler exhorted. "It is not safe out there." Her voice lowered to a crackling hiss of warning. "Particularly in this neighborhood. Particularly around this house."

"Miss Tyler, you don't mean to say that someone could have it in for you because you rescued these cats?"

The old woman shrugged, letting her age-shrunken eyes disappear into the sagging pouches of her skin. "I'm old. I live alone. I don't approve of how they like to entertain themselves. They resent me, and my cats. Sometimes someone calls and threatens to inform Public Health. Other times, someone just calls."

"Threatening phone calls?" Temple perked up. "You can report that."

"They can report me for too many cats. It all comes to nothing. The police won't believe either of us, they don't want to mess with a crazy old woman and her cats."

"But you don't have to just wait here like a sitting duck!"

She smiled and caressed her cane. "Too bad cats are not good watch dogs, hmm? But I couldn't bring a noisy, enthusiastic dog into their refuge. They prefer quiet and the company of their kind."

Temple looked around. Were so many cats kept so close happy together? They didn't look unhappy. And they were safe, as they certainly had not been just beyond these sturdy old doors. She could no longer smell the strong animal presence; it had become natural. This was their safe house, and they had a right to leave their scents upon it.

"That's a wonderful cane," she told the old woman.

Miss Tyler held it out into the cool, bright light. "Mexican-made," she said proudly. "By an old wood-carver near Cuernavaca. I used to get around before I got so old, before I had all these cats. My last trip, he carved it for me. For luck."

Temple studied the strongly colored figures carved into the cane: parrots and donkeys, wagons and cacti, sombreros and coyotes. No cats. "The colors are hand-painted?"

"All hand-carved, hand-painted. No one does handwork like this anymore. If time must handicap me, if I must limp and lean, at least I will have a magical cane."

"And cats." Temple looked around again, smiled and finished the last of her ginger cookie. "You will have magical cats."

"Oh, don't let Father Hernandez hear you say that. He's down on my cats as it is. He is a serious man. He has no time for magic."

"Father Hernandez? Oh—from the church down the street. Does he object to having so many cats near the church property?"

Miss Tyler snorted. "How could he? Do I object to the kids playing and yelling at recess day in and day out?" She pounded the cane tip on the floor for emphasis. "No, we have had a parting of the ways on theological grounds, Father Hernandez and myself."

"Theological grounds? You mean matters of dogma or conscience?"

"No, I mean matters of cats."

Temple looked down. Perhaps in theological circles, cats had become a subject of grave debate, such as how many cats could pirouette on the head of a pin.

Miss Tyler looked down—and around—to her sprawling, meowing pride of pussycats. "Father Hernandez," she said in dire tones, "will not concede that my cats will be waiting for me in heaven, and vice versa."

"Oh. Isn't that the standard position in most religions?"

"I don't know about most religions. I am a faithful Roman Catholic, always have been. My house has stood here longer than the church. Until now," she added grimly, "I planned to leave most of my estate to Our Lady of Guadalupe, with a bequest for the care of the cats, but since Father Hernandez has revealed his foolishness on the issue of pets in heaven, I changed my will. Everything goes to the cats now. If they can't be guaranteed passage through the pearly gates, I'll see that my house remains a paradise on earth for them."

"I'm sure Father Hernandez feels he must adhere to the letter of the law. Maybe adults tell children that their dead pets will go to heaven, but I don't think even kids believe it nowadays, any more than they believe in the Tooth Fairy."

"I don't care what kids believe in." The cane rapped the floor again. "All the animals were in the Garden of Eden with Adam and Eve. Why would God separate us from the very creatures He created with us—in heaven, where He can have everything just the way He wants it? If a sparrow cannot fall without His notice, how can He let so many cats suffer without any hope of an afterlife? Besides, there is no one I'd want to see in heaven, except these."

She surveyed her collection with approval.

Temple wasn't getting embroiled in a debate on cat heaven. She discreetly checked her watch. "My gosh, it's late. I've got to go!" Jumping up was a bad idea. Something underfoot squalled in protest. Obviously, the cats in this house weren't used to sudden movement.

Just then the phone rang. Miss Tyler sighed and began to push away from her stool.

"I'll get it," Temple offered with Girl Scout quickness.

But where was it? Follow the trail of the telephone trill. Miss Tyler was making sputterings of protest behind her, but they slacked off.

Temple found a supple phone cord emerging from behind the refrigerator, and traced it for the space of two more rings through tendrils of hanging ivy to the actual instrument's lair: atop the refrigerator. She grabbed the receiver and pulled it down to her ear.

"Hello," she answered a bit breathlessly, realizing she should have prefaced that with "Tyler residence" in case some elderly phone mate of Blandina's was puzzled by a new voice.

Apparently she sounded enough like Miss Tyler on that one hasty word to reassure the caller.

"S-*s*-*s*-sorry," he, she, it whispered, the esses sharp and sibilant. "You'll be s-*s*-*s*-sorry."

Temple tore the phone from her ear as if scorched. She had just heard Peggy's famous Hissing Caller; only, Peggy hadn't said anything about outright threats.

Temple brought the receiver close and listened again. Nothing to be heard now but the sinister *ssssss* on the open line. Either Miss Tyler was getting calls from an asthmatic masher or a defective radiator, both of them elderly.

"Hello?" Temple repeated in a high, breaking voice, making herself into a querulous old woman who didn't hear too well. Playing that sweet, elderly poisoner in the high-school class play, "Arsenic and Old Lace," hadn't hurt.

But the caller would not be lured into further words. The hiss continued, interrupted by a slurping, breathing sound.

Temple stretched up to hang up the phone, then turned to poor Miss Tyler, who was watching her with sharp eyes.

"What did they want?" she asked.

"Not much, just hissing on the line." Just like the odd phone calls Peggy had been getting.

"You heard it, then!" she crowed. "I am not crazy. I have a witness. They've never called before when Peggy was here, or Sister Seraphina."

Temple checked her watch again. Past seven. "When does Peggy come for the evening feeding?"

"Five or six, at the latest. I've never told her about the calls; no point, she wouldn't believe me. Nobody does."

"Then you've never had company this late before?"

Miss Tyler smiled. "You're right. Sister Seraphina is careful not to walk back to the convent after dark, though it's only a few doors. This neighborhood has changed," she added in disgust. "But the phones have never hissed before."

"Does it stop?"

"Only when I hang up."

"Has . . . the caller ever said anything?"

Miss Tyler shook her head and used her cane to shoo away from her ankles the large cream tiger-stripe that had come in with Temple. "You've mooched enough, you big galoot. Gone over to the enemy, haven't you, Peter, even though they won't make room for you in the afterlife? And you with nine of 'em to go through, too!"

"What about the caller?" Temple repeated patiently. "Has he spoken?"

Miss Tyler shook her head again. "Nope. Don't even know if it is a 'him,' though the phone people said most of these callers are. Hims. Or kids. But I've never heard a word, just that strange hissing sound. I've heard noises, though, and seen lights at night. Outside the house."

"You need to notify the police," Temple advised, wondering whether to mention that brief, unsettling phrase, *You'll be s-s-s-sorry*.

"Huh. I did. Many times. They ignore my calls now. They never find anything outside and I don't want 'em inside. They might take my cats. No one believes me. No one believes a crazy old woman who keeps a lot of cats."

"I believe you," Temple said stoutly—or was that Girl Scoutly? "I heard the hissing with my own ears. Do you have good locks on the house?"

The woman came slowly across the uneven floor, her cane prodding the yellow cat ahead of her. "Go on, go on. Usually it's his partner Paul who visits. Go on, Peter, you traitor. Just as in the New Testament, yellow through and through, until the cock crew thrice. And then they make you gatekeeper. Huh. No justice, not even in church." She eyed Temple as she came even with her. "Good locks, and the windows are nailed shut. Still, it's scary, alone at night. And no one will come."

Temple waffled. Should she offer to stay? Here, with all these cats? Blandina Tyler wasn't her aunt; her problems weren't Temple's responsibility. She was already doing far more than she should. And the police were probably right; old ladies alone heard things, saw things, worried about things. Many became slightly paranoid, or even clinically so. Still, it was eerie that both the aunt and the niece were being methodically hissed at . . . or not so odd if you concluded that the aunt had been included in the harassment of the niece, or that it had something to do with a shaved Birman cat at the cat show.

Temple stood on the threshold with the ejected Peter and waited to hear Miss Tyler turn her lock and deadbolt. She spun to face the street, which was dark now. Her Storm was a huddled shape blacker than the evening. Only Peter by her legs was a reverse shadow, a beige pool of motion.

Then he took off, trotting around the side of the house.

Curious, Temple followed his pale form in the dark. Had she heard a dry twig snap? The ground was sandy and uneven. Her heels sank with every step, and she imagined them getting scuffed beyond repair. The oleander bushes clinging to the side of the house loomed as tall as Max Kinsella and scratched gently on the screens as she passed.

This was hopeless, she thought, stopping. The cat was no longer visible, and Temple felt lost in an unknown stretch of underbrush.

She retreated, coming at last to the front flagstones and clicking down them as softly as she could. Neighborhood kids—even gang members—could be tormenting Miss Tyler. She had taken their living toys away, hadn't she? Such kids, if you could call them that, would be coming out for the night now that it was dark, to hang out, drag race, do drug deals.

Scary stereotypes, but not unrealistic. Matt's self-defense instructions started droning in her head as she trotted for the safety of her car. Somewhere a sinister-sounding motor throbbed, its muffler growling in the empty night like a lion roaring out a challenge over the African savannah.

Why were there so few streetlights along here? She glanced up to see the church's square tower black against a still-backlit, charcoal-gray sky. Old neighborhood, that's why; now a poor neighborhood, with no clout for civic improvements.

She had her keys out before she reached the Storm, had unlocked it and hurled herself inside, locking the door again. Relieved, she started the car. The loud churn of the engine was an answer to the idling lion's roar down the block. Her headlights stabbed the night, announcing her presence. But she was secure in her metal island and, rolling into gear, glad to get away and now inhale—ah, air that was not cat-clogged.

She turned on the radio for the company of its lighted dial as much as for any music. But before she turned up the sound on Rod Stewart's latest hit cut, another, less upbeat sound replayed in her head: *You'll be sorry.*

Would she?

Chapter 11

Prize Pussycat

Here is my problem. I must find many cats. Normally, this is a piece of catnip for me. I am a first-class finder with a world-class sniffer, particularly if the subjects in question are cats. However, I have no desire to hit the most conspicuous locale for a surplus of cats, which is the animal pound.

The deliberately mysterious Karma has indicated that a large portion of Las Vegas's cat population is in danger of a blanket snuffing. The animal pound is too obvious a site of feline slaughter. Karma is anything but obvious. So. Where do scads of cats gather? I do some walking around, which is conducive to thinking, and come up with nothing but the Cat's Meow retail establishment, a clearing house where wandering strays are promptly seized and made into other than what they were; that is, eunuchs. Some of the more successful products of such experiments end up as window-dressing, not for sale, but for display in their diminished state.

I am the first to admit that the feline gene pool is more than somewhat vast, not to mention mathematically staggering. Still, some sense must be used in determining who to turn off and who to leave free to turn on. I am not about to put my particular genes lower on the evolutionary ladder than any other dude's of my acquaintance. In fact, I have been thinking of making a sacrifice for my community by offering a donation to one of these sperm banks that specializes in providing material of a superior sort. My kind of street smarts is just what the species needs, but there is a foolish prejudice against dudes of a free-wheeling background.

I say nature, not nurture, makes the feline. These pampered purebred pussums are not worth one of my used-claw sheaths. Where and when have they demonstrated their survival suitability? Dudes of my sort, of which there are damn few, *excuse moi français,* are just what the doctor ordered for my besieged and rapidly degenerating species.

Speaking of which, I encounter a bit of unforeseen luck. I have returned to the Circle Ritz and my dear little doll's apartment, and am reclining on one of my favorite spots, the latest edition of the day's newspaper (before Miss Temple Barr has had a chance to read it), when I begin to knead my powerful front limbs in the Sports Section of the *Las Vegas Sun,* which is *my* form of aerobic exercise these days.

In the process of this exertion, I inadvertently crinkle back the top pages. What to my wandering eyes should appear but the Classifieds section, the "Pets" part in particular. And what do I see advertised but another of these disgusting auction-block debacles for my kind: a purebred cat show at the Cashman Center. Now there is where a cacophony of cats could be found! What if some demented soul, some mad bomber, perhaps, were to strike while the clans were gathered, so to speak? Such a scenario would fit Karma's vague predictions of death on the grand scale.

I rise and go now, to enter an arena I hold in the greatest of contempt: a cat show. Let no one say that Midnight Louie does not give his all for his kind.

Within an hour after making my noble resolution, I am inside the Cashman Convention Center, crouching under an avalanche of empty cartons once home to bags of Pretty Paws scented, clumping cat litter. I do not know many cats, not even the clumping kind, that enjoy the aroma of mentholated grass, which is the aftersniff that Pretty Paws leaves in its footsteps.

One would think that a prime specimen of rampant felinity like myself would be in-like-Flynn when it comes to crashing a cat show. I regret shattering any such delusions, but a cat show is perhaps the one venue most closed to one of my sort, for a very simple reason. These precious pussums—and I do mean "precious" in both senses of the word—are too valuable to be let loose on these vast premises. Hence any cat present is either caged or carried. Since neither condition appeals to me, I will indeed have to make like a feline Errol Flynn to storm this castle of kittydom without getting tossed into the nearest dungeon, i.e., a cramped cage with sanitary facilities that are much too conveniently close for one with my supersensitive sniffer.

So I peek out from under a Pretty Paws box and plot my course. At the moment, I shelter under the admissions table, where two-footed individuals are paying a pretty penny to get in and gawk at the crème de la crème of catdom. I eye the jungle of table legs surmounted by rows and rows of common cages hidden beneath enough poufs, swags and drapes to clothe Little Bo-Peep for a Gilbert-and-Sullivan operetta.

I am not fooled for a moment: froufrou does not transform a steel-mesh cage into a pleasant site for Midnight Louie. But speaking of pleasant sights, I notice one such resident not too far away: a long-haired platinum blonde who has nothing better to do than yawn, with no one in attendance.

I decide to begin my interrogation there. During a lull of passing shoes, I tippy-toe over the concrete floor and hurl myself behind a drapery intended to conceal the under-table clutter. I shudder to see a basket brimming with torture equipment: combs, brushes, powder and—my nemesis—nail clippers. Nobody gets near these retractable shivs unless I am forced to use them. I also spot something I recognize only from my brief sojourns in various veterinarians' offices: a battery-operated clipper equipped with jagged steel teeth. Such an instrument is frequently applied to dogs, who, through thousands of years of domestication, have allowed humans to modify their body hair like topiary trees, and to some unfortunate feline souls who found themselves in circumstances where they could not attend to their daily grooming and ended up in one solid snarl. If you have never seen a clipped cat, you have been spared a terrible sight; most of my kind look best in their dress coats.

Since I dislike spending much time in the vicinity of these fiendish so-called grooming instruments, I slink out from under the cloth and vault atop the table.

I find myself face to face with the strangest creature I have ever seen: it is long, lean and the color of a nice dollop of kidney-and-liver pablum—a tastebud-terrifying brown-gray shade. And it is wrinkled all over. I would take it for a shar pei, an ugly customer of the canine persuasion that looks like everything but its skin shrank in the wash, except there is no mistaking the scent of a feline.

It hisses at my sudden appearance, and the sentiment is mutual. I feel I am looking in a mirror and seeing the image of a ghoul. If it were a girl ghoul, I might be tempted to linger, but this is definitely a dude, and nobody so naked should be gawked at without somebody collecting a fee, usually at a side show.

I return unceremoniously to the cool concrete floor and resume my two-yard dashes from tablecloth to tablecloth, avoiding human feet—and eyes—with my usual subtle and almost supernatural skill. I told you that these genes were A-1!

Never have I encountered so many weird-looking members of my species. The people on parade here are no prizes, either, but luckily they are oblivious to ordinary dudes engaged in surreptitious spying when they have so many extraordinary dudes and dolls, to whose every sneeze and sniffle they are attuned.

I do encounter one rather ordinary, albeit famous, face. This is a big, brown-and-black kisser of the variety called tiger-striped. I have paused to admire the solid-brass nameplate on the cage when I glimpse the inhabitant, who is almost as large as I am.

"The notorious Maurice, I presume," I say.

His ears perk up. "What do you know about my notoriety?" he asks in a throaty growl.

"I have seen your television ads. Is that Yummy Tum-tum-tummy stuff any good?"

"Naw," says Maurice, yawning. "They have to spice it with tuna fish in order to get me to look like I am eating it. And with all the time those commercials take, the Yummy Tum-tum-tummy is half rotted anyway."

I wrinkle my nose as if smelling a rat. "That spokescat gig pay pretty well?"

"Perhaps. You would have to ask my trainer."

"You have a personal trainer? What is the matter? Has the Hollywood life made you forget how to leap, look and listen?"

"Fame—even without fortune—is better than warming a cage floor at the Big House."

"You have been on Death Row, too?" I ask, impressed. Not too many of us end up with a commuted sentence, and our own series of television commercials to boot.

"Plucked from the jaws of death," he affirms in a bored tone. "My autobio is available in children's book sections everywhere. It is called 'Maurice, the Miracle Cat.' " He fans his nails—clipped, of course—in an affected way to examine them.

For all his down-home looks, this dude loves to put on airs.

"You have not heard any rumors of an attempted uprising against cats?"

"What nonsense!" Maurice says with a superior sniff. "I am told that cats are now more popular than dogs. Who would want to harm them?"

"You have been living the soft life for too long," say I, scowling. "The animal shelters work night and day shuffling cats out of their mortal coils, not to mention the random pieces of ricocheting metal that charge down the street, known as cars. You also overlook the bad old days, when our kind's association with what some authorities regarded as the wrong people led to a witch-hunt that consigned millions of our forebears to the fiery furnace."

"Ancient history," snarls the tiger-stripe before me.

Easy for him to say: he was not the wrong color in the wrong century. Given that ancient history, it is lucky that a dude of my particular dark dye lot is here at all.

I see that Easy Street has made Maurice—bet his original name was something simple like "Boots" or "Tuffy"—insensitive to social issues, and move on. It occurs to me, however, that any evil-doer wishing to do cats in general a public disservice could do worse than to begin with a visiting celebrity like Maurice. Perhaps I do not want to stop this fiend.

But duty comes before poetic justice. As I wend my careful way between cages, avoiding cooing humans and raised stainless-steel combs, I come across a strange rumor. It begins with a coy Siamese whose baby-blues hold a come-hither look. I have never cared for the oriental type—too skinny, too often cross-eyed and kink-tailed, and always temperamental—but I sashay over to find her chocolate-brown tail tapping impatiently outside the grillwork of her cage.

"What is the scoop, Big Boy?" she asks, nothing infantile about her baby-blues now that I am closer. "How did a he-man like you bust into this sideshow? Are you an escapee from the Household Cat Division?"

"Heaven forbid," I say with sincere shock. "I am an independent operator."

"Oh," says she, arching her back and edging near the grille, "a P.I. You checking out false pedigrees?"

"Nope. I am looking for terrorists of the cat kind."

Alarm narrows her pupils to tiny vertical slits you could barely poke a thread through, which leaves a lot of sky-blue for an impressionable fellow to dive into. Perhaps I have not given these Siamese a fair opportunity to engage in a bit of intraspecies getting-to-know-you. But visions of detente die a quick death in my head.

The dark brown tail jerks itself into an unattractive kink. "Listen," she hisses in a voice gone harsh with fear. "One of our number was brutally attacked by someone wielding a pair of dog clippers."

"Who is the unlucky topiary bush?"

"A Birman, name of Minuet of Celestial Sunrise. I hear the poor dear is so distraught she can barely lift her head from beside her water bowl."

"Where is this denuded dame? Any material damage?"

"Row L, numbers sixty-six and sixty-eight. And just to her competition chances. Purrsonally, we competitors think another owner went amok. You know how high-strung these breeder types can get." Her narrow, chocolate-masked face regards me seriously.

"Right," I respond, leaping over the table edge to a surface a guy can trust, cold concrete.

The brutalized Birman is right where the Siamese said she would be. Luckily, the area is deserted, and even the neighboring cages are empty, so I have this little doll to myself.

I am not up on every breed of fancy cat, but it does not take a genetics degree to see that the critter in question is only a hair or two away from the great and glorious Karma herself. Make that about six thousand hairs. This little doll looks like a toy lawnmower has been run up and down her spine and around her slender midsection. This Mohawk-in-reverse does nothing for her looks and apparently has plunged her spirits into a deep depression, for despite my rubbing back and forth on her cage side for some moments, she does not lift her despondent head.

"Where is everybody?" I finally ask.

She sighs and lays her head to her paws. It is a rather ludicrous head, with two rows of fluffy yellow hair bracketing a bald patch. I manage not to snicker, for a cosmetic mishap is tragedy indeed to these show girls and boys. Let us just say that the little Birman is having one bad hair day.

"I do not know," she answers at last. Few can resist my manner of dignified, steady support. "I think that they are judging my . . . my . . . category," she spits out, a wail on the way.

I cut off the sound effects with another question.

"Who did it?"

"I do not know," she says again. "I am sleeping quietly in my safe little cage when someone picks me up from the rear. At first the sound is like a mother's purr. You know how loud that sounds when one is just a tiny thing?"

I nod, gruffly. My dear mama was forced to give up her offspring due to a stroll down some street or other from which she never returned. I do not like to think of my litter days, but I do recall a time when the roar of my mama's purr signaled safety and—even better—satiety.

"I must have been . . . drugged, I think." When Miss Birman wrinkles her blond brow now, a dude can really see it without the intervening hair. She would not care to know that her new hairdo has added years to her looks, and I would not like to be the one to tell her this.

"I fell asleep again on being returned to my pillow, and knew nothing more until I heard my owner scream."

"This would be—"

"She howled in that peculiar human way called a yell. She screeched. How else could I describe it?"

"I do not mean what was the scream like, but who is your owner?"

"Oh. She calls herself Peggy Wilhelm. A most unimaginative name. She is all right, but now she has taken Snow-upon-the-Mountain Spring into the judging ring, and I am left behind to shiver."

I study the rough roller-coaster ride of her bare spine. It is indeed a defenseless stretch of skin and bone. It will be spring before she sprouts a decent crew-cut. Although her plight is unfortunate, her life was never threatened. I find this funny business with a dog clipper most perplexing. After a reassuring pat on the victim's semi-stripped tail, I bound down to earth again and stalk away, thinking hard.

Perhaps my problem is putting any credence in Karma's doleful maunderings. After all, I have just met the lady and I have no proof of her reliability. It is easy to forecast disaster these days, and easy to set up as a prophet. What it is not easy to do is to figure out why any person or persons unknown would wish to crop a show cat within an inch of her life.

It is while I am occupied with pacing out the limits of this conundrum that I hear a human voice cry, "Hey!"

Somehow I know that I am the lowly object of this admonition.

I look up to see that I have been spotted ranging free by a guard. I can tell that he is a guard because he wears a uniform accoutred with insignia and a big black-leather belt bristling with vaguely threatening equipment, including a walkie-talkie. He could be a refugee from a marching band. On the other hand, he is running in my direction and I do not believe he needs another tuba player.

I take off, cross-country, under tablecloths, over boxes and baskets, in a zigzag course that would even confuse a Singer sewing machine. Of course the aisles are choked with passing feet and I dare not skitter across them for fear I will trip an unobservant person, flinging him or her to the unforgiving pavement, and even worse, risking a crushing and giving away my location.

What to do? Clearly, a runaway feline will stand out like a shaved Birman in this atmosphere. Clearly, I must go undercover—fast.

I spy a line of cages on a table, and the last one is empty and bare, its door thoughtfully ajar. I zig, then zag, take advantage of a gaggle of cooing breeders carrying a lolling handful of Persians. I float atop the table like a butterfly and dash inside the cage like a gerbil heading for home.

Then I assume a casual pose—on my back with my limbs in the air, hoping I will not be taken for dead.

Apparently not.

A voice booms out above me, but I do not open my eyes, the better to keep up my disguise.

"Will you look at this one!" the voice, male, urges. "This old boy is ready to nap for the afternoon." He sounds rather envious, if you ask me.

"What is the name on the cage?" a woman's voice trills.

Through my eyelashes I can see them both bend down to consult a piece of white paper affixed to the steel wire. What have I got myself into?

"Percy," the man reads. "Strange name for a big bruiser like this."

I cringe. Percy. If my peers, not to mention my inferiors, hear this namby-pamby name on the street, my tail will be mincemeat.

"Well, this *is* the 'Household Pets' category, all-breed mixes and types allowed," the woman notes. "Oh, look. The cage isn't even closed. Some owners!"

She slams it shut while I subdue a shudder.

"You must remember that these people are amateurs," the man tells her. "Who else would enter a cat this overweight?"

Overweight? Look who is talking, Jell-O-Belly! I quash my indignation. Sometimes playing dumb is the best disguise. When the two toddle away, I raise my head to see the lay of the land.

It appears that I have an audience—a handful of people arranged among those cold, cocoa-brown metal folding chairs every convention center is so fond of. Between me and my public sits a long, bare table that has the look of an accessory in an experimental laboratory. Only the lightning bolts are missing.

It soon becomes all too obvious what is up here. One by one, the cats are removed from their cages and carried to the table, where they are publicly posed and prodded while the man—a judge, apparently—announces their bad points to all and sundry. I can but agree with him as I size up the competition: a spindly collection of nine-pound weaklings, heavy on stripes and calico patches, with whiskers barely long enough to catch in a cobweb.

At last my turn comes. The cage latch opens and I am hefted out, a hand pushing hard into my soft underbelly.

"What a heavyweight, folks!" the jocular judge announces, pounding my four feet to the tabletop. "A fine, glossy coat, however, and well maintained."

At last, a modicum of praise.

"And nice white whiskers. This is Percy. Percy's owner should note that this big fellow could use a diet of Free-to-be-Feline Lite and some exercise."

I stifle a growl as the crowd laughs, not daring to attract attention to myself. Although playing the pusillanimous pussycat goes against my grain, I know better than to talk back to any judge.

My examiner strokes me to the end of my tail, then shuffles some papers. "Despite Percy's deplorably self-indulgent condition, he is a fine specimen, a strong, big, juicy cat and he gets best of category."

A smattering of applause erupts. All right, sizzles. Apparently my stunning victory has not encouraged sufficient enthusiasm in this ignorant group.

I am carried in triumph back to my commandeered cage, reinserted and then latched once more behind a wall of gridwork. The woman trips over, beaming, to affix a rosette of blue satin ribbon to my cage front.

I bat its twin tails with one lethargic paw. Blue ribbons do not open steel latches. I do not know how I am going to get out of here, but I do know that the AWOL Percy will be of no help. Shortly, another batch of contestants will be brought to these show-and-tell cages and it will become all too obvious that Midnight Louie, aka "Percy," is in the wrong place at the wrong time.

Chapter 12

Wakeup Call

A ringing sound in his ears awoke Matt. He sat up in the dark, his body pounding with sudden alarm, his mind trying to remember. He often dreamed of the phone ringing, natural enough when his working life was spent answering it. Had that awakened him, or—

Another ring of the phone, a falsetto wobble from the main room. No dream, but who would call him at—he focused on the bedside clock-radio's LED numerals—four-thirty in the morning? Who even knew his phone number besides the hotline?

Awake, and even more alarmed now, he got up and stumbled into the dark, trying to avoid the boxes of books he still hadn't unpacked, trying to find his way quickly through the rooms that still didn't seem his.

"Yes?"

He expected a pause and a hangup. Wrong number. Or someone looking for a crack-of-dawn pizza.

"Matt?"

No mistake. Woman's voice he couldn't quite place. "Yes?"

"Thank God!"

"Sister Seraphina! What—?"

"You've got to come."

"Come . . . where, why? Now?"

"Now. To the convent."

"What's wrong?"

"Our neighbor lady—a very old lady—is terribly ill, and Father Hernandez . . ."

"Yes?" he prodded.

"Father Hernandez is not functional. I need your help."

"Have you called an ambulance?"

"It may not be necessary, but you must come at once. More is needed."

He didn't want to get caught up in this, couldn't get involved in this. "Can't you handle it?"

"She's an old, old lady, Matt, from a generation that trusts only men in a crisis. It would be better if you came. Please, Matthias—Matt."

He kept silent again. He had been asleep for only an hour; waking up so suddenly put his brain in deep-freeze. "I—I don't have a car, no transportation." Even to him, it sounded like an excuse, although it was true.

"Oh, Matthias, you must come quickly!"

He had never heard Sister Superfine sound so out of control, an old woman with a dysfunctional priest, an obscene phone-caller and now an injured neighbor on her hands.

"I'll get a car," he said, "and be there as fast as I can."

"Please hurry."

It was the last thing on earth he wanted to do, but even before she had hung up, he had switched on the small lamp by the phone and opened his almost-empty address book to a number at the beginning.

Chapter 13

Extreme Urgency

Temple was waiting outside her apartment door in a double-knit navy-blue jumpsuit, with her car keys and a tote bag, two minutes after Matt called.

"Of course you can have my car in an emergency," she had told him, not taking time to ask why.

Now she wondered. He hadn't sounded panicked, only deeply distracted beneath the haste, and oddly reluctant. Footsteps pounded down the distant stairs and Temple went to meet them. At least he had remembered to forget calling the fatally slow elevator.

The low, night-wattage of the hall sconces made the Circle Ritz's interior seem eerie and isolated, like the limitless maze of corridors on an ocean liner. Temple almost expected the floor to lurch. What could be so urgent?

She met a running Matt by the elevator, where he reached for her car keys like a drowning man for a line.

She pulled her hand away. "I'll drive."

"You don't have to—" He reached again.

"Matt—no! This is an emergency; you might have to go fast. It's my car; I'll drive. Come on."

Temple headed for the door to the stairs and bulled through, Matt following and arguing too loudly.

"Temple! I don't want you involved," he insisted behind her. "I can drive fast—and safely, for heaven's sake. Give me the keys."

Even with their voices lowered to hoarse whispers, the words echoed up the concrete stairwell and buffeted at the safety doors separating them from resident sleepers.

Temple kept going—fast, clattering down the hard stairs in her slide-on wedgies, the loose shoe backs slapping the soles of her feet as she skittered tight around each turn of the stairwell.

She charged out into the still, hot Las Vegas night, heading for the Storm until Matt caught up and hooked her arm, stopping her and spinning her around to face him in one economic gesture.

"You don't need to go," he said, insisted.

He must have dressed as quickly as she, yet in appearance he was the same unruffled Matt she always saw in his knit shirt and khaki pants. Casual, calm. Except that now his voice vibrated a hint of exasperation she had never heard before, maybe even . . . desperation.

She hated to 'fess up—she didn't need to rise in the dead of night like a misdirected zombie on an errand of mercy—but if he wanted, needed, her car, she would have to admit what she knew.

"Yes, I do need to go, Matt, because you don't have a driver's license and I'm responsible if anything happens."

Stunned, he froze for a moment, then followed without protest as she made for the car again. "I forgot, but—how . . . did you know?" he asked over the Storm's top as she unlocked the driver's side.

Temple leaned across the seat to open the passenger door. "Lieutenant Molina." Matt really froze at that one. She was sorry the nearest streetlight was too distant to illuminate faces. "Come on, get in." Temple started the car so suddenly the ignition gargled a protest. "Where are we going?"

Her question seemed to interrupt a series of questions he was asking himself. He shook his head to clear it. "Do you know where Our Lady of Guadalupe Church is?" He sounded resigned now. "Seguaro and Del Rey?"

"No, but I know the intersection. Just tell me where to turn when we get there."

Even at five in the morning, Las Vegas streets sported traffic: if Chicago was the city that never shut down, Las Vegas was the one that never shut down or shut up. Temple guided the Storm along the fastest route at a slightly racy forty-five miles an hour. "What'll I say if the police stop us?"

"How did Molina know?" asked Matt, still dazed that she knew about his status—or lack thereof—with the Nevada State Motor Vehicle Department.

"How did she know about your license? Or your absence of same?" Temple flashed Matt a glance as a streetlamp flared overhead. His habitual calm looked more like numbness. "She checked you out. Bet you didn't dream that I would be so dangerous to know. Yes, sir, Lieutenant Molina has a nagging curiosity about men of my acquaintance."

"Damn," he said, the only time she'd heard him swear. Why he said it was not clear.

"Yeah, Molina makes me say that a lot, too," Temple put in to lighten the atmosphere. "She is one stubborn daughter of a dork."

"Daughter of a dork?" That had shaken his unnatural calm.

"Well, son of a bitch is sexist, and besides, Molina's the wrong sex for it."

Matt's laugh sounded less like amusement and more like surrender. Obviously, things weren't going his way tonight, and Temple was one more unpleasant surprise. She wasn't supposed to know about his errand, and she wasn't supposed to know he didn't have a driver's license. Why? She was becoming almost as curious as Molina, Temple reflected.

"What are we riding to the rescue about?" she asked as she turned onto Seguaro.

He laughed again, wearily. "I don't exactly know. I recently . . . heard from an old grade-school teacher of mine from Chicago. She called out of the blue a few minutes ago, begging for help. I don't even know how she got my number."

"Chicago? I thought you were raised on a farm."

He turned to face her at last. "What do you mean?"

"That's how you knew Midnight Louie was a he, you said on the day he came, that day we met by the pool. You said you learned that animal-husbandry sex stuff growing up on a farm."

"What a memory for detail! And checking out an animal isn't that arcane as long as it isn't big enough to kick you." Matt leaned forward to adjust the air-conditioning fan. "The farm was my grandparents'; we went there almost every weekend when I was a kid, but I lived in the city, the old, inner city."

Temple nodded and eyed the neighborhood the Storm's headlights revealed in bright snatches. "Funny, I was here just today on an errand of mercy, I guess you'd call it."

"Errand of mercy?" He sounded struck by the phrase.

Temple took her right arm off the wheel and flexed it weight-lifter style, while declaiming:

"*Cat feeder for the world,*
Litter-lugger, stacker of Tender Vittles,
Player with kittens and the nation's pet-sitter . . ."

Matt's laughter was relaxed for the first time that evening. Temple knew that her impromptu paraphrase of Carl Sandburg's poem "Chicago" wouldn't amuse him if he hadn't told the truth about growing up there. She sighed. Here she was, expecting every word to be a lie, like Molina, just because Molina had proved that Max Kinsella was living a lie. All men did not lie just because Max had, and besides, Max's sins were of omission more than commission. What were Matt's sins? Maybe she'd find out tonight, Temple thought with interest.

"Turn here," he said tersely.

"Are you sure?"

"Yes, why?"

"I can't believe it! I was just on this street a few hours ago, yesterday evening. I could have found my way here solo, even in the dark. The Cat Lady I visited lives near here. Does your old teacher keep cats, by any chance?"

"Only two, Peter and Paul."

"Peter . . . ? A pumpkin-colored—"

"There she is! She shouldn't be waiting outdoors at night in this neighborhood," Matt hissed under his breath, opening his door and bounding out of the car before Temple had fully stopped it.

She followed as soon as she could wrestle her tote bag from the backseat, where it had fallen to the floor and wedged itself behind the driver's seat. Then she remembered Matt's concern and locked the Storm. By now he was conferring intensely with a woman whom the streetlight etched in pale grays.

She eyed Matt's former teacher with interest: tall and white-haired, she was leading Matt down the block at a rapid pace. "It was easier to tell you to come here than to direct you to a new address," she was explaining in the breathless voice of one who's been handling a crisis alone for too long.

"Fine, Seraphina," he said, turning to make sure Temple was all right. "This is a neighbor, Temple Barr."

The woman turned to give Temple a glance that took her in from top of the head to tippy-toes. Then she bustled on down the overgrown sidewalk, a bag like a doctor's swinging against her leg. Temple wondered if the woman was a doctor—or a nurse—and if so, why did she need Matt? And what kind of name was "Seraphina?" And why just that?

"We look in on this elderly neighbor lady," Seraphina was explaining to Matt. She turned right at a walkway leading to the shadowy bulk of a house. "She's a bit . . . eccentric, and sometimes confused. She isn't always the most reliable person, cries wolf, but she called tonight again in a very credible panic. When I came over, I couldn't decide if her distress was physical or mental, but it was distress—"

"Then you didn't send for an ambulance?" Matt demanded, almost accused.

"I thought we'd decide about that . . . after." Seraphina had stopped at the front door to grope in her pocket for a key.

Temple reflected on how only elderly women came equipped with routine pockets nowadays. Her own jumpsuit had none, no doubt to preserve its sleek, wrinkle-free modern lines; too bad people didn't come with the same guarantee.

"None of this may be necessary—" Matt was saying with an impatience new to him "—me, Temple's car and Temple, this . . . entire emergency."

"It is necessary!" Seraphina retorted fiercely. "Do you think I would call on you if it weren't an extreme matter?"

Matt didn't answer for a moment. "You might think you were doing it for my own good," he said at last.

"For *her* good. I gave up on you when you graduated grade school; you're on your own, Matthias," she answered, then pushed a key into the lock and worked the heavy door open. "I left Rose with her," she added, to Temple's mystification, if not Matt's.

Temple could only follow along like an unneeded comma, a trailing, expendable body tacked to the end of the mysterious rescue party. Her floppy shoes had made a disgraceful racket on the walk outside; they were no more discreet on the interior tile floors. But after four steps into the house, she stopped dead.

Even in the dark of night, even distracted by the emergency and the puzzling, unspoken byplay between Matt and this Seraphina woman, Temple knew where she was. Her nose told her so. Her nose said "Cats ahoy!" Cats to bow and port, and cats amidships. Cats high, cats low, cats large, cats small. Cats in hats, maybe, but most certainly cats in litter boxes, oh my.

A light switch flashed on at the older woman's sure touch, illuminating a staircase rising into the dark of a second story. Sure enough, cats were sprawling on the treads and balancing on the wrought-iron handrail and playing patty-cake through the bars of the decorative bird cage.

Matt and the old woman were working their way upward, stepping around cats as called for. He had taken the bag from her and from the rear, looked like a doctor making a house call.

Temple rushed to catch up with the pair, even though she felt redundant to their drama. The upstairs hall led to a bedroom, of course, where another old woman sat beside an even older woman who lay on the bed, her head tossing, her hands wringing. Blandina Tyler looked waxen and harried at the same time. Her eyes roamed the room's perimeter as if seeking escape—or an unseen enemy trying to enter.

"Noises again," she was murmuring in a monotone. "Betrayed by noises and lights and hisses. And Peter could not be found. They were coming for the Lord, and Peter could not be found . . . . Has the cock crowed yet?"

"Hush, Blandina." Seraphina rustled over like a veteran nurse and passed a calming hand over the woman's brow. "The neighborhood roosters will be screeching soon enough." She glanced at the attendant. "Any change?"

The woman named Rose shook her grizzled head. "She may have hyperventilated while you were gone, but her condition got no worse, just the nonsensical ravings—"

Temple watched the two women, puzzled. They were past seventy, bespectacled, plain and rather dumpy, yet both radiated an air of cheerful competence polished to a high gloss, like retired nurses. Matt, she saw, watched the woman in the bed as if hypnotized by her. Did he know Blandina Tyler?

"They want me to die," Miss Tyler wailed suddenly. "They will take all I have and draw lots for the rest. For the cats. I was in the garden when they came, with noise and lights—and where was Peter? Run away. I wasn't going to struggle, but then—oh, it's horrible, horrible! Profanity.

'Pray for us now and at the hour of our death—' I don't want to die that way!"

Her clutching fingers reached for the women trying to calm her agitated body. She clung to their hands as if to sanity.

"She's no better," Seraphina judged. "Call the ambulance, Rose." As her friend rushed from the room, Seraphina bowed close to the stricken woman. "I've brought the sacrament, Blandina. You needn't worry about dying untended."

"Not . . . Father Hernandez!" Blandina both begged and ordered. "Not . . . him. He wants me in heaven without my cats, and I won't have that. I'd rather go to hell!"

"Now, you don't mean that, and it won't happen. And not Father Hernandez. Someone else."

"I won't have it from you!" Blandina Tyler said with a trace of her earlier sharpness. "You go too far, with your short skirts and bare heads. Sacrilege. Profanity. And so cruel—" Her face contorted as if seeing a nightmarish vision.

"Not Father Hernandez," Seraphina said firmly, stepping aside to reveal Matt, looking like an angel of the Lord, all golden-haired and as handsome as a prince in a fairy tale.

The sight of him struck Blandina silent for a moment. Then she looked him up and down with the old suspicion that Temple recognized; she had been its recipient only hours before. "He's not wearing—"

"I called him in the dead of night," Seraphina reminded her.

"Isn't it . . . dawn yet?" the old woman asked in a sudden, pathetic, trembling tone. "The nights have been so long lately."

Matt drew a side chair to the bed and sat on it. Sister Seraphina lifted the black bag onto the bedside table she had emptied of clutter. She opened the bag and drew out a shining length of pale satin as long as an albino snake, wider than a ribbon but not as broad as a scarf.

Matt took it and put it around his neck. Temple had a momentary vision of a World War I pilot with his silk scarf

. . . but that was off-key. She kept trying to place this scene into some context she could recognize, and failed utterly.

Matt glanced at her briefly, the first time he had acknowledged her presence since introducing her to Seraphina, then lifted one end of the satin length to his face and kissed it.

Seraphina handed him a small glass bottle holding clear liquid, leaning near to whisper something in his ear.

"We are gathered," Matt said, "at the side of our friend Blandina to bring health and healing to her spirit and body." He stood, and with several ceremonial shakes, sprinkled the bottle's contents on the bed and around the room. When a strong sprinkle came in Temple's direction, she started as if it were acid, but Matt no longer noticed her, nor anyone in the room but the sick woman.

"She attended daily Mass," Seraphina murmured to Matt, adding with a smile, "despite Father Hernandez. And made her confession every Saturday."

He nodded, then leaned forward with great concentration and almost visible compassion to place his palms on the old woman's head. She sighed deeply, then the tortured tossing of her head subsided.

Seraphina took another small glass bottle and some cotton balls from the bag. Curiouser and curiouser, thought Temple.

"Should I leave?" a voice asked. Temple was startled to find it had been hers.

Matt did not look up, but Seraphina smiled and shook her head. Temple backed up until a piece of furniture stopped her, and set her heavy tote bag on the floor as slowly and quietly as she could.

Matt pressed his thumb to the bottle, then tilted it. His thumb-tip glistened as it reached toward the sick woman, touched her forehead and made a mark there. He repeated the ritual, anointing the palm of each hand.

Temple squelched a wild wondering if that gesture tickled. Clearly, it did not. Blandina Tyler calmed even more as Matt intoned: "Through this holy anointing may the Lord in His love and mercy help you with the grace of the Holy Spirit.

Amen. May the Lord who freed you from sin save and raise you up. Amen."

Matt then leaned forward and spoke intently, in a low tone, wishing Blandina peace of mind and body, true serenity of soul and spirit. Temple couldn't absorb all the words, just as she could barely absorb the meaning of this scene, but she absorbed the same calm that visibly quieted Blandina moment by moment.

"Our Father," Matt began, "Who art in Heaven . . ."

Seraphina joined in, and Temple was surprised that she still knew the words as well as she did—okay, an Our Father was like the Pledge of Allegiance or riding a bicycle; once you learned to do it, you never forgot—except that she alone charged ahead at the end with her favorite, thundering, dramatic line, "For thine is the Kingdom and the Power and the Glory—" The others stopped, even Rose, who had returned to the room and stood in the doorway watching and nodding with a solemn look on her round, woebegone face.

Temple sat down on what was behind her—an old-fashioned trunk, she saw as she turned—and caught Blandina's cane, which had been propped against the trunk, before it fell to the floor. When she reinstated it, she noticed that the rubber tip was damp and dotted with curds of fresh dirt.

Blandina had been out in the garden, Temple realized. Maybe that's where the ravings about a garden, the Garden of Gethsemane, had risen to haunt her mind. And that comment about Peter and betrayal and cocks crowing . . . obviously, the woman was very religious. Obviously, Temple was attending a religious rite. Obviously, Matt had presided here at Seraphina's behest.

Except that nothing was obvious to Temple beyond the incomprehensible obvious. Who was who and what was what—and did she really want to know?

She heard Matt's voice murmuring again, and this time she didn't listen. She was beginning to feel like an eavesdropper, after all.

Then she heard the thin, pale wail of a nearing emergency vehicle and felt relieved that something, something she understood, was coming to take charge of this situation that was so perplexing and even, in its way, frightening and disturbing.

When the heavyset man and woman pounded up the stairs—the siren had apparently banished all cats—with their equipment and their gurney and when Blandina Tyler was checked fore and aft and was being noisily bounced down the stairs, Temple finally looked up from her front-row-center seat on the trunk.

The black bag was shut. Matt was silent and scarfless. Seraphina was looking much relieved and toward Temple, then to the person referred to as "Rose."

"Forgive me for forgetting introductions," Seraphina said. "I am Sister Seraphina O'Donnell and this is Sister Saint Rose of Lima. This is Matt's friend, Temple—"

"Barr," Temple was proud to find herself reporting. Sister Seraphina O'Donnell. Sister Saint Rose of Lima. The words made no sense. "Rose" did. She smiled at the woman, who beamed back.

Temple decided that only good Girl Scout behavior would save her. "I . . . um, was supposed to come in the morning and help Miss Tyler feed her cats. I suppose if I stopped at your house—" she carefully included both women in her glance "—you could let me in. There are . . an awful lot of cats."

"We know." Rose chuckled a little. "You're a darling girl to suggest it," she added with a tinge of Irish brogue, "but we can do it. We're used to Miss Tyler's fascinating felines. In fact, we adopted a couple of them."

Temple didn't try to argue. A person lost in space, time and sense does not argue, as Alice in Wonderland had proved long ago.

"I'll ride with her to the hospital," Sister St. Rose of Lima told Sister Seraphina, who nodded and retrieved the black bag from the bedside table.

Matt did not offer to help her with it, Temple noticed, and Matt was always polite beyond belief.

"What about her cane?" Temple asked with belated concern, hefting the colorful stick.

"She won't need it until she comes home," Sister Seraphina assured her, following Rose out into the hall.

Temple nudged Matt, who had not yet moved, then went out in turn.

Downstairs, the rooms glowed with the silent red strobe of the ambulance light outside the open front door. Cats' eyes gleamed in the dark, as green as Christmas foil.

"Apparently she has a lot of cats," Matt said when he came downstairs, still sounding dazed.

Temple was able at last to have something in common with the odd old women named "Sister"—wry laughter.

"That's an understatement," Temple said. "Do you know how many there are?"

Sister Seraphina answered while Sister St. Rose of Lima—what a long name; no wonder it was shortened to "Rose"—went out to the ambulance.

"We think seventy-three."

"Aren't there laws?" Matt asked.

"City regulations," Seraphina corrected in a voice that was pure schoolteacher. "Her cats keep her happy. Who's going to complain about how many she keeps?"

"Maybe . . . somebody," Temple said.

Both of them looked at her, the Silent Woman through all of this.

"Miss Tyler was getting odd phone calls," Temple began, thinking. "No wonder she ended up so hysterical tonight. That's a lot of pressure for an old lady living alone to take, with nothing but watch cats around."

"Phone calls?" Matt was suddenly incisive, as he had not been all evening, but just as he had been when Temple had limped home after being assaulted in the Goliath parking ramp a few weeks before. "What kind of phone calls? Obscene?"

Sister Seraphina, in shock, which seemed foreign to her, sat down on a shapeless easy chair—and half-rose when a sleeping cat rocketed off the cushion and into the darkness.

"Obscenely weird," Temple said. "Hissing sounds. Maybe wheezy breathing. And when I was over here feeding the cats this evening, she mentioned sounds and lights outside the house."

Seraphina shook her head. "She was always calling the police about that, but they never found anything. They finally stopped coming."

Matt lifted a tiny, but adult, white cat from the third step of the stairs and sat down. The harsh hall light above painted his face with deep shadows of strain, or of thought.

"I got a call at the hotline from an elderly woman not long ago . . ."

"That must have been Blandina," Sister Seraphina said. "She called us at the convent at least twice a day."

After a silence, Temple spoke. "She was old, she was alone and frightened, she cried wolf to everyone who would listen. What if there really is a wolf?"

"Why?" Matt demanded.

"Well, the reason I'm here—" Matt looked alarmed as Sister Seraphina's expression grew alert, but Temple wasn't about to tattle on Matt's missing driver's license to old Teacher Seraphina, no way. The generations had to stick up for each other, no matter what "—is that Miss Tyler's niece, Peggy Wilhelm—"

"Darling girl," Seraphina interrupted enthusiastically. "Never abandoned her aunt."

"Anyway," Temple went on for Matt's benefit, "she raises purebred Birmans, and is exhibiting them at the cat show downtown this weekend. And one was shaved."

"Shaved?" The question came simultaneously from both listeners.

Temple, assured of a rapt audience now, nodded solemnly. "Shaved from head to tail, and around the body. Birmans are long-haired cats, and this one was a potential champion in its class, maybe even a Best of Show. Birmans are the sacred cats of Burma, but they're not supposed to have tonsures like monks. This one does. Peggy has to stay and guard her other cats, so I came over in her place to help her aunt feed the kitties last night. I can't help wondering if the incidents are connected."

"Not," said Matt to Seraphina, "to mention the obscene calls to the convent."

"Convent?" Now Temple could express full indignation and ignorance. "What convent?"

"Ours," Seraphina said serenely. "It's really just a large house; there are so few of us left. We Sisters of Charity belong to Our Lady of Guadalupe now," she added for Temple's benefit. "Rose and I and a few others. Blandina was our neighbor and we looked out for her—and the cats—when Peggy wasn't around."

"Someone is making obscene phone calls to a convent?" Temple demanded in disbelief. Oh, Alice, lend me your Tylenol-3, your caterpillar and a full deck of cards!

"To one of our nuns, Sister Mary Monica."

"She's over ninety and seriously hearing-impaired," Matt explained quickly, as if that made any difference.

"So that's why you're here," Temple charged.

"Guilty," he said, sounding exactly that. "Sister Seraphina called on me because she thought that I, being a hot-line counselor, would know about the creeps that do this."

Matt and Sister Seraphina exchanged a quick glance that was not lost on Temple. More was here than met the eye. Oh, boy, was that an understatement!

She decided to stick to the facts she knew, Ma'am, just the facts, and Sergeant Friday could take a flying . . . fillip.

"So," said Temple, toting insanities, "two houses practically next door to each other are receiving nuisance calls, and now one resident is . . . I don't know, either ill or hysterical. Miss Tyler seemed to have her marbles all in a row when I was here this morning."

"She's been under a lot of pressure," Seraphina said firmly. "Recently she's had a little feud with Father Hernandez, our parish priest. Despite her devout ways and the parish development program, they came to a parting on the issue of whether cats go to heaven." She sighed.

"Oh," Temple said. "I was raised Unitarian. I'm not good on this theology stuff."

Seraphina's smile was the kind that would melt barbed wire. "Neither was Father Hernandez," she said. "We tell children that heaven will be what they imagine. Why can't we tell old people, who are closer than us to both childish simplicity and heaven, what they need to hear? Father Hernandez refused to allow even a scintilla of chance that cats could cajole Saint Peter for entry. Blandina was furious, and worse, frightened. Those cats are all she has."

"Besides her niece," Temple put in.

"A niece, however devoted, is not the same as the creatures she saved, as the creatures who came to this house and found a haven here. Her rescued cats made Blandina feel useful, and that is a boon at any age." Seraphina sighed again, though she did not strike Temple as the sighing type under other circumstances.

Temple considered that old nuns were not so different from elderly maiden ladies who had too many cats and thought that their time had passed, that they could save no one but themselves and a few dozen abandoned animals. Except that nuns tended to go in for abandoned souls. Was Matt one?

In the dark of early morning, the cats hid and moved and hungered for food. Like a school of silent fish, they shifted through the vasty deeps of this old house, now missing its mistress. Temple thought of the tinfoil troughs she had filled not a day before, and of how empty they would soon be, and of how empty this house would be without Blandina. She saw the cane abandoned against the bedroom wall, and heard the cats crying for love and food, food and love.

She saw an Outsider who railed at the safeness of all little worlds, who dialed deaf, ancient nuns with even more ancient obscenities, who harassed old women and cats. She remembered the things the old woman, wandering, had said in her bed, and became profoundly disturbed.

"Blandina had no hearing problem," Temple said. "Maybe she went out to face the night lights and sounds.

Tonight. What made her sick? What made her so sick at heart and soul that she thought of Christ betrayed by Peter? I'm not particularly religious," Temple confessed, "but wasn't there a lot of the New Testament in what she said tonight?"

They were watching her, the old woman and the man she did not know.

"There was fresh dirt on Miss Tyler's cane tip," Temple said. "In the bedroom."

When they rose, it was a foregone conclusion.

Seraphina led them through the house's labyrinthine ways to the back. Dawn was bleaching the horizon white. The bushes flared like black fires against the sky.

Cats milled around their feet in the kitchen. Cats clamored for milk and honey and Yummy Tum-tum-tummy.

They went outside. No cocks crowed.

The garden was still and empty. Blandina would not trust her precious cats to an outside environment, and most rescued cats disdained the cold, cruel outer world that had orphaned them.

The three of them went their separate ways in the garden, lost in separate thoughts, searching separate ways.

Light blotted up the darkness slowly, hardly seeming to win, but sure to.

Temple had more to think about than old women and cats, but she kept looking for Something.

She found magenta-flowered oleander bushes burning bright against the indomitable dawn, scrub cactus and strange flowers, sluggish lizards hissing away in the underbrush.

The backyard was large, and fenced in with stone five feet high. The sky was blushing pink. She walked back toward the house, thinking of feeding the cats, even though it was early. It would save a trip later.

She came to the back door, and the light was just enough that she saw what they all had missed seeing on the way out.

She didn't think that she screamed, but the other two were there in what seemed to be too long an instant.

"My God!" said Matt.

"Peter!" Seraphina said in shock, then repeated the name in a voice of distraught love.

Temple saw what Blandina had seen, in her own backyard, on her own back door: the beige convent cat, half of Peter and Paul, nailed—crucified—by his outstretched front paws to the heavy wooden back door.

Chapter 14

Cat Crime

"He's not dead," Matt said, coming into the kitchen's bright fluorescents. "Can you find a towel?"

Temple and Sister Seraphina scattered in shocked relief: Temple for the terry-cloth dish towels that she had spotted yesterday under a stack of unused foil roaster pans in the pantry, Sister Seraphina upstairs for parts unknown.

Both women had scurried into the house—averting their eyes from the open door—as soon as they had found the claw hammer Matt had asked for in the shed at the back of the garden. Temple felt guilty about failing to rise to the occasion while she comforted Sister Seraphina in the kitchen, but—after all—Matt had spent his summers on a farm and was better prepared to deal with animal tragedies.

Temple was a city girl through and through. She had to avert her eyes from roadkill, even if it was a bird or a squirrel or a rat, although she noted the exact location and invariably called animal control to pick up the remains, hoping they would do so before she had to drive that way again. In fact, she would often change her route for a while to make sure the road was clear. If everyday traffic fatalities upset her that much, a crucified cat was more than even a good Girl Scout should have to cope with when there was (thank God for the small favors of long-institutionalized sexism) a man around to see to it.

So, still feeling guilty when Sister Seraphina leaped over cats to hurtle down the stairs with a bath towel, Temple manfully offered to take the towels out to Matt.

The cat lay on its side on a wooden bench, unconscious, Matt said.

"Are you sure?" she asked, handing him the towels.

"I think it's in shock. We may be too late. But the . . . foot injuries weren't enough to kill it. Do you know of a vet?"

"Yes, and—" Temple checked her watch. "They've just opened, thank God." She instantly blanched, wondering if invoking the deity over a cat was disrespectful.

But Matt didn't notice. He was wrapping the cat up like a baby in swaddling clothes.

"I'll drive; you carry," Temple suggested briskly, heading back into the house to collect her tote bag.

Sister Seraphina was waiting in the kitchen, white-faced. "I'll feed the cats," she said as they came in. She peeked gingerly into Matt's bundle. "Will he—"

"We'll try."

"It's too bad you couldn't stay for seven-o'clock Mass. I'd like you to meet Father Hernandez."

Matt didn't look at all sorry, just worried. "I'll have to pass on that."

"Of course," Sister Seraphina murmured.

"And we'll call with news," Temple promised, jingling her car keys.

She and Matt rushed out, avoiding cats, and into the Storm as fast as she could unlock it.

Temple barely noticed the morning warming up and brightening all around her; she was just glad she could drive in daylight as she pushed the Storm around corners and down lightly traveled streets at forty miles an hour, getting a slew of dirty looks from more moderate drivers.

"Hold the bundle up," she suggested to Matt. "Maybe they'll think it's a sick baby."

He obliged; the cat was too unconscious to care.

"That's the most awful thing I've ever seen in my life," Temple said by way of small talk. Her knees were inclined to shake, she noticed, and so had her voice on the last sentence.

"Quite a night," Matt answered in his usual understatement.

She wondered what it would take to jar his composure. She just may have seen it. She had a feeling that the cat's plight had restored Matt's equilibrium, even as it had almost tipped her totally off the scale of sanity.

"Who would do such a thing?" she asked, knowing the question was expected, and useless, and unanswerable, but needing to ask.

"I don't know. Someone sick is the obvious answer. But in what way?"

"And why the convent cat on Miss Tyler's door? Who was the target of this act?"

"Usually the kind of people—or kids—who torture animals aren't too fussy about the targets. They just want to find someone who cares, who'll be hurt and shocked and frightened."

"It could be kids, couldn't it? That's even creepier."

"Adults don't normally do this sort of thing. If they're inclined to atrocity, they've graduated to abusing people by the time they're all grown up."

Temple shivered at Matt's cynicism, new from him. It bespoke a darker world view than she had suspected he glimpsed.

She spun the Storm around the last corner and pulled into the lot, relieved to see only a sprinkle of cars for staff members. She ran around the car to open the door for Matt and clattered ahead to open the vet's door.

An empty waiting room. Good, Temple thought as she stormed the desk.

"We've got an emergency, a terribly abused cat."

The woman on duty looked up, her face struggling to blend an expression of anger with sympathy. "Take it right in. I'll buzz Dr. Doolittle."

"Dr. Doolittle?" Matt mouthed in amazement as he followed Temple into the first examining room.

She shrugged and watched him lay the bundle on the tabletop, then reached out to stroke the cat's forehead.

Energy and a rush of air came in with the vet. "What happened?" she asked, peeling back the towels to reveal Peter's inert form.

Temple and Matt consulted each other with a glance.

Matt spoke. "We found him nailed to a door. He's not dead, but I don't know how bad—"

"Your cat?" Dr. Doolittle asked. She knew Temple had Midnight Louie.

"No," he said quickly. "A . . . friend's. An elderly lady's."

Dr. Doolittle made a sound of disgust as she put on a stethoscope. An assistant hurried in. "You two had better wait outside until we get a good look at him."

They edged out into the antiseptic hall, then into the waiting room, where they could read dog and cat magazines or peruse free literature from manufacturers of dog and cat products—Yummy Tum-tum-tummy or Free-to-be-Feline. Not easy to forget where you were in a veterinarian's waiting room, Temple mused. Not easy to forget what brought you there. . . .

She and Matt sat on adjoining free-form plastic chairs and stared at the vinyl-tiled floor.

"Reminds me of the hospital emergency room," Temple said finally.

"Yeah."

"At least Lieutenant Molina isn't here."

"She might have to be here yet."

"What do you mean?"

"It's not homicide, but it's pretty close."

"A tortured cat is not the kind of thing the police can deal with," Temple objected, for the idea of Lieutenant Molina being drawn into her life again was just too awful to contemplate. "Animals are legally viewed as property. That poor cat is worth what somebody would pay for it, period, and you know that's not much."

"Still," Matt said, "the police Gang Unit might be interested, especially if they've got satanist activity in the area, and they usually do."

Temple sat forward on the chair designed to slide her deep against its back. "Satanists?" she whispered. "I never thought of that!"

Matt shrugged, looking uncomfortable. "The cat's owners are nuns who live in a convent next to a church; the cat was nailed to the door of a devoted churchgoer who takes in stray cats. Crucifixion is a potent symbol to modern Christians, no matter the victim, no matter the denomination."

Temple resisted the chair seat's slick pull on her weary and stunned body, resisted slumping into her seat like a scarecrow who'd seen too much and was finally too scared to scare back.

"Satanism," she repeated, truly chilled to the bone.

Dr. Doolittle was there almost as soon as they heard her coming. She sat down on an empty chair.

"He *is* in shock. He's lost a lot of blood."

"Yeah, the door was pretty smeared," Matt said.

Temple stared at him. "I didn't see any blood."

"It was still darkish. I noticed it as I was getting him off and daylight was breaking."

"We need to transfuse him." Dr. Doolittle was being professionally brusque. "As soon as possible."

"Then do it," Temple gave permission. "I'm sure the owner will okay it, if Peter needs it."

Dr. Doolittle sighed. "That's just it. We usually have one of our office cats available, but a customer fell in love with the last one and adopted it. We haven't taken in a replacement yet."

"I don't understand," Temple said. "Office cats?"

Dr. Doolittle took off her tortoiseshell-rimmed yuppie glasses and rubbed her face with a bony hand bearing the battle scars of her profession.

"We're a vet's office. Everyone's always dumping unwanted or wounded animals on our doorstep. Some we place. Some we keep. It's handy to have a healthy cat around when blood donations are called for. We just happen to be out at the moment."

"What are the qualifications for a blood donor?" Temple asked.

"We prefer a big, strong, healthy donor. And of course it must be a cat."

"Louie!" said Temple, standing.

Matt was standing, too. "The Circle Ritz?"

"We'll be right back," Temple told the vet on the way out the door.

Getting into the Storm fast was becoming a habit. The driver and passenger doors slammed simultaneously. Temple gunned the motor and headed for home.

The Circle Ritz was quiet. Late workers hadn't left yet; early birds were long gone. They raced up the three flights of stairs, automatically ignoring the elevators.

Temple flubbed putting her key in her own front door, her hands were shaking so much. "Let's hope he's here. Come on, Louie, you old layabout, be laying about—"

Inside, the apartment was cool and serene, like a scene from a decorating magazine on another planet. So much had happened since Temple had left here in the wee morning hours at Matt's urgent behest.

They stood stock still, absorbing the unoccupied peace of the place like refugees from a far uglier world. Temple eyed her pale sofa. Only black cat hairs, like the trail of the Yeti in the Himalayas, all advertisement and no substance.

She ran into the small kitchen, looking high and low. Free-to-be-Feline untouched in the bowl, but the tempting top layer of Shrimp Oyster Aloha was gone.

To the office, Matt behind her, and no familiar dark form sprawled all over her paperwork. To the main room again and—no help for it—her bedroom, which Matt had never seen, through no fault of her own, but now. . . .

Oh, Lordy, she hadn't straightened up in here. Clothes everywhere and toppled shoes and—oh, to die; how had she forgotten about them?—four *Cosmopolitan* magazines fanned like a hand of playing cards by the bedside table; she read them only for the horoscopes, honest.

And there, like a fat black spider, smack dab in the middle of her crumpled zebra-striped, red-piped coverlet.

"Midnight Louie!" Temple squealed, picking him up in one surprised, limp, large armful. "I knew I could count on you!"

"Have you a towel?" Matt asked.

"No, a carrier in the storage closet."

"No time," Matt pronounced, going into her bathroom and coming out with a bath towel that featured a top-hatted Fred Astaire doing a signature glide.

He wrapped Louie and headed for the front door.

Louie wasn't going to like that, but Temple jangled her key ring and ran after them.

Once more into the Storm. The Fred Astaire towel was doing a cha-cha in Matt's grasp, but Temple was too busy driving unsafely to watch.

The vet's. Out of the car, into the office.

Matt bearing Louie like a veiled sacrifice into an examining room. Temple trotting alongside, wailing apologies as she patted Louie's only visible part, the top of his head.

Dr. Doolittle there, talking seriously as an attendant whisked Louie away. "Your cat should stay here all day to recover, but he'll be just fine. We won't know anything until this afternoon. Call at four."

Temple and Matt stood outside the veterinarian's office, watching the sun glint off the second-story windows across the street. He had called Sister Seraphina from the receptionist's phone. Diagnosis: still alive. Prognosis: we won't know till four o'clock.

Temple threw herself behind the wheel again and hit the bucket seat like a sack of couch potatoes.

Matt was in the passenger seat as if materialized there, as if he were the Mystifying Max and had always been there, but invisible.

"Where to?" he asked, but he sounded as if he didn't care.

Temple started the car engine, not blaming it one bit for choking.

"The emergency room," she said. "My style this time."

Chapter 15

Soul Food

Not another car was parked between the slanted parallel lines pointing to Fernando's Taqueria, which could have more accurately been called "Fernando's Hideaway," so modestly was it squeezed between a dry cleaner's and an old-fashioned barbershop that didn't open until eleven o'clock.

"Breakfast," Temple said, turning off the Storm's engine with a happy sigh to know that the car would stay idle and stay put for a while, "is on me."

Matt looked dubious in a disinterested sort of way. Granted, Fernando's was not impressive from the outside. And as they entered to face garish yellow walls, mercifully softened by dim lights, and bare Formica tables and gray plastic chairs, Temple had to admit to herself that it wasn't impressive on the inside, either.

"Isn't a *taqueria* for takeout food?" Matt looked around,

his doubtful glance pausing on a blackboard with the menu written entirely in Spanish.

"Normally." Temple plunked herself down at a table for four and set her tote bag on the empty chair beside her. "Fernando's isn't normal, but it's clean, out of the way, and the food is fiery enough to compete with a shooting star. Plus, the coffee is so strong that your spoon will stand up and do a Mexican hat dance in it."

Matt pulled out an opposite chair, looking around in a shell-shocked way that Temple just knew an order of *Heuvos Rancheros Fernando* would do much to overcome.

"You *do* like Mexican food?" she asked in an anxious afterthought.

"Normally," Matt said, "but today isn't normal." He eyed the empty little restaurant again, so bare of frills. "This place is pristine, though, for a hole-in-the-wall."

"I figured that's what we needed at the moment—a hide-out, a modest little hole-in-the-wall for two."

Matt nodded slowly, looking as if he would rather be adjusting the silverware and the place mat or turning his water glass in his hands, only there wasn't any of that.

A Hispanic man emerged from the rear and deposited a bouquet of stainless steel silverware wrapped in a doily of plain white paper napkin in front of each of them.

"I'll order," Temple said, because she knew the menu and because she didn't think that Matt would be good at small decisions right now. "I'm having the House Heavenly Hash—onions and cilantro on the side of *huevos*—that's eggs—swimming in the house sauce, which is very green, very thick and very spicy-hot. And coffee." She repeated the order in fairly decent Spanish to the waiter, who nodded, disdaining to write anything down.

Matt shrugged. "The same, I guess."

"Okay, but I'll order your sauce on the side—they have a great tomatillo salsa that will leave your tonsils unscalded. Y *agua*," she told the waiter last, pointing to them both.

Now Matt would soon have plenty to fiddle with.

"This doesn't strike me as your kind of place," he said.

"It is now. But you're right." She hated mixing metaphors, mixing Max and Matt, but there was no escape, not even for a verbal magician. "Max found it," she admitted. "I'm not that adventuresome. Max always said that the best thing about Fernando's was that nobody here speaks English. It's perfect for six-cups-of-coffee mornings."

"Oh." Matt leaned back to let the waiter set a tall, olive-green, nubbly plastic glass before him. "Did Max have a lot of six-cups-of-coffee mornings?"

Temple smiled, shakily. If she wanted to find out the scoop on Matt, she would have to dish up a bit of her and Max. "No, and not too many mornings, either. He usually slept until eleven. Fernando's is a little more lively then."

"I keep the same hours," Matt noted after a slow sip of water.

"You going to be able to get off of work tonight?"

"Maybe, if they can call someone else in. But there's no point. I won't get any sleep anyway. I'm not used to normal work hours now."

Temple nodded. "Then the best thing to do is to start mainlining caffeine and keep going until . . . what time do you usually get home? Three-thirty A.M.?"

He nodded.

"And Sister Seraphina called you at—?"

"Four-thirty."

"Then the cat was attacked before four."

He nodded again, clearly not as interested in the night's exact chronology as she was. "Temple, you must be wondering—"

"I am beyond wonder," she said quickly. Nothing was worse than an ex-reporter's need-to-know, and right now she was so very needy. "I'm too tired. But I am congenitally nosy—"

"You've got a right to know," he began, leaning back again as a heavy, white-porcelain cup filled to the brim with molasses-dark—and thick—coffee was placed before him.

"*Leche, por favor,*" Temple asked the waiter before unfurling her paper napkin and drawing out the spoon. How long could she put it off?

A small blue pitcher of milk arrived, and then the waiter left. Temple poured a pale stream into her coffee, stirring until the black color softened. The cup was too full. She'd have to drink it down a little before she could mix the just-right shade of tan.

"I don't have a right to know anything," she said after another moment. "Of course . . ." She sighed. "Given my wild imagination, it might be in your best interests to head me off at the pass."

He sipped the steaming coffee as if to gather Columbian courage. "I was a priest."

Four little words. Hearing them put Temple in the kind of daze Matt had visibly occupied ever since Sister Seraphina's call. She was getting hooked on a *priest*—after the debacle of Max? Oh, puhleeze. No. . . .

"You'll have to bear with me," she made herself say. "I'm a fallen-away Unitarian. We know a little about everything and not much about anything. You *were* a priest?"

He nodded.

"An . . . Episcopal priest?"

He shook his head, but couldn't help smiling at her hopeful tone. "No."

"No." Temple contemplated her coffee cup, then added enough milk to bring the contents lapping at the brim. She concentrated on spilling not a drop as she lifted it to her lips and sipped, saying a little prayer so she wouldn't spill, so she wouldn't spill her overflowing uncertainties. "I didn't really think that Our Lady of Guadalupe was big in the Episcopal Church, but they do have nuns, I think, and they do call them 'sister'?"

Matt nodded. "You know more than you think you do."

"But you were a Catholic priest?"

"Yes."

"The kind with the usual vows—um, poverty, chastity and obedience?"

"Yes."

"The celibate kind?"

He tried hard not to hesitate. "Yes."

"And now you're not a priest, officially."

"Yes."

"But if you *were* a priest, why did Sister Seraphina call you? Why didn't she ask this invisible Father Hernandez everybody talks about but nobody sees? And why would an . . . ex-priest perform some kind of rite?" Temple knew her spate of questions was a form of denial, yet she denied on, like poor befuddled Peter in the Garden. "I know you didn't want to do it. Aren't you . . . disqualified from doing that now? Isn't it a . . . sin?"

Matt leaned forward, his arms and hands curved around his coffee cup as if defending it, or seeking warmth.

"It's a judgment call and a delicate situation. In an emergency, if the person is dying, Sister Seraphina could administer the sacrament herself, even a lay person could. But if the person's condition is more uncertain, and a priest is available . . . Father Hernandez was not. Miss Tyler had been having a fierce feud with him and would have been even more distressed to see him."

"I know about that," Temple put in. "Father Hernandez had this perfectly silly notion that God doesn't allow cats in heaven. If poor Miss Tyler had seen Midnight Louie, I'm sure she would have seen the point in that."

"The theological point," Matt said, "is that animals don't have souls, and only those with souls can get to heaven."

"Only those with souls in apple-pie order," Temple added solemnly, wondering about Matt's.

"The . . . sacrament used to be called 'Extreme Unction' and was associated with the dying. Nowadays the church recognizes the healing nature of the ritual and it's given under much less rigorous circumstances. It's called the anointing of the sick, and the reason you were so puzzled by it—besides being such a fierce Unitarian—is that a lot of Catholics haven't witnessed it, even today. It was the most private of the sacraments, and to some, the most frightening. To a devout Catholic like Miss Tyler, the sacrament could have a strong healing and calming effect, as you saw. Sister Seraphina was right that she should have it, was right to decide that Father Hernandez would upset her, was even right to call on me. A woman of Miss Tyler's generation would not have accepted a nun administering a sacrament; priests and doctors are like gods to such women."

He laughed wearily at their delusions, then said with the intensity of someone convincing himself: "I was part of the necessary psychological efficacy of the sacrament, as well as its spiritual aspect."

"But Miss Tyler is feuding with Father Hernandez! How can she do that if she's such a devout Catholic?"

Matt smiled, his first full-wattage smile of the morning. "Devout Catholics, more than anyone else, consider themselves privileged—no, obliged—to point out personal failings to their parish priests."

"Oh. It must not be fun to be a parish priest."

"No."

"Were you?"

"For a while."

"Oh."

Out from the kitchen came the waiter bearing two large oval plates heaped with mounds of food. Mexican food had an earthy, yet limited color range—yellow to red to brown—and was not highly textured; everything was chopped into such tidy, digestible piles. Yet it was . . . Temple searched for the proper mental tribute: it was Yummy on the Tum-tum-tummy. Especially when that tummy was dancing a solo of uncertainty.

She and Matt studied their plates with awe after the waiter left.

"That's a lot of food," Matt said finally. "I don't know if I've got the stomach for it."

"One taste and you'll know you don't. That's what makes Mexican food so much fun; it's an endurance contest."

He offered a pale smile and spooned some of the milder salsa on his eggs. Temple made sure her eggs were basted in green sauce and took a big bite.

Umm, who would believe minced vegetables could have such zip? That scrambled eggs, no matter how fluffy, could taste so substantial?

"This isn't bad," Matt admitted, forking up another bite.

The warm food and hot coffee, the combination of bitter and fiery tastes—the very alienness of eating Mexican food at eight o'clock in the morning—revitalized them both, as Temple had hoped it would. It was hard to stay down in the mouth when your taste buds were on fire. Temple doused her eggs with a speedy helping of onion-potato hash with cilantro.

For a few blessed moments, they just ate. When they had to take a respite from the culinary fireworks, they sat back by mutual agreement. Temple broke the silence first. Again. She always was doing that sort of thing, rushing in where fools would keep their lips zipped.

"You still didn't explain why an ex-priest can administer a sacrament in an emergency."

Matt dabbed his lips with the flimsy napkin, as if to brush away the meal's heat as well as its traces. "Once a priest, always a priest." He used the rueful, solemn tone that announced a truism said long before he had repeated it. "In any emergency, I'm called upon to perform priestly duties if no other priest is available. If I came upon a dying accident victim, for instance."

"Why did I get the feeling that Sister Seraphina was . . . I can't say glad, but why did I feel that she was challenging you to do this?"

"She was a grade-school teacher of mine. She knew when I went into the seminary, although I entered from college. She knew when I left, although I was years and miles away by then. Talk gets back. Every parish is a news bureau; nuns have some kind of nationwide intelligence system . . . or the Holy Spirit whispers deportment reports on former students during prayers, or my Guardian Angel tattles on me—I don't know. But she knew, and she knew where to find me now, when she needed me. And she needed . . . she's disappointed in me, in my leaving, on some level that maybe she doesn't even admit to herself. She didn't mind forcing me to face my ambivalent position. I've left the priesthood, but the priesthood will never leave me."

"That's . . . cruel," Temple said.

"No, just harsh. A religious life does not fear harshness."

Temple shook her head. "I never would have guessed it." She thought for a moment. "Say, that's how you dredged up that black suit you wore when you played the organ for Chester Royal's memorial service! That's why you can play the organ at all!"

Matt held up his hands in surrender and laughed, out loud this time, and long. "You always have to put two and two together, did you know that? You're insatiable."

"Yeah, but what do I do when two and two add up to three?"

He sobered immediately.

Temple took another stab at her eggs, then rolled the corner of her napkin. "Matt, I have to tell you, we ex-Unitarians are pretty tolerant, but I have severe problems with religions that can't let others live and let live according to their honest lights."

"So do I," he said promptly.

"I mean, fundamentalists basically concentrate on judging other people and finding them guilty on all counts, whether they're Christian or Muslim."

"That's why there are so few Catholic fundamentalists, although there are a goodly number of conservatives."

"But, I mean, a church that in this age of AIDS won't condone safe sex with condoms because it's also birth control! Well, that's more than a harsh position; that's insanity."

He stirred in the hard plastic chair. "I don't want to argue theology or logic with you. A lot of these issues have liberal and conservative positions within the church, especially in America."

"Now I may be wrong," she said. "I don't pay a lot of attention to religious matters, to tell the truth. But. Isn't the church against premarital sex?"

"Yes."

"Against all forms of birth control?"

"Well . . . there are natural methods—"

"Against divorce?"

"Yes . . . but again, there are instances—"

"Against . . . masturbation?"

"All sexual acts must be open to the conception of children—"

"Matt!" Temple leaned forward, over her decimated plate of cooling food. "What are you going to do?"

"I don't have to take positions on any of these things anymore, now that I'm not a practicing priest. I don't have to tell anyone else what to do anymore." He seemed relieved, but he still didn't get it.

"Matt!" Temple knew that she sounded even more exasperated, but she couldn't help it. Conundrums demanded solving and she was sitting across from a walking, talking human conundrum who wasn't facing the facts of his new—how new?—existence. "What are *you* going to do? What *can* you do, now that you're not a priest? You move in any direction that's middle-class comfortable, reasonably independent and sexually active—in other words, normal—and you sin, right? Well?"

Chapter 16

Catechism

"Most of us marry ex-nuns. Fast."

"Isn't that a little . . . limiting?" Temple asked.

"The blind leading the blind? Yes, but who else has anything in common with us? Why do you think I'm here—doing my nightline job, living at the Circle Ritz? There were many good reasons I went into the priesthood, and some wrong ones. The church agrees that the wrong ones outweigh the right ones. Now it's up to me to figure out how to live postpartum, if you will; to decide what kind of ex-priest I'm going to be, what kind of Catholic, what kind of man."

Matt drank his cooling coffee, down to the dregs—and dregs did inhabit this bitter, strengthening brew; Temple could taste the grit of fresh grounds when she was halfway through her cup.

"I'm sorry you had to find out," Matt went on, almost to himself. "Sorry that Sister Seraphina had to find out, sorry that what I am is still less than what I *was*. I've got a lot to work out, more questions that I can't answer than even you could ask."

"I'm sorry. I'm nosy. I'm pushy—"

"You're right," he interrupted, without denying her unflattering self-description. "I'm facing a lot of contradictions."

He spun the oily black dregs of his coffee in the white cup as if looking for tea leaves to read—nope, too superstitious, Temple thought; an ex-priest couldn't even do that.

Temple studied the contradiction sitting across from her. She was attracted to Matt, had been from the first, even though—fresh from Max's inexplicable desertion—she knew better.

She found Matt handsome, but then, that was obvious. She had always squirmed at her attraction to the obvious, but she also understood that the very things that were not obvious about Matt attracted her even more. Now she was getting down to that nitty-gritty—with escalating interest! If she didn't know why he had left the priesthood, she could wonder why he had entered it.

"The girls in high school must have gone crazy when you went into the seminary," she mused, knowing she was dangling for history, for answers, for rivals.

He quirked a smile. "Girls always want what they can't get."

"Boys do, too. That's high school, isn't it?"

"High school must have been a piece of cake for you," Matt said matter-of-factly, expertly, easily, turning the spotlight from him to her.

"Why?" Temple was indignant.

"You're outgoing . . . I was going to say irrepressible. You're so easy with people. I bet you were the most popular girl in your class."

"Bet again! I was the shortest. With glasses. I never could adjust to contact lenses. I was known to get good grades and to be a 'good sport,' although I couldn't play sports worth a stinky pair of sweat socks."

"I wasn't good at sports, either," he said quickly. "Except for the martial arts."

"That's hard."

"But it isn't a team sport."

"Still, I bet the girls were angling for you."

His expression grew dreamy, softened as hers had when she had thought back to the adolescent wilderness of high-school days, which did great things for a face that didn't need any help. "A couple of them actually asked me to the senior prom. They didn't know yet," he said.

"*They* asked *you?* I'm impressed, but not surprised. Didn't you go?"

He looked down, away. "No."

"But you could have. What harm would it have done? Senior proms are such a rite of passage," Temple said in her dreamy turn. "Maybe you were better off not going, though. I went, and was I sorry."

"Why?"

"Why?" Temple wanted to clutch her hair, although she knew such a gesture was theatrical. "Because I was forced to go! Wouldn't you know that in front of the whole debating team, I would get asked by dweeby Curtis Dixstrom because I was the only girl shorter than he was—and the creep knew that I was too 'intellectual' to hold out for a jock or a class president. So I went."

"And you surprised yourself and had a good time?"

"You sound like my mother did then," Temple said sourly. " 'Oh, go, dear, and maybe you'll meet somebody else nicer.' I didn't want anybody 'nicer,' I wanted somebody cooler. So I went, and loathed it, and Curtis got seriously drunk at the after-prom party and I ended up driving him home, and me too, in his father's dweeby Volvo station wagon."

Matt tried not to laugh. "You always end up taking responsibility, don't you?"

"You always turn personal questions back on the interrogator, don't you? You don't much like talking about you."

"No, I don't. We wouldn't be now if Sister Superfine

hadn't used her nationwide nun intelligence network to track me down."

"Superfine? Oh, Seraphina/Superfine. Isn't it . . . disrespectful to call a nun that?"

"You bet it is. Catholic kids nowadays are almost as disrespectful as public-school kids. And it isn't really disrespectful. Only popular nuns get nicknames."

"I was going to ask you where these nuns get their names. Do priests change their names?"

He shook his head. "Only nuns. I never thought about it that way, but it's probably sexist. Nuns are expected to give up their old identity, but priests aren't. Of course, brothers take new names as well."

"Brothers? Oh, brother. There's a lot about the Catholic Church that's Greek to me."

"There's even a Greek Orthodox Catholic Church." Matt mustered a teasing twinkle. "And in it, priests can marry."

"And still be Catholic? Amazing. Maybe you could . . . change churches."

Matt sobered and shook his head. "Celibacy wasn't the reason I left; it isn't the reason for a lot of ex-priests."

Temple's heart sank. Celibacy made a lot of sense in the current uncertain social climate, but she couldn't imagine any healthy prime-of-life person contemplating it forever.

"In the old days," Matt was explaining in his informative, neutral voice that so efficiently distanced him from the listener, from himself even, "boys entered the seminary from grade school. Now they enter after high school, or even after college, so there's no way the candidates haven't had a chance to experience a normal social life."

"You mean that some priests aren't virgins?"

"The promise is for the duration of their priesthood."

"Forever."

"Forever."

"Except . . . in certain cases," she parroted his earlier answers about matters of ironclad dogma.

He nodded ruefully. "Except in certain cases."

"I'll never figure it out," Temple said, pushing her plate

away and resolving to change the subject. "Any more than I'll figure out why anyone would harass an elderly woman like Miss Tyler."

"Kids would," Matt said promptly, "and this is gang territory."

"What isn't nowadays?" Temple asked with a shudder. "And making obscene phone-calls to a convent." She contributed another, deeper shudder to the conversation. "Were you serious about satanists?"

The waiter retrieved their empty plates. Matt braced his elbows on the table and scrubbed his face with the palms of his hands. "There's not as much of it out there as the alarmists think, but it is a possibility. Satanists are known to be cruel to cats."

"And the attack on Miss Tyler's niece's cat at the show is strange. That seemed more of a prank, or the work of a malicious competitor."

"Could people get that worked up over a cat competition?"

"There's status and money in it," Temple said promptly, "and where there are status and money, there also is a motive for mischief."

"Sounds like another beatitude, only I'd call it a maleficitude."

"It's the oddest coincidence," Temple said, reaching for the small green chit the waiter slapped to the table before Matt.

"You drove, and then some," Matt said, sliding it off the table and pulling out his wallet.

New, Temple observed, like a lot of his clothes looked. Why hadn't she noticed that and come to correct conclusions before? Because nothing about Matt was particularly noticeable, until you knew his history, and then everything was more fascinating than ever . . . oh, dear Lord. Could a congenitally curious woman ever have had a more perfect subject of interest?

"What are you doing the rest of the day if you're not resting?" she asked.

"If you don't mind dropping me off at the convent, I'll see how Sister Seraphina and Miss Tyler are doing. I can get home all right during the day."

"I'll stop by the vet's and check on Louie and poor Peter."

"How free are you today?"

"As free as a rock-concert ticket at a radio station. Why?"

"Want to practice your self-defense techniques at four?"

"Not really, and you'll be dead tired—"

"That's why I'll need to do something like that."

"You must think I need intense help."

"No, but not many weeks ago you were confronted by thugs looking for Kinsella; now you're driving me around bad neighborhoods in dark nights. You need it. By the way, have you gone to group yet?"

"I will, I will, when I get a minute!"

"Four o'clock okay?" he asked, eyeing her hopefully.

"Okay." She thought he was crazy to push himself this hard after a night's lost sleep, but maybe that was exactly the way he kept himself sane.

Chapter 17

Cross Not the Cat

"You looked tired, Matthias," Sister Seraphina said in the cool visitors' room of the convent, the elderly air conditioner's hum as domestic and comforting as a refrigerator's.

"You lost as much sleep as I did," he countered, "and it's just Matt now."

Her eyes shut in brief, placid admission of the correction. "I do not work a night shift like you do, and the old don't need much sleep—luckily so, for we seldom get it. Nor do we change old habits easily. Matt, I think that you should meet Father Hernandez now."

Matt maintained silence. He had no desire to meet this Father Hernandez who was reduced to feuding with parishioners about the afterlives of cats, with managing fund drives to keep the parish alive, and with retreating to the bottle when the maddening daily wear and tear had become too much. Mostly, he didn't want to meet Father Hernandez because no matter how badly the man had failed, he had not deserted his post, he had not yet left the priesthood. Father Hernandez's mere existence, with all its cracks and fissures, would seem a rebuke. Matt realized that he was still raw from his severance with his vocation and only imagining that a man whom he was not willing to judge would be a harsh judge of Matt Devine. Father Hernandez would not even know Matt's history, unless Sister Seraphina had told him. Had she?

Matt finally rose without comment and let Sister Seraphina lead him out into the hot, post-meridian sun, which already fell less scaldingly on his fair skin. Autumn was coming.

He was given the grand tour on the way to the rectory. Our Lady of Guadalupe Church had a cool, old and ornate interior, laced with white plasterwork and pastel statues of the saints that most other Catholic churches downplayed now, confining even the Virgin Mary to a discreet side altar. The blinding, blue-collar magnificence reminded him of his home church of St. Stanilaus in Chicago, the architectual opposite but spiritual cousin to Our Lady of Guadalupe. Working-class people were inspired by churches of blatant beauty, perhaps because their daily lives held so little of it.

The school was a pair of dull, one-story adobe wings enfolding a sandy-surfaced, scruffy playground. The once-bright, painted-metal monkey bars and swing sets had paled and peeled to a dull burnt-sienna undercoat in the dry desert sun. Now the playground was empty and not even the dust stirred. Behind the schoolrooms' glinting glass windows, shut to keep out the heat, lay teachers tried to inspire the restless students for another nine-month school year, that everlasting pregnant pause between the blessed deliverance of too-short summer holidays.

Matt was remembering everything he wanted to forget, but he could regard this unexpected odyssey into another priest's parish as a form of penance. The church was too successful at converting confrontation into endurance. He had not yet found a new place in the church, or outside of it.

At least the rectory was foreign. St. Stan's had been red-brick-grand, with tidy white trim, and peopled by three priests and the eternal housekeeper: that prototypical elderly, devout and devoted (if sometimes waspish) cook and cleaner and dorm mother—always female and always above any kind of depraved suspicion—who committed herself to serving a houseful of religious men.

Here a large, lumpy Mexican woman whose charcoal-dark hair glinted with silver strands as shiny as fresh paint opened the door, not one of those forbidding Northern gatekeepers whose severe gaze would make any caller feel properly guilty for being there and disturbing Father.

Spanish coos urged them into the artificially cooled dimness. The tile floors were hard and so was the heavy, dark Spanish furniture, as plain and somber as a cross. Colorful cloths draping the backs of wooden chairs provided welcome warmth and softened the austerity.

"Is Father Hernandez in, Pilar?" Sister Seraphina asked.

"*Si*, *si*. But he is now with Mr. Burns, the lawyer." Pilar sounded most impressed with this visitor.

"We will wait," said Seraphina, who did not sound impressed. A successful teacher never sounds impressed by anything, Matt reflected, and she had certainly been that.

She claimed a hard bench in the hallway. Matt, after strolling down the passage to examine the wall decorations—a citation from the Knights of Columbus, a modern chrome cross with a gilded figure of Christ on it—joined her. He was reminded of benches placed outside of the principal's office for misbehaving students to warm until a higher authority was good and ready to deal with them.

"You'll like Father Hernandez," Seraphina said suddenly, in a warmer tone, "although lately he seems lost in some labyrinth of his own. Before—"

Before, he had been a good priest, as Matt had been. Matt leaned his elbows on his thighs and clasped his hands, the fingers dovetailed, then realized the position could be construed as an informal one of prayer. He had so many reflexes to disconnect.

At last the closed door down the hall cracked open. Voices bled from the room beyond. Intense voices.

"You must concentrate on the developmental fund-raising program, Father, or there will *be* no OLG! I can't understand your distraction at such a critical time. And you must make up with Blandina Tyler. What is this nonsense about cats in heaven? You mustn't allow an old woman's silly fantasies to affect your fiscal judgment. She's recently been threatening to leave her estate to her cats—so the Ladies' Flower Guild says—and not to Our Lady of Guadalupe. That would be disaster."

"She may do as she wishes," a testy voice answered. "The church does not tailor its theology to fit the notions of its wealthier members."

"Yes, yes, Father—"

The men were moving into the hall now, ending their meeting.

"But—" continued the first voice, soothing, reasoning, warning, "this is such a minor matter. Cats! Sneaky, selfish creatures, but people who fancy them can be fanatics. It's bad for the peace of Miss Tyler's body and soul to work herself into a state over such a triviality."

The attorney was fully in the hall now, an earnest man in his worried mid-thirties, wearing a blue-striped seersucker suit that would look at home in a barbershop quartet. Horn-rimmed glasses perched on his rather prominent nose, giving him the prissy look of an accountant, oddly contradicted by a smile exposing a thin silver line of braces.

Such was the lot of a parish priest nowadays, Matt ruminated unhappily: keeping well-meaning parish volunteers happy while facing the realities of a waning congregation, sisterhood and priesthood, and a youth population that was eroding into the camaraderie of the gangs instead of attending Mass, and regularly receiving stolen goods instead of Holy Communion. Not to mention the unwed-pregnancy problem.

Matt stood, Sister Seraphina rising beside him, as the parish priest came out into the hall, wearing black slacks and a short-sleeved black shirt with the usual pastoral notch of white clerical collar showing.

Traditional garb for today's more modern priests and hot in a desert clime, Matt couldn't help noting. His neck broke out in a sympathetic rash as he remembered the imprisoning circle of starched linen. Father Hernandez's appearance surprised Matt even more. He had expected someone roly-poly, like the housekeeper, someone warm and cheerful and now obviously incompetent and harassed. Instead, Father Hernandez reminded Matt of the late Bishop Fulton J. Sheen, Catholicism's only televangelist in the late, unlamented fifties. Father Hernandez was tall and thin, his skin the color of rich Corinthian leather. His attractive, rather ascetic face was framed by a handsome halo of silver hair.

"Visitors," Father Hernandez announced with an air of relief. "Sister Seraphina, is this your . . . friend from Chicago?"

"Matt Devine," she said quickly. "Father Rafael Hernandez. And Peter Burns here is the parish attorney and also a dedicated parishioner who donates much time to Our Lady of Guadalupe."

Matt shook hands with both men, surprised by the priest's anemic grip, but not by the lawyer's businesslike, Toastmaster knuckle-cruncher. Matt gripped right back, but got no reaction, just a curt acknowledgment and farewell.

Odd, but Matt would have picked the lawyer as the tormented man who had recently hit the bottle that Sister Seraphina had described, not the priest.

"Come in." Father Hernandez gestured them into a study equipped with the mandatory four or five comfortably upholstered chairs, useful for receiving prominent community members offering money, or bereaved families making funeral arrangements, and fellow religious.

Matt sank onto old leather with relief; it was cooler than cloth, and the rectory air conditioner was old, audibly cranky and patently ineffective. No wonder a sheen of sweat had polished both the priest's and the lawyer's faces—or maybe the discussion of parish fiscal matters had produced the moisture.

Father Hernandez threw his long frame into an old-fashioned leather swivel chair behind a massive glass-topped desk. Pen-holders, papers, a calculator, the large glass ashtray for guests or the occasional parishioner bearing a rare cigar, a missal and breviary—the flotsam of a religious and administrative life—met and mingled on the parish priest's desk. Matt had used one like it once, and knew its makeup as a geologist knows the strata of the various geological ages of the earth. Here and there amid the scattered papers, loose paperclips glinted like veins of silver.

Father Hernandez leaned his weight on one leather-upholstered arm and swung the chair into a familiar and favorite position. "Before you say anything, Sister Seraphina, I'll tell you that I called the hospital. Miss Tyler would have nothing to do with a visit from me, as I told you; besides, the emergency-room doctors diagnosed hysteria, gave her a prescription of Valium, and are sending her home with her niece. Now that we know the cause of her . . . episode, it's clear that her condition was due to mental shock rather than a physical breakdown."

Seraphina nodded. "You're quite right, but we didn't discover . . . the animal until Blandina had left in the ambulance."

Father Hernandez tented his long fingers and shook his solid sterling head, bishop material if looking the role had anything to do with it. Matt envied the man's air of churchly charisma, of an attractiveness untainted by movie-star good looks. Why should such a man—and Matt had seen the type before, the kind who could charm money out of a cuckoo clock and make it seem a privilege to the donor—worry so much about a fund drive that he risked everything: career, parish, fund drive, and even his priesthood, which was quite a different matter than a mere career, by diving into a bottle? Perhaps Seraphina had jumped to conclusions there.

"The cat," the pastor was musing with impressive melancholy. "Poor . . . Peter, did you say? I could never tell him and Paul apart, but then, I'm not much of a cat person. It must," he added with a mahogany glance at Matt from under bristling pewter eyebrows, "have been traumatic to take him down, given your situation, Mr. Devine."

He knew. Of course. Seraphina would consider it only right that he know. "You mean the implication of blasphemy?"

The pastor nodded solemnly. "Most disturbing. We are used to graffiti on the school walls, obscenities scratched into the rest-room doors, but then the vile phone-calls to Sister Mary Monica, and now . . . this."

"You think that they're related? Miss Tyler was receiving bizarre phone calls as well."

Father Hernandez laughed, the sound's harshness as disturbing as the sight of a crucified cat. "Miss Tyler's cats and calls and health and will! I'm tired of such . . . unworthy speculations on Miss Tyler. Something worse may be abroad, eh—Matthew, was it?"

"It was Matthias; now it's Matt."

Father Hernandez spread his hands to show calm acceptance, the gesture as broad as a blessing. Veteran priests often assumed the unconscious mannerisms of the vocation; Matt saw that now, as he saw residual gestures in himself. He was surprised that anyone would be shocked that he had been a priest, given the signs, but Temple certainly had been.

"Sister Seraphina tells me you mentioned satanism."

The question's directness sent Temple flying to the farthest fringes of Matt's mind. "I meant that only in the sense of misguided individuals playing at the trappings of satanism, Father, not a . . . serious . . . outbreak."

"Hmm." Father Hernandez balanced his chin on his tented fingertips. The dark eyes that regarded Matt grew suddenly haunted. "It wouldn't surprise me if it were the real thing, Matt. Not with the unholy mischief that's been happening around Our Lady of Guadalupe lately."

"What do you mean?" Sister Seraphina interjected.

The pastor's eyes avoided hers. "I . . . haven't told you everything."

"There's more?"

He shrugged. "I found the holy-water fonts in the church filled with red liquid before six-o'clock Mass last week."

"Red—?" Sister Seraphina couldn't bring herself to ask more.

"Dye," he answered quickly. "In the holy water. Red food coloring. Disposing of it properly will be quite a challenge. And the communion wine was also colored water."

Sister Seraphina's lips folded. She said nothing, but her eyes held such a look of disapproval that Matt could imagine her saying, "And was that too great a disappointment, Father?"

Still, the tricks around the church tugged at his interest. No wonder a sober and steady priest might find his grip slipping. Matt imagined himself celebrating Mass again, concentrating on the ritual and the prayers, achieving a recognizable spiritual state and then, at the most sacred, sacramental moment for priest and congregation, saying, "This is my Body, This is my Blood," and sipping from the gloriously gilded chalice—thin, colored water, not wine. Transubstantiation indeed.

Add other, more brutal harassments, such as a convent cat crucified, and Matt could understand that a priest might need more than meditation to steady his nerves.

"Maybe your friend could help us," Sister Seraphina said into the lengthening silence.

It took Matt several long moments to realize that she addressed him and finally look up. His face remained blank.

"The plucky Miss Barr," she prodded him. "You mentioned that she has had some involvement in detection."

Temple came winging from the back of the beyond with a fiery crown of red hair and a shining sheriff's badge in the palm of one hand, like a pixyish saint.

Matt laughed. "She handles public relations, and happened to have murder rear its ugly head at a couple of events she stage-managed, that's all. She's no professional, although—"

He stood up, hands jammed in pockets, stunned. "Although . . . the reason she was working the cat show this weekend is that there's been some funny-business there. Miss Tyler's niece had entered some cats, and one of them was shaved."

"Shaved," Father Hernandez echoed in complete confusion.

Matt nodded. "To disqualify it from competition, they thought. It was done with animal clippers, down the length of the body from head to tail and around the middle."

"My God—" Father Hernandez's warm-toned skin, as dark as a George Hamilton tan, turned sallow. "Don't you see? Remember the legend of how the donkey's back was marked at Jesus's birth for all time?"

"A cross," Matt heard his own hoarse voice say. "The cat was shaved in the shape of a cross. Then it's related!"

"To what?" Sister Seraphina exploded. "Pranks? Except for Peter, that is all we're talking about. Childish pranks. We sit next to a building housing two hundred and sixty-five children and teenagers, after all."

Father Hernandez's eyes slid away from her again, Matt noticed. The gesture was guilty. Most good Catholics had a hangup going back to grade school about deceiving nuns, but Matt would bet his best—and now useless—clerical collar that Father Hernandez wasn't telling anyone the full story. Maybe that was the secret he kept between himself and his most recent confessor, José Cuervo.

Chapter 18

Blue-ribbon Blood Sacrifice

I have been ill-used a time or two in my multitudinous lives, but nothing can quite compete with serving as a combination feline pincushion and a victim of the late great Count Dracula.

The average person would not believe the sort of ghoulish rituals that go on in the hidden back rooms of the local veterinarian's office, such as blood extraction through the victim's (me!) jugular vein.

When my little doll hands me over to the enemy, even I have no idea of the torments in store. And this indignity comes after my debilitating day at the cat show!

No doubt the attentive reader is wondering how I escaped the cage labeled "Percy" to return to the soon-to-be site of my newest betrayal—that is, home to the Circle Ritz in time for Miss Temple Barr to scoop me up unceremoniously and hasten me off to see the vet.

I wish that I could say that my great strength, savage nature and wily feline brain were responsible for tripping the latch on my steel cage. Alas, these are modern times and such primitive attributes are seldom necessary. Nowadays it is who you know that counts. In this instance, it is who it is that knows me: one Electra Lark, cohabitor with the reclusive Karma, landlady of the Circle Ritz and a bosom buddy of mine for almost three months now.

Naturally, she would know me in a darkroom, and she does almost as well across a crowded hall, even at a cat show.

"Louie!" I hear bellowed in dulcet tones.

I turn to scan the indifferent passersby. The judging is temporarily over and, yes, Midnight Louie is the last one left behind, stranded high and dry under the odious pseudonym of Percy, may his offspring have tape worms!

How could I have missed the slinky muumuu in electric shades of magenta, silver foil and chartreuse? For once I wish that I was as color-blind as certain erroneous experts insist that my kind is.

This vision bustles over, and I see that it is carrying a straw bag the size of Rhode Island. Miss Electra Lark is not the least inhibited at subjecting me to an interrogation I cannot begin to answer.

"Why, Louie," says she when finally and fully positioned before my cage. "What are you doing here?"

The answer should be obvious, so I say nothing. She fingers the ribbon affixed to my prison, then spots the paperwork and roots in her gigantic bag. Finally she draws out a pair of rhinestone-trimmed Ben Franklin glasses, pokes them up to her eyes and frowns at the news that I am "Percy."

She looks at me again, just to make sure, and I give her a one-word greeting to let her know she's got the right dude and the wrong name and number.

"You've got to be Louie," she mutters under her breath. "Percy is described as a tiger-stripe." She eyes me again and begins to speak as if I can understand every word, which I can, but this is not supposed to be generally known. I fear that Miss Electra Lark has developed some eccentricities from her clandestine association with the ineffable Karma.

"Temple must have entered you in the Household Pets category," she informs me quite incorrectly. "Then . . . she was called away by that early morning emergency of Matt Devine's—I would sure love to know what that was about!—and so she asked me to come over here and watch Peggy's cages while Peggy went to the hospital to see her ill aunt, and then . . . Temple forgot to mention in all the excitement that she'd entered you yesterday in the Household Pets contest today!"

Satisfied by her convoluted logic, she beams at me. "And look at you, Louie! You won." She leans forward to unhook the ribbon, then hesitates. "Unless this Percy won and you somehow ended up in his cage."

I nose my ribbon fondly to tell her it is mine, all mine, and show my claws, delicately, for further evidence.

"No need to get testy about it! All right, here goes the ribbon, pinned to my shoulder, and here goes my back—"

With which mysterious comment she swings open the cage door and lifts me up, and onto, her capacious bosom. I told you that we were buddies. A scent of gardenia nearly gags me, but I control my distaste.

After all, I am being borne out of the cat show with my Best of Class blue ribbon in plain view of all and sundry by my own personal bearer.

It is not a bad exit, if I do say so myself.

Chapter 19

Confidence Game

At four o'clock that afternoon, Temple found Matt waiting for her by the pool, sitting cross-legged in his gi on the blue mats, meditating.

Only twelve hours had passed since he had received the frantic call from Sister Seraphina. Temple marveled at his cool, collected calm. He did not look frazzled, worried or weary.

Temple, on the other hand, felt all of those things, and was sure that she looked it. At least the mirror over the bathroom sink had told her just that after she had slipped on her gi and paused to drag a brush through her thick red curls. She resembled a Raggedy Ann doll with a blank, bloodless, white-muslin face. Shock, she thought, and aftershock.

The last thing she felt like was a lesson in self-defense, but—from what Matt had implied—the martial arts had been his sanctuary even before the church. She sensed that learning—and teaching—kept that cool of his impeccably in place, and that his hard-won tranquillity was a shield.

"How is Miss Tyler?" she asked abruptly, breaking his reverie.

He looked up and nodded reassuringly. "She's home from the hospital already, with her niece. She was simply showing the effects of being terrorized at her age. What about Louie—and the other cat?"

"Dr. Doolittle says they're both resting comfortably."

"Do cats ever rest any other way?"

"No, I guess not. Louie can come home at six. Peter will have to stay a couple more days."

"How are you doing?" he asked next.

"Too tired to give in to it. I found the strangest thing on my living-room sofa. A blue ribbon. Do you suppose a good fairy is giving me a commendation for doing good deeds?"

"Maybe it's a reward for progress in your self-defense lessons."

"Hardly. I asked Electra to watch Peggy Wilhelm's cats at the show as long as needed; maybe she left me a ribbon to cheer me up. But she's not back yet. That's really odd."

"Minor League compared to what we've been involved in lately. Let's get to work." Matt rose with the supple ease that always surprised her. She had associated martial arts with kicks and grunts, not control and serenity.

Feeling far from serene herself, Temple kicked off her slip-in wedgies and stepped barefoot into the shade with Matt and back in time to their first lesson. The plastic of the mats was slick and cool on the soles of her feet. For a moment, the stress of the past few hours seemed a lifetime ago. Then Temple reminded herself that the reason they stood here doing this was that two men had assaulted her with their fists only a couple of weeks ago. She wondered if the blows she suffered then were any less stunning than the gantlet Matt had recently run through the byways of his hidden past—only, he had been forced to drag along an unwanted witness: her.

She pushed these distracting thoughts from her mind.

Matt was serious about teaching; she must be serious about learning.

"Did you find the pepper spray I left in your mailbox?" he asked.

She nodded. "A couple of days ago. Where did you get it?"

Matt shrugged. "At a gun show at the Convention Center." His mouth tightened. "If I had known, I would have bought some for Sister Seraphina and Miss Tyler's niece."

"Gun show? You?"

"That's where you readily get that stuff. It's legal. The point is, use whatever defensive weapons you carry—and you know what they can be?"

She nodded. "The pepper spray, ah . . . the wheel-lock device in my car, my car keys, a rolled-up newspaper—"

"Right. Whatever you can lay your hands on is fine, but in the end, you are your own best defensive weapon. You have to be prepared to resist with nothing more than yourself."

Temple sucked warm desert air between her teeth. "That's just it. There's so little self when it comes to me. I wouldn't intimidate a gerbil."

"That's not the point. Intimidation may not be the weapon you need; on the other hand, if it is, you can do it. Say you're attacking me—"

Temple quashed any smart remarks. He was an ex-priest, after all, and she found it horrifying how much that new knowledge inhibited her usually flagrant imagination.

"Come toward me," he advised, "as if you meant to do me harm."

Temple charged gamely.

Matt's stance changed to braced feet and slightly extended arms. "No!" he bellowed in a deep voice, straight from the gut of a Marine drill sergeant.

Temple was so shocked that her heart nearly stopped. It resumed with cumbersome, heavy beats.

"Jesus!" she said, clapping her hands over her throbbing organ. She felt like a hero in a romance novel. Then she realized that her expletive had its origins in the sacrilegious and should have been deleted. "I mean, oh, my goodness—"

Matt waved away her apologies. "Authoritarian rage can give even a rapist pause. The loud 'No!' brings back that scared three-year-old inside everyone who's ever confronted a parent. You try it."

"Me? Bellow like a wounded bull? I don't think so."

"Weren't you P.R. director for the Guthrie Theater in Minneapolis? Didn't you say that you acted in school drama productions? Aren't you an ex-TV reporter? You must have some dramatic instincts—"

Goaded, Temple answered all those questions with a wrenching, growling, basso, Greek-tragedy "No!"

Matt jumped, unprepared for the little girl with the big voice, and Temple almost scared herself. Then he smiled. "You ever heard that a gun looks scarier in a woman's hands because they're smaller than men's, and the gun looks bigger?"

"No, I can't say that I have, but then, I don't frequent gun shows," Temple answered with great virtue.

Matt only shook his head. "Well, from you, a rock-bottom 'No!' sounds much more definite precisely because you are so petite. Surprise is your best weapon. Use it."

"The mouse that roared."

"Exactly."

"What else can you teach me?"

"Well, the human body has two vulnerable areas. Can you guess what they are?"

Temple was at a loss. She felt vulnerable everywhere, especially since the attack.

"What's covered and protected in professional sports?" he prompted her in the approved style.

"For women? Nothing, unless they play men's contact sports. For men . . . heads, I guess. Faces."

"Good."

Temple paused. What she had to say next would not be polite. Especially to a priest. Jesus. Should she be a good student or a sensitive friend?

"What else?" Matt prodded.

Temple sighed. "Groins." That was better than balls, at least.

"Right," he said, not the least nonplussed.

He was all instructor now, and Temple saw that naked wasn't the best disguise; distance was.

"The human body has its limitations, because it's erect," he went on. "We can either lunge forward or retreat backward."

Matt mimicked those motions, making a mock dive for Temple and then retreating. "What happens?"

"If you attack . . . you drive forward and your face is vulnerable."

"And if you attack my face?"

She pantomimed his suggestion, her fingernails going for his eyes, and watched his upper body flinch away.

"You can step in," he prompted, "and—"

She stepped in, lifted a knee, jabbed with it, then froze the motion. He was right. An attacker exposed either his face or his groin; he could not protect both. All Temple had to master was the willingness to attack one or the other with all the skill and power at her command.

Self-defense, she realized, was a dirty business. Almost as dirty as having no defenses at all had been.

After learning another dozen ways of turning an attacker into creamed corn, Temple retreated to her apartment to take a shower. She wasn't accomplishing a lick of work, but she had never been so busy.

Matt had insisted on getting to work in his usual fashion, so Temple dashed out again in the Storm solo, this time to the vet's to pick up Midnight Louie.

Dr. Doolittle was gratifyingly positive about Peter's prognosis.

"He's such a mild little guy," she said by the front counter, where Louie, looking as unhappy as Nero Wolfe on a forced outing to a five-and-dime, lay in lackluster disarray after he had been retrieved from the place's mysterious private regions. "What a shame someone had to sneak up on such a good-natured cat and commit mayhem."

Louie yowled plaintively at that, no doubt identifying with the injured Peter now that he had been shanghaied into blood-donor duty.

"As for this big galoot, give him lots of meaty food, maybe kidney and liver," Dr. Doolittle advised. "He'll need to rest and recuperate for a while."

Louie's ears had perked up at the mention of food. Temple feared that her battle to convert him to Free-to-be-Feline pellets had encountered another setback, this time on doctor's orders.

She pushed her tote-bag straps as far up on her shoulder as possible and then lugged Louie out to the car. She had to put him down to open the door. He stood twitching his back on the asphalt, looking groggy. She was afraid that he might take off in sheer disgust, but when she opened the passenger door, he hopped up on the front seat in the disconcertingly doglike way he exhibited at times.

"Well, Louie," she told him as she put the Storm in gear and backed out of her parking spot, "you missed a lot of exciting developments yesterday while you were at home lounging and today while you were taking a rest cure at the veterinarian's. Now you'll have to stay put for a while longer. I think I'll shut your escape hatch until you've had a chance to recover your strength."

Louie blinked and curled up on the seat in a big, black ball. He really was such an intelligent, docile cat, Temple thought as she patted his ears.

Chapter 20

Blood Brothers

Granted I am weak in the knees from my involuntary blood-letting at the House of Dr. Death. This does not mean that I cannot lift my head a little and do some brain work. Contrary to Miss Temple Barr's notions, when I am laying about is when I do my most intense cogitating.

As for the charge of "lounging" about yesterday, she is, of course, utterly unaware of my unofficial outing to the cat show. In addition, the mysterious blue ribbon she puzzles over when she brings me home is no mystery. The perceptive Electra Lark brought both me and it home, and by then I was in a mood to be transported, although I usually prefer my transports to be made in the company of a female of my own species, if I have any say in the matter.

Nonetheless, people will believe what they will of me and my kind, and it suits me to be underestimated. I get a lot more done that way.

While I am sequestered behind the innocent facade of the veterinarian clinic, in what I can only describe as a kennel, redolent as that word is of my least favorite species, the canine kind, I do a little mild sleuthing.

How, you may ask, can Midnight Louie, flat on his side—well, not exactly flat; I do have a generous amount of muscle around my midsection—accomplish what Mr. Matt Devine and Miss Temple Barr have not achieved in running from pillar to post in a car all day?

For one thing, I have reached an age where I know how to produce the most results with the least effort. This is an art, like myself, that is much underestimated in these hectic modern times. For another, I speak the lingo of the chief witness to the mayhem.

Poor old Pete is a little jaundiced around the gills, and he was yellow to begin with. He lies on his side, looking quite flat and pathetic, a tastelessly cheery lime-green bandage on his foreleg holding a thin, transparent tube in place. Through this elongated straw can be seen the slow, rich trickle of a ruby-red substance: yours truly's life blood.

Despite public opinion, I abhor unnecessary roughness, especially when it is directed toward me. And although I have drawn my share of blood in my day, I do not resort to fancy technology to do it. Yet I cannot begrudge the poor schmuck in the adjoining cage a second chance at life, especially when he is the prime witness to the bizarre goings-on in the shadow of the convent. So I interrogate him gently.

"Say," begin I in a growling undertone that the attendants are likely to overlook. (I am a past master at passing for an innocent bystander in stir.) "Who did your nails?"

My breezy reference has all four of his limbs twitching, although only two were assaulted. Sometimes shock is the best incentive.

He spits weakly, then asks, "Who wants to know?"

"Your blood brother in the cell next door; Midnight Louie

is the name; crime is the game. What is the name of your attacker?"

"I am a pacifist," he says after a moment's silence.

"You are a pincushion," I point out brutally, "and unless you come clean and tell me the truth, who is to say that your pal Paul or some other neighborhood dudes might not get the same treatment or worse?"

"What can you do about it?" he demands in a thin, yet derisive voice.

"More than you can," I inform him. "Now talk."

So he does, off and on, between visits from attendants. The story I squeeze out of him is not much help. It seems he was not accosted, but snatched. Only, he says "abducted." These pacifist cats are somewhat unnatural, but everybody has a right to his political position.

This I find interesting. It betokens a crime of premeditation rather than of opportunity. Many a dude or doll of my type has been rudely run over—or more intentionally rubbed out—just for being in the wrong place at the wrong time: i.e., on the public street when a wacko of the human sort is feeling mean. Few have been the victims of premeditated mayhem. I will not speak of the unspeakable—of the attraction my species holds for the murderous actions of satanists and so-called scientists then and now. But there are less nefarious reasons that we might become victims of crime. The corporate cats, Baker and Taylor, were kidnapped from a bookseller's convention to confuse a murderer's trail. I wonder if a scheme of the same sort is in play here and now.

The unforthcoming Peter, with prodding, reveals more: a damp cloth was slapped over his kisser, he recalls, that smelled "sweet" and "heavy, like a baby diaper."

I diagnose a dose of chloroform, and Peter also admits that he was not conscious during the distasteful deed of hammering his extremities to the door.

Was the perpetrator infected by mercy—or by a desire for quietude and swift action? I favor the latter, not finding much mercy in the method of Peter's suspension.

After I pull what I can from the poor dude, I lean back to mull over the few pathetic facts I have obtained. One, Peter was plucked unwilling to be the object of this experiment in suspended animation; he did not stumble into the perpetrator's hands. Two, the perpetrator was prepared to execute just this act; it was not a spur-of-the-moment impulse. Three, the perp is either one sick puppy, or he—or she—had some unsuspected hidden motive in mind, beyond terrorizing Miss Tyler and any inadvertent passersby, which happened to include my good friend Miss Temple Barr and her good friend (and getting better) Mr. Matt Devine. There is nothing like shared shock to bring persons of the opposite sex closer.

It is a pity that the shock of awakening to be whisked off to a vet's office to have blood drained does not do much to endear the feline sort to the aforesaid whisker-offers.

Chapter 21

Mortal Complications

When the phone rang, Temple awoke, aware that stilettos of morning light were stabbing through the mini-blinds on the French doors to impale themselves in the bare wooden floor.

She wanted to lurch upright to answer the phone, but King Kong was sitting on her chest. Her mildly nearsighted eyes strained to focus. Holy cats, make that *Kitty* Kong! And make that her entire torso, not just her chest. Midnight Louie was arranged thereon, tail end pointedly turned to her face, front paws kneading her abdomen in alternating rhythm.

"*Ooof!*" Temple struggled up. "Off!"

She caught the phone on the fourth ring, before her answering machine could kick in, but she was panting.

"Hello?"

"Miss Barr?" By then, Temple had felt for her glasses on the nightstand and clapped them to her face. The clock read seven.

"Yes."

"Sister Seraphina O'Donnell," the voice cut in, using such an efficient tone that Temple unconsciously sat up ramrod-straight in bed.

Beside her, Louie remained lying on his side, where he had rolled when she had risen, licking his disheveled fur and casting dirty green looks over his shoulder at his ex-mattress. Too bad that wasn't his ex-*mistress*, Temple thought in irritation. She never did wake up well, God and the Mystifying Max knew for very different reasons.

"How did you get my number?" she asked.

"The yellow pages. You are listed under public relations, you know."

"Oh, and Matt mentioned my profession yesterday," Temple remembered. "You don't forget a thing."

"I hope not." Sister Seraphina sounded grim. "I shall have to remember a great deal shortly. And you as well." She sighed. "I'm sorry to call so early—"

"And I'm sorry I forgot to call last night," Temple interrupted. "Sister." She found the title awkward. Using it as an afterthought separated from the preceding sentence didn't help hide that. "Peter is going to be fine—"

"Good." The nun's tone was strangely flat.

Before Temple could react to this odd disinterest, the nun's voice was crackling over the phone with brisk sentence after sentence, each one more shocking than the next.

"I'm afraid that you'll have to come to the convent again. Miss Tyler was dead when Rose stopped by to collect her for six-o'clock Mass. It could be a . . . suspicious death. We called the authorities. Lieutenant Molina wants to question you as well." There was a pause. Temple could hear a rustling sound as Sister Seraphina covered the phone receiver with her hand to listen to someone else at the other end of the line. "Actually," her voice amended when it returned, "Lieutenant Molina doesn't want to question you, but fears that she must," the nun reported dryly.

"That's me, the obligatory interviewee. What about Matt?"

Sister Seraphina paused for a long moment. "I haven't told him yet. He'll be upset. It would be better for you to tell him when you collect him. Lieutenant Molina wants to see him, too."

Temple noticed *that* statement required no amending, and she couldn't blame Molina. If the lieutenant had to interview people about a murder at seven in the morning, beginning with Matt Devine was as pleasant a prospect as any.

As soon as Temple clicked down the interrupt button to end the call, she lifted a forefinger and punched in Matt's number, which she was beginning to know by heart. Beginning? She had memorized it the first time she saw it.

When the phone stopped in mid-ring as it lifted off the hook, Temple winced. This time Matt had had only three hours of sleep. He sounded like it.

"Yes?"

"Temple."

"Temple—?"

"I know this is the middle of the night for you, but we're wanted by the authorities."

"What are you talking about?"

"Your favorite long arm of the law, Lieutenant Molina."

"Temple, what's going on?"

"Miss Tyler died during the night. Make that passive tense: was probably killed."

Now he was strangely quiet, so Temple went on.

"Apparently Molina is conducting interrogations at the convent. As some of the parties who were the last to see the victim alive, I imagine our testimony will be of high interest to her."

"She'll be highly interested in our testimony, period." Matt sounded chagrined. "My cover's really blown now, isn't it?"

"Well, yes," Temple admitted, "but I won't tell anyone about your ax-murdering days, I promise."

"Thanks. Did Sister Seraphina say how Miss Tyler died?"

"No. Maybe we're supposed to be surprised."

"I bet we are," Matt said. "Give me three minutes and I'll be ready—or at least dressed."

"Too bad," Temple muttered as she hung up. Things were all backwards lately; she and Matt were always getting each other *out* of bed instead of into it. Given the recent revelations, that was probably for the best.

"Another golden dream pounded to glitter dust," she told Midnight Louie as she swooped her legs over his grooming bulk and to the floor.

He favored her with a glance implying that anyone so cavalier about his comfort deserved some discomfort of her own. Then he resumed stroking his glossy side, red tongue raking along black fur under a flare of white whiskers.

Temple shivered in the tepid air conditioning. However groggy, she was not too dazed to realize that an old woman was dead. She had just met Blandina Tyler, but somehow she had spiraled deep into the old lady's life—and now death. She wondered what Molina would make of that. She wondered even more what Molina would make of Matt now.

They were both too sleepy and too stunned to say much in the car.

Matt turned to her when they were halfway there and announced, "I applied for my driver's license yesterday. I figured I didn't need one until I got a car, but now I see that it could come in handy in an emergency."

"You mean every other day."

He smiled at her. "Looks like it." Then he sobered. "Much as I . . . blamed Seraphina for overreacting the other night, it's a good thing I did the anointing. That turned out to be Blandina Tyler's last rite."

"So it was worth coming out of the closet for?"

His glance was grim. "We'll see. Now Lieutenant Molina will be on *my* case."

"Yeah!" Temple wiggled her toes in her high-heeled sandals and grinned. "Maybe not mine, for once."

By the time the Storm crept along the curb in front of the convent and stopped, terminal sobriety had set in again. She and Matt sat in the car for a few seconds after she'd killed the motor.

"I wonder who will take care of the cats," Temple said.

He shook himself out of a reverie. "Miss Tyler must have made some provision. Whatever, they'll be well-to-do; Seraphina told me that she had inherited family money."

"Maybe she left a bequest to Peggy Wilhelm to look after them. You've never met Miss Tyler's niece?"

He shook his head, then cracked the door and got out.

The morning sun hadn't reached enough height to sizzle yet. The air was balmy, pleasant. Birds sang in the bushes, invisible but enthusiastic.

Sister St. Rose of Lima opened the door, a wizened, bespectacled elf now wide-eyed in dismay. Spry, she led them along the hall to the visitors' room, then scurried away as if what was inside was too painful to confront.

Temple saw why when she stepped over the threshold. The plain room was crowded with people ill at ease with each other. Peggy Wilhelm sat on the carved wooden chair, her eyes as raw as uncooked eggs, biting her lip while Sister Seraphina bent over her, murmuring.

A priest, Father Hernandez apparently, paced impatiently by the window in a long black cassock topped by a white, choirboy smock edged with lace along the hem and the sleeves. Obviously, he'd come straight from early morning Mass.

Paul, the cat, perched in the ajar window, watching the priest's trapped-mouse movements with sharp, certain feline eyes.

Molina's brunette razor-cut hair was bent over a notebook in which she was making some cryptic memo. She looked up when Temple and Matt entered, her intense blue eyes registering a tricky blend of disbelief, suspicion, curiosity and relief.

"And there isn't even a convention involved this time," she noted to Temple. Almost everybody else looked perplexed.

"Wrong, Lieutenant," Temple retorted in cheerful contradiction. "A cat show closes tomorrow at the Cashman Convention Center."

"Cat show?" Molina's wrinkled nose indicated she'd had enough of cats in Chez Blandina to last her for some time. "Step across the hall for a moment. I've got some questions." She eyed Matt. "For you both."

Molina brushed past them in her bell-bottom navy pantsuit while Temple reflected that she hadn't seen bell-bottoms or a pantsuit on anyone since her grade-school days. Molina was showing an alarming new tendency to be trendy. Was it Matt, or Memorex?

The room across the hall was plainer and smaller than the visitors' room, furnished with a bare blond table and several cafeteria-style wooden chairs with forest-green and chartreuse vinyl seats. A heavy, Spanish-style wooden crucifix clung to the pale wall like a large, eavesdropping fly.

"Looks like an interrogation room, doesn't it?" Molina suggested in a satisfied voice. "Father Hernandez hears the nuns' confessions in here."

"Don't expect any from us," Temple warned.

Matt flashed her a cautioning glance. He wasn't aware of her long-standing, and tart, verbal fencing-match with Molina. He wasn't used to being under suspicion, and he certainly wasn't used to having something to hide.

"How did you get involved in this one?" Molina asked Temple, nodding to the chairs and perching on a corner of the uncompromising table.

"Electra Lark, my . . . our landlady, thought I could do the cat show some good." Temple sat down and crossed her knees.

"Did you?"

Temple felt herself flush. "Not really. I haven't had time and there wasn't much left to do to promote it. Electra really thought I could help Peggy Wilhelm."

Molina flipped through her notebook pages, but Temple suspected it was a gesture meant to hide the fact that Molina didn't need to look up anything. "This Peggy Wilhelm is

Miss Tyler's niece?" Temple nodded. "What kind of help would she need from you?"

Here's where it got uncomfortable. Temple squirmed on her unattractive and utterly rear-numbing chair and crossed her ankles.

"Peggy had been getting weird telephone calls."

"So I heard. That doesn't answer my question."

"Electra thought I might be able to . . . find out what was going on."

"Since when do you work for the phone company?"

"It wasn't just the calls," Temple said, well aware that she hadn't made any progress on that problem at all. "The first day of the cat show, Peggy's prize Birman was sheared like a sheep."

"So what has that to do with what happened next door last night?" Lieutenant Molina could not have sounded any more weary, bored and disgusted.

"Maybe nothing, but it certainly made Peggy frantic about staying with her cats at Cashman Center, so I volunteered to come over here and help Miss Tyler feed *her* cats, which I did, Thursday morning."

"That was the first time you met her?"

Temple nodded.

"And the last?"

She eyed Matt. "Not . . . no."

"We came over here early the following morning," he said, stressing the "we."

Molina was too busy frowning down at her notebook to see Temple's relieved smile.

"Sister Seraphina indicated that she called on you two for help. Why, I can't imagine."

Temple was sure that Molina had never spoken truer words.

"Sister Seraphina seemed reticent to discuss that predawn expedition," Lieutenant Molina went on. "Nothing makes a cop more suspicious than reticent nuns, especially this cop. Nuns are used to cooperating with authority, and when they go wishy-washy on me, I get very nervous."

" 'We' didn't come over here," Matt volunteered into the ominous silence. "I did. Temple drove me."

"Now why was that, Mr. Devine?" Molina asked, folding her arms.

He smiled at her with serene understanding. "I think you know why. After all, you yourself told Temple why I couldn't drive. No license."

"You woke up your neighbor at—what was it?"

"Four o'clock."

"At four o'clock in the morning, because you're such a law-abiding soul that when Sister Seraphina called, you knew you needed a driver."

Now Matt squirmed on his slick, plastic chair seat. "No, I knew I needed a car. Temple reminded me of my illegal status."

"So Miss Barr is the rigorous upholder of the law. How interesting."

The lieutenant's bright baby-blues consulted Temple with exaggerated wonder. Was Molina attempting to be sarcastic?

"It was an emergency," Temple said flatly. "We both did what we had to do: get there as fast as the law would allow."

"Not a little faster?"

Temple swallowed. She had been driving. "Maybe a little."

"Did you know the nature of the emergency?"

"Only that it involved Miss Tyler and there was no time to be lost."

"Why? According to the ambulance report, she was agitated but generally well. The hospital didn't keep her."

"Sister Seraphina said—" Temple began.

"Sister Seraphina said a lot to a lot of people in the past couple of days," Molina observed. "Too bad she won't say much to me. In fact, she wouldn't say anything until you arrived." Here the sapphire gaze as sharp as broken glass landed—and stayed—on Matt.

"Maybe I should leave," Temple offered. She had already seen Matt forced to explain his background once in the past forty-eight hours. She didn't need a repeat performance, and he probably didn't relish witnesses to his recital.

"Stay." Molina pointed to Temple's chair like someone disciplining a dog. "You witnessed the first night's disruption. If I'd needed to question you separately, I'd have done it. Now, Mr. Devine, the floor is yours. Just tell me what happened, in sequence."

Matt thrust his hands in his pants pockets and stared at the tabletop alongside Molina. "Sister Seraphina called."

"How did you know her?"

He didn't shift position at Molina's interruption, probably realizing that there would be many such intrusions. "She was a teacher at my grade school in Chicago."

"Chicago?" Molina purred like a puma at this crumb from Matt's mysterious past. "Catholic school?"

"Saint Stanislaus."

"Polish?" Molina asked, her narrowed eyes flashing to Matt's blond hair.

He nodded, oblivious, concentrating on his story, on the sequence of events.

"She was vague about the trouble, but I never doubted her. Nuns from teaching orders never kid around."

Molina nodded, then started as Matt suddenly stared up at her and continued. "She said to come fast. I thought of Temple's car. I wanted to borrow it. I never remembered, or cared, about the license. Temple insisted on driving. That's when she told me you had looked into my 'background' and found out that I didn't have a driver's license."

"Does that bother you, that I checked?"

"Yes. You had no cause."

"I'm a cop. Cops are curious. That's cause enough."

"No official cause."

Molina fanned out a hand—strong, no-nonsense nails, heavy class ring. "Enough for official instincts."

Matt glanced back to the table. "Temple drove, not too fast."

"Not too fast and not too slow, just right, like Baby Bear,"

Molina mocked. "Miss Barr always treads the line of legality on those high heels of hers. One day she might fall off."

Matt flushed but didn't look up again. "We met Sister Seraphina at the convent door. She explained that Miss Tyler was deeply distressed, possibly physically, certainly emotionally and spiritually. She wanted me to administer the anointing for the sick, to calm Miss Tyler in case her condition was . . . serious."

"You?" Molina stood up, arms still folded over her chest. "Where was the pastor of the parish?"

Temple could see truth and loyalty battling in Matt. "Miss Tyler was miffed with Father Hernandez over the issue of whether cats go to heaven or not. She would have been disturbed rather than soothed if he had come to her bedside."

"Still, parish spats come and go. Surely she wouldn't object to his attendance in a grave illness?"

"Seraphina didn't think her condition was that serious, and she didn't think that Father Hernandez was suitable."

"He was the parish priest. He should have been called. Wasn't he furious to have been ignored?"

"I don't know."

"This is odd! Everybody is walking around Father Hernandez like cats on a hot tin roof. He has always struck me as the autocratic type who wouldn't take kindly to that. Why was he not called and you were? Why?"

"That was the problem, and what Sister Seraphina felt too loyal to tell you." Matt sighed. "He was incapacitated."

Molina drew that in, mangled her lower lip for a few seconds, digested the information. "Confessions indeed. You are saying that Father Hernandez was—what? Spit it out."

Temple could see Matt's hands knot into fists in his pockets. Her own hands tensed. Molina could be a chain saw at times, and Matt was ready to explode at the touch of a scalpel. Temple realized that he was hiding more than she knew.

Molina missed nothing, and would pass up no advantage.

"Tell me; otherwise, I'll have to force it out of Sister Seraphina. Or Father Hernandez himself. What was he?"

"Drunk on tequila, I suppose," Matt said in a dead, disowning voice.

It wasn't Father Hernandez he disowned, a shocked Temple thought, but his own feelings about this shameful news.

"I see." Molina sank back against the desk, as if borne down by the tawdriness of the revelation. Temple saw that she hadn't liked forcing this particular secret into the open. "Now I can understand Sister Seraphina's reticence. Nun or not, she's acting as an enabler by hiding the problem, you know," she added almost gruffly. "Religious loyalty aside, she needs to get him into treatment."

"Maybe now," Matt said.

"All right. Scandal in the parish, but couldn't she have administered the sacrament in an emergency? She doesn't strike me as someone who would crack under pressure."

"She could have, but she knew that Miss Tyler was of an age and an era that would be scandalized by a nun taking on such sacramental duties, even in an emergency."

"So she called you. Because . . ."

"Because I was a priest."

Molina stood again, sincerely shocked. No, not shocked. Startled.

"You're a priest? I suppose the hotline is pastoral work, but—"

"The hotline is a job," he interrupted, looking up with chilly control. The cat, so to speak, was about to emerge utterly from the bag and the worst was almost over. "My job, now. I said I *was* a priest. Past tense."

Molina's dark head nodded slowly. "Of course you would be obligated to act as necessary in an emergency. What are you doing in Las Vegas?"

He didn't miss a beat. "My job, just my job. There aren't many available for men with my educational background."

Molina suddenly spun to Temple. "Are you Catholic?"

"No. Unitarian. Sort of. Well, I *was* a Unitarian."

They both looked at her.

"I'm sorry." Temple shrugged. "I know it's supposed to be an undemanding faith, but I just sort of . . . fell away. What is this, the Spanish Inquisition?"

"What is that comment, an ethnic slur?" Molina retorted.

Temple gulped, then she got it. "*You*'re Hispanic—and Catholic?" Minnesota had a small Hispanic population, and Temple had always assumed the name "Molina" was Italian.

"Hispanic, yes. Catholic, sort of," Molina mocked Temple. She scowled, annoyed at having to explain herself. "My daughter attends Our Lady of Guadalupe School."

Daughter? Temple couldn't imagine Molina as a mother. Well, maybe as a mother, but not as a wife. And Hispanic, with those Celtic-blue eyes?

"Now that everybody knows where everybody is coming from," Molina resumed with a wry tone, "maybe we can get back to the facts. You—" she nodded at Matt "—anointed Miss Tyler. You—" she quirked an eyebrow at Temple "—watched in stupefaction. Then what?"

Temple answered, figuring Matt needed a break. "Then Sister Seraphina decided that Miss Tyler wasn't improving and called nine-eleven. Rose—Sister Saint Rose of Lima—accompanied Miss Tyler in the ambulance. After the medical crew left, we all got to talking and realized that maybe Miss Tyler's ravings about Saint Peter and being betrayed in the Garden weren't just religious confusion and death fears. I had noticed that the tip of her cane had fresh dirt on it, so—"

"Wait." Molina's hands elevated like a traffic cop's. "*You*—you noticed that the cane tip had fresh dirt on it. I can see that you are riveted by religious ritual, Barr, but what made you even think of the cane at a time like that?"

"It's a riveting cane. No, really! It's hand-painted and carved. I noticed it leaning against the trunk I was sitting on in Miss Tyler's bedroom and . . . I saw the dirt crumbling onto the floor. So we all hurried out to the garden, and that's where Matt discovered the crucified cat on the back door."

Lieutenant Molina didn't move, she just glanced wearily at Matt, who resumed the tale. So the atrocity done to Peter surfaced, down to how Matt had freed the animal. Temple cringed to think of bracing a claw hammer on the wood and delicately pulling long carpenter nails through a cat's paw, not once, but twice. Even Molina looked impressed.

That's when Temple decided that Molina would also be relieved to hear that Peter was doing well, thanks to Midnight Louie's blood donation. She did remember Midnight Louie—?

"Miss Barr, I remember every scintillating detail about your exceedingly bizarre circle of acquaintances including the feline," the lieutenant assured her in exaggeratedly lucid tones. "In fact, I am developing quite a fascinating file on the whole kit and caboodle."

"Happy to oblige you with entertainment," Temple answered.

Molina resumed the interrogation. "And neither of you saw Miss Tyler since then?"

"No," they answered in unison, like well-trained schoolchildren. Then they glanced guiltily at each other and looked away. They had sounded rehearsed.

"Neither of you returned to the Tyler house, or to the convent or to the church?"

"I did." Matt seemed relieved to have the floor to himself. "I came back here to confer with Sister Seraphina."

"What did you confer about?"

"Miss Tyler. Father Hernandez."

"You knew that Miss Tyler was coming home from the hospital, with her niece?"

"Yes."

Molina turned to Temple, who wondered why this double interrogation wasn't giving the tall lieutenant whiplash. "You knew that?"

"Matt mentioned something about it later."

"When, and where?"

"Four P.M. Friday, in the pool area of the Circle Ritz."

"Taking a dip?"

"No . . . learning how to take out a drip. Matt was teaching me some self-defense moves."

Molina's head whipped toward Matt again. "What do you know about self-defense?" Her skepticism was not quite a sneer.

"I've practiced some martial arts."

"Well. Mutant Ninja ex-priest." Molina's head swung toward Temple again. "Did you learn anything?"

"How to combat persistent bullies who are bigger than I," Temple said quite deliberately. "The eye gouge, the groin kick, the biting-off-body-parts technique."

Molina grinned. "Not much art to that."

"I wasn't teaching Temple tae kwon do," Matt put in. "Just the basics of sidewalk self-defense."

"Then what happened?"

"I went to get ready for work at seven," Matt said.

"I went to the vet's to retrieve Midnight Louie and check on poor Peter," Temple added when Molina looked her way again, before turning back to Matt.

"Anything odd happen on your shift at the hotline, any out-of-the-ordinary calls?"

Matt's smile was charmingly crooked. "All our calls are out of the ordinary, Lieutenant, but none last night were noticeably so. Are you thinking the nuisance caller might have wanted to leave a message last night?"

"Maybe." Molina stood up with an air of finality. "The crime-scene team is working over the house. When they're done, I'll want to hear what the three of you have to say about the cat incident, so stay around."

"Where?" Temple mouthed at Matt behind her back as the lieutenant drifted out the door like a navy-blue shadow.

Matt grinned with relief that the interrogation was temporarily over. "That's one question I can answer. The convent kitchen. A great place to stay out of the way. Come on, let's find it."

Temple couldn't help feeling like a trespasser as they wandered the convent's many halls. Maybe a former priest had the right to make himself at home here, but she didn't. Perhaps she had been infected by years of Protestant superstition about Catholic clergy and Catholic Church structures. She kept expecting to run into something she shouldn't around a corner, something mysterious and semi-creepy—a shadowed statue with a bank of lit candles twinkling eerily before it, or one of those kitschy red-velvet upholstered kneelers you saw in the background of cheap European vampire movies.

This convent showcased only spanking-clean walls and floor and simple pieces of furniture. When they located the kitchen, down two steps at the back of the house, they found Pilar rattling around in the space big enough to hold an empty table for eight.

Pilar shook her head and began a litany of commiseration without waiting for a more formal conversational cue.

"Oh, terrible, so terrible, what happened to Miss Tyler! I was shocked. The sisters all stirred up before breakfast . . . police cars in the neighborhood, sirens."

Matt pulled out a chair near the table's corner for Temple, then another at the head for himself, so they sat at right angles.

"We had to leave the apartment building without breakfast ourselves," he put in.

"No breakfast?" Pilar repeated, scandalized. "The sisters all are over at the church praying for Miss Tyler's soul—those who are not here waiting for Lieutenant Molina to question them. Questioning the good sisters, can you imagine? I do not know what that woman is thinking, and a member of the parish, too."

"Oh, she attends church here?" Temple pursued.

"Not often enough," Pilar responded with a frown, banging around in the cupboards. "Not morning Mass, but most Sundays. I suppose her work might call her away, but that's hardly an excuse for missing a Sunday obligation. This police stuff is no job for a woman and a mother." She snapped a pair of pale orange Melmac plates down before them with unnecessary emphasis.

"Women do everything nowadays," Temple said.

"Not good work for a woman with a child, who cannot even guarantee to be home at the same time every evening."

Pilar sniffed with contempt. "Poor little Mariah, and what kind of a saint's name is that? I pretend that it is Maria, but no—I am corrected. It must be pronounced 'Mah-rye-ah.' "

Her back to them like a disapproving black wall bowed by print apron strings, she rattled pans and mixing bowls by the stove.

"Mariah. It's better than Tiffany," Temple put in.

"What's wrong with Maria, as in 'Ave Maria'? Nothing stays. No family discipline, no respect for the church, for the saints' names. The neighborhood is a dumping ground, and now poor Miss Tyler is killed in her own home, while her niece is sleeping there."

"Were . . . the cats all right?" Temple asked.

Pilar's bulky body twisted from the stove. "And what was done to that cat—!" She crossed herself hastily, her long middle finger tapping forehead, chest and each shoulder in turn. After a shudder of distaste, she turned back to her stove top. "A cruel but calculated thing. Blasphemy."

When she faced them again, a plate of thick, steaming pieces of French toast was in her hands. She bore it to the table, putting it down beside Matt's place. "There you are," she said in a gentled tone. "You like raspberry preserves, syrup?"

"Yes," Temple and Matt answered again in irritating tandem.

Pilar knew just what to do. She fetched servings of each, later bringing them cups of fresh, midnight-dark coffee and a small, rose-colored pitcher of half-and-half.

Then she stood beside them, stubby hands crossed over her apron front, and, like some gruff guardian angel, watched them eat.

"This is wonderful," Temple said, realizing how hungry she was when her stomach growled at the mere sniff of food.

"Sisters won't eat it," Pilar said in disgust. "Too upset. Even cats won't eat it. Good that you do. Do you want sugar, Mr. Devine?" she asked solicitously, hovering over Matt's coffee cup.

He took her anxious presence in perfect stride. "Everything is fine as is. Thank you, Pilar. I can see that the sisters are well taken care of here."

"And Father Hernandez. I also cook for him at the rectory, and must run back and forth, back and forth." She rolled her hands into the apron folds. "He is not much for breakfast lately. Do you suppose that Mrs. Molina will have the nerve to question Father Hernandez?"

Temple nearly choked on her coffee to hear the name of Molina preceeded by the honorific of "Mrs." Molina an ordinary Mrs? Never!

"What does Mr. Molina think of his wife's occupation?" Temple inquired demurely.

Pilar's sniff was a snort this time. "No Mr. Molina. Maybe there never was one. Who is to say? All I know is that Mariah Molina is in the fifth grade at the school, and I have never seen a wedding band on her mother's hand."

"Many widows don't wear wedding rings," Matt pointed out charitably.

"More divorcées," Pilar answered with scorn. "Some even have the nerve to come to church and up to the communion rail. You can't tell anymore who is who and what is what. Even the church is confused. Priests and nuns are priests and nuns no longer, and married people get dispensations—"

"I think you mean 'annulments,'" Matt suggested quickly, obviously stung by her dismissal of ex-anythings.

Pilar didn't pause for corrections. "No wonder poor Miss Tyler is dead. Nobody respects anything about the church anymore. Next they will be slaughtering nuns and priests in their beds, like in the heathen countries. I only pray that Miss Tyler did nothing foolish with her will, like leaving her money to all those cats, instead of to Our Lady of Guadalupe."

"Lately she'd been saying that she would, hadn't she?"

Pilar eyed Temple with skepticism. "Old ladies are tyrants around the parish priest. They want attention like a small child, and they use the promise of their money to get it. Father Hernandez was foolish to anger Miss Tyler."

"What could he say?" Temple asked. "Apparently cats in heaven is not a kosher Catholic concept."

"He could have talked around the matter, without lying. Instead, he told her no, no cats in heaven. Now there may be no dollars in the development fund. In my day, a priest did not have to scramble for money; the Sunday baskets were full. We were all poor, but we all gave what we could. Today churches must rely on the rich, like any other beggar. Are you done?"

The question came so sharply it sounded like an accusation. Temple studied her empty plate with its free-form design of syrup contrails.

"Yes," she admitted, only to have the plate whisked away.

"And you, Mr. Devine, do you want more?"

Temple frowned. She had not been offered more.

"This was plenty," he said, looking up at Pilar with that six-million-dollar-man smile. "The toast was wonderful."

"More coffee?" Pilar coaxed.

"Perhaps a bit more coffee, if it's not too much trouble."

"No trouble," Pilar said, clumping to the stove in her lace-up shoes.

When she returned to refill Matt's cup, she gave Temple a cursory glance. "I do not suppose that you want any more."

"No," Temple said, too amazed by the byplay to consume anything at the moment.

She analyzed the situation. Pilar treated Matt like a favorite pupil, but Temple like some unwanted playmate dragged home from school unannounced.

And Matt Devine just sat there, soaking up this female consideration like he was born to it. Maybe Pilar could smell a priest; certainly Matt knew exactly how to handle a devout woman who lived to cater to the clergy. Particularly the male clergy.

Temple sipped the last bitter drop of coffee in her cup. She had pictured priests as totally isolated from women, but in a parish setting, she saw, they were surrounded by them.

Utterly off-bounds, of course, but interacting daily, and even in the most intimate domestic setting with a housekeeper.

She had assumed that celibacy went hand in hand with innocence, with perhaps a secret and noble struggle underneath. She would expect a priest's ignorance to render him slightly gauche and awkward, despite the education of the confessional. Matt Devine was neither gauche nor awkward in this setting. He knew his way around these women like a master thief knows the layout of the Metropolitan Museum of Art. He knew how to handle them without seeming to, without their noticing it any more than they should. He was forever "Father"; they relied upon him and deferred to him and considered him their own.

Pilar didn't think about all this, of course; she just reacted from instinct, as did Matt.

Temple's own instincts grew uneasy at this insight. Matt's background made him a smoother customer than she had thought, than maybe he realized himself. He was a performer of sorts, after all, a spiritual prestidigitator.

He was beginning to remind her a lot of a missing magician named Max Kinsella.

Chapter 22

Hissturbing Questionsss

The door to the kitchen snapped open and a wizened face peered around the dark walnut doorjamb.

"Psst!" Sister St. Rose of Lima hailed Matt and Temple loudly enough to pass for a screaming steam kettle.

Pilar's stolid back remained turned to the room as water ran and her elbows cranked in and out over the sink. Apparently no dirty dishes lasted longer than an angelus bell in a Catholic kitchen. Temple mourned the last sweet licks of syrup on her plate that were disappearing under a baptism of sudsy water, leaving a plate that would now be squeaky-clean and innocent, unlike the rest of them, except maybe for Sister St. Rose of Lima, whose ancient, baby-doll face was wrinkled with unconcealed conspiracy . . .

Temple and Matt rose quietly and went to the door, where a whispered conference revealed that Sister Seraphina wished to meet them in the rectory while the lady lieutenant—that is the way Sister Rose put it with an awed precision—was interviewing Miss Wilhelm in the convent.

Temple and Matt exchanged one mystified glance and went out, not speaking until the warm light of day was bestowing hot haloes of amber sunlight on their heads.

"Sister Seraphina is showing signs of giving Lieutenant Molina as much trouble as I do," Temple mused. "I thought nuns were sworn to respect authority."

"Authority isn't as obvious as it once was," Matt said, "neither religious nor civil. I'm sorry to learn that Lieutenant Molina is a member of this parish. It could prejudice her."

"In pursuing the case?"

"In pursuing my past."

"Why do you think she'll bother to do that?"

"In her own way, she's as curious as you are and she has all the official means of prying at her fingertips. I suppose the crucified cat points to a religiously troubled killer. Why not me?"

"Listen, Devine, you *are* trouble, you are not troubled."

"I thought *I* was the self-defense teacher."

"In matters of physical prowess. In criminal matters, I'm the expert. Why do I feel that 'prowess' is something that has to do with 'lady lions' on the African savannahs and not me?"

"You've got plenty of prowess," he assured her, "in unexpected areas."

Matt paused at the rectory door, then pulled the wrought-iron hinges open with a mighty tug, as if he expected the door's weight and was ready for it.

They submerged themselves in another passage through cool interior shade, in a peace perfumed with lemon oil and candle wax and a faint odor of old incense.

Voices drifted into the silence like swimmers floating onto a deserted shoal, striving voices, one male, one female.

Matt's pace quickened as he made for Father Hernandez's office door. Once there, he paused and turned to Temple with an expression of firm regret.

"I'd better go in alone."

"She summoned both of us."

"Yes, but—"

Beyond the door, Father Hernandez's voice rose to an angry rail, reminding Temple of the keening associated with an Irish wake. There was nothing Irish about this place, this time, this cast of characters, although the wake notion was all too apt with Blandina Tyler soon to become the centerpiece of her own.

Matt slipped through the door without seeming to open it.

Magician! Temple's resentful thoughts hissed after him. Subtle and self-concealing. Discreet. The bitter words surged back and forth in her mind like angry surf. Max had confided nothing, revealed nothing unnecessarily, had shut and locked doors behind him that he never came again to open, and too many of them bordered Temple's emotional premises.

She waited outside this new closed door, unable to keep from overhearing snatches of dialogue; unable to avoid dissecting and interpreting it.

Father Hernandez's voice came louder, deep and uncontrolled, a berserk organ rambling in a minor key. It ebbed and flowed in time to her softer mental surf. Temple could picture him pacing, his dramatic cassock skirt straining against his long, lean strides, his figure erect despite its distress. He did not look like a bendable man in any respect. Yet the voice was unkempt and slurred, touched with the tequila's thick, tart tongue.

Seraphina's mission was obvious to Temple whether she was invited in or not: to restore reason, if not sobriety, to Father Hernandez before Lieutenant Molina sat him down and peeled his mind like a muscat grape fat with foreign intoxicants.

"I have failed," he raged in a threepenny-opera voice, rich and sonorous for sermons and now directed at himself like an accusing Greek chorus that would be heard through closed doors no matter what. "A serpent is loose in our little Garden of Eden, of Gethsemane."

Sssserpent loossse. As in Eden. But a serpent sounded more at home in Gethsssemane, the garden of purely human betrayal, Temple thought.

Matt's calm murmur—so damned priestly—was harder to decipher. Maybe Temple was irreverent to put it that way in her mind; maybe it was immaterial and irrelevant to care how she put it to herself. She paused before the sealed door, guilty but determined. Matt was the core of her concern. What would this crash course in troubled Catholicism do to him?

"Falsely accused!" Father Hernandez's best pulpit tones cried. "There is a Judas among us."

How he hissed the incriminating words! Falsssely accusssed. A Judassss among usss.

"Scandal!" the drunken voice raved.

Sssscandal, Temple heard.

"This is the Man!"

Thisss isss the Man.

Could Father Hernandezsss be the hissing caller? Certainly his rich, Hispanic voice, blurred by liquor and desperation, broadcast a susurration that an old woman on a phone might mistake for hissing.

"Snakes!" he ranted.

Ssssnakesss. On the phone. In the parish. In the pastor's raving words.

Matt's voice suddenly came clear and strong, urging control and sanity, banishing the bad dreams. Or the memories? Did Father Hernandez harbor bad memories of driving an elderly parishioner to distraction and ultimate death before she could change her will and cut the church from it like a plump plum doomed to wither on the apostalic vine?

A priest who killed? How? How, when he was drowning himself in tequila and paranoia?

Temple couldn't stand it. Eavesdropping was not her long suit—in hearts, clubs, or even when it came to aces up her sleeve in spades. She needed to confront her suspicions in person, which is no doubt why Max's disappearance had so thoroughly confounded her. Her hand reached for the dark iron doorknob, then turned it.

The overheard dialogue clarified the instant that she entered the somber study. She felt as if she had walked onto the set of a play and the actors were now enunciating with Masterpiece Theatre perfection for her benefit. Certainly the scene was striking.

Father Hernandez was facing Matt, as dark and brooding as a tragic hero in his coloring, his old-fashioned black cassock, his tortured priestly passion.

"Some priests walk away," he was saying. Bitterness and regret seasoned his accusing voice. "I cannot."

Ssssome priesssstsss, the snake hissed in Eden, in Las Vegas.

Matt, as innocently blond as any first-communion angel of seven years in a winsome white suit, answered the challenge with a lift of his head and his voice. "Some priests stay when they do more damage than if they left."

That reply caused Father Hernandez to recoil, to sink into one of the upholstered armchairs designed for the comfort of his flock and put his face in his hands.

In the ensuing silence, Sister Seraphina wrung her wrinkled old hands and glanced from one man to the other. "We must give each other the benefit of the doubt," she urged. "We must support each other in our separate ways."

Father Hernandez withdrew his hands and turned to the peacemaker, his red-rimmed eyes empty and wounded. "Separate is different for all of us. Don't worry, Sister. I will pull myself together for the police lieutenant." He smiled as he shook his head to clear it. "She is only a parishioner, after all. I have heard her confession." That assertion made Temple blink. She would love to hear—even overhear—C.R. Molina's confession. "I have always been able to appease my parishioners," he added with a touch of the old arrogance. "Except for Miss Tyler."

"A priest's role is not to appease," Matt put in.

"Walk in my shoes, Fisherman!" Father Hernandez's

black-coral eyes blazed. "What is most unappeasable is Satan, and he is out there, be certain of it."

Shoesss of the Fisssherman. Mossst unappeasssable. Ssssatan. Isss. Csssertain.

Temple heard hisses, and there was no one there—only a conscience-wracked parish priest. Conssscience-wracked parisssh priessst. And Ssssissster Sssseraphina. And Matt Devine, who could not possssibly be party to this cssselebration of disssassster and doubt.

"You look tired, my dear," Ssssissster Sssseraphina whissspered to Temple.

She was; no point in denying it. She was even beginning to look forward to the nexssst ssstage of Csss. R. Molina'sss inquisssition. My asss, Temple thought, fed up with suspicions that hissed through everybody's most unconscious word choice. Pardon, she thought again contritely, in deference to the religious environment. Balaam'sss asss.

Lieutenant Molina found them, of course, even in the refuge of the rectory, about ten minutes later. She skeptically eyed the assembled foursome, then addressed only Father Hernandez.

"I'll need to ask you some questions. Alone."

The other three left without any parting pleasantries. No good days or good-byes. It was obviously not a good day, and they would obviously see each other again.

"I should talk to Peggy," Sister Seraphina muttered as much to herself as to Temple and Matt on the way back to the convent.

"So should I," Temple said. "We," she added in deference to Matt.

He was more intimately involved in this death than she, after all. Temple had only fed Blandina Tyler's cats—once. Matt had administered her last sacrament.

"Why?" Matt asked, his eyes distant and troubled.

"She's the only one who's going to tell us what really happened to Miss Tyler. Molina won't."

"What would Peggy know?" Sister Seraphina asked with a wrinkled brow.

"She should know as much as Molina saw fit to tell the victim's only relative. I'm hoping that will be time of death, the method, maybe even a speculation on the motive."

At this pronouncement, Sister Seraphina and Matt exchanged a lightning glance. They were doing a lot of that lately, Temple had noticed. She wondered if the same suspicions that danced the polka in her active imagination were making a slow, reluctant saraband through their minds: Father Hernandez had a lot to lose if Blandina Tyler had lived to leave Our Lady of Guadalupe out of her will. That worry could have turned him to the bottle. Could it also have goaded him into the unreasonable acts bedeviling the convent and its neighbor: the crude calls, the midnight ramblings and rustles, the brutal attack on Peter? Could it have caused him to kill the old parishioner before she made good on her threat?

Sister Rose admitted them to the convent, and they returned to its one public room, where Peggy Wilhelm nursed a cup of tea that smelled of apple and almonds. Not even hot, pungent herbal tea could steam the pleats of worry from Peggy's pleasant round face.

She stirred at their entrance. "I'll have to contact the neighborhood funeral parlor—Lopez and Kelly, isn't it?"

Sister Seraphina nodded.

Peggy went on. "I don't know when the police will . . . release the body, but no doubt the funeral people can see to all that. I'll have to go back into the house and . . . pick some clothes for the funeral, feed the cats."

"I'll go with you," Sister Seraphina said promptly.

"I'll feed the cats," Temple volunteered. "I know the routine."

Matt said nothing. The practicalities of death were always women's work, Temple supposed. He was designated to come along later, in cassock and vestment, to intone and bless and bury, only he didn't do that kind of work anymore. Father Hernandez would have to do it, whatever his condition—or involvement.

"What," Temple asked, unable to restrain herself any longer, "did Lieutenant Molina tell you about the . . . crime?"

Peggy's eyes were as dull as tepid tea, scummed over with sorrow and shock, their expression deadened. "The medical examiner at the morgue will determine the cause of death. I found her at the bottom of the stairs with a broken neck, with numerous bruises and contusions. She could have tripped on a cat, or several cats, but the lieutenant admitted that she didn't like the severity of the marks around her head and throat. Her cane was broken into several pieces. I guess it didn't take much to kill Aunt, either way: accident or murder. It must have happened after midnight, the lieutenant said. I was sleeping in the downstairs back bedroom, and no one next door at the convent heard anything."

"Whose rooms are nearest the Tyler house?" Temple asked.

"Only Sister Mary Monica's," Seraphina said in wry tones.

Matt nodded wearily. "She's virtually deaf."

"Convenient," Temple noted grimly. "If it was murder, it looks as if the killer knew the neighborhood. But was he—or she—the one who made the nuisance calls and harmed the cat?"

"Paul's the roamer," Seraphina said suddenly, nodding at the statue-still ocher figure of a sitting cat on the windowsill. "Peter rarely goes out. He's the homebody."

"Then someone came *inside* the convent to get him," Matt realized with growing alarm. "Someone who had easy, unchallenged access to the place."

They mulled that without comment. Temple's mental list included Father Hernandez, the loyal but narrow-minded Pilar, even Peggy Wilhelm, who was often at her aunt's house and often visited the neighboring nuns who were her backup cat feeders. And she had been at the scene of the crime the whole time, ostensibly asleep. So if Father Hernandez was suspect, why not a nun, or assorted nuns? Even virtually deaf Sister Mary Monica?

"The entire matter rests on the will," Temple said half-aloud. "Did Molina say anything about that?"

"She asked about it," Peggy admitted. "Not too nicely. She pointed out that it didn't much matter whether Aunt Blandina left her estate to the cats or the church; I was out of the picture either way."

"Did that bother you?" Matt asked.

Peggy paused for a moment before shaking her head. "Why should it? I'm a cat breeder. That means I'm a little nuts about the species. I'm happy to see so many abandoned animals have a chance at a decent, protected life. As for the church, I really didn't have that much contact with my aunt. I didn't earn a place in her will; if she wanted the church to have everything, fine. I just hope the cats weren't left out entirely. But she wouldn't have done that, no matter what."

That was all Peggy knew, all they could know. When Sister Rose bustled in to tell them that an officer wanted to see Miss Wilhelm, they tensed in concert.

Their visitor was not Molina, but another detective, a wiry man with a luxurious mustache who identified himself as Detective Sanger. The crime-scene team was through. Miss Wilhelm could collect some clothes for her aunt's funeral, but otherwise the bedroom and stairs were still off-limits.

"What about the cats?" Temple asked indignantly.

Detective Sanger rolled his eyes. What about the cats?

"They need to be fed and watered twice a day."

"Do it then," he told her, "but stay downstairs."

"What about the upstairs cats?" Peggy wondered, the ones that preferred to stay on the second floor.

"They'll just have to walk down the stairs to eat," he said. "They've been all over that place since forever. I guess they can't do any more to mess up the crime scene."

"It was a crime . . . then?" Sister Seraphina asked.

The detective eyed her sincere face. "We don't know for

sure yet." His voice was the standard detective-issue gruff. "Just do the essential business and get out."

They chirped agreement like doves in their little nests who are reputed to agree, then eyed each other after the detective had left. Maybe, Temple was thinking for them all, they would find some overlooked clue in the chaos.

Temple, Seraphina and Peggy decamped with a will for the Tyler house and their designated duties. Where Matt went next, he didn't say, but his face was a study in graceful abstraction when they left.

The trio was greeted at the Tyler door by a coven of milling cats—thirteen pairs of eyes the gold, copper and verdigris color of old coins gazing up to heaven and human faces for manna and Yummy Tum-tum-tummy.

It was messy, sometimes smelly, bend-and-twist work, but Temple was glad she could concentrate on feeding the multitudes while Peggy and Sister Seraphina went about unearthing funeral clothes upstairs. She counted their slow overhead steps in a series of loud creaks, then stopped with a can of Finnyky Feast half-open and smelling to high heaven.

This old house made more sounds than the mews of its many feline residents, and Blandina had not been in the least deaf. Suppose she had heard a step in the hall and come out to investigate? Her cane could have been ripped from her hand and used to strike her until she fell down the stairs, the victim of an apparently nasty accident.

How could Molina prove or rule out murder in such murky circumstances, with such ambiguous clues as bruises, and stairs the murder weapons? Perhaps the cane . . . now broken and in police custody. Was it the murder weapon? Temple would have liked to see it again, for more than the dried dirt on its rubber tip.

A raucous meow reminded her that standing with an open cat-food can in hand and two dozen open, empty mouths at her feet was not a particularly safe occupation. *Thump.* A big brown-and-white tom had leaped atop the cabinet. *Mer-oww,* he said.

He was not as eloquent as Louie, but he made himself understood. Temple dropped a dollop of what looked like minced eel bellies into an empty pie tin. Boston Brownie was at it in a twinkling, and so were the lithe, lean cats that joined him atop the cabinet for a feast.

Now that their benefactress was dead, Temple wondered, would the authorities evict these cats from their overcrowded haven? Miss Tyler's death exacerbated everybody's problems. Lieutenant Molina was forced to investigate a suspicious death in her own back yard. Matt was confronting his past in great, stunning wallops. Father Hernandez, hiding from something past or future, now stood in an unavoidable spotlight. Sister Seraphina fended off obscene phone-callers and held everything together, while Peggy Wilhelm nursed a shaved cat and buried a well-to-do aunt whose cats and money were sure to be bones of contention for the framers of city statutes and decipherers of legal complexities equally.

A vibrating fur boa suddenly encompassed Temple's ankles. Cats curved around her calves, making her wobble on her usual high heels, turning her into an island of comfort and consideration, making her a prisoner of their endless needs.

Temple wondered if Blandina Tyler had ever felt that way.

Chapter 23

It's in the Cards

It is never possible for the born overachiever to rest on his laurels.

Actually, what I normally rest upon is a lot more personal and less prickly than laurels, but that is another story.

I am recovering from my ordeal as Blood Bank Boy of the Year when a certain irritation, a rather noxious itch in my ears, a haunting restlessness, indicates that I am being summoned by the imperious, if not imperial, Karma.

I must confess that I am sorry to have sniffed out this telepathic dame. Like all advocates of alternative realities, she is more than somewhat flaky. I am not referring here to the state of her skin, but to that of her mental capacities.

Now that she has got my number, I foresee that I will rue the day I ever investigated Miss Electra Lark's premises and discovered the resident prophetess. (This foreseeing is not restricted to psychic cats, you will observe, but is also accessible to the ordinary street dude if he is so foolish as to think he has anything to look forward to.)

Right now I am anticipating a hot climb in the dark to the fifth-floor penthouse, where I will find the sublime Karma hiding behind something and teasing me with whatever it is she has to hide.

These telecats would be a pain in the neck if they were not already a pain in the previous life. I have a feeling that I have felt Karma's hooded claws riding my destiny in other places and at other times. I am no more amenable to that idea now than when I was a hot-blooded kit accepting worship and mummification at the hands of long-gone Egyptians. Why is it that those who are gods in one culture end up as garbage in another? I could go on about my noble origins and sadly fallen state, but time is fleeting and I do not have too many lives left.

I bestir myself, which makes me feel like last week's stew, and slip through Miss Temple Barr's accommodatingly loose French doors. (These French are notoriously loose in every manifestation.) I naturally recall that my normal egress—the small, high, open bathroom window—has been closed for my own good. This means that I will have to put myself to considerable trouble to achieve another escape route, which cannot be doing my own good much benefit, but those who determine one's own good do not worry about such trivialities.

So I am out on the patio and up in the blink of an eye, if it is a lizard's peeper and rather slow to blink. I stand on the penthouse patio, girding my loins for another encounter with the elusive Karma. This loin-girding is a figure of speech and somewhat obscure. It certainly is not the fun it should be.

I push my way back into the shadowy interior. All is still, which means that Miss Electra Lark is nowhere in the vicinity. I have nothing against Miss Electra Lark, other than her taste in household companions and furnishings, but I am not eager to be caught trespassing on her turf.

She is a buxom lady who is quite capable of sweeping me out the door without so much as a by-your-leavings.

I am in luck, as usual. Faint light flickers from the many prognosticating orbs—otherwise known as crystal balls—stationed around the room. The light glows green, and I realize that I have once again stumbled upon the hypnotic eyes of the prescient Karma.

"You rang," say I in a bored, Maynard Krebs manner. (I am fond of vintage television reruns on the cable channels when I can get my mitts on a remote control.)

I cannot say that Karma uncorks a sigh, but she certainly looks askance.

"Louie . . . Louie . . . Louie," she breathes. "Such a common and undistinguished name. Sometimes one must descend to the cruder tool. I see a cogitation of cats in disarray, abandoned. Threatened. At sea."

"Maybe they met up with an owl with a three-pound note," say I. "I myself might skip town with some bird with dough about now."

"Louie . . . Louie . . . Louie. You are incorrigible."

"Flattery will get you nowhere," I warn her wan-coated silhouette.

A pale paw flops out from under the sofa fringe, which begins doing a distracting hula at this interruption. I almost miss seeing the several oblongs of pasteboard pinned to the carpet by four admirably sharp claws.

"I have been studying the Tarot," Karma announces.

"I am not unfamiliar with the pharaoh," I riposte. "We go back a long way together."

"Tarot," she repeats. "T-a-r-o-t."

"As in tommy-rot," I answer.

"More like tomcat-rot," she purrs, "but unfortunately, your health appears to be splendid. "Oh, Louie . . . Louie . . . Louie. Do you recognize this card?"

"I am not unfamiliar with cards," I assert as I train my discriminating peepers upon the oblong she shoves forward with one agile claw. I see a picture of a dude in a funny hat who looks as if El Greco has scratched his portrait in a sandbox; he makes a mighty odd Jack of any suit I ever saw.

"The Thin Man," say I.

"Oh—" She no longer uses my name as an expletive. "This is the Hierophant, fool."

"Say, I knew a few of these Higher Ophants in my early days. They usually led the parade when Ringling Brothers came to town."

Karma's sky-blue eyes cross with consternation. I do like to ruffle her fluff. "The card of the Hierophant represents the figure of the Priest," she announces in high disdain. "In ancient Greece, far from my lost Burma, he was the interpreter of mysteries. Here, I fear he is the heart of the mystery. I have drawn the Hierophant repeatedly in the past few days."

This I do not doubt. I can see the claw marks on the card. In fact, the figure of the Hierophant, now that I look more closely, wears that funny pointed headdress reminiscent of either a dignitary in the Ku Klux Klan or a bishop of the Roman Catholic Church. Strange bedfellows, even on a Tarot card.

I have not encountered any animated bedsheets, otherwise known as Grand Dragons, lately, though I have heard a lot about the Catholic Church all too recently from the person of the abused Peter, but no bishops. So who is supposed to be the dude on the card?

"Does not sport the big ears of a Crosby," I say. "Does not look like Dumbo."

"Neither," Karma says with great precision, "do you, but that is no excuse. Do you not sense the connection instantly?"

"I do not know many priests, not to mention even fewer elephants."

"But . . . you know . . . more priests than you know."

I hate it when she leaks cryptic words like they were precious drops of Bailey's Irish Cream. From eavesdropping on my little doll, I have my suspicions about a certain person, but they are vaguer than Tarot cards.

"One," I snarl, "but he may be in the past tense."

"There is no past tense in life, Louie. All present problems merge past and future. I fear that you are not capable of distinguishing such differences, but you are the only tool available."

"Listen," say I. "I am sick of being compared to a pair of household pliers. I am not a tool, or a fool, I am a feline being! If you insist on being abstruse, I will have to resort to my own methods."

"Your methods?" Karma sounds particularly scornful.

"I have my ways."

"Your ways! Study *my* ways, and learn." One long, pale scimitar of nail, the blood showing pink through its pearly surface, taps the dude with the upstanding headdress. "I have often drawn the Hierophant reversed of late. You, of course, realize what that means."

"He has undergone sex-change surgery?"

"At times," Karma says, "I suspect that you deliberately play the fool to claim some connection, however remote, with the symbols of a higher consciousness. At other times, I do not. The Hierophant in itself represents a third party, a dark horse suddenly on the scene, a surprising development, and of course the church, or he who represents it. Reversed, it denotes a rude rejection of all religious beliefs, perhaps during youth. It speaks of emotional disturbance; someone is distrustful of others, or to be distrusted."

I say nothing, not knowing what to make of this gibberish, and Karma tilts her head at me. "Speaking of the Fool, you will see that I have drawn this card, too, as well as the Emperor, which is heaven and spiritual things under the all-important sign of Libra, as I mentioned before, and the Emperor reversed, which is chicanery. Also see here the Tower reversed, another Libra card, and the sign of an obsessive, distorted mind and spirit, of reality skewed to suit an unscrupulous, twisted mentality."

I wait for her to associate this last description with me, but am disappointed. "Quite a cast of characters," I comment, cocking my head to denote intelligent contemplation. I am getting the hang of this oracle routine.

"These are not from a single cast of the cards, but the same figures have appeared repeatedly. Obviously, your task is clear, and formidable. You must find the true Hierophant, who will lead you to these other cards whose roles are less clear: Death, Deviltry, Justice and Judgment, as well as Temperance."

I hold my Temperance and say nothing. Death, Deviltry, Justice and Judgment are fully familiar to me, if not as cards, and I have always handled them well, in my own unenlightened way.

Having done my penance at the feet of Karma and her magical, mystery cards, I bow my way out of the Arcane Presence and head for my particular ever-fruitful source of wisdom and all knowledge—the hot, bustling sidewalks of Las Vegas, Nevada, and whoever I can find on them with a tale to tell—man, woman or four-footed friend.

Chapter 24

Money Business

Matt was waiting in the shade of a tall stand of oleanders when she came out of the rectory.

Lieutenant Molina paused for a moment, then regarded the notebook she had been tucking into the deep side pocket of her navy jacket. "Will I need this?"

He smiled. "It's not confession time. I just wanted to talk to you."

"I'm not good to talk to right now," she said, without a softening smile.

Matt could understand why she intimidated Temple. Lieutenant Molina was serious, direct, and competent to the point of a matching plainness of dress and manner. All women who competed in a once thoroughly masculine field like medicine or police work adopted that protective coloring—or lack of coloring. Women who would be priests shared that same single-minded purity of performance that sometimes made them seem slightly inhuman.

"Did Father Hernandez offer any new information?" he asked.

"Only that the pranks around the convent phones had spread to the church. Red dye in the holy-water fonts, that kind of thing." She frowned, her expression abstracted.

Matt wondered if she envisioned her daughter's hand dipping into a still surface of blood-tinged water. "Did he consider satanists, or would-be satanists?"

"He didn't mention it. I thought of it. Look, I can check with the ritual-crime team, but I doubt it's anything like that. Father Hernandez certainly is frightened of something he wasn't a few weeks ago. He puts on a good act, but he's scared white down to his cassock hem. Perhaps it's fear of losing the Tyler estate. I've got a call in to the parish lawyer's office."

"There's something I don't know if I should pursue," Matt began.

He realized from the instant, hungry flare in her eyes that even by mentioning it, he had gone too far to retreat. His false sense of familiarity with Lieutenant Molina through Temple tended to make him forget that she was a seasoned homicide detective, and was not about to play games with anyone's conscience.

"What?" she demanded.

"Father Hernandez," he continued, wishing he hadn't mentioned it.

"So he drinks," she finished for him in a clipped, unshocked voice. "That rumor's been running riot over the parish for two weeks. Something new for Father Rafe, all right. He's Old World, autocratic, often an infuriating pastor, at least for those of us who don't feel that clutching rosaries is the beginning and end of devotion. But he was never a drunk."

"Then you agree that this new behavior is disturbing."

"Sure it is. So's yours."

Matt blinked as if to shake the hypnotic gaze of a cobra. Lieutenant Molina's eyes were such a deep, lucid blue that it was hard not to fall into them, and fall into her eternal trap, maybe. Everyone in the so-called helping professions dealt in charisma of one kind or another.

"Mine? What's so disturbing about my behavior?" He used the disarming tone that worked so well on lady librarians, nurses and church housekeepers. "I'm pretty low-key."

It did not work on Lieutenant Molina. Her narrowed eyes reduced her compelling blue pupils to fractured glimpses through bristling eyelashes. "That could mean that you've got something to hide, or that you'd prefer to hide. Something more than your past profession. This case—if it is murder and it is a case—reeks of some sort of religious kink. Anybody with a religious background is a suspect."

"At least that leaves Temple out for once," he retorted. "She'll be pleased to learn that lukewarm Unitarianism has such protective qualities."

"No, it doesn't. Miss Barr is a born victim of guilt by association."

"You're referring to the magician."

"And others." Molina's single arched eyebrow had far more effect on her stoic face than it would have had on anyone else's. The Mr. Spock syndrome.

"That's what I was going to suggest, that you check the background of everyone involved with Miss Tyler. You must have ways of finding out everything from how many fillings they have in their teeth to what their confirmation names are."

"We have ways, as you well know. Are you still miffed about my discovering your absent driver's license?"

"No."

"Or reporting it?"

"Maybe."

Lieutenant Molina had turned so that they were strolling into the hot sun and back to the convent. Matt glanced at the sports watch on his left wrist as a burst of childish screeching exploded somewhere behind the church. Mid-morning already; the kids had been let loose for recess.

Molina stopped dead, her head lifting like an animal's—alert and relying on some secret sense. Did she consider her young daughter, playing so near what could be the scene of a particularly cruel murder of a defenseless old lady? But all murders were cruel.

Then her corrosive gaze rested on him again.

"So you're still annoyed that I looked you up?" she pressed.

"I still wonder why. Maybe you were trying to protect Temple from another mystery man."

"She needs protection." Molina's voice grew low, almost angry. "That woman should not be let out without a leash, or at least a license. No, it's not Miz Barr I worry about." Molina leaned nearer. Matt was struck by her solid size, her height so like his own, the training that made her formidable in many ways not expected in a woman. "I want Max Kinsella," she said, her words underlined with an intensity he had never heard from her. "Nobody does a vanishing act without leaving traces. In his case, the only clue so far is a dead body at the Goliath Hotel. Nobody gets away scot-free with an open file on my desk."

"You think he'll come back," Matt said with sudden insight. "For Temple."

"Why not?" Molina's tone grew defensive, as if she'd had to defend her interest in this old case before, to colleagues and superiors. "Look at how Kinsella arranged for the condo, even before he vanished. Everything set up in both their names so Miss Barr could simply take it over. He knew he might be leaving."

"You think Temple knew that, too?"

She backed off suddenly, even gave a small laugh, a laugh that dismissed her own passion and pursuit. "Maybe. Maybe not. Certainly she didn't stage her own attack. Those men meant business. It's a good thing you're teaching her some self-defense. If she's going to keep sticking her neck out, she should learn how to keep it from being chopped off. How does—did—a priest get involved in martial arts?"

"We're allowed hobbies, you know. And prayer and meditation aren't too different from the contemplative side of many martial arts. But, to answer your question, I wasn't always a priest. I started tae kwon do in high school."

"Catholic high school in Chicago?"

He nodded.

Lieutenant Molina stopped walking again and glanced toward the church, past it to the unseen school and playground. The streets were quiet now. Recess was over. "I don't know if I'll keep Mariah in Catholic schools. It's a solid education, and God knows, there's less violence and gang activity than in the public schools, so it's good for her now. But later it might betray her."

"Too Catholic, you mean?"

She nodded, then looked away. Matt realized that she had fallen into the trap everybody did, that of consulting him, without him even trying to encourage it. She stuck a hand in her jacket pocket, angry about forgetting herself, her position, her authority, and his position as a possible suspect, however remote.

"Did they betray us," he asked softly, "or did we betray them?"

She recognized an ambiguous question, too, especially when it was so germane. Her look was swift, and as swiftly reestablished their relationship of hunter and hunted.

"Maybe it was a victimless crime," Lieutenant Molina said briskly, stepping up her pace toward the convent. "I'll check out everyone's background—I was going to do it anyway—beginning with you. What seminary did you attend?"

"Saint Vincent."

"Where?"

"Batesville, Indiana."

"How did a confirmed Midwesterner like you end up in Vegas?"

"Looking for luck, I guess. Aren't you from someplace else?"

"I'm asking the questions."

"I couldn't find a job anywhere else," he admitted after a moment. "Too much Catholic education."

Her smile was wry, but not unfriendly. "I couldn't either.

Do me a favor and get Miss Barr to drive you home or something. I could use a vacation from her inquisitive face."

He nodded and waited in another patch of shade by Temple's Storm, Las Vegan enough to know to get out of the UVs. In Chicago, snow had been the element worth fearing; here, it was unheard of, and something as simple and treasured as sunshine could be lethal.

When Temple did come out, it was from Miss Tyler's house. She joined him by the car.

"That is an excessive number of cats," she commented, "especially when you feed them and clean their boxes."

"That going to be your job for a while?"

"Super pooper-scoopers, I hope not! Peggy was busy selecting clothes for the funeral with Sister Seraphina, so I pitched in. Literally." Temple pantomimed pitching out something, presumably feline waste. "Say, you don't want a cat or two, in case they're not covered in the will?"

"Not after what you've described," Matt said hastily. "Ready to go?"

"Yeah. I want to close down the cat show and make sure no more malicious tricks have been pulled." She started around to the street side of the Storm, then stopped and stared almost as narrowly as Lieutenant Molina, down the road to the church. "Say, isn't that the wimpy lawyer we met yesterday who just pulled up at the rectory in the silver Camry?"

Matt squinted into the bright sunshine. "I'm not sure—"

"Well, let's find out."

Temple threw her jangling key ring back into her tote bag, hoisted its straps high on her shoulder and began pacing toward the car in question in a no-nonsense manner.

Matt was startled to find himself jogging to keep up. "Temple! It's none of your business."

"Do you spell that 'nun'?" she shot back over her shoulder with a grin. "Sister Seraphina called you in as a consultant, and I came along for the ride, or the drive, rather. I bet what's-his-name has got the will, and inquiring minds want to know what's in it."

He caught up with her. "Do you think the lawyer or Father Hernandez will tell you?"

"No, but I'd bet that Father Hernandez will tell *you*. He looks like a man desperately in need of a sympathetic ear of the right sort."

"What sort do you mean?"

"Someone in your unique position."

They were huffing up to the rectory door now, the effort of walking fast in unshaded sunshine sheening their faces. Matt began to see what Lieutenant Molina meant about a leash. He stopped Temple at the threshold by grabbing her arm. She did not seem to take exception to the contact.

"What's so unique about my position?" he demanded, knowing he was asking for it, whatever it was, but inquiring minds need to know, as she had pointed out.

"You know the priesthood, its pressures and rewards. You're out of it, so you're hardly one to point fingers, no matter what Father Hernandez has done."

"And what has he done?"

"Dived into a bottle, for one thing." She bit her bottom lip. "But there's more to it than that. I bet you could find out if you went about it the right way."

"Why would I want to?" he asked stiffly.

"Because it might be important to why Miss Tyler was murdered."

"The jury isn't in on that yet."

Temple sighed and rolled her eyes. "Of course she was. And maybe all the other stuff—the phone calls, the cat shaving and crucifixion—was just diversion." She shrugged. "You can keep me in custody if you want, but what would it hurt to go in and ask?"

He released her quickly, realizing that his grip had become tight, almost desperate. He definitely did not want to become unofficial confessor to Father Rafael Hernandez. He had left all that, hadn't he?

Temple was shameless. Public-relations work must do that to even the most sensitive soul, Matt concluded. Once inside the rectory, she clicked down the hall on her pert high heels and didn't pause until she reached the ajar office door. Then she nudged herself through.

"Sorry to disturb you, Father Hernandez," she apologized brightly. "I didn't know you had company. Oh, Mr. Burns! Do you happen to know yet if the cats were covered in the will? I've just been feeding them, and I don't know how long poor Peggy can fend off the animal-control people once their number is generally known."

Matt groaned inwardly at her bull-in-a-china-shop routine, except that with Temple, it was more like Bambi in a Baccarat-crystal showroom. Unlike Lieutenant Molina, she was not physically impressive; in retaliation, she could on occasion become as cute as hell and achieve the same ends. Her victims talked, despite themselves.

He heard the surprised—and dazed—voices invite her over the threshold and tagged along behind.

A legal-length white document of several pages was indeed splayed atop the flotsam on Father Hernandez's desk.

The pastor was looking far more dazed than the attorney. Neither man challenged the newcomers' right to know. Matt suspected that had less to do with Temple's unruffled chutzpah than with the contents of the will. He found himself becoming seriously curious.

Temple settled with Shirley Temple confidence in one of the comfortable chairs built to hold more than twice her bulk. Matt took another and assumed a neutral expression.

"The cats." Father Hernandez ran his fingers through his thinning, sterling-silver pompadour. "It appears that they are indeed in limbo." He quirked an apologetic smile at Temple. "You may not be familiar with the term."

"Oh, but I am. Does that mean that they're to be . . . evicted?"

"No, no . . ." He waved a soothing hand.

Matt recognized all the proper murmurs and gestures—patented Good Shepherd, parish-priest style—and recognized that they were being performed by an automaton. Father Hernandez had just had an unexpected shock. He turned, as Temple had, to the lawyer.

Lawyers love an audience.

Burns riffled lovingly through the long pages that had been folded four times and tended to curl shut.

"I know that this document created much speculation," he admitted, "but I couldn't reveal the late Miss Tyler's latest will until it was a matter of record, as it certainly is with her unfortunate death. Father Hernandez has just had some excellent news." He cast a puzzled, almost hurt glance at the shell-shocked priest. Lawyers are not often the bearers of good news and when they are, they like to enjoy it. But Father Hernandez wasn't doing that, so he turned to his new audience, announcing with a smug flourish, "Miss Tyler did not change her will as she supposedly threatened to do. She was more bark than bite, if you will forgive a canine analogy used in connection with a feline-lover of such long standing." He bowed to Temple, then glanced triumphantly back to Father Hernandez.

"I happily report that Our Lady of Guadalupe is the sole beneficiary of the will. That means a considerable boost to the parish-development fund, but first I must inventory the contents of Miss Tyler's safety deposit box to estimate the exact amount."

Father Hernandez silently tented his prayerful fingers and propped his long face upon them. He did not look like an administrator who had been granted his dearest wish.

"She made no provision for the cats at all?" Temple asked in surprise.

Burns shrugged. "No. I mentioned it, as a matter of fact, but she insisted that when one is facing the afterlife, one must not be bound by the things of this world."

"But—" Temple was not taking this well. The intrepid investigator had vanished into the persona of a crusading animal advocate. "They'll be caged and shipped off to the animal shelter! In sixty hours, most of them will be dead, and they're house pets, not feral animals. It's . . . awful. Can't anything be done?"

Father Hernandez bestirred himself. "The church is also heir to her house?"

The lawyer nodded.

"And its contents?"

Again, a nod.

"I suppose we can delay the disposition of the cats." His hand brushed his forehead as if checking for a headache that he could not quite feel but suspected was there. "The . . . sisters can take care of them, perhaps arrange some better solution."

"The city authorities will not tolerate substandard conditions for long," Burns put in discreetly.

"No one is living in the house any longer," Father Hernandez said impatiently. "Why is it anyone's business but ours?"

"Because it is public knowledge now," the lawyer replied.

"Yes." Father Hernandez sounded depressed even further by this obvious news. "Public knowledge is all, even in matters of life and death. What will the public think? Well, be damned to the public!"

Matt winced at the fury in Father Hernandez's voice. He sensed that this very fury was what the pastor had been trying to douse in quarts of tequila.

"You don't mean that," Burns was saying in obvious contradiction of the facts.

When priests and lawyers tell each other lies, what is to become of the rest of us? Matt wondered. He felt his own unacknowledged bitterness rising like bile in his throat.

He glanced at Temple. She was watching the two men's interchange with the bright, uncommitted gaze of an observant bird. She cared about the cats, but at the moment she was measuring these men and their motives as the best way of defending the defenseless.

He wanted to be out of here, this room of subtexts and unspoken thoughts. To be alone in his bare rooms at the Circle Ritz, so devoid of personality and past, or back in his safe, soundproofed cubicle at ConTact, listening to long-distance agony. Eavesdropping on life.

Matt's palms felt damp. Much as he hated to admit it, Temple had been right. Something was drastically wrong with the state of Father Hernandez's body and soul. The will in the church's favor had done nothing to restore his peace of mind. The church development fund was the least of his problems. Might murder be the worst of them?

When Lieutenant Molina did as he had suggested, as she had meant to do anyway, and looked deeply at every person involved in this sad and apparently well-plotted death, what would she find?

Chapter 25

One Less Orphan Animal

"This is great!" Chortling, Cleo Kilpatrick pointed to the photos of bizarre-looking cats in both Las Vegas's Saturday morning and evening papers.

Temple nodded at the naked Sphinx on the *Review-Journal* second front and the semi-naked curly coated Rex in the *Las Vegas Sun.* She hadn't noticed her successful handiwork, mainly because she'd skimmed the papers for news of the possible killer's successful handiwork—the death of Blandina Tyler.

Beyond the two women stargazing at the local papers, cats, cages and breeders were bustling around the huge exhibition space in the process of shutting down the cat show. An entourage passed. From their midst, the exiting Maurice, the Yummy Tum-tum-tummy cat, gazed out majestically from a carrier emblazoned with his name and a portrait of the product he represented.

"I'm so glad," Cleo went on as her glance paused on the procession, "that you didn't get any more publicity for that dreadful Maurice. Frankly, commercial cat foods are not the best feline nutrition."

"Oh, are you a Free-to-be-Feline advocate?"

"Most definitely."

"Then tell me one thing: how am I supposed to get a cat to eat it?"

"It will take a bit of patience at first—"

"Wrong. It takes patience to the bitter end."

"Cats can be finicky."

"Louie isn't finicky. That's the only stuff he refuses to eat."

"Sometimes they have to be encouraged to do what's good for them. Don't feed him anything but Free-to-be-Feline. If he gets hungry enough, he'll eat it."

Temple nodded, not bothering to say that if Louie got hungry enough, he'd leave home. She wanted to avoid explaining that Louie was free to eat elsewhere, lest she get another lecture on roaming cats. Miss Tyler's cats seemed happy enough confined indoors, but they had been abused on the street. Louie hadn't; he had survived quite nicely without Temple or her Circle Ritz condominium. Any cat that showed the ingenuity to ensure that he could come and go deserved his freedom and whatever free lunch he could find, Temple thought.

Then her eye fell on another exiting cat. "What about that little black one?" she asked, pointing to the undecorated cage near the front registration table.

"You mean the Humane Society cat? Apparently no one adopted it. It'll go back to the shelter."

"Oh." Uh-oh. Temple edged over on tentative heel clacks. She didn't need another cat. More untouched mounds of Free-to-be-Feline. More black hairs all over her off-white sofa. As soon as she approached, the cat rose from its sitting position and began rubbing its face against the grille, gazing at her with big harvest-gold eyes, its little pink mouth opening in a series of silent meows. "How old is it?"

"Looks about nine or ten months," Cleo said.

"What is it?"

"Basic domestic shorthair in basic black. An ordinary alleycat, in other words."

"I meant the gender."

"Oh. Probably female. It would have to be fixed."

Temple read the small card affixed to the cage. "Caviar." Forty-five dollars with shots and a discount on spaying.

Temple reached out a hand, which the cat's jet-black nose instantly nudged. She stepped back as if the cage grille were electrified. This is how it began with Miss Tyler, she told herself: such a pretty, sweet cat; such a shame that no one would take it, that it would have to go back to the Humane Society. What was the matter with people? No one would probably take it there, either. Not a kitten, too old already.

Cats in cages were streaming out the open rank of exhibit-hall doors in their owners' firm grasps, fancy cats that were guarded, groomed and displayed like expensive dolls. Louie would probably go nuts with a competitor in the home place, but he was gone so much. She would enjoy having a calm, spayed female, a loving homebody, around.

A woman stepped up to the table and began gathering the Humane Society literature that surrounded the cage. Temple watched her resentfully.

"Excuse me." The woman stepped in front of Temple to take the card from the cage and stuff it into a canvas bag with the other unclaimed pieces of paper.

She opened the cage door, a pushy woman who didn't care about shoving a potential customer aside, so sure was she that it was too late and little Caviar had lost her last chance.

The woman reached in and took out a stainless-steel bowl of water, a small plastic litter box, somewhat used. Then the cat was trained. The Humane Society woman, who certainly didn't seem that humane if she was going to snatch this poor cat right back to a place where its life expectancy was maybe three days, reached in and removed a stainless-steel bowl of unappetizing green pellets.

Temple experienced an epiphany of the cat kind. "Oh," she heard someone saying in an enchanted voice. Hers. "Does she really eat Free-to-be-Feline?"

The woman, who would have had a perfectly ordinary, nice face if she hadn't been intent on whisking a caged creature back to its doom, looked at Temple oddly.

"Sure," she said.

"Well, then—" Temple dug in her tote bag for her checkbook. "I've got a whole case of Free-to-be-Feline at home."

"Temple, are you sure?" Cleo Kilpatrick asked in an undertone at her elbow. "What about your other cat?"

"He's very . . . versatile. I'm sure he'd love a little friend."

Cleo drifted back to supervise the chaos of the disassembling cat show while Temple bent over the table to make out her check. The little black cat rubbed and purred like a wind-up toy behind the silver grille.

Temple soon discovered that purchasing a homeless cat was a lot harder than finding one. The Humane Society woman went from Madame Defarge to Lieutenant Molina, reeling off a roster of highly personal questions. Was Temple married? No. Were there any children under seven in the household? No, Temple said, surprised by that question after answering the first in the negative. Other animals? Only Midnight Louie. What was he? A stray cat she had taken in. How old? Possibly eight or nine, said the vet.

Madame Inquisitor did not inquire into Louie's sexual capabilities, which was good, for Temple had to sign a document stating that she would have the female called "Caviar" spayed at the first opportunity. Of course she would have done it without signing her soul away to the Humane Society; with Louie around in an unaltered state, it would be irresponsible not to.

As for what Midnight Louie did in his unaltered state when he was out and about on his rambles, Temple tried not to think about that. She supposed she would have to bite the bullet one day and deal with Louie's rampant masculinity, but he was such a fine, clever cat the way he was, and quite valuable as a bodyguard. She would hate to "alter" any of these desirable characteristics. Maybe he was too old to get into much trouble; certainly he never showed any signs of having indulged in a cat fight for the favors of a lady.

While Temple rationalized away her worries about Louie, the Humane Society lady accepted the check, gave her a copy of the adoption agreement, then handed her Caviar, who, recognizing this as her big audition for life, liberty and the pursuit of happiness—and Free-to-be-Feline—was still purring madly.

The cat fit atop the flotsam in Temple's tote bag, hardly adding to its weight, unlike Louie. Also unlike Louie, she showed an admirable inclination to sit still and be carried.

Temple, heart pounding as if she'd just left the biggest designer-shoe sale in six states, couldn't help showing off her impulse purchase. She trotted down the aisles cooing at her tote bag and oblivious of stares until she came to Peggy Wilhelm's stand.

Minuet had been taken home after her assault, but the other Birmans sat calmly in their carriers and regarded Temple and her animated tote bag with delft-blue saucer eyes while Peggy broke down the show cages into flat pieces for easy transport.

Peggy looked over her shoulder to register Temple's approach, then brushed a hand through her mop of grizzled hair and shook her head. "Such a sad show, in every respect."

"Not every." Temple tilted her tote bag to show its contented contents. "I've adopted the Humane Society cat."

"Oh." Peggy Wilhelm looked hungrily into the bag at the furry black wedge of face staring up at her. "What a great thing to do! You mean no one had taken it? How sad." Peggy's voice thickened as she turned away. "Sorry. This has been a lot of strain, with Aunt Blandina dying, and Minuet. Now I've got all of Aunt Blandina's cats to worry about . . ."

Do you ever! Temple thought, remembering that the will had ignored them. It wasn't her place to inform Peggy of this latest blow, but she could confirm her suspicions in a roundabout way.

"You're sure that your aunt would have made provision for their upkeep, though?"

"Oh, positive. Aunt Blandina would have never, ever left her precious cats out in the cold, even if she did leave most of her money to the church. I mean, she would have died first."

The oddity of the expression under the circumstances made Peggy grimace as she realized what she had said. "Oh, I am exhausted silly over all of this! You know what I mean. I was happy to help her out with the cats, but she did have much too many, and couldn't stand the idea of giving up a one. Even letting the nuns take Peter and Paul was a wrench. So she'd hardly leave her babies out of the will."

"What about you? Don't you mind being left out? Everybody assumes that you will be."

"Oh, I've got my own life and a decent job at the library. I don't have any needs, any family of my own. Spinster and overenthusiastic cat person, just like my aunt. We weren't much alike otherwise. But I do hope she didn't leave her money to the church!" Peggy added with surprising passion. "A lot of evil can be done in the name of religion, especially if it has money."

"Do you mean all religion, or just Catholicism?"

"Well, the Catholic Church isn't exactly enlightened on the matter of sexual repression, is it?" she asked brusquely, slamming sheets of cage grilling together with such energy that the clashes made her Birmans' chocolate-colored ears slant back in distress. "Or premarital sex or birth control or looking after inconvenient babies that aren't aborted."

"Then . . . you're not a practicing Catholic?"

"Not since I was old enough to move away from home. Look, maybe I sound . . . disillusioned, but the only people who slavishly toe the church line these days are old-fashioned old ladies like my aunt. They wear their tiny little silver feet against abortion and send money to the missionaries and get sent tons of holy cards and cheap rosaries and requests for money. And they *are* courted for their money, you better believe it. Most of them need that attention so much that they'd rather leave their money to the church and the foreign pagan babies and the unborn babies than to their own kin, than to their own flesh and blood."

Peggy's hands and voice were shaking now, and she had given up stacking cage sides. The Birmans crouched in their carriers, sensitive to their owner's strange tirade. Temple's tote bag stirred as Caviar thrust out a curious and unintimidated head to see what was the matter.

"It's just been too much."

Peggy said that quickly, before Temple could say anything, could back off or apologize . . . or even pose more questions that might answer the suspicion that was now rising in her mind—the notion that Peggy Wilhelm was far more than what she had seemed, and had far more reason than previously suspected to commit unreasonable acts involving cats, her aunt and the Catholic Church.

"Too much," Peggy repeated. "I don't care what that damn will says, what she did. I won't let them hold their damn money over me again. It was always a trap, and it was always the church before me. I did my duty by her, by her precious cats—I paid my debt—and now my life is my own again."

"Who are you talking about—'them'?"

"You obviously didn't grow up Catholic," Peggy said with an uneasy laugh. "My parents, my parish nuns and priests, my aunt—they all ran a tight ship when I was young and couldn't do anything about it. Well, now I can, and I'm not going to let their guilt trips get to me, that's all. I'm going to take my cats home and I'll come and feed Aunt Blandina's cats as long as they need it, and then it stops. It finally stops here."

She pushed the dishwater-brown frizz off her flushed forehead, then glanced again at the quizzical black-cat face in Temple's bag. Her white face crumpled like a used Kleenex.

"Oh, just take your damn cat and go," she urged with waves of the hand that wasn't covering her mouth. "I haven't gotten much sleep and the show is over. This time it's really over. Sorry."

Temple backed away, nearly stumbling over a clutter of cat carriers at the table behind her. She had seldom seen a personality come apart like this, even among friends and family. Now she knew why Matt was so reluctant to play Father Hernandez's confidant. Confession might be good for the soul of the penitent, but it swamped the recipient in a confusing, aimless barrage of unspecified ancient wrongs and festering emotions.

In some way, Temple had innocently triggered this upsetting deluge of emotion. Now, almost as disturbed as Peggy Wilhelm, she walked through the cold, echoing, gray-concrete vault of the exhibition hall, which looked like a school gym the night after the dance, when all the illusion has been stripped away.

She glanced from time to time at her docile passenger, as if to comfort it against the miasma of human emotions now churning around them both.

But the cat was calm, only the people were agitated.

What a good thing that cats couldn't really know what was happening to them! Temple hated to think that Blandina Tyler's cats might sense that they had been disinherited, or that Midnight Louie might somehow know that he was about to get an unwanted roommate before it happened. That was the great thing about animals; they never laid any burdens on their human companions. All they asked for was food, shelter and affection.

Come to think of it, they weren't too different from your average self-sufficient human being, either.

Chapter 26

Cat Inquisition

As soon as my dear departed Miss Temple Barr is safely off to the cat show Sunday afternoon, I whisk out the French doors to do some investigations of my own. I cast one quick glance at the penthouse before I put the Circle Ritz in my wake.

I dare not let my thoughts linger on the elevated occupant of that address, for that might tip her off to my itinerary. Much as I would hate to admit it to the object of my spiritual anxiety, the Sublime Karma (as opposed to the Divine Yvette, the object of my carnal devotion), I have found the clutter of cats she was yammering about being in danger just days ago.

I am bound—not to the animal pound, or even to the Humane Society shelter for the poor and infamous. I am headed into Hierophant territory, off to Our Lady of Guadalupe, whose name I hear bandied about in recent days by my dear soulmates at the Circle Ritz. I include Mr. Matt Devine in that group, now that I and Miss Temple Barr have been seeing more of him.

The cathouse I am in search of should not be hard to find, with three key pieces of information in place: from what I overhear, it is very near Our Lady of Guadalupe Church; the grievously attacked Peter was a next-door neighbor, which means that his sadly diminished spoor should be all over the place; and it is home to seventy-some residents of the feline persuasion, which means that the supersniffing powers of my nose alone could find it from a six-block radius.

I have overlooked a fourth tattletale clue, ring around the collar, so to speak: a yellow police tape reading "Crime Scene: Do Not Cross" circles the house and tends to give away the location just a teensy.

I slip past it like a fleeting shadow. Getting in is another trick. These feline pensioners were not intended to get out. I explore the no-man's-land between the place and a neighboring house that no doubt is the convent famed in song and story, as I have been overhearing it lately. Sister Seraphina and her calling nuns. Or called-upon nuns, to be more precise.

The house is old by human standards, but I am a veteran at finding my way in and out of forbidden places. Some crumbled stucco near the rear leads to an under-porch crawl space. If there is anything I am into faster than a flesh-hungry flea, it is a crawl space.

I box aside spiderwebs and occasional spiders the size of a well-fed mouse. I range over broken boards and rats' nests and a whole subcontinent of creepy-crawlies, including scorpions. I finally find an opening and push my way into what people call a utility room via the dryer vent pipe, which is not only loose, but just the size of my circumference.

After sneezing my way past a colony of dust bunnies the size of chihuahuas, I shimmy between the shiny white walls of washer and dryer and am home free. Actually, I am free to take measure of this home, which is now entirely occupied by my own kind.

A thousand rich scents sprinkle the air with fur, dander, and perfumes mostly neuter. *Quelle* disappointment! This is a house of eunuchs! At least I know that no physical force will be called for with either sex. I am torn between triumph at finding so many of my kind safe and sound and consternation that the price of safety is censorship in the ultimate degree.

Oh, well, we cannot all be tough, swaggering, fearless examples of our species.

I wade into this wilderness of my kind, swimming like Jacques Cousteau amongst an exotic cornucopia of creatures—cats striped and spotted, shaded and solid, black-and white- and zebra-striped; caramel-colored and brown; white and cream; calico- and rum-tum-tiger; long-haired and short; tailed and tailless; big and small, tall and squat; male and female, and most often, neither.

I am struck by the vast variety and the noble sense of community among my kind. On the street, it is one for one's self. Never have so many coexisted so peacefully. The house, with its two stories and many rooms, is a sort of rookerie, a shared territory both crowded and oddly orderly. I am humbled by this refugee community, this coagulation of every kind and kin until survival and mutual dependence have overcome the more territorial urges of instinct. Young voices mew while older ones purr caution. I am greeted by open meows showing sharp teeth and line-fine whiskers.

No one heeds my progress. I am the ultimate outsider. The inspector-general. The cop. The Lone Ranger. I am recognized, but not claimed, so finally I must get down to business and start taking testimony.

No one has bothered to interview these key witnesses to many crimes. I hear tales of telephone calls, closely observed. Of an old woman growing older and more tremulous with each cowardly attack by ring and by wire.

I hear of her rushing to the closed windows and doors,

watching, her anxious cane occasionally impinging on an innocent extremity. Of long night vigils, of lights teasing the edges of the house.

I hear of the coming of the Chubby Lady With Birman Breath, distracted and worried, and oddly resentful of the cats coming to stroke her legs. Of the Sister Ladies, who are cheerful and loving with each other as well as with those of our species, who pet and coo and feed, whether it is the dear old Keeper or the numerous Kept they tend.

I hear, with some pride, of the sweet efficiency of my current roommate, who is known as Delicate Heels, and who has never spiked an inconvenient extremity to a floorboard and whose litter-box dredging abilities are second to none.

Speaking of none, none of these residents has been confronted with Free-to-be-Feline. Luckily, Delicate Heels has left the cooking to other, more experienced hands—such as Friskies and Yummy Tum-tum-tummy—during her tenure.

And I hear voices of worry, telling of having heard hissing over the telephone with their sensitive ears.

What kind of hissing, I ask. Like a snake's?

No, not like a snake's.

Like a fellow or sister feline's?

No, most definitely not.

Like a machine's?

They pause to consider that, and I recall the hiss of a television set that is not properly tuned to a channel.

Not like that, Mr. Midnight, they cry in chorus.

Then what is it like? I demand.

Like nothing, they say in cat concert. Like nothing on earth.

Perhaps that dratted Karma is right. We are not dealing with natural disasters here, not even with ordinary murder—for I trust the testimony of my kind's ears above their eyes and mouths—but with unearthly chaos.

This murderous snake may hail from beyond Eden to Gehenna itself.

Chapter 27

A Face Card from the Past

It was a scene from an English mystery: the principals gathered for the all-important Reading of the Will.

Temple wriggled her skimpy, tender derriere deep into the well-upholstered behemoth of a chair just like the other chairs gathered around Father Hernandez's now-familiar desktop.

Her dangling toes brushed the floor as she swung them all the better to kill time and to admire neat, Charles Jourdan navy pumps piped in red, so smart for the unexpected country-house killing, even though they required—ugh—pale gray pantyhose on a hot day. Miss Barr with a humid spike heel in the rectory. Ooh.

Actually, the occasion that brought them all together here, wondering, was not exactly the reading of the will, although the terms of that will would come to public light here. The meeting's real purpose, and the only reason she was included, along with Matt Devine, was the disposition of the late Miss Tyler's cats rather than her money.

How convenient, Temple thought, that Father Hernandez's office came with just the right number of chairs for such a group. Sister Seraphina sat on the edge of her cushy seat, uncomfortable on the visitor's chair, her sensibly shod foot tapping oh-so-subtly. A woman of action, she barely kept herself from fidgeting at the ahems and haws that proceeded from the church attorney at regular intervals. For a relatively young man, he was uncommonly fussy.

Peggy Wilhelm let her half-glasses lie docilely on her ample chest, suspended by their leash of silver beads. She had no expectations of anything in the will, and was not even ready to cast a cursory eye over its terms.

Peter Burns sat forward, the mahogany-colored calfskin briefcase on his knees serving as a table for his voluminous papers. Oddly, he seemed nervous and expectant, glancing from the priest to the nun, then to Matt and Temple, whom he regarded with obvious disfavor and a look behind his round glasses that said: What are you two doing here? He never even glanced once at Peggy Wilhelm, which spoke to how utterly she had been left out of the will, and out of everyone's consideration, except as convenient cat-tender.

Temple felt a flash of anger at the way Peggy had been overlooked. She was the Cinderella figure in the tale: overworked and overwilling, asking for nothing but her fireside ashes and an unshaven cat.

Father Hernandez remained the cipher. Handsomely harried, his features seemed to sink deeper into his skull on every occasion, along with the maroon circles cast by his dark eyes, until the man himself was likely to disappear behind his own hidden worry. Max revisited.

Worry. Matt worried her. Temple glanced at him, his calm as evident as Father Hernandez's incipient hysteria. Ice or instability. Temple couldn't decide which facade was the least healthy.

But she had nothing to worry about. She was mere witness to other people's follies on this occasion, included only because she had shamelessly begged Matt to let her know if anything of the sort should transpire. Besides, somebody had to add a touch of flagrant footwear to this occasion: Matt wore rubber-soled Hush Puppies, as effacing as his everyday manner; Sister Seraphina, her habitual Red Cross battleship-gray model; Peggy, a battered pair of Famolare sandals; and the attorney, brown wing-tip oxfords—in a Las Vegas September!

Temple discreetly turned an ankle to refresh herself with a glimpse of an artfully curved vamp. Shoes were such a comfort, except when they were walked in! Perhaps the spiritual should never be expected to turn physical.

As Burns cleared his throat for the thirteenth time, Temple swept her feet together and demurely touched toes to the floor beneath her chair.

"I presume," Burns said, "that you all know that Miss Tyler did indeed keep and remember Our Lady of Guadalupe in her latest will."

Sober nods all around.

"When was this will dated?" Sister Seraphina asked out of the blue, a vertical line etched between her eyes just above the pale, amber-plastic glasses frame.

He consulted the document itself to make sure, although he obviously knew the date by heart. "August twelfth."

"And she wanted to omit the cats?"

"Apparently they had palled."

Peggy Wilhelm frowned in her turn. Mr. Burns was obviously no cat person. Cats were like Cleopatra; age could not stale nor custom wither their infinite variety.

"I knew about her nineteen-ninety-two will," she put in. "The cats were definitely left a bequest."

"For how much?" Father Hernandez asked.

"Twenty-five thousand."

"Perhaps I should allow that sum toward their . . . keep or disposition," he said. "She surely wouldn't have wanted them put to sleep."

"No," Peggy agreed with a shudder.

"Before you commit funds to the cats, Father," Burns

offered in an apologetic tone, "I should warn you that Miss Tyler's assets were not as ample as everyone, including Miss Tyler, imagined. She kept her funds in CDs; you know what the interest rates on those have been like in the past few years."

Father Hernandez sighed as heavily as anyone in the room at this comment, reminding Temple of Matt's comment that parish priests were often harried administrators more than they were ministers.

Peggy Wilhelm frowned again. "She was getting forgetful, but Aunt Blandina hinted that she had plenty of money to take care of the cats and the parish, too—at least before she got annoyed with the parish."

"Old people lose touch," Burns said flatly. "Lawyers see this all the time. I still may uncover some unexpected resources; she had notes and unexplained keys tucked into drawers all over the house, as many as cats." He granted Father Hernandez a cautioning glance. "But I wouldn't count my chickens, financially speaking, before I counted my cats. And I wouldn't count on having much bounty to share with those cats."

"What about the harassment?" Matt asked. "Did that cease with Miss Tyler's murder?"

A thrill ran visibly through the people in the room at this reminder of unexplained events.

"Lieutenant Molina suspects murder," the lawyer said precisely, "but the harassment may have been mostly in Miss Tyler's elderly imagination."

"Not Peter," Seraphina said stoutly. "Not Sister Mary Monica's phone pal."

"Does he still call?" Temple asked.

Sister Seraphina shook her head abruptly. "No. And that worries me more than if he did."

But no one bothered to ask why. Seraphina was another old woman, an unreliable or even insignificant reporter of phenomena. Temple found her fingernails digging into the tapestry-upholstered arms of her fat chair. Why would the caller stop now? Seraphina was on to something. A glance at

Matt's still—too still—face told her that he thought so, too. Scary, she was beginning to read his lack of expression better than any expressiveness.

She was also beginning to guess where he had learned such patient stoicism—in the seminary, where young men were expected to listen and learn and not to challenge authority.

"It's so odd," Peggy said. "Her finally ignoring the cats after all this time. I feel cheated for taking care of them so much if she didn't care—"

"But *you* did," Seraphina put in quickly, with a smile. "You cared."

Peggy Wilhelm's face remained leaden, lost. She nodded without conviction. "Aunt Blandina used to mean what she said. It was the one thing I respected about her."

The young lawyer's pale, manicured hands hit the arms of his chair with a thump of emphasis. "It's too soon to do anything. The police have made no determination. I have possibly not tracked down all the estate assets. Be of good cheer," he urged with a hopeful smile that showed the dull silver flash of metal wire on his front teeth. "Perhaps Providence will find some answer for the cats. Certainly the story in the *Review-Journal* may help."

"Story?" Peggy wailed in concert with Temple.

Burns looked blank and a little hurt. "A reporter heard about the police report on all the cats, and a rumor that they might be legatees. I didn't see any harm in explaining their possible plight—"

"Oh!" Sister Seraphina seldom sounded disgusted, but she did now. "Mr. Burns. Don't you see? You've brought all the forces of animal control and flaky animal advocacy down on us before we're ready to deal with it."

Father Hernandez swiveled his bulky leather chair away from them all, putting his—and its—back to the desk.

The conference was officially over, with little resolved.

Nobody knew for sure that Miss Tyler had been murdered, except maybe Molina, and she wasn't talking.

Nobody knew how much money was coming to the church, not even the operative attorney.

Nobody knew what to do with all the cats, except the deluge of cat-lovers and cat-haters who would be sure to make their opinions known far and wide once the story hit the street.

Temple looked at Matt, to find Matt looking at her.

They needed to nail down something, and the obvious place to start—curses!—was with Molina and the issue of murder.

"I'd rather you called her," Matt said when she drove them back to the Circle Ritz.

"Why? She hates me."

"She doesn't hate you. Police lieutenants aren't allowed to hate. Bad public image. I don't want her to waste her time digging into me."

"Why? Are you a good suspect?"

"I'm a diversion, when the real case needs to be solved."

"Funny, I always thought you were a diversion, too."

He shrugged off her smart comment and opened the car door to a slow seep of Las Vegas heat. "I've got to work tonight. I'll see if any calls have come in from other old ladies. Miss Tyler's death may have forced her harasser to move on."

"Or to stop," Temple said.

"You think it was part of the whole . . . scenario?"

"Scenario. Very good, Mr. Devine. Yes, I do. And so was Sister Mary Monica. And Peter."

"But what was the scenario? Or more important, the point?"

"I don't know." Temple glanced up at the Circle Ritz's round, black-marble-encased exterior, her eye pausing on the third floor. "I hope my new kitty hasn't been too lonesome this morning. On the other hand, I hope Louie hasn't come in, discovered her and raised holy hell."

"Louie with a rival?" Matt cocked a blond eyebrow. "I don't think it will fly."

"Caviar's not a rival; she's a little sister."

"I don't think Louie is into little sisters, either."

"He must not be a Catholic cat," Temple said demurely.

Matt bit back a reply and vanished into the building at a trot, ahead of her.

Temple took her time getting her tote bag out of the Storm and walking into the air-conditioned lobby. Her thoughts were as sharp and as aimless as the blows of her heels on the sidewalk, and later, on lobby marble.

She took the elevator upstairs—Matt had probably used the stairs, but her high heels demanded more civilized methods of transport.

She turned the key in her door lock, eager to greet her new baby—and scared semigloss white that Louie would be there and in no mood to discuss new roommates of the feline kind. What had she done? Louie was a loner, an individualist, a me-only cat. How could she have thought he would welcome this dainty little pussycat simply because it desperately needed a home and was his favorite color, jet-black? What had Temple done? What would she say to Louie? Oh, Louie, Louie. . . .

Louie was nowhere about the apartment, Temple discovered after she tiptoed into the cool depths of her empty rooms. Caviar was curled atop the *Cosmopolitan* magazines in their Plexiglas rack, polishing a paw to shining ebony.

Temple sighed in relief and ran to check the two bowls of Free-to-be-Feline in the kitchen. One was mounded high, wide and handsome. One sported a dainty dip in the middle. Obviously, Louie had not been in, or he had left in disgust.

Temple went back to kneel by her new acquisition. Caviar tilted her sleek head so Temple's long nails could scratch her chin. She purred, stretched and displayed a long, lithe torso, quite different from Louie's well-upholstered midsection.

Then the tender interlude was over. Duty called. Or rather, Temple must call to do her duty.

She looked up the Las Vegas police number, dialed it and waited through the super-smooth and polite, *Star Ship Enterprise* female computer voice, expecting it to purr "Captain Kirk" at any minute. After rejecting pressing a series of numbers that would connect her to a dozen unneeded departments, Temple stayed on the line and asked meekly for "Lieutenant Molina, please."

She got her on the first throw.

"This is Temple Barr. I—"

"Fine. Are you at home?"

"Er, yes."

"Good. I'll be by in twenty minutes. Think you can stay put?"

"Yes, Lieutenant."

"I've got something I want you to see."

"Er, don't you want to know what I called about?"

"No. Be there."

Another gracious conversation with the Amy Vanderbilt of the Las Vegas Metropolitan Police Department. Temple hung up with a sigh. She wasn't any good at interfacing with police personnel. Why did she have to keep doing it?

She changed her clothes and ditched the pantyhose, but she kept the businesslike pumps on, with footlets, just because. She wasn't about to sit back and let Molina catch her napping at five-foot-zero.

She dangled her key chain in front of Caviar and was rewarded with several spirited boxing motions. "That's it, girl, you show that Midnight Louie what a tough cookie you are!"

She paced to the window and looked at the empty pool. No Matt waiting by his namesake mats, no Louie glaring resentfully up at her. She was glad not to confront Louie's reaction to her impulse purchase, but what if he had already come, seen and decamped?

Her doorbell rang, a lovely *ding-dong* sound straight out of the fifties and "Father Knows Best."

She skittered to the door and opened it to face Lieutenant Molina, looking her most official and towering.

Temple ebbed before the law, into her living room. "Is it about Miss Tyler's . . . death? Has the cause been determined?"

"No—and no."

Surprised to hear it put so plainly, and so cavalierly, Temple sat down on her shapeless sofa.

Molina stood there, glancing at Caviar. "Shrunk your cat?"

"This is Caviar. She was going to be sent back to the Humane Society."

"Your Midnight Louie may shrink her head—and then send her back to the Humane Society, from what I've seen of that black devil. You do rush in—"

"If you're not here about the Tyler case—"

"Why would I bother you about the Tyler case?"

"I was . . . a witness."

"Not to the murder. But you may have been a witness to this."

Molina flashed a card from the depths of one of her ever-useful jacket pockets. A flash card, Temple thought, like I'm in school and I have to get some equation right.

Molina's eyes shone with brilliant blue triumph as she slapped the card faceup on the sofa's broad, canvas arm.

Also faceup was Max Kinsella, in profile and full-front views, looking about—oh, eighteen, his Adam's apple prominent in the profile shot. A lot of type supported the double images, and some bigger type ran across the top. Letters. Initials. I-n-t-e-r-p-o-l.

M-i-c-k-e-y M-o-u-s-e.

And Molina was the cat who had caught the canary.

"Interpol—?" Temple queried.

"That's why I couldn't find anything on him," Molina announced with the glee of Lieutenant Gerard pouncing on Dr. Richard Kimball. "Look at the name. Look at it."

"Michael," Temple repeated dully. "Michael. Aloysius. Xavier."

"Kinsella!" Molina finished. "Michael Aloysius Xavier Kinsella. That's why I couldn't trace him."

"Max," Temple pronounced slowly. "He didn't lie. What's this about the IRA?"

Molina began to pace. "He was suspected of being a member. Of course it was a while back. According to that card, he was sixteen. Still . . . that's an international terrorist organization. I knew he had a record somewhere!" She paused, as if her euphoria had let her down with a bang. "This doesn't explain the dead man at the Goliath, or his supposed career as a magician, but I knew he was more than he appeared to be."

"I always knew that, Lieutenant," Temple said quietly.

"Not this!"

Temple looked at the card again. She had never pictured Max that young, that raw, that unfinished, but even here she saw the magician half-hidden behind the flat, unflattering black and white. Michael. Mike—? No, Max.

"Look at the description," Molina prodded.

Temple knew Max's statistics by heart, and the damning card confirmed them, only the height off. Height: six feet (and three inches yet to come). Hair: black; eyes: blue. . . . She gaped up into the icy aquamarine of Molina's waiting eyes, which glittered with true-blue triumph.

"Max's eyes aren't blue!" Temple said. "They got that wrong." Maybe they got everything else wrong too. . . .

"Did they? I always wondered why a man with green eyes—a performer used to projecting a well-groomed stage image—kept a beige-and-blue sweater. I assume you're as sentimental as ever and it still hangs in your closet."

Temple flushed to remember an intent Molina taking Max's sweater to the French doors a few weeks before. "I'm just lazy, not sentimental, Lieutenant; no time to houseclean. And I never saw Max wear that sweater."

"Exactly. Why did he have it?"

"Most men are careless about color-coordinated clothes."

"He wouldn't be." Molina almost sounded as if she spoke from intimate knowledge. "Don't you get it? Contact lenses. We know he was a wanted man at least once in his life. Who knows what he's been up to since he was sixteen?"

"I do!" Temple stood up, her voice and hand shaking, the Interpol card quivering. "I never saw any contact lens equipment; I never saw Max take them in or out, and I lived with him."

"Long-wear lenses. And he *was* a magician, after all. You only saw what he wanted you to."

That allegation hurt worse than anything Interpol might have had on Max. Temple lowered her eyes to the familiar stranger captured in cold type. "What did they say he did wrong?"

"Not enough," Molina admitted. "Enough to be suspected, to sit on some search roster for a while and be forgotten. The IRA is dirty, brutal business. I wouldn't get my hopes up, if he started there that young."

Temple rubbed her nose, which itched and maybe wanted to do something else undignified, like sniffle. "It's politics," she said. "Politics is always dirty if you're the underdog."

"I imagine he was, Mr. Michael Aloysius Xavier Kinsella."

"If you're the underdog, you're used to surviving."

"What would you know about it?" The question was personal.

"I knew Max, and you didn't."

The lieutenant reared back, then blew out a breath like a winded horse. "You didn't know enough."

"Neither," Temple said evenly, "do you."

"It's my job to find out."

"Thanks for the tip."

"You're not disillusioned, are you?"

"It's hard to disillusion a magician's assistant."

"You were more than that."

"Was I? I wonder. What are you going to do about the cats?"

"Cats?"

Temple told her about the will and the forthcoming article and the furor likely to arise over their collective welfare.

"Oh, rats," said Molina, her good mood ruined by the coming storm. "All I need is a raft of animal extremists all over the scene of the crime."

She snatched up her card like it was the ace of hearts. "You do admit that this is the same man?"

"This is the man," Temple said, echoing Miss Tyler, who

had echoed a classic scene of betrayal with a kiss in the Garden where Peter had betrayed yet again—and had been betrayed. Temple betrayed nothing but the facts, Ma'am, just the facts.

Molina read that in her eyes and had another reason to lower her triumph a notch.

"I thought you'd like to know."

"No, but I'm better off knowing. I'm not sure that you are."

"Why?"

"Politics, Lieutenant, are a lot less clear-cut than crime. You should know that by now."

Molina tapped the card on her palm, then pocketed it. She was gone as fast and furiously as she had come, not with a magician's smoothness, but with sound and fury signifying nothing.

Temple went to the dormant cat. "Michael Aloysius Xaviar. Kind of rhymes with Caviar at the end, doesn't it, kitty? I just hope Midnight Louie hasn't done a disappearing act, too."

Chapter 28

A Clerical Error

"You look beat," Sheila said when Matt walked into ConTact at six-forty-five Wednesday evening.

He didn't argue, but slipped into his donated office chair and let it swivel him outward to face the sparsely furnished room instead of into the instant isolation of his phone niche.

"Lines been busy?" he asked.

"Quiet so far. They're all waiting until the weekend to explode." Sheila regarded him curiously. "Want some coffee?"

"Yeah, thanks." He was surprised. Everybody took care of their own needs around ConTact, but Sheila was a social worker and she sensed his mental fatigue.

She brought him a Save-the-Whales mug steaming with a full shot of coffee from the big aluminum urn in the corner. "What's going on?"

"Oh, some friends of mine have problems. Thanks." He

toasted her with the cup before taking a careful sip of the scalding brew.

"Don't you encounter enough problems here?"

"Sure, but old friends are old friends."

"They aren't tourists—?"

"No!" He laughed at the idea of Seraphina and company as tourists, then realized that Sheila had finessed him into explaining why the idea was so absurd. "An old teacher of mine ended up retiring here. I help her out with the odd problem now and again."

"Mr. Goodwrench," Sheila said with a joking smile. "Kind to old ladies and dogs." She looked relieved that an obviously old lady was the object of his attentions.

"Cats," he corrected without saying more, turning his chair to face the dead-end white walls of soundproofing.

"So you're tuckered out from playing handyman," Sheila pressed.

"Yeah," Matt answered, wondering what category of household task taking down crucified cats would come under.

He didn't want to talk about it, even think about it. So he jumped on the phone when one of the lines lit up, jamming on his headphones. He sensed Sheila standing behind him, hovering over him.

"ConTact," he announced to the caller. Whoever it was, that person would not stand breathing above him, brimming over with questions.

The voice began, a man's, sounding wired. Matt felt his pulse speed up for the crisis, beat to the rhythms of agitated speech, as his mind began sketching a mental picture of the speaker. He was plugged into the anonymous, distant night again. The presence hovering behind him lingered, then whispered away, defeated.

Matt breathed a sigh of relief that the caller was talking too fast and too hard to hear the ebbing presence. Then Matt heard only the caller, his troubles, his fears, his gravelly, desperation-edged voice. Connected again to someone who needed help and would demand nothing more than that,

Matt breathed deeper, steadier, like an athlete, and entered his listening, concentrating, problem-solving mode. Nothing was as soothing to the psyche as other people's problems.

To his relief, the lines kept ringing and he kept jumping to answer them. That kept Sheila from offering any more favors and expecting any more answers. He was already obligated to answer to more than enough women. Lieutenant Molina, Temple, Sister Seraphina.

Still, at the back of his mind, the problems of Our Lady of Guadalupe swirled like leaves caught in an eddy.

His watch showed 2:30 A.M., when the first line rang again and he punched the button.

"ConTact. Can I help?"

"If you can help an old lady who has mysterious disturbances around her house," came a now-familiar voice.

"Sister Seraphina, what's the matter?"

She sighed. "I'm sorry to call you, Matthias, but the police won't do and I know your number now, so you're stuck."

"You can call anytime," he assured her. "What's the problem?"

"First, Sister Mary Monica heard some disturbance from Miss Tyler's house."

"Sister Mary Monica *heard?*"

"Exactly." Seraphina's normally booming, cheerful voice grew grim. "I looked out her window and glimpsed a light in the second story, then it went out. So I settled Monica down and watched. I never saw another light in the house, but several minutes later a flashlight bobbed along the side of the house to the garden. Mind you, Matt, I saw only a few firefly-fast glimmers; maybe I was staring into the dark too hard for too long. But I remembered poor Peter and got worried, so I called Father Hernandez at the rectory."

During the long pause, Matt imagined a dozen equally unfortunate scenarios. Temple would have been proud of him.

"He was . . . very bad, Matt. He insisted on coming over and stumbling about in the bushes with his own flashlight.

Of course he—we—found nothing, not after all that sound and fury. I finally got him back to the rectory. Matt, he needs you."

"No one needs me! I'm no longer practicing—"

"Father Hernandez is crumbling before my eyes. He made so little sense. I know his drinking isn't the primary problem; it's a symptom. The only alternative is to go to the bishop, and Father Rafe is such a proud man, and the parish is at such a delicate point in its fund drive—"

"And I'm the best that you can do," he interrupted a bit bitterly.

She refused to be buffaloed by his anger. "Yes," she said simply. "Please."

"What do you want me to do?"

"Come here when you get off work. Talk to him. I think Father desperately needs to share his problem, his sorrow, with another human being. He won't talk to me, to a woman, about what he must regard as a terrible failure."

"But to me he would?"

"He might. I don't know what else to do, Matt."

"Do you think you're going to win me back by making me function as what I used to be?"

"No. But I think you might win Father Rafe back to what he used to be."

"I'm that good?"

"You're the one person he might think would understand."

"He doesn't understand me."

"That's not what's needed here. We need to understand him, and to let him know that nothing can be as bad as he thinks. His isolation has distorted his thinking."

"So has the drinking. You're asking for a miracle here."

"No miracles. Just good pastoral care."

Matt's weary laugh came out as a brief bark. "I can call a cab and be at the rectory by three-thirty." He didn't want Temple in on this, not anymore. Besides, he couldn't use her indefinitely as a taxi service to his past. "You're lucky we live in Las Vegas, a town that never shuts down."

"Chicago's supposed to be the town that never shuts down, Matt, but the recession has done a pretty good job of forcing it to. I guess counseling is the one profession that never runs out of customers."

"Maybe." She had given him an innocuous-sounding name for this dangerous, unrequested intervention in another man's struggle with his own soul. Another priest's. Counseling, not ministry. All right. "I'll be there," he promised.

"God bless you, Matt."

Las Vegas cab drivers, like their Manhattan counterparts, have seen everything. So the ponytailed driver of the Whittlesea Blue cab Matt called didn't raise an eyebrow when he was directed to Our Lady of Guadalupe Church. Las Vegas had more churches per capita than most U.S. cities; why shouldn't a midnight meanderer want to save his soul as well as spend a wad at some casino?

The neighborhood was dark, still and well-behaved. No lights glimmered now around the Tyler house, supposedly empty except for cats, or around the convent next door, but Sister Seraphina had made the proverbial "candle in the window" literal at the rectory.

Matt saw one thin, ivory wax candle winking in the rectory's kitchen window. He wondered if it was left over from last Advent or St. Blaise's February feast day, if it had been blessed or was merely an ordinary candle pulling ordinary candle duty.

Matt listened to the cab's wheels peel slowly away on the gritty pavement as he walked to the side of the rectory, then pushed the night's last button—the doorbell.

He heard the faint, hoarse ring of an elderly buzzer within, waited, then rang again.

Finally, other sounds came, like a blind man boxing his way through a maze. The door opened all at once, fully wide, filled by Father Hernandez, who looked smaller and older in civvies—a navy turtleneck and dark slacks. Matt would be willing to bet that he wouldn't touch a bottle while in uniform; even his breakdown would be regimented.

"Seraphina called you," Father Hernandez challenged. "What would we do without nuns to meddle?"

The question required no response, and Matt gave none. He simply entered when Father Hernandez faced the inevitable and stepped aside.

"What are we supposed to do?" the pastor asked, traces of both bafflement and self-mockery in his voice.

"Talk," Matt suggested.

Father Hernandez turned and moved through the semi-dark kitchen, bumping into a countertop. Matt followed, avoiding comment, avoiding judgment.

The priest buffeted down the narrow, dark back hall ahead of Matt like a babe down a birth canal, caroming from wall to wall, blindly driving toward the light that poured like pale syrup from the open office door.

He lurched through that door into the room beyond, into his chair, which creaked to accept the body he threw into it. A green-glass-shaded banker's lamp lit the desktop's jumble without casting much light on Father Hernandez's face behind the desk, or on Matt's when he sat down in front of it.

Despite the hour, despite the situation, rectories had an ineffable cozy feeling, and Matt felt that trickle of warmth even now. Familiar ground, once his own. But not quite.

The desk lamp also illuminated the tall, clear bottle of tequila sitting under it, and the plain kitchen glass fogged with fingerprints beside it.

José Cuervo was evidently the friend of Father Hernandez that Sister Seraphina had suspected.

"Care for a glass? I almost said, 'Father.' " Father Hernandez gestured with a host's broad, sweeping hand to the solitary bottle and glass.

Matt realized he had never before confronted anyone who could be so dangerous to his own hard-won equilibrium. He nodded. He would get nowhere if he began on a holier-than-thou platform. Besides, he could use his own dose of Mexican courage.

Father Hernandez's dramatic eyebrows rose, but he pulled out a drawer and extracted a glass as plain and smudged as the one already in sight. He unscrewed the bottle cap and poured three inches of liquid into each smeary glass. No ice, no niceties.

Matt leaned out of his chair to accept it, then sipped. He'd had tequila before in a different form: the festive, salt-rimmed, pale jade bubble of an oversized cocktail glass. Straight tequila burned like rubbing alcohol and had a sour, acrid aftertaste. He set the glass down on the desk, careful to place it on a clump of papers rather than on the naked wood, where it would sweat a pale ring into the finish.

Down the hall, the rectory's aged air conditioner droned like a snoring giant.

"What does she think you can do?" Father Hernandez asked after taking a long, almost loathing gulp of his drink. His voice wasn't slurred, but a bit loud and contentious. Matt didn't take offense; Father Rafe wasn't angry with him, although he might act like it.

"Sister Seraphina always had greater expectations of me than I could live up to," Matt replied.

"Don't they, though? Don't they all?" Father Hernandez leaned over his desk. "I don't blame you for leaving, you or any of the other thousands. It's not like it used to be. Everything's changed—the liturgy, the bureaucracy, the clergy, the parishioners." He eyed Matt carefully, as if he had to concentrate to see him, and maybe he did. "Was it the usual, celibacy? I can see that a young man who looks like you—"

"It wasn't celibacy," Matt said quickly. "Nothing so simple."

"Ah. You think celibacy is simple, do you? How long were you in?"

"Including seminary, sixteen years."

"It gets harder," Father Hernandez said, sitting back to drink again. "Not the celibacy, everything. Raising money, cutting corners when there are so few other priests and nuns to be found. We used to run on our clergy—our dedicated hundreds of thousands sworn to poverty, chastity and obedience. Now we have all the worries and the expenses and none of the resources."

"I've seen the frustrations of parish life, Father."

"Yes, came, saw and left. Not like Caesar, were you? No conquering, just accounting, and accounting for yourself and your parish to the bishop, who hardly knows your name unless you become involved in some untidy abortion fracas or sleep with a teenager or disgrace your cassock by slopping a little liquor on it."

Matt winced at the corrosive tone. "Will the bishop have to hear about you?"

"Has already, I suppose. Spies everywhere. 'Father Hernandez is tippling a bit nowadays, Your Eminence. Perhaps you should send him somewhere to dry out.' If only that were the worst of it!"

Matt sipped from his glass again, wondering whether he should probe for some indiscretion with a woman or with the abortion issue. Father Hernandez answered that himself.

"Women were never my weakness," he announced with boozy satisfaction, almost as an ordinary man would boast the opposite. "Not sex, and never the bottle, until lately. Did Sister Seraphina tell you about those odd calls to poor old Monica and the late Miss Tyler, who was so generous despite my lamentable lack of tact toward cats?"

Matt nodded. Father Hernandez leaned forward over his desk, clutching his glass in both hands.

"Do you still observe the sanctity of the confessional?" he demanded, staring into and through Matt's eyes, his gaze as piercing as laser light.

"I left officially, I didn't just walk away like some do. I . . . underwent laicization. I'm not a priest anymore. I can't observe what I can no longer practice."

"You can treat anything I tell you with the same seriousness, can swear to keep it eternally secret, as privileged information, even as a lawyer or a psychiatrist must do."

"The obligation no longer has the spiritual element," Matt objected.

"But if I asked you to . . . revert to that degree of confidentiality, would you?"

"I would have to," Matt answered unhappily.

He hated being asked to perform as a quasi-priest again, but he also understood that those were the only terms on which Father Hernandez would accept him as a confidant.

"If you were my confessor," Father Hernandez went on, "I would have to begin my confession, 'Father, forgive me, for I have not sinned.' "

He laughed at Matt's partly appalled, partly puzzled expression, then sighed long and deeply. "You know about the convent getting anonymous phone calls? I have been getting letters."

"Letters?"

Father Hernandez disappeared behind the desk as he bent to wrestle open another old, and sticky, drawer. He surfaced with a large manila envelope, but before opening it, he refilled his glass and nudged the tequila bottle in Matt's direction.

"I'm fine," Matt said, indicating his almost untouched glass and registering the irony of the expression at the same moment. He was not fine, and neither was Father Hernandez.

"All right." Father Hernandez gulped more white lightning, then licked his lips. His hands came down hard on the plump manila envelope. "First, these are lies. I believe the term is 'damnable lies.' But we don't call Satan the Father of Lies for nothing. Lies can undo a life."

Matt nodded.

Father Hernandez sighed again, shakily. "I can hardly bear to show another human being such lies, but I'm sick of swallowing them by myself and saying, doing, nothing to defend myself. I think you will see why I can do nothing. Nothing. But this." His hand waved at the bottle. "It's a coward's way out, and no way out at all, but it slows my mind from eating at itself so I can pretend to function. Every time I say Mass, I hope I will receive the grace to face this, and every time, I gain only enough strength to keep up the mockery. Now I understand why even Our Lord asked His Father to take the cup of His coming sacrifice from His lips in the Garden of Gethsemane. If what is in these letters becomes public, I will be crucified."

Matt steeled himself to receive the envelope Father Hernandez passed over the desk. Gethsemane again. Where Christ went to contemplate his foreordained suffering and death. And yet the act was not foreordained, according to church teaching; Christ could have refused; that was what made the fruition so significant. Matt never thought for a moment that Father Hernandez was exaggerating his situation.

He drew the rustling bundles of paper from inside the envelope as if they were snakes. He opened one white, business-size envelope, unfolded a crisp piece of typing paper and read.

He read three before he looked up again. Sweat crystallized on Father Hernandez's anxious face. He watched Matt like a child gauging a parent's reaction to a bad report card, uneasy but defiant, afraid but proud.

"And there's nothing to this?" Matt asked.

"Nothing. I swear on the Cross."

"Nor the charges about your previous appointments?"

"Nothing, there or here, then or now. You know what will happen if this . . . garbage becomes public."

"A media circus maximus."

"Bring on the Christians," Father Hernandez intoned with bitter drama. "Bring on the priests."

"So it should be," Matt said, his tone stern as any archbishop's. "Child abuse of any kind is a heinous offense. The sexual abuse of children by the clergy is unspeakable. I confess that I can't imagine how any man of God can shut his eyes to such acts, yet several have been proven to have done just that."

"Not me." Father Hernandez's dark eyes glowed like embers as his fist pounded his chest, not in the humble throb of a *mea culpa*, but in the emphatic rhythm of a Spanish dancer. "And now it has become fashionable to allege such things. You know how disturbed minds leap in when such ethical chasms open up, swallowing even the innocent. I am innocent!"

Matt spread his hands. "If so, you would be cleared, ultimately."

"Perhaps. And I say only perhaps. But the stigma." Rafael Hernandez held up his pale, damp palms from the glass they curved around. "Stigma. We know where that word comes from, from the nails through the wrists and feet; the stigma is the Crucifixion."

Matt nodded.

"You know the position the church faces on such matters nowadays."

Matt nodded again.

"What would you have me do?"

Matt said nothing.

"If I went, as I should, to the archbishop, he would be forced to take the most stringent of actions. There would be publicity. Now, the church is anxious to demonstrate its eagerness to root out what it once covered up, and rightfully so. Yet mistakes can be made when such zeal is employed, when an institution of any kind is fighting for its integrity, its reputation. There is a new Inquisition at work."

Matt could not deny that.

"You talk to people on that hotline; you must speak to many disturbed souls, some quite unappealing. What do you think of the writer?"

Matt moved the three envelopes through his hands as if weighing them. "The police could do a better psychological profile. Yes, I know why you feel they mustn't be involved. I'm no expert on anonymous letters, but I'd say an organized person did this. They seem to be printed on a laser printer, which rules out the ancient clue of the uneven typewriter keys. I sense someone intelligent taking almost a vicious pleasure in the perversity of the charges. Does the writer never ask for anything?"

"Nothing!" Father Hernandez clutched his head instead of his glass, his face taking on a distracted look.

"Then it could be a crank, some disaffected parishioner, or even an anti-Catholic bigot."

"I know what it could be. I also know what will happen if the letters are made public: a full-scale investigation, no matter how unsubstantiated the charges. After that, neither I nor Our Lady of Guadalupe will be worth much. Matthias, I have been a decent priest, perhaps not the brightest or the best, or the humblest, but to the extent of my abilities, I have been faithful to my vows and have tried to be of service to my parishioners and my duties. I don't know what to do. Perhaps this . . . correspondent will tire of baiting me and stop."

"Perhaps he—or she—will go public when you least expect it."

"True."

"The police would be your better bet," Matt said.

"Go to Lieutenant Molina? Never."

"Pride goeth before a fall, to be sanctimonious. Besides, this isn't a case for a homicide lieutenant."

"She would learn of it."

"Probably, but forget your image in the eyes of a parishioner. Lieutenant Molina is also a professional, and professionals don't buy what every anonymous crank might charge. The police investigate this sort of thing all the time and are well acquainted with anonymous letter-writers. They might give you more benefit of the doubt, and they certainly would investigate quietly. If they leaped to conclusions and filed false charges, they can get sued."

"What you're saying is that the church, my church, to which I have devoted most of my life, is more likely to persecute me than to defend me."

"Now, given the political climate on this issue, it has to avoid any appearance of favoritism, of sheltering anyone."

"So they will crucify me, with a mockery of a trial, as was done to Christ. We priests claim we walk in Our Lord's footsteps, or try to, but confront something like this, Matthias, and say then that you are prepared to face the Crown of Thorns from the hands of your own bishop and the whips and the scourges of the press."

"I believe your innocence," Matt said. "I do believe you, Father Hernandez. And if I do, so will others. Yet I see your point. Why pull down disaster upon yourself? Still, the pressure will draw attention to you in any event."

"You mean this?" He lofted the two-thirds-empty bottle. "I try, but my thoughts run around and around like mice on a wheel. Who? Why? When will the attack escalate? How?"

"That's why the good news of Miss Tyler's bequest hardly seemed to matter to you."

"Money." He shook his silvered head. "It is the means to a good end, one hopes. It is essential to life and bureaucracy. I wish the cats had gotten it, do you understand? No one would accuse the cats of misconduct."

"Father, we both should know more than most that false accusations are a terrible cross to bear. You, too, should ask our Father to take this cup from your lips." Matt pointed to the bottle. "Whatever happens, that is the first bridge to cross."

Father Hernandez shrugged and ran his fingers through his elegant hair, turning it into a ruffled halo. "I'll try. Harder."

"And I'll think about this letter-writer. It could be the same person who called Sister Mary Monica, and who tried to crucify the cat. We could be dealing with a truly demented individual."

Father Hernandez looked up, and actually smiled. "Thank you for that 'we.' That is more than I was willing to grant you when we first met. Forgive me."

Father, forgive me, for I have not sinned. . . .

Matt ran that ironic phrase through his mind as he left the rectory. His watch read, by the candle still burning in the kitchen window, five-thirty in the morning.

Dawn was a vague, teasing lightening of the dark along the eastern horizon. He jammed his hands, cold hands from tension felt but not shown, into his pants pockets and began walking back to the Circle Ritz.

Daylight would begin to shadow him soon, and he was not

afraid of the neighborhood. He was not afraid of anything he might encounter on Las Vegas's stirring streets. He had spent two hours staring at the face of true, spiritual fear, and ordinary fear would never look the same again.

Chapter 29

Trespasser and Transgressor

After my fruitless explorations at the cathouse next to the convent, I pad my weary way back home. Interrogating some three-score possible witnesses—or do I mean witlesses?—makes me eager to lay my considerable length on the cool black-and-white tiles of the kitchen floor and contemplate the full bowl of Free-to-be-Feline while I decide which of Miss Temple's food stores I should raid instead.

Actually, the challenge of finding a suitable substitute for this odious health food has added a piquant character to my several daily meals at the Circle Ritz, providing an element of uncertainty reminiscent of my untrammeled days on the streets and sidewalks. I need to keep my survival skills sharp, just in case my current cushy situation becomes too confining.

I scale the building's exterior along my usual, well-worn

route, lofting from patio to patio to decorative cornice ledge to open bathroom window in the twinkling of a private eye.

My street-worn tootsies make a four-point landing on the bathroom's cool ceramic tiles. Ah, home, sweat-free home, after a hot day on the job.

I hightail it for the kitchen, partly because the tiles there are cool, too; partly to indulge in my daily stare-down with the unbanishable Free-to-be-Feline.

I crouch before the elegant glass-footed banana-split dish that my attentive companion has seen fit to heap with Free-to-be-Feline. There it sits, an army-green mountain of pellets that would serve equally well entering—or exiting—a rabbit. I have seen more appetizing vitamin pills from the health food store.

I will, of course, not touch one crude pellet. I contemplate busting into the lower cabinet for a raid on Miss Temple's hidden stock of Finny Flakes, a toothsome, sugar-coated cereal product thoughtfully shaped into the miniature likeness of our piscine friends. Yum. I can put away whole schools of these little nibblies.

Then I notice a new variation in the unspoken food war that has been waged between us ever since my usually sensible roommate saw fit to introduce the foul Free-to-be-Feline to my menu.

Another bowl—in fact, a pink Melmac saucer from the upper cupboard—of the questionable comestible sits beside mine, this mound of pellets surmounted by a suggestive valley at the apex. Has some intruder been at my rejected food? My rear extremity swells to irritated proportions as I growl to myself, "Who's been eating my Free-to-be-Feline?"

The usual suspects come quickly to mind: the invasive mouse (but my alert presence alone would banish any vermin of that persuasion); the rapacious insect (but even the largest cockroach could not dispose of the apparent amount of missing FtbF); the unexpected visitor (but neither Mr. Matt Devine nor Miss Electra Lark has previously shown the slightest inclination to snack on my food, whether I favor it or not).

There is, of course, one party so depraved, so predictably greedy, so . . . unclassy as to vacuum up any foodstuff to be found on a floor. I refer, naturally, to the domesticated dog.

I have become lax on my own turf, I realize, and did not sniff for intruders before bounding to the buffet. I lift my head and sniff for dog. Actually, dogs possess an overbearing scent that I should have noticed even in my mad dash for the eats.

I do not sniff dog. Instead, I detect a delicate scent of an unknown nature, not unpleasant, but not native to this environment. I press my sniffer to the floor near the second bowl of FtbF and reel at the flagrant trail of a foreign feline.

Now that I am alerted to the intruder, I race into the living room . . . to find a stranger ensconced on the off-white sofa, fast asleep.

My proprietorial instincts have given way to something quite different. Both my nose and my eyes are right on target: the individual who has been tastelessly filching my Free-to-be-Feline is a dainty, nubile number who is not hard on either of my prime senses, who is, in fact—free, black and female!

In an instant, I bound up beside her, anticipating a most enjoyable interrogation.

In the same instant, she is awake and transformed into a hissing banshee with a croquet-hoop back, bushy tail, poisonously slit golden eyes, bristling silver whiskers and as many sharp white teeth—all showing—as a barracuda with an overbite.

"Whoa! Wait a minute, Miss," I soothe in my best growl, which is only slightly intimidating.

She is having nothing of it, but backs against the rear sofa cushions, her admirably unclipped claws snagging the fabric, a phenomenon that will not please Miss Temple Barr.

"These are my digs," I point out diplomatically, "although I do not mind an occasional attractive visitor."

"Possession is nine-tenths of the law," she responds without softening her defensive posture.

I hold my temper and back off to the sofa's far end. It is obvious, despite her furry fireworks, that my intruder is of a tender age and experience; so young, in fact, that she has not yet had that odious operation known euphemistically as "fixing." Obviously, she needs someone to show her the ropes.

"You must have sensed my previous possession," I point out.

She shrugs, allowing the ebony halo around her head to settle down a bit. "It was either this or Murder Inc."

"I take it, then, that my tenderhearted roommate has saved you from the animal pound."

"I encouraged her to intervene, yes."

I nod sagely. "She is a delightful companion, Miss Temple Barr, but not the best cook. Did you really eat that *Flea*-to-be-Feline?"

"It is a highly nutritious food, well balanced in all essential vitamins and minerals."

"I can see that you and Miss Temple hit it right off," I note sourly. "I can be magnanimous. However, I must insist that you desist from eating Free-to-be-Feline. I am training Miss Temple to forget it."

"I will eat what does me the most good." She looks me up and down with less than an admiring flick of her long, black-mascara-coated eyelashes. "It would do you a lot of good, too."

"Listen, I am head dude around here. You'll do as I tell you. If you're nice to me, I might even let you stay a while."

"What does that mean?" she snarls quickly.

I have never heard such ugly sentiments coming out of such a beautiful little doll-face before. I wonder where she got her feisty temperament. A life on the streets can do that to some, but it is a shame to see such a comely little doll so warped.

"I mean that it is my place, and if you want to stay, you have to play to my hand of cards, and right now I am holding all the aces."

"If you mean to imply that I must extend you any personal favors because I happen to need a home for the moment, that is an extremely sexist and patriarchal statement, not to say coercive. I am sure, however," she adds with a satisfied purr, "that you did not mean any such thing."

"Uh . . . no." I frown, which wrinkles my broad forehead and is—I am told—a dignified, attractive expression. Her last statement sounded oddly like a threat of some kind, which I am not used to hearing at my size and age, and especially from a petite little doll of tender years. No doubt her rough months on the streets have made her somewhat . . . touchy.

"What is your name, kid?" I ask in a kindly, avuncular manner that it costs me much effort to produce.

"They call me 'Caviar.' "

I nod, savoring the moniker. "A tasty choice. I sampled some of the best beluga from Russia when I was house dick at the Crystal Phoenix. You have heard of the Crystal Phoenix Hotel and Casino, of course, the classiest joint in Vegas?"

"No," she says shortly, sitting down to lick her luxurious rear extremity into shape. I admire her tongue-and-teeth work.

"Anyway, this beluga stuff is like little black pearls, very costly and quite succulent, full of the salt of the sea. My old man has his own yacht, and is quite an expert in seafood, wherever he is."

"How nice. My old man was a scamp and a tramp and he left my mother flat. I do not care where he is, and I do not judge anyone by paternal lines. We cannot help who our fathers are."

"I can see that you have had some tough times, kid," I growl. "You need someone older and wiser—and bigger—to look after you."

I get a solid gold eye cocked full at me. What gorgeous—and searing—peepers this doll has!

"I do not think so," she says.

"What are your plans?"

"To rest for the moment. I am tired of cages."

"Yeah, I know what you mean. I have been in the stir a few times myself, even with a sixty-hour death penalty."

She eyes me with respect for the first time. "Why are you still here?"

"I broke myself out."

She looks impressed, a little. "I guess you are big enough to manage it."

"Actually, I used brains, not brawn."

Now she stares at me again, as if I am a bowl of Free-to-be-Feline and she is on a diet. "You are quite amusing," she concedes.

Well now, this is progress. I stretch out along the sofa, until my mitts are almost within touching distance. I have met these embittered street girls before. They take delicate handling, but soon recognize the wisdom of putting themselves under the protection of a powerful dude, like yours truly.

"I have to warn you, if you stay here, you are in some jeopardy."

"Miss Barr seems most thoughtful and civil."

"Yeah, but she has scruples. These are things people get from time to time. She will probably have you undergo an unpleasant operation that will not do much for your future sex life. I know you are a young thing and not aware of what you might be missihg, but believe me, this 'spaying' is a fate worse than death."

"I am quite familiar with this form of birth control," she says coolly.

"I can find you a cozy place nearby where you will not be subject to forced sterilization."

She eyes the comfy surroundings, then me. "Some hole-in-the-wall love nest? With you? I think not. I prefer the knife."

"You do not know what you will be missing?" I argue, appalled.

"Oh, but I do know. I have had these alley dudes trying to jump me since I was a kit. No loss."

"But these were not worldly, suave, accomplished dudes—"

"Can it, bud. I have seen it with my mother and others. Some dude jumps you from behind, and all you get out of it is a bite on the back of the neck, some pawing and mauling and a lot of hungry little faces nobody wants who are doomed to be run down, locked up or gassed at an early age. No thanks."

"You do not want kits?" I try not to sound too skeptical, as I never did either, but I was a guy and that was natural.

"Not in this rotten world."

"What about . . . love and sex?"

"What about it? I told you my father was gone as quick as he had come, no pun intended. My mother walked herself to a rail to feed us four. She always said I take after my father more than somewhat, but he took off before he even knew my name."

"Sure, it is a mewing shame, but that is the way it is, kid. I know my old man only from hearsay, too. And you must admit that our mothers are A-one."

"Yes, but they dare not spare we kits more than a few weeks, because some other guy on the run comes through, makes like Dracula in heat, and more kits are on the way. Plus, if the old man sticks around, he gets jealous of the babies and might break their necks some night so Mama will go back into heat. I do not much cotton to persons of the male persuasion."

"So I notice," I note with alarm. Most of the ladies I have known considered a dude a necessity of life. This little lady seems to have sworn off a lot of things formerly considered necessities by the general population. She is one scary little doll, although as cute as hell.

"You say they called you 'Caviar' in captivity?" I ask for

lack of anything sensible to say. I am more than somewhat shook.

She retracts her last set of claws and licks her front mitt into the sheen of a black-satin glove.

"Yeah, but that is not my street name. Actually, I am named after my missing, unlamented father, who appears to have made quite an impression on my deluded mother."

"You are?" I ask to gain time and collect my wits. Could this little doll be on the level with all this?

"Yes." She pauses in her elegant grooming to lift her head and regard me with the icy disdain she apparently extends to all of the male persuasion. "My real name is Midnight Louise."

I would pale, if that were possible.

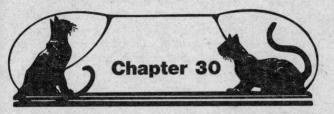

Chapter 30

Willy-nilly

Temple, Peggy Wilhelm and Sister Seraphina stood outside the Tyler house, eyeing its impressive bulk with an awe much resembling Dorothy and her friends regarding the Emerald City of Oz.

Temple was guilty of a lifelong identification with Dorothy, at least from the Judy Garland movie: she was a Midwestern girl with an inborn optimism in everything to be found over the rainbow; she really dug those ruby-red slippers; and now she had—instead of Toto—a black cat named Midnight Louie as she ventured and adventured into ever-more exotic terrains personal, professional and quasi-professional, if you count crime-meddling as a quasi-profession.

"You say that Lieutenant Molina okayed our going through the house?" Temple asked Sister Seraphina again.

"Cleaning the house," Sister Seraphina modified scrupulously. "It seems that there is no hard evidence of foul play.

The injuries that killed poor Blandina could have been received in a fall. The police have gathered what physical evidence there was, in case new information turns up, and the house with all these cats in it is a white elephant. If we don't deal with it, it will be declared a public health hazard, and Our Lady of Guadalupe is morally obligated to do something positive about the cats, having benefited from the will."

"And if we find anything . . . interesting in the house?" Temple prodded.

Sister Seraphina winked through her trifocals. "Then we give it to Lieutenant Molina and reopen the case."

"Forget it," Peggy said. "Sure, some flaky things happened at the fringes of Aunt Blandina's death, but there were no more incidents at the cat show. I bet a competitor just wanted to ruin poor Minuet's chances. She was a prime contender. And this phone and lights stuff—you know the way kids in this neighborhood act up."

"What about Peter?" Seraphina reminded her in a suddenly sober voice.

"How is he?" Temple asked, for she had delivered the cat, hot-pink bandages wrapping each front paw, to the convent the day before.

"Fine, but he won't be wandering for a while. Sister Rose is keeping him close to home." Sister Seraphina smiled at Peggy. "I know this is hard on you, dear. You've taken responsibility here from the first, with no hope of personal gain. I can't say I approve of your aunt leaving you out of her will, even if the church benefits. You will know you did your duty, as years go by, and that will be a comfort."

Peggy nodded sudden gratitude at the nun, then glanced around through tear-glazed eyes. "There's a lot of history in this house."

"And cats," added Temple, pushing up the sleeves on her CATS! sweat shirt.

Peggy glanced at her sweat-shirt logo, as did Sister Seraphina. They all three linked elbows and skipped up to the gates of this feline Emerald City.

Emerald eyes greeted them at the door, and meows and upturned bewhiskered faces pleading not just for food, but for attention. The cats were obviously missing the daily ministrations of Blandina Tyler.

Temple marveled at the dead woman's stamina. She was like the Old Woman in the Shoe with her flock of children. Temple was already wondering if she could handle two cats, and here Blandina had opened her door to dozens of hungry mouths and hearts.

The trio soon found that Blandina Tyler had been a collector of all sorts of things. String, for instance. Balls of it occupied the kitchen drawers. Temple threw them down for the cats, which schooled like piranha around the playthings.

"Look at this!" Peggy pulled a fistful of what looked like a limp tan octopus from the bottom vegetable drawer of the refrigerator.

Temple blinked, while Sister Seraphina came over with a puckered face, then grabbed the booty and laughed. "Support stockings! you know, those cast-iron things that require girdles and garter belts that old ladies wear. These things are as stiff as rubber bands." She looked suddenly demure. "I think the best invention in the past thirty years was pantyhose."

"Amen," said Peggy Wilhelm. "I remember wearing this awful little garter belt that put welts into my skin, and in the early seventies, shorter skirts were always pulling up to show everything, until pantyhose came along."

"Early seventies," Temple repeated. "Gosh, I never got to wear long stockings in those days. My problem was socks that sagged around my ankles and those overbig toes that made wrinkles in my tennies and hurt my feet."

"Now you wear high heels and hurt your feet," Sister Seraphina reproved, sounding rather motherly.

"They hurt less than those tennies jammed with oversized socks," Temple protested. "Besides, I'm wearing tennies now."

"Yeah, hot metallic-pink," Peggy jeered in good humor.

"You wouldn't recognize low-profile shoes if they tripped you."

"Everybody has to have a hobby," Temple said in her own defense. "I also like to explore. Let's 'clean' some more."

By eleven-thirty they had rooted out six thirty-three-gallon garbage bags of support hose.

"Where do old ladies get these things?" Temple demanded as she opened a tempting, hard-sided suitcase from the forties in a back bedroom and spilled out another cornucopia of support hose.

Sister Seraphina laughed and shook her head. "It's the Depression mentality, which I'm depressed to admit I'm old enough to understand: save everything in case it might somehow be of use later. Save, save, save."

Temple shook her head and began exploring a 1930s' dressing table she would love to have: big round mirror, pillars of drawers bridged by a low shelf. Paint it white or silver and—wow! Maybe there'd be an estate sale. . . .

The shallow drawer in the bridge piece was filled with ancient tortoise plastic hair combs, hairnets, wads of thin, gray-brown hair, safety pins, and a plastic box filled with buttons, all of it resting on a yellowed piece of cockatoo wallpaper serving as a drawer liner. Temple removed everything, figuring the dressing table might bring some money in a sale—if she couldn't buy it beforehand.

Then she pulled up the lining paper.

Something lay beneath it. Something long and white and made of paper that would be folded four times. . . .

Oh, my seldom-sensible shoes! Temple peeled the elderly paper out from the drawer. A will. An old will.

She sank onto the tapestry-covered stool in front of the dressing table and read. I, Blandina Tyler, etc. To wit, etc. Sound mind, etc. She was quiet for so long that Sister Seraphina peeked in to see if Temple was still working.

Temple glanced at her with wide eyes, then went back to reading. Seraphina came and read over her shoulder.

"What is it?" Peggy Wilhelm asked from the doorway, her hands trailing more of the stockpiled support hose.

Temple jumped. "I found—"

"It's a will, Peggy," Seraphina said.

Peggy moved into the room, her face flushed from hours of housework. "A will?"

"An old will," Temple said gently. "From the sixties." She held it out to Peggy.

Peggy took and read it by the dim light of the single ceiling fixture. Temple and Sister Seraphina waited, having no right to say anything until Peggy knew what they already did.

"But . . . this names me as the sole heir. To everything. I don't understand. I was . . . in my twenties then."

Temple rose to go to her, but Sister Seraphina's staying hand held her in place.

Peggy shook her head, then sat down on the edge of the nearby bed, onto which Sister Seraphina's steadying hand guided her.

"My parents had died," Peggy added with dawning insight. "I was alone by then. I—I didn't know Aunt Blandina ever cared that much."

"She did," Sister Seraphina assured Peggy. "And here's proof."

"She didn't have the cats then—" Peggy said slowly.

"She was a lot younger," Seraphina reminded her. "Perhaps more sensible. As we age, we get . . . peculiar. It's true. My dear, Pilar was making us a lunch. Let me run next door and get it. You read this over. It's a gift, Peggy. A gift from the past. Accept it, and let it go."

Sister Seraphina left, an obvious believer in the efficacy of food easing shock. For Peggy Wilhelm was in shock; Temple saw that, and seeing that, she wished that the will was dated nineteen ninety-four. Apparently, Peggy had never accepted being left out of her aunt's will as philosophically as she had pretended.

Temple, however, was now alone with the stunned woman, not a comfortable position for a public-relations specialist who liked to put the best face on things.

"Sister is right," she found herself saying. "Here's proof that your aunt didn't discount her only living relative. She just got caught up in caring for the stray cats and became obsessive."

Peggy scanned the pages of the will again and again. Then her face crumpled like old support stockings. "Oh, Temple, you don't understand—you can't understand what this means to me."

"I understand that you realize you were not always left out."

"No!" Peggy squeezed Temple's hand, forcing her to kneel beside her. "I can't tell Sister Seraphina, but—" Her free hand stroked her forehead, as if to install order within her cluttered mind. "Temple—! Oh, this is astounding. You don't know, and Sister Seraphina can't, she wasn't anywhere near this convent then. I *lived* with Aunt Blandina in nineteen fifty-nine, for almost a year. Here, in this house, before the . . . cats."

"You came to stay with her?"

Peggy nodded.

"You attended Our Lady of Guadalupe Church?"

Peggy nodded. "Yes, for a while."

"A while?"

"Until it was a scandal," Peggy said in bitter tones. Her muddy brown eyes met Temple's. "I was pregnant," said this fifty-year-old woman with grizzled gray hair. "I was fifteen years old and pregnant. I was sent to Aunt Blandina's by my parents, so no one around home would know. Another city, a scandal twice removed: me and the baby."

"Oh, Peggy, I'm so sorry."

"You don't know what it was like back then. So hush-hush. So much shame." Peggy pursed her lips as she folded the will shut. "Such grim business. Clandestine arrangements. I even had the baby in this house to avoid a public record, to quash suspicion. A Mexican midwife." She smiled weakly at Temple's shocked face. "It was an easy birth, I was only fifteen. The baby was fine—and whisked away to some clandestine adoption process. A good Catholic home was promised. Infertile parents who ached for a baby. Mine."

"Peggy—!"

"It had to be. They were all so disappointed. I was such a good girl, such good grades in school. They didn't want to know who, or why. I was such a good girl."

"You are," Temple said blindly, wishing for Sister Seraphina back, for Matt, for someone who knew how to talk to broken hearts, yet understanding that her very own age difference and religion gap made this confession, this release, possible.

"Now people are more realistic about it," Peggy said. "Then was the Dark Ages. It must be kept quiet at all costs. I was to forget it. My . . . my baby."

Temple had never felt more inadequate. She had never had a baby. She had not got religion. She was talking to Peggy from the dark side of the moon as far as experience was concerned. The only loss she knew was Max's disappearance.

"Did you . . . ever try to find the baby?" Temple whispered.

Peggy shook her head. "I tried to forget, like they all told me to. I thought they hated me. I thought they never forgave me. I even grew angry with Aunt Blandina, my keeper, and her cats. She couldn't keep my baby, but she could take in cat after cat in the years afterward. We never spoke of it, and my parents had died so soon after, only seven years. They left everything to her, to Aunt Blandina, at their deaths. I thought that was . . . punishment. I didn't want to speak of it, think of it, find anybody! But . . . cats. Eventually, I created cats, bred cats. I don't know why."

"Maybe the cats were your aunt's way of making up for letting that child go," Temple said. "Maybe they're your way of having something that depends on you." Maybe Midnight Louie was a Max substitute, right?

"She did care about you, even after it was all over," Temple forged on. "Look, Peggy, this will is dated after you said all of this happened. You were her sole heir then. She did care. Only, like Sister Seraphina said, she got old and . . . queer."

Peggy folded the will against her breast, like a baby. "Can I . . . keep this?"

"Sure. But let me copy it first. I guess we've got to keep a record. I'll get it back to you."

Peggy's troubled face threatened rebellion, then subsided as Temple gently tugged the will from her grasp.

"Don't tell Sister Seraphina," Peggy begged her. "Don't tell anyone."

"No," Temple promised. "I won't."

But she was almost as troubled as Peggy. Somehow, she was sure, this discovery of the old, forgotten will altered every assumption anyone had made about Blandina Tyler's death, including those of Lieutenant C.R. Molina.

Chapter 31

Curious Confessions

Louie still wasn't home when Temple checked in again, but Caviar was reclining on the sofa looking especially pleased with herself.

Temple untied and kicked off her metallic sneakers and settled beside the cat, stroking its silky head. Caviar had longer, finer hair than Louie, but her wise silence made her as good a thinking companion as the larger cat.

"Louie isn't boycotting us, is he?" Temple ruminated aloud. "I hope I didn't send him over the edge by bringing you home."

Caviar's purr was soft and steady, unlike Louie's sometimes rough and rowdy one. It made an ideal background of "black noise" for Temple's darkening thoughts.

What a quandry! Should she inform Lieutenant Molina of the newly found will, which was far too old to affect the current will, but which might point a suspicious finger at

Peggy? It proved, at the least, that at one time Peggy had been the principal heir. Despite Peggy's gratified and even touching surprise at the discovery, it did not escape Temple that Peggy could have playacted that reaction, that she could have known years ago that she was an heir. That would mean that she might not have accepted her aunt's new resolve to endow the cats—at least not with the equanimity she apparently displayed.

Then there was the matter of Peggy's forgotten past. Temple twirled her finger into a lock of Caviar's ruff and frowned. Unwed motherhood still was not something to shout from the rooftops, but such young women today had many more options: they could keep their child and finish school. They could have an abortion, depending on where they lived and if parental consent was required, and if required, was given. They could bear the child and give it up to adoption.

In Peggy Wilhelm's day—the end of the fifties—unwed pregnancy was such a scandal, particularly in religious families, that she'd had only one choice: bear the child in shame and as much secrecy as possible, then give it up and forget it as quickly as possible.

Temple kicked her sock-clad foot against the sofa base, startling the droning Caviar, who flattened her ears back and moved down the sofa.

No avoiding it, Temple thought. Peggy Wilhelm could have been nursing a thirty-year-plus grudge against the aunt who helped her parents stage-manage the situation. Did she resent being forced to give up and give away the child? What about an aunt who now felt no responsibility to anyone or anything but her stray cats? Had Peggy come to resent her so bitterly, along with her devotion to the cats, that she attacked her own Birman to divert suspicion and eventually caused her aunt's "accidental" death? She was in the house that night. Motive and opportunity, as they say on TV.

Temple sighed again, driving Caviar a few inches farther down the sofa seat.

She had promised Peggy not to tell Sister Seraphina. But

not Lieutenant Molina. Yet the suspicion was so farfetched, and Blandina Tyler's death could be so innocuous. Old people are prone to debilitating, even fatal, falls.

The phone calls to Miss Tyler and Sister Mary Monica showed the workings of a sick mind, but anonymous callers were the least likely to act out their fantasies, whatever they were.

Or was Peggy Wilhelm shredding slowly through the years? Did she blame the church and her aunt for her disgrace and loss of self-esteem, especially now that attitudes were becoming more enlightened and less censorious?

The last question Temple confronted was the thorniest. She had been confided in. She had, in a sense, received a confession. She had promised not to tell one specific person; did that bar her from telling others?

Temple hashed the matter over until it was so shopworn she could hardly tell one end of the argument from the other.

One thing was clear: Blandina Tyler's intentions were not as cut-and-dried as everyone assumed. Another unavoidable clarity also tugged at Temple's mind and conscience for attention after the day's cleaning expedition: Blandina Tyler collected more than unwanted animals—string, stamps, stockings, maybe even . . . wills.

At four in the afternoon, Temple rattled around the apartment one last aimless time in search of Louie. Nothing. She put on her shiny sneakers and decided that since she had snooped in a dead woman's house, she might as well compound her sin and go snoop in a live man's apartment.

She slipped up the steps in rubber-soled silence and down the curving, dim corridor one floor above until she came to the short hall that led to Matt's door.

She had never been here—had never been invited—but she knew from the number of his unit, Eleven, where it had to be. Right above hers. The carriage lamps beside the doors were kept on day and night, not only for a homey touch, but because there was no daylight in this cul-de-sac.

For the first time, it struck Temple that the Circle Ritz's design, besides being forty years old and quaint, reflected the confidence of a simpler, crime-free time. These private entrances were isolated, and possibly more dangerous than desirable for that reason.

Temple recognized the beige cardboard in the brass frame beside the doorbell as the back of a ConTact card. "MATT DEVINE" was printed on it in ballpoint in the measured block letters of someone who has been carefully taught to be legible in matters of public record.

She rang the bell, surprised to hear the muffled yet mellow *ding-dong* from within; she had never heard another resident's bell, except Electra's, which was different, being in the penthouse.

Matt answered it, looking rumpled in a beige T-shirt, Bermuda shorts and bare feet.

"Were you sleeping?" Temple asked guiltily.

"No, but I, ah, didn't get to bed until seven this morning." He glanced at his watch. "Did we have an appointment for a lesson? I don't doubt I forgot—"

"No, no. I'm not up to making like Sue Jujitsu today anyway, but I wondered—"

He stepped back, opening the door and looking reluctant. "Come in. It isn't much, or rather, I haven't done much with it."

Temple stepped over the threshold, feeling the move was momentous. A person's rooms could tell you a lot about the resident.

She glanced around, trying to look as if she was not. Bareness hit her like a heat wave: bare wood floors, bare French doors and windows, a secondhand sofa bare of pillows. Bracket-mounted bookshelves mostly bare of books and knickknacks. Boxes serving as tables, or simply clumped here and there as if clinging together for company.

"I'm not used to providing my own decor," Matt admitted with a shrug, ruefully eyeing his warehouse landscape. "And then, I'm not sure how long I'll stay in Vegas."

Temple tried not to look startled. Of course Matt would

stay; she was far too interested for him to just fade away on her and move on. And of course her feelings and wishes had nothing to do with what he wanted to do, and would do.

So her sudden pall of disappointment as she stepped into the room so exactly like her own, but so much emptier, was not because of the blank slate of his surroundings, but due to the General Unpredictability of Anyone, which led her back to her conundrum.

"Have a seat." Matt gestured to the black-and-tan plaid sofa, wisely selected to conceal dust, dirt and wear and tear, then corrected himself, "Have *the* seat."

He sat on a piled pair of wooden crates.

"I'm sorry to bother you, but I'm disturbed about something I can't see around."

"What's that?" he asked, instantly interested. Problems did not dismay him; in fact, they were a kind of security blanket, Temple saw. As long as he could concentrate on someone else, he wouldn't have to look too much at himself.

"I know something about somebody nobody else does," she said, realizing she sounded slightly childish.

"And you're trying to decide whether to go into blackmail or not?"

She wasn't in the mood for humor. "I'm trying to decide if I'm obligated to keep it to myself—or the opposite."

"Why is your knowledge a problem?"

"It's about someone involved with Blandina Tyler."

Speculation ruffled Matt's face like wind on water. "You're usually one to unearth information, not suppress it. Why does this instance bother you?"

"It's . . . very personal, and it's sad, and the person just poured it out to me because I happened to be there at a critical moment."

"Isn't that what crack gumshoes love?"

"I'm not a professional, Matt. I'm not even a dedicated amateur. I can't help it if I keep . . . finding out things about people. And this is so remote, so farfetched—"

"Nothing about a possible murder is farfetched."

"I know. That's why messing around in one can do so

much damage. And this person has been damaged enough."

Matt's brown eyes grew as distant as such a warm shade can manage. "We're all damaged enough," he murmured as if thinking of someone else. "By the age of three," he added ruefully. His gaze snapped back to her, sharp and intent. "Look, I'm in the same boat you're in, only my silence has been invoked on professional grounds. I'm still uneasy about it."

"Someone confessed to you?"

"In a manner of speaking. It's not official, but ethically my hands are tied, so I guess I'll just keep sitting on them."

Temple felt her eyes widen and her voice lower. "Matt, do you suppose we're both talking about the same person?"

"I doubt it," he said dryly, "but you've got me awfully curious about who your confider is. You aren't bound by the confessional, Temple. You're free to serve your conscience or your civic duty or your instincts—"

"Or my curiosity," she finished in brittle tones. "Why do people keep telling me things?"

He laughed at her exasperation. "You don't seem like you'll harm them."

"That could make me the most dangerous of all," she said.

He nodded. "Let's hope none of your 'confiders' figure that out, especially if your suspicions are correct."

"Oh, I don't know. I don't seem to be doing much of anything right lately."

"Why do you say that?"

Temple lifted her hand and then let it fall despondently to the sofa cushion she was sitting on. "Oh, Midnight Louie's been gone for a long time. I'm afraid that it's that Humane Society cat I brought back from the cat show."

"You're not surprised about that?" Matt sounded shocked. "No, Louie wouldn't like that. Cats are very territorial."

"But she's such a little darling, and all black, too."

"Color coordination does not soothe the savage beast when his territory is involved. Is she spayed?"

"Not yet."

"Then Louie might overlook the obvious, but you could end up with kittens on your hands."

"Just what I don't need. Poor Caviar! I don't know what to do. Maybe I can find another home for her. Louie will come back, won't he?"

Temple's voice took a sudden, husky dive as she contemplated driving Midnight Louie off for good by bringing a rival home.

Matt watched her for a long moment, looking shocked again. Then Temple realized how much her fears of Louie's desertion echoed her earlier desertion by a black-haired, much bigger, two-footed male roommate—Max Kinsella. Only this time, she may have brought it on herself.

"I'll get the other cat out of the place as soon as possible," she swore, already distracted from her moral dilemma.

Matt proved what a superbly insighted counselor he was by forbearing to point out that it might be too late.

Chapter 32

Cross-examine Not the Cat

I take a long, long walk while I count the follies of my youth.

Then I take an even longer stroll while I enumerate the follies manufactured during my middle age. This brings me up to the present day, and by chance to my old stomping grounds, the Crystal Phoenix Hotel and Casino.

Though it is the usual hot day—say a hundred and ten in the shade—a cold chill has me in its icy grip. When the precocious Caviar, aka Midnight Louise, inquired where I was going, I told her I had business of a spiritual nature to conduct. She looked the usual dubious, so I informed her importantly that I am working on a case involving the welfare of hundreds of cats, and that I cannot be expected to sit around and chat with some wet-behind-the-ears upstart.

Perhaps I was hard on the little doll, but I had to get out of there and think. Never have my past sins come back to haunt me so unexpectedly. In fact, I have never thought of my past activities as sinful until I have seen what my devil-may-care ways have wrought: an utterly unnatural female feline. Obviously, this misguided young doll is in desperate need of a protective male influence. In the past, I have regarded a protective male influence (mine) in a completely different light. Now I am saddled with the sudden responsibility of a . . . sire.

No doubt scads of my unacknowledged—even unconsidered—offspring run to and fro in Las Vegas. However, I have never confronted one in the flesh and fur before. This new, mature responsibility gives me the willies. It is as if I have seen my own ghost; in a sense, I have.

I slip around the side of the Crystal Phoenix and to the lush landscape between the hotel's two embracing white-stucco wings out back. Broiling tourists turn French-toast brown around the light-dappled pool, but I ignore the roar of the crowd and the smell of the grease—cocoa butter—with which they are well basted.

Under the tall calla lilies I shift like a shadow until I reach my Walden Pond, my still, mysterious center, my place of contemplation and retreat.

Carp glide just beneath the pond's shining surface—a golden argosy of glittering scales and tender, hidden flesh. Also orange, black, blue-and-white, et cetera. These carp are very showy fish, especially when they are called koi.

Yet even their flashing fins do not distract me from my black mood. I think over my options and decide that the only noble course is to proceed to the scene of the crime and redouble my efforts to save the orphaned cats. When a dude is down and out due to some domestic upset, there is nothing like hard work to clear his brain and conscience. Well, there is nothing like work.

Who knows? According to recent events, some of these abandoned felines may be my kin. In fact, if I tote the mathematical odds of my lifelong activities of the procreative sort, *most* of them may be kissing cousins to a carp-lover of my all-too-close acquaintance.

Day has turned to dark by the time I arrive at the residence in question. Not only does the lack of light match my mood, but it suits my investigative m.o. This "m.o." stands for a fancy Latin phrase, "modus operandi," which I believe has something to do with computer communications and cool operators like myself.

I am determined that these household types will not elude my incisive questioning this time, even if I have to resort to my incisors, which are sometimes called "canines," a lousy word to hang on a fellow of another species entirely.

I have overheard a good deal about this case, one way or another. In addition, I am the recipient of the mystic Karma's confusing hodgepodge of clues. Most of these latter are closer to chopped liver than useful hints, but one incoherent bit has got me thinking. This is not always easy to do, especially when I am under a severe personal strain. I have not even had a chance to publicly spurn my Free-to-be-Feline in more than twenty-four hours.

If my hunch is right, I am on the trail of a twisted and complex plot combining revenge and larceny that has been hatched by a thoroughly despicable, twisted and complex person. If my hunch is not right, at least I can pick up a little Midnight snack later during my investigations.

I belly-crawl down the sandy space between the Tyler domicile and the neighboring house of holy repute in the approved U.S. Marine boot-camp manner. I am as silent as anyone whose delicate underbelly (and lots of it) is doing the equivalent of fire-walking over an emery board. Then I slip through the secret entry and work my way into the heart of the house.

Along the way, I find the usual buffet rest stops—Tin Pan Alley with hors d'oeuvres. Once I have dined, I reconnoiter the premises. I am happy to discover that the residents are in a restless state of mind. The uneasy witness is always more forthcoming.

Now the residents do not pooh-pooh my interest in the case, preferring to leave it to "the authorities," but bend my ears back with tales of things that go bump in the night. So many of them swirl around me, each with his own tale to tell—not to mention tails whipping past my kisser—that I do not know where to begin.

Settle down, I tell them. I did not bring a notebook. After I swear that their testimony is for my ears only, the conjunctive caterwauling begins:

Oh, whines a red tabby with a cream shirtfront, we have been unable to get a wink of sleep, with all the comings and goings, day and night.

That is what you have to expect in a house that has been visited by violent death, I reply.

But, purrs an attractive Russian Blue who has unfortunately been rendered sexless, that is the point. We have been visited repeatedly by someone who is obviously Up to No Good.

How, I ask, does she know?

She does not know, only has "a suspicion."

I harbor a strong suspicion that even when Miss Tyler's dependents are willing to talk, little of any worth will be forthcoming.

Who, I demand, has been in the house since last I visited?

That nice old lady from next door, volunteers a petite tiger stripe.

I ask for a description and get it: navy coat, silver head-markings, and a strange, translucent appliance sitting on the bridge of the nose.

Apparently these benighted feline fools are unaware that they are living cheek by cowl with a nunnery. This description could cover any one of the old dolls next door, none of whom are suspects in my book, pardon the nun pun. (Anyone who is familiar with the intricacies of my first case, the Wreck of the Remaindered Editor, is aware that such homophones as "none" and "nun" can be critical clues, but in this case, they are mere wordplay.)

A Great White cruises past me—all white, all muscle and, luckily, fully neutered—and informs me that Delicate Heels has also been back. This does not surprise me, though Miss Temple Barr's flagrant infidelity of late is getting harder and harder to take. First there is the black banshee camped in the middle of my pied-à-terre, who unknowingly claims an intimate connection to yours truly. Second, there are Miss Temple Barr's long absences while she cavorts by the pool and elsewhere with Mr. Matt Devine. I am not against some moderate, healthy exercise, but not at the neglect of family and friends. Then there is my little doll's skipping off to venues where dozens of my kind convene, such as the cat show, and last but not least, this entire house full of unclaimed cats panting for a new full-meal deal.

So pardon me if I am not enthralled by the praise heaped upon her from several dozen honeyed throats, all with an eye on a new home, sweet home. Mine. I almost snicker to imagine them encountering the current inhabitant. Let them match switchblades and repartee with the hard-as-snails Caviar and see how well they do!

I also hear tell of other visitors. "Birman Breath" is not highly regarded by the crew, most of whom are not pedigreed and are highly scornful of such pampered creatures and their personal pamperers. The description—grizzled-head female, portly and often leopard-spotted or tiger-striped—puts me in mind of Miss Temple Barr's hapless contact at the cat show, whose prize-winning entry was savaged by a dog clipper.

I perk up. I did not know for certain that the cat with the new punk haircut was a Birman. I picture Karma shaved to the skin in a two-inch swath from eyebrow hairs to tail tip, and once around the middle. The effect is both amusing and demystifying.

The description of the most mysterious visitor proves to be the most provocative also. The particulars vary from witness to witness, perhaps gaining embellishment with repetition, but I think that at last I am on the trail of the villain who did such violence to Peter the convent cat.

As the residents tell it, this person is a monster indeed: dresses in my colors from head to toe to mitts, including soft-soled shoes that do not smell of natural materials, such as leather. A faceless, hairless tan head. Sex undetermined.

I favor the male, and—given the black—either a burglar or a . . . priest.

This person has come and gone surreptitiously outside the house since before Miss Tyler's demise, a shy and elderly cream confides:

Since her death, the Great White puts in gruffly (this ex-he is evidently boss around here), this same person has become an intruder. He seems to be looking for something.

What of the night of her death? I ask.

Here there is a marked difference of opinion. Most of the witnesses were sleeping. It is only since their mistress's absence that they have become nervous by night and day, and notice more. Before, the only people around out of doors were repair persons and the like.

The quiet cream claims to have glimpsed the intruder's legs running down the stairs after Miss Tyler fell.

I ask why this news was not forthcoming on my last visit.

After an awkward silence, the cream confesses that the assembled residents "did not know whether to trust an outsider or not."

Just such an attitude, I remind them testily, has led to much grief for the great sleuths of history, from Sherlock Holmes up to my personal favorite, Seymour Katz, the Peoria P.I. whose exploits in *Undercover Agent* magazine I have followed since I was a kit.

Where, I ask them next, has the intruder been intruding about the house?

After an unclear chorus of replies, I get the gist: upstairs, downstairs and in my lady's chamber.

I decide to investigate the same turf and so I trot upstairs first. Naturally, the crime scene is a mess. It has been tainted by Lieutenant Molina's scene-team, which has laid a trail of unnatural chemical substances over everything. Then a convention of handy helpers has been through, among whom I recognize the subtle scent of my own little doll, which is music to my nose, unless she happens to be confusing a crime scene, which she is.

I trot down the fatal stairs, observant for any telltale traces. I see nothing but the expected cat hair gathering into dust bunnies here and there.

Finally, on the first floor again, I am struck by something one of the witnesses said. "Downstairs," I repeat in a contemplative monotone. "Is this downstairs, or is there more below?"

The Great White finds this question too obvious to answer, but a half-grown black-and-white with a freckle on his pink nose steps forward to say that a further set of steps beckons beyond the kitchen.

There I go, to find a painted wooden door handily ajar.

They are not allowed down there, the cream cautions in a quavery voice. The Great White sneers and says that doesn't mean that some of them have not been down there plenty.

I am not fond of basements. They are dark, damp, spider-webbed, crammed with old, forgotten junk, and usually escape-proof. Luckily, they are rare in Las Vegas, except in the older houses, of which this is one.

It occurs to me that others may have overlooked the basement, too. If people are searching the house, whether honestly or clandestinely, it behooves me to do so as well. I growl a warning to the others to remain upstairs, no matter what happens, and I trot down the dark stairs.

Ugh. Painted wooden treads, with those nasty black-rubber safety covers tacked on. Nothing says "dirty, dank, possibly haunted basement" to me like that shifty stairway to the lower depths.

My eyes adjust slowly to the eternal twilight here. Contrary to legend, my kind's sight is not keenest in the dark. My ears and super-sensitive whiskers serve me better. I hear a clink and a scrape in the farthest, darkest corner.

I slink in that direction, waiting for my fabled night vision to adjust and let me detect a scintilla of difference between darkness and shadow. Apparently my fabled night vision is waiting for another legend, the Robert E. Lee.

Before I reach the corner, I hear a single, grinding step.

A full moon of light beams into my bedazzled pupils, which slit tighter than the eye of a needle unreceptive to camels and rich men like the late, great Aristotle Onassis. Even as my vision adapts to the blinding glare, a pair of dark, shapeless human mitts looms toward me, bearing something white like a wadded-up, wet diaper.

"A black cat! Perfect for the church door on Friday," intones a voice more distant than the announcer in a bus station. I see nothing but my approaching doom in the form of a wet, white cloud.

The revolting material is slapped across my kisser. At first I think I smell Pampers, but the odor is heavier. I struggle, claws boxing the air. I snag something—cloth, and then I am swaddled like an infant in a tough outer fabric that my flailing limbs tear at but cannot escape.

As I involuntarily slip into Lullabye Land, I recognize the means of my capture: the storied cloth soaked in sleep-inducing chloroform that P.I. Katz is always encountering—and the equally fabled, and feared, burlap bag. Could it be that Louie is going for a Midnight swim?

Chapter 33

The Fur Flies

Temple, still despondent and now feeling guilty, in addition, entered her foyer without enjoying the usual glow her smart accommodations gave her.

Worse, Caviar acted agitated from the moment Temple returned from Matt's apartment, as if the cat knew that her fate—not to mention her reproductive future—had been decided.

She had been pacing the living room when Temple had peeked in, and she'd resisted all attempts to be picked up and calmed, despite her earlier docile behavior. Now she was yowling, regarding Temple with piercing owl-gold eyes and regaling her with even more piercing cries.

Temple just couldn't ship her off to the vet's, but she had to isolate her in case Louie returned. She wrestled Louie's cat carrier from the front storage closet, then struggled to push Caviar inside, feeling like a monster. Caviar complained in a soprano shriek en route, and even more loudly once locked inside.

Temple showered Caviar with soothing chirrups as she left the carrier in the kitchen, feeling like she was waving a cheery toodle-oo to Sidney Carton on the way to the guillotine.

Temple frowned. The cat's reversal of behavior was most odd, almost as if she were . . . well, upset about something. Had Louie come home?

In a lather of guilt and urgency, Temple began to search the premises. Perhaps now that Caviar was corraled, Midnight Louie would deign to show himself. She looked under the bed, in the darkest reaches of the bedroom closet, behind the bathroom doors, atop the office bookcases, under the desk, behind the green plant, on the dining-chair seats in one corner of the living room. No Louie anywhere.

Finally, she went back into the kitchen and opened every cupboard. The only track of a cat she found was an overturned Finny Frosties box. Caviar's yowls reached operatic heights. Glumly, Temple righted the box and turned back to the room.

Her eyes fixed on the feeding bowls as her mind mused on the tale of two kitties: Caviar's Free-to-be-Feline was nibbled down to the bowl's bare bottom. Louie's was . . . what was Louie's? Temple certainly couldn't see the untouched mound of food beneath the newspaper tented over it.

She snatched up the newsprint like a magician expecting to reveal . . . missing Free-to-be-Feline, proving Louie had been here, and even recanted. All was forgiven, he was just hiding—

The Free-to-be-Feline rose to its customary heights. But, Temple realized, that didn't prove that Louie had not been here. Unless the newspaper. . . .

She looked at the open pages and saw for the first time the fine print of the Classified Ads section. Was this a mute message from Louie? For instance, was it opened to the "Pets" section, implying that he was off in search of a new home?

No, the top page was the first page of the Classified section. All that was on it were strange self-help group and service ads that sounded vaguely illegal—such as for piercing parlors—and, of course, the obituaries.

Of course. Temple skimmed the entries, horrified to read of a thirty-six-year-old man who had succumbed to a heart attack and a twenty-nine-year-old woman who had perished from an unspecified long illness. Good thing that she didn't peruse these things daily. It was a lot less safe out there than one realized.

Yup. Blandina Tyler had an entry, sans photograph, a scant two-inch listing of name, address, birthplace, former occupation—nurse—date and place of funeral: 10:00 A.M. Friday at Our Lady of Guadalupe. Suggested charities: Our Lady of Guadalupe and the Humane Society.

What did this obituary say, if it had been left as a message, which was ridiculous, because Louie couldn't read, no matter how smart he was. Yet Caviar had been so agitated . . . and now she was strangely silent. Temple glanced at the carrier to see a sober feline face following her every move with unblinking intensity. The words came into her mind as if seeded there by some supernatural agency and now bursting into full, logical bloom: Blandina Tyler. Funeral. Tomorrow. At the church so conveniently close to Blandina's own door, just down the street. Address.

Temple folded the paper. This was silly. She just had a feeling, and it had nothing to do with finding the Free-to-be-Feline under an Obituary section, as if the absent cat had meant to imply the stuff should be buried. Louie still couldn't read, not even to make a macabre joke. Yet only a cat could have batted the paper so neatly over the bowl. Caviar? Temple eyed the eerily quiet carrier again. Really, *she* couldn't read either.

Temple decided to check on the Tyler cats anyway. Peggy had given her a key. What good was a key if she couldn't use it?

First, Temple investigated her tote bag to make sure the Tyler house key was there—it was. She grabbed the big brass ring of her own keys, moved along the apartment's French doors to make sure they were latched, and went into the guest bathroom to be certain that Louie's high transom window was open so he could get in if—when—he came back.

Satisfied that the apartment was both secure against human invaders and still offered sufficient feline access, Temple went out the front door and locked it behind her.

If anyone saw her at the Tyler house and questioned her presence, she would say she was worried about the cats, plural. Mostly though, she was worried about the cat, singular. Very singular.

Temple had not counted on how creepy a house in which a person had died could look at night in a seedy neighborhood.

She stood beside the parked Storm, its cheerful aqua color now a flat charcoal gray under the faintly coral glow of the distant sodium iodide streetlights.

She knew that only cats moved in the dark, empty house in front of her, yet she remained reluctant to enter.

No rectangles of light checkerboarded the convent next door. Its windows at the side and rear were obscured by tall oleander bushes, except for Sister Mary Monica's second-story observation post, and she was probably abed by nine.

Temple jingled her huge key ring for the companionship of its familiar chime, then regretted the noise. Although she could claim that she was concerned about the cats, she couldn't explain her presence here in any really rational way.

The odds of Louie being inside, no matter how widely he got around, were nil. And this house had been the focus of unsettling phone calls and prowlers. However much Blandina Tyler's elderly and lonely imagination may have amplified these incidents, someone of ill will lurked at the edges of the events that had brought both Temple Barr and Matt Devine to Our Lady of Guadalupe.

Matt would consider her a bit looney if he knew she was standing here planning to enter a deserted house on the evidence of a disarranged newspaper and her own instincts.

Temple hitched up the tote-bag straps, straightened her shoulders and started up the walk. What did she have to lose? Still, she kept her weight on the balls of her feet, so her snappy red high heels wouldn't slap the sidewalk and alert someone who would question her right to be here—or alert someone else, who had no right to be here either.

Out of nowhere, the dark loomed up and ambushed her with a crushing sense of personal peril. A fist of fear squeezed her heart, making her pause to heed its wild pounding. The cooler night air chilled the goose bumps of sweat that had blossomed all over her body. She was alone in the dark in front of a house where someone had died a possibly premeditated, violent death. Suddenly the empty street and its distant lamps reminded her of a deserted parking ramp.

She dared not turn back to the curb to verify that her car stood there, alone, that she was not once again in that dangerous parking ramp, that two men were not even now behind her waiting to pounce and pound. . . .

No safety beckoned ahead, only the mute, dark house. The exterior entry light had long since burned out. She forced herself to walk to the doorway, every loud footstep a declaration of defiance. She couldn't let her recent beating turn her into a mouse. Temple's key scraped at the lock mechanism for many seconds, making surreptitious noises that she figured would attract at least a brace of Dobermans. On the other hand, a dog attack would be something different.

Nothing moved but a warm tease of breeze through the bushes. Sweat prickled Temple's scalp, and her heart still hammered.

Then the lock snicked and the door opened.

She slipped inside and quickly closed the door behind her to mask her presence, and to commit herself to the deeper dark before her. She stood there listening to the silence and the inner thunder of her circulatory system, then envisioned the daylit house in her mind and groped for the light switch beside the door.

Evidently Peggy, or Sister Seraphina, had lowered the air

conditioning now that only cats were in residence. The interior air was lukewarm, and thicker than ever with the smell of fur, fishy food and litter boxes.

Temple heard a thump deep within the house. A stirring cat, alerted to her presence, perhaps. She fumbled over the rough interior stucco wall for the switch and finally touched the plate's smooth, plastic surface.

Flick. Nothing.

That had happened somewhere else recently. Where? Ah, in Electra's entry hall.

Maybe this entry-hall light had burned out, too.

Temple kept her palm against the rough wall and moved forward by baby steps, wary of the many rag rugs waiting to trip the visitor in dark or daylight.

Her foot kicked something soft that scrabbled away. Not a rug, a sleeping cat.

"Sorry, kitty," she whispered.

Immediately her active imagination painted a room full of mortally insulted cats, schooling in the dark to wash over her until she tripped and fell among them. Then they would swarm her, their barbed tongues preparing the way for hundreds of feral, piranha-like teeth.

In the dark, even pussycats took on a sinister presence, especially if they were unseen.

Some light did penetrate the rooms as her eyes adjusted, but the dim, vaguely recognizable forms she saw only confused her more. Was that the edge of the refrigerator glimpsed through the dining-room archway—or the archway itself?

She tottered into the living room, leaving the safety of the perimeter. Her foot kicked something again, something heavy and inanimate that lay unmoving and didn't roll away when gently prodded. A dead cat?

Temple bent like a blind woman to pat the lump at her feet, not knowing what she would find, what she would touch.

A rag rug rolled into a cat-sized mass. She sighed and pushed it out of her way, starting at a shrill, hollow sound.

Oh, an empty tinfoil roaster pan, driven over the hard floor by the moved rug.

Maybe the cats did need more food; maybe that was the inexplicable instinct that had brought her here: a psychic cat chorus chanting for Yummy Tum-tum-tummy.

She edged into what she hoped was the kitchen, her arms flailing ahead of her, although it was her high-heeled feet that were in the most imminent danger of encountering obstacles.

Cats must have eeled away from her in the well-populated dark. She never felt another brush with anything animate or inanimate. When her shoes hit the kitchen's ceramic tiles, her tension eased. Surely a light would work in here, at Commissary Central. Peggy must come over for an evening feeding. She would instantly miss a burned-out light. Now, where was the switch?

Temple cruised the room's perimeter, moving her feet in a soft shuffle now and then accented by the *ting* of a kicked tinfoil pan. *Step, step, step, kick. Step, step, step, kick.*

Her first circuit was hard on her shins and revealed no light switch at the expected level. Was the central overhead light operated by a dangling cord? Temple couldn't remember that either. Amazing what you *don't* look at in an unfamiliar house.

So she shuffled her way to the presumed middle of the room and began swinging her right arm to and fro above her head, trolling for any dangling strings. Of course she could be too short to reach it, and her hand might be missing it by inches.

Frustrated, she edged around the room's perimeter again, checking under cupboards, behind the countertop microwave oven and the breadbox, which both smelled strongly of tuna fish.

Inspired, she clasped the refrigerator, working her way around the predictable bulk for the wall behind it that she remembered. Halfway around the behemoth, she became aware of something that told her it didn't matter if she found a light switch or not, something that chilled her blood.

The refrigerator did not vibrate with a low, throaty hum, although it could be temporarily at the off cycle. Still, every working refrigerator she knew exuded a clammy exterior chill. This one was as warm as hour-old dishwater. Her questioning hand found the handle, slightly sticky with—sniff—halibut halitosis, and cracked the door, her eyes reflexively squinting shut against the expected glare of the interior refrigerator light.

Nothing. When she finished her shuffle at the hoped-for wall behind it and patted her hand up and down in the dark, she was not even mildly exhilarated to finally find a light switch under her fingers. The button stood at attention: up in the "On" position, but no light prevailed. Electrically speaking, the house was dead.

Temple clutched her tote bag to her side for company—fully loaded, it was almost that big—and thought. Had the electric company jumped the gun and turned off the service? Had Miss Tyler's bill payments been delayed by her death and her power turned off? What about the cats? When had the power gone out? After Peggy Wilhelm's last feeding, but Temple wasn't sure when Peggy made her nighttime visits. Obviously, before it got as late and dark as this. Peggy would not want to be caught in a deserted house too late. Smart woman.

Well, Temple would just have to feel her way back to the front door and consult with Sister Seraphina next door on what to do now that the house was without power.

Or she could feel her way forward in the opposite direction, deeper into the house, where she now heard scuffling sounds that didn't sound like cats. Noises that sounded like feet, moving in the distance.

Sure.

Blandina Tyler was worried about her cats and had come back to take care of them.

Sure.

Temple tried to ignore the anxiety that sent prickles rushing down her arms, the numb disbelief reaching out to paralyze her mind.

She was alone in someone else's deserted house. Someone else, who was dead. Yet she could think of a half-dozen perfectly ordinary explanations for why another person—a concerned individual like herself, a neighbor, a caretaker, a cat lover, a congenitally curious idiot with a suicidal streak—would be in the house.

Perhaps Sister Seraphina had noticed the power failure and come over to investigate.

This theory seemed even more likely when Temple realized that the scuffling sounds were coming from below. Sure, a good old-fashioned Midwest basement! The house was old enough for one. And someone had gone down to check the electrical box because of the power outage.

It would be a bit embarrassing to explain her unannounced presence, but not impossible. She was glib in awkward situations—most of them, anyway. She could talk her way out of anything; what else was a P.R. person if not convincing?

Temple was not convincing herself.

She edged quietly closer to the sounds, down a back hall jammed, she remembered, with brown-paper grocery bags full of newspapers. And support hose.

Hadn't there been a door there, another back door? Or a door to the basement?

Now she heard a voice.

Singing.

Okay. Must be a repairman. Who else would sing in a basement in the dark?

"Heav-y dev-il," came the first lyric.

Singing heavy-metal music?

"Up and up we go, where we stop nobody knows but Jesus."

Temple cocked her head to interpret the singsong voice and the odd words. Jesus? Must be a nun from next door, checking on the house, but what kind of song—psalm?—was that? "Nobody knows but Jesus . . ." Familiar. An old spiritual. Nobody knows but Jesus—*Nobody Knows the Trouble I Seen!* Odd song for a Catholic nun.

Then the song changed, and was even odder for a Catholic nun to sing . . . unless she was an exceedingly odd Catholic nun.

"That old black devil got me in its spell, that old black devil that I know so well."

The voice was closer, but Temple couldn't tell the sex or the age any better. And the last words and melody were so familiar, too, but from another side of the compact disc to the first familiar phrase. Old black *magic!*

A streak of white magic suddenly outlined the door, edging it in a thin frame of light.

Temple retreated to the refrigerator, rounding its side to seek shelter just in time.

The basement door swung open until it smashed into the paper bags. Bright light bobbled around the back pantry in nervous shafts—a flashlight. A repairman would need a flashlight in a house with no power, she told herself. So would a burglar, her self talked back. Or a killer.

"*Baa, baa, black sheep, have you any wool?*

No, sir, no, sir, only old bags full."

The voice was so near, and it panted between the lines of the old nursery rhyme. Something thumped at the singer's rear.

Temple peered around the edge of the refrigerator.

The flashlight's erratic beam illuminated the pantry. A figure, humped and twisted, hunkered before the closed basement door. A big burlap bag lay on the floor, obviously filled with something.

Temple's horror-movie mentality filled in the blanks. Dirt from a basement grave? A pod person left by aliens? Dead cats?

No, live cats. The bag had moved, though the semi-human silhouette was turned away and did not see.

"Heav-y dev-il," came the singsong voice again as the figure turned to lift its burden. "You'll swing for it from the church door. *Pox vobiscum.*" A chuckle punctuated the gibberish.

Whoever it was bent over farther to hoist the bag up on

a shoulder, straighten to human height . . . and spot Temple.

Like a rabbit, she took off, through the dark and the cats, feeling things fly from her milling feet—tinfoil food dishes, water dishes (she felt her ankles splashed), surprised cat bodies.

She heard equipment—flashlight, bag, bowie knives, boomerangs, bullwhips, whatever—thump to the floor, and heard the softer thump of running shoes behind her. Like a jogger downtown, yeah, coming up from behind on the poor ordinary walker.

Temple's ankle crashed painfully into a barrier that would not give, twisting her foot until the high heel slipped sideways. A step. She didn't want to climb, but had no choice. Maybe she could find Sister Mary Monica's window and heave a brick through it; all right, heave her tote bag through it. Then she could scream out the open window, and by the time anybody came, the bogeyman from the basement would have ground her bones to powder.

Temple stumbled upward on her shaky heels, tripped and banged her knees on the steep steps. She was upright and running again before the pain registered. When her foot lifted and came down on level ground, she almost jolted herself into losing balance. Teetering on her high heels, she glanced back.

Darkness was rushing up the dark stairs. A shape like wind incarnate, as black as the night around it. No pale pattern of face or hands, just darkness.

Temple rushed down the hall, not wanting to bottle herself in a room but having little choice. She felt an open doorway and dashed through. She slammed the door shut behind her, knowing it wouldn't lock, and felt for something to drag across it.

At her back, the subconscious warmth of light beckoned. She found a trunk and pushed/pulled/kicked it in front of the door. It was heavy; maybe there was a body in it. Then she had to turn and see the light. Now *there* was a phrase for religious revelation—

She recognized Miss Tyler's vintage dressing table, saw it

clearly . . . fire was creeping across its dusty surface, up behind its round mirror, around its twin columns of drawers.

Fire! And in a house full of cats. Temple grabbed a small round rag rug from the floor and began beating at the dresser—top, bottom, behind. Flames flared from the wind, then sank at the first blows. The dark returned, and so did the sounds. The scrape of the trunk as it groaned across the wooden floor. Wooden floor—oh, no! The floor would catch like tinder and drop into the rooms below and turn this place into an inferno, and she was stuck on the second floor. Forget cats! What about her?

Temple cast away the smoky, charred mat and caught up another of the pesky rugs. They worked pretty good as fire dampers. The dresser, made of old, tough mahogany, was slow to catch flame. Temple continued to beat the flames down into the dark from which they sprang, thinking. The fire had not been meant to flare until the person who set it was out of the basement and the house.

Now that person was up here, with her. What to fight first? Fire, the unknown intruder or her own fear? She ran to the window, a blotch of gray beside the bed, grabbed the bedside table—a spindly, old-fashioned model that would probably splinter, she remembered—and hurled it at the window glass. Once, twice, three times until they shattered together, glass and wood.

In the dark of night, the sound was small, liable to be mistaken for a pint of whiskey dropped in an alley, or dogs overturning garbage cans again. In neighboring houses, television sets were blaring and windows were shut against the heat, air conditioners humming away and muffling all exterior sounds.

But some people in this neighborhood were too poor for central air conditioning, and their windows stayed open on a pleasantly cool, early autumn night—

"Fire!" she yelled, as instructed to do in case of rape. "Fire!" It really is!

Her answer came from behind, a white, suspended object

that closed in on her face like a wisp of cloud smelling of hospitals.

At first the wet coolness was a balm to her overheated face. Then the sickly odor seeped into her nostrils and some force kept it pressed there. Chloroform. And a fire. If she passed out now, she was French toast.

Lessons. Do the unexpected. Don't tense, relax.

She went limp, let herself sink, against all her instincts, into the unseen person behind her. Air, blessed air, slipped between her face and the encompassing cloth.

It was enough. She ducked, half falling, and spun to face her attacker, grabbing her tote bag by the handles and swinging it in an arc over her shoulder. At the same time, she kicked a heel into what she hoped was the right height for a knee.

Her bag connected with a solid something.

"Jesus Christ!" hissed a voice that was neither man nor woman, neither brute nor human. *Jesssusss Chrissst.* The caller! No face to recognize, only a burlap-sack mask over the head, glaring at her as expressionlessly as Jason's sinister hockey mask.

Temple's left hand was digging in her bag for the big brass ring and came up with keys bristling between every knuckle.

A strong hand grabbed the bag from her grasp, but she had ducked to the floor and now she felt with her right hand until it closed over a smooth wooden pin—one of the table legs.

She struck again at the shadow closing on her. Struck for the side of the neck and the carotid artery underneath the thin skin. Hit right, hit hard enough, and caused instant unconsciousness.

The impact jolted her arm and shoulder, even as she lurched to her braced feet. Matt would disapprove of the incapacitating high heels, but she hadn't had time to lose the shoes. She did now. The dark form had crumpled to the floor. She bent and snatched off her shoes, then glanced at the dressing table. It had flared again. The mirror, framed in tangerine curlicues, reflected a faint image of her own figure, her face haloed by wildly disheveled red curls. She resembled a barbecued cherub. This fire was getting too hot for her to handle, even with a rag rug.

She stepped toward the door.

A hand closed around her ankle.

Temple gave. Fell, still facing the half-open door with the trunk against it.

She turned and kicked out both stocking feet, as hard as she could, then leaned inward and struck out with the table leg, again and again, until it met resistance, until it knocked on bone and her ankle was free.

She scrabbled away, eeled out the door.

In the distance, someone screamed and kept on screaming.

She was sure it wasn't her. She was running downstairs in the dark, feeling soft, furred forms fleeing at her passage, like fish in an unlit tropical sea.

Oh, poor kitties!

The screaming grew louder and sounded like a siren.

She was at the bottom of the stairs when she heard their top echo to soft-thudding feet descending in a staccato beat.

Then she tripped. On level ground, and she tripped over another of those cursed rag rugs. She pushed it away, but it was heavy and . . . warm . . . and heaving and scratching.

The big front door heaved, too, and then groaned as something hit it from without. A few more crashing blows and solid wood splintered like veneer. The door broke open, swinging against the wall on screaming hinges. More horror-show effects: huge, clumsy figures filled the opening, backlit by lurid red.

Temple looked up the stairs. The shadow had stopped in the leak of red light, pinioned by the glare of the incoming firemen's powerful flashlights.

"Upstairs," Temple shouted. Two men charged past in heavy rubber boots, smelling of cinders. "Careful! That's a killer."

These men weren't the police, but they were armed against a bitter, flesh-eating enemy, fire, in body armor and with axes. Two thumped past her to collect the shadow, two thundered all the way up to confront the fire; another turned and stomped out again, perhaps to radio the police.

Beneath Temple, the burlap bag writhed and hissed as if housing a dozen snakes. Then it growled. Fascinated, the returning firemen, with the shadow in custody, stopped to watch, focusing their flashlights on the bag.

A portion of the burlap was soaking wet. It proved to be torn as well when a black snake shot out of a four-inch slit. A furry black snake. Temple squealed hoarsely and scrambled away.

The black snake retreated, to be replaced by a black muzzle.

Snarling, Midnight Louie boxed the bag until his shoulders and forelegs were through, then twisted and turned until the burlap was dragging from his hindquarters like a comical train. After a few more acrobatic antics, he finished delivering his bedraggled, nineteen-pound self from confinement.

Temple watched in admiring delight. "Louie! What are you doing here?"

"Are you all right?" A fireman plucked Temple up from the floor to her feet as easily as if she were a mislaid cotton ball. "You know this cat? What's going on here?"

Boots pounded down the stairs. "Fire's out. Arson."

"Can we get some lights on in here?" another big and booted man asked.

Footsteps pounded down the basement stairs behind a beam of powerful light.

In moments, lights blinked on around the house. The refrigerator burped into a happy hum again, and the distant air conditioner hiccoughed once, then began droning dully.

At Temple's feet, Louie growled and spit and tried to walk. He swayed like a drunken sailor and sat down suddenly, looking surprised and cranky.

"I think he's been drugged," Temple told the nearest fireman.

One of the men keeping the shadow in custody kicked at a white rag half out of the burlap bag. "Chloroform."

The fireman who had lifted Temple looked down at

Louie, then addressed his mate. "We better get this fire victim some oxygen pronto." He scooped up Louie and strode outside. Temple followed on shaky legs.

A crowd had gathered around the huge, light-flashing fire trucks. If Louie had intentions of clawing the fireman who carried him, he was foiled by the heavy, waterproofed slicker the man wore. *Thump-thump*, the word was passed. *Thump-thump, clump-clump*, a medic came to the front door with the needed gear.

Louie was pinned to the ground and treated, though he was not fond of the plastic mask and struggled as if his tomhood were in jeopardy. He didn't relish the flash photo that was taken of him under care, either, but he calmed down when he could sit up and breathe ordinary air again.

Temple frowned at the photographer, who wore a *Review-Journal* I.D. card. She wanted to know Louie's name, anyway.

"I hope I'm not in that photograph," Temple grumbled after providing the information. It did not behoove a P.R. person to irritate the press. "I must look a mess."

"Fire survivors often do," the woman noted dryly, moving away to take an overall shot of the crowd.

"What about the intruder?" Temple asked the firemen once the photographer was gone. She nodded toward the house.

"We're holding him for the police," said her fireman, who was young and freckled and struck her as fearless. "As is."

"Him? Are you sure?"

The fireman was amused by her incredulity. "Yes, Ma'am."

Temple thought about the suspect that assertion eliminated—Peggy Wilhelm—and breathed free again. She leaned toward the fireman, who didn't look too alarmed by a rescued maiden offering confidences.

"Couldn't we peek behind the mask before the police get here?" Temple whispered as close to his ear as she could get without hitting the hard and inconvenient fire hat. "I'm just dying to know who it is."

Chapter 34

The Bishop's Tea

"Temple!"

Sister Seraphina separated from the crowd and enveloped Temple in a big brown blanket that she definitely didn't need after so much exertion on such a warm night.

Temple was interested to know that formerly sleeping nuns wore voluminous navy-velour bathrobes that she had not seen the like of since a fifties' television sitcom. Sister Seraphina's bathrobe, especially with its long satin rope tied at the waist, more resembled Temple's notion of a habit than anything the nun wore in the light of day.

Sister Seraphina seemed unaware of her attire's fascination.

"When I heard that someone was found in there," she said, "I feared it might be Peggy—never you." She turned briskly to the identically clad woman behind her. "Sister Rose, you had better call Peggy Wilhelm and let her know.

She'll want to tend the cats—they're all right, aren't they?" she asked Temple in sudden anxiety. "What about this one?" She eyed Midnight Louie, who was remarkably content to sit at Temple's feet and groom his own, for the moment.

"That's not a Tyler cat; that's mine. He's been given some chloroform, but he's fine now. Sister, where is Father Hernandez?"

Sister Seraphina twisted to scan the crowd. "I . . . I don't know. Perhaps he was sleeping and didn't hear—"

Sleeping like Peter in the Garden, Temple thought grimly. Or perhaps he was not sleeping at all.

"Sister Mary Monica saw the flames from her bedroom window," Sister Seraphina went on, "so we called the fire department. And then we did call Lieutenant Molina. And Matt."

Temple grimaced. Sister Seraphina had mentioned the two people she least wanted to see in her current state. Fire survivors, she guessed, couldn't be choosers.

In fact, one of the firemen was stomping over. He arrived to request the same information the news photographer had: name, address, a short statement. Temple complied and then asked a question of her own.

"What about—?" she began, still seriously seeking answers, when tires squealed and an unmarked Crown Victoria pulled up behind the Storm, followed by a squad car.

Like the Red Sea parting for Moses, the crowd parted for Molina, her partner and two uniformed officers. Temple cringed when Molina's crowd-scanning glance spotted her. Molina rolled her eyes and did not pause, disappearing into the house with an escort of police and firemen.

A uniformed officer remained outside to disperse the crowd, which was reluctant to return to late-night TV talk shows when something much more interesting to talk about was happening live on their very own street. Grumbling, people straggled off.

"We live next door," Sister Seraphina objected when her turn came.

"You the nuns?" the officer asked.

Temple, still clutching her blanket, bristled, but nobody noticed.

"The lieutenant wants to speak to you later at the convent." He frowned and looked up and down the street, obviously not seeing anything that resembled his idea of a convent.

"We'll go quietly, Officer." Sister Seraphina turned Temple toward the convent.

"I'll carry Louie." Temple bent down to scoop up the cat in her blanket and almost didn't unbend again.

What a mistake. Even freshly oxygenated, Louie weighed as much as a potbellied pig.

"Wait!" Temple cried, remembering. "My tote bag's in that house."

"Your purse?" The officer frowned again.

"In the bedroom where the fire was started."

He nodded. "I'll check. If we don't need to impound it for evidence, you can have it."

"Evidence? Impound? My daily organizer is in there, my apartment and car keys. I'll be helpless."

"I'm sure something can be worked out—" he glanced uneasily at Seraphina, than back to Temple "—Sister, Ma'am."

"Oooh!" Temple protested as he walked away. "Do I look like a nun?" she demanded of Sister Seraphina.

"You look like a slightly scorched madonna-and-cat right now," Sister Seraphina said with a chuckle. "Come on. We'll get you some nice hot tea."

"I could use a nice hot toddy," Temple corrected.

Waiting in a convent visitors' room for Lieutenant Molina was not her idea of how to recover from severe physical and emotional stress. Carrying Midnight Louie wasn't an antidote, either.

She started to slog along the sidewalk with Sister Seraphina, her curiosity temporarily stanched and her stamina quashed. Another vehicle with a light on the top cruised to a stop by her car—a Whittlesea Blue cab.

Matt Devine took one look at her car and began running toward the Tyler house. The uniform stepped into his path; for an instant, it looked like a confrontation brewed.

"Matt, over here!" Sister Seraphina caroled. "We're all right."

He glanced at the Tyler house's ashen facade, which radiated red emergency lights, then started for them at a trot.

"Temple?" He anxiously searched her face, which was probably pale and smoke-smudged. "No one said *you* were here. And Midnight Louie! Are you okay? Really?"

"Well, I may have broken a nail or two—and Louie a claw, too."

"Let me take him."

Temple sighed relief when the nineteen-pound burden was lifted from her arms, which were shaking with strain for some reason possibly having to do with fighting off an arsonist—and maybe a murderer—only half an hour earlier.

Matt wasn't too enamored of Louie's bulk, either. He set the cat down as soon as the party was inside the convent door.

A yellow cat came to investigate—Peter or Paul—and the pair suspiciously sniffed noses, but no fireworks threatened.

"Come sit down, dear," Sister Rose urged in the kindly tones of a great-aunt, escorting Temple as if she were Belleek china.

Sister Seraphina was soon on their heels, but not Matt. At Temple's questioning look, she leaned near.

"I sent him to the rectory to see about Father Hernandez."

Temple let herself be shepherded into the overbearing visitor's chair. Sister Rose even scooted a needlepoint-covered stool under her feet, which naturally failed to reach the floor, then darted out of the room.

"Sister Seraphina," Temple beseeched, protesting as a needlepoint pillow—this one a tasteful scene of Christ in the Garden of Gethsemane—was inserted behind her back. She shrugged off the smothering blanket. "I'm fine."

"No, you are not. You've had a dreadful shock. As much as Matt might be reassured by your offhand remark about only breaking a fingernail, I can see that you've been through a good deal more than that."

"Well, yes, actually," Temple admitted, intimidated by Sister Seraphina's air of stern concern. "The awful man inside the house had Louie chloroformed and in a sack—God knows what he intended to do with him—and he had set the bedroom dresser on fire and I tried to stop the fire, and stop him, and I really put some good moves on him. I'm new at this, but I think I had him cold before the firemen came."

"So that's what Mary Monica saw," Sister Seraphina said with a sigh of relief, sitting heavily on a nearby chair. "I was a bit afraid for her sanity. She said she saw the Devil dancing with an imp in Blandina Tyler's bedroom while the fires of Hell burned around them."

"I was the . . . the imp?" Temple demanded.

"Apparently. Her eyesight is not the best, and you do look a bit disheveled. When Rose and I looked out the window, we saw only the fire, but we called nine-eleven from Monica's room-phone right then. Poor Mary Monica. She has been sorely tried these last few weeks." The nun's softened glance sharpened again. "Did you see the intruder?"

"Yes, but not without a burlap mask. The firemen are sure it's a he, though. I wasn't, not even when we 'danced.' I thought of Peggy—"

"Peggy? Rummaging through her aunt's house in the dark, in disguise? Why?"

"Well . . . the will we found. She might have been looking for another version, a later one that left her everything, too."

Sister Seraphina shook her head. "Not Peggy."

"You don't know Peggy like I know Peggy."

"What do you mean?"

"I can't say, but I had good reason to suspect her."

"Apparently good reason to suspect Father Hernandez as well."

"If the intruder was a man, he wore black."

"Lots of men wear black, not just priests. And would a priest up to no good wear the clothes of his calling?"

"He would if he were a little . . . demented."

Before Sister Seraphina could answer—and her face was full of doubt, even outrage, at Temple's suggestion—Sister Rose tiptoed back into the room with a small silver tray upon which sat a tall glass of iced tea.

Temple's heart sank. What she definitely didn't need now was iced tea. Sister Rose's watery eyes were too solicitous to refuse, however, and she braced herself to take a swallow of the dreaded, cold beverage while bravely repressing the shivers of aftershock that were threatening her composure.

She took a ladylike sip, then her eyes widened. This iced tea packed quite a kick.

Sister Rose leaned near. "We keep a little something in the brandy line for the bishop in case he might call."

"How much of a little something?" Temple whispered back in a raw voice.

"Well, I didn't know how much for tea, so I put in a juice-glassful."

"Oh," said Temple, who began to think that she might make it through this night, no matter how long and dreadful, after all, thanks to Sister Rose's heavy hand with the bishop's brandy. At least it wasn't the pastor's tequila. Temple couldn't stand tequila outside of a margarita.

"I thought Matt would be along by now," Sister Seraphina commented to the room at large. She glanced at the schoolroom clock mounted on the wall.

Temple was startled to see that it read only ten-fifteen. She felt as if midnight was long since past.

Sister Rose settled on a side chair and they all regarded one another nervously.

"Those are . . . wonderful robes," Temple said, for lack of anything else to offer.

She was pretty sure that Father Hernandez wasn't coming, for the simple reason that he was under police custody in the house next door. But . . . why? The church had received the Tyler estate, lock, stock and barrel of cats. Yet the pastor had seemed little pleased and not at all relieved by that fact. Whoever had done whatever had been done—and Temple was not at all sure of the extent or intent of it—would have interesting reasons.

Sister Seraphina picked at the satin rope tie of her robe, looking chagrined.

"A gift from a well-to-do woman in my last parish. She insisted that we old nuns must need something, and when I told her robes, she was ecstatic. She purchased twelve."

"Twelve." Temple was impressed by the parishioner's generosity. In lamplight, she was even more impressed by the robes' sober but lush quality.

Sister Seraphina shrugged. "She got them on sale. At Neiman Marcus."

Temple frowned, then started to laugh.

Sister Seraphina began chuckling. "They are very useful and quite durable, and probably cost the moon originally."

"What's Neiman Marcus?" Sister St. Rose of Lima inquired brightly.

"Just a department store," Seraphina said.

"Like Mott's Five and Dime?"

"Exactly," Temple said, shaking her head. She took a stiff sip of her tea and let her toes wiggle. Her pantyhose toes, she saw, were sprouting runs like weeds. "My shoes!" she wailed. "I forgot about my Italian-leather shoes. They're over there, too. The firemen probably soaked everything with water."

Sister Rose tsk-tsked in bewildered sympathy. Her faded pink terry-cloth scuffs were washable and had weathered several cleanings. Of course they were not Italian.

Sister Seraphina swiveled alertly to the hall. A moment later, Matt appeared in the doorway.

No one dared ask anything. Temple could see that he read their anxiety—at least hers and Seraphina's—but he could not guess the cause.

"Father Hernandez wasn't in the rectory," he said.

Temple and Seraphina settled back into their chairs with a mutual sigh and a significant look.

"Is it important?" Matt asked.

"It may be," Temple said. "Someone was in the Tyler

house. Someone had captured Louie and chloroformed him and stuck him in a burlap bag."

"Why?" Matt asked.

She went on wearily. "I don't know. Someone had started the house on fire in Blandina's bedroom."

Another voice added to the narrative. "Someone stopped him."

Lieutenant Molina appeared in the hall behind Matt, who quickly eased into the room to allow her entry.

Molina eyed the room's occupants, her glance pausing appreciatively on the nuns' robes before it rested on Temple and her libation.

"Apparently Queen Victoria here has been practicing her marital arts' p's and q's. She stopped him from setting the house afire and perhaps committing other violence." Molina sank down in one of the brocaded side chairs. "I could use some tea myself."

"We all could." Sister Seraphina nodded at Sister Rose, who scurried out like a dormouse on a secret mission.

Matt leaned on the edge of the desk near the door and watched them all, thoroughly perplexed.

"What exactly has happened?" he asked.

"My question precisely." Molina pulled out her notebook. "We have a rather . . . distraught . . . suspect in custody."

"Suspect?" Seraphina emphasized.

Molina nodded neutrally. "We have the professional detective's bane, Miss Temple Barr, on the scene and heavily involved. We even have an unauthorized cat on the premises, the equally baleful Midnight Louie. Where is he now?"

"Somewhere in the convent," Temple supplied.

"We found a burlap bag somewhat . . . damaged, and a cloth soaked in chloroform. Apparently it had been used on the cat."

"Peter!" Sister Seraphina sat up. "That's how someone captured him for that horrible attack; they chloroformed him. Was it satanists, Lieutenant?"

"You tell me. We found a satchel of . . . tools near the bag.

Hammer. Spikes. Looks like more of the same was on the schedule."

"Louie was a candidate for crucifixion?" Temple shuddered with a sudden chill and reached for the fallen blanket.

"Possibly."

"Has your prisoner said anything about that?" Matt asked.

Molina's blue eyes regarded him with the clear, emotionless stare of a Siamese cat. "Nothing . . . sensible. Yet."

The eyes returned to Temple. "I hesitate to ask this. I am not in the mood for original answers, but yours surely will be more coherent than his at this point. Why were you there?"

"Well," Temple began, "it was the state of Midnight Louie's Free-to-be-Feline that first made me uneasy . . ."

Molina shut her eyes, and Temple continued, glossing over the obituary page tented over Louie's dish and concentrating on her great specific and general concern for cats singular and plural, on her impulse to check on the Tyler cats, on her shock at finding an intruder and a fire in the house, and especially on her amazement at finding Midnight Louie in the bag.

"So it was all a wild coincidence," Molina summed up in a deadpan voice.

At that moment, Sister Rose appeared beaming on the threshold, a tray full of tall, iced-tea glasses in her hands, with Midnight Louie massaging her ankles as if begging for catnip.

"Sometimes things happen that way," Temple said as Sister Rose distributed the glasses.

They were accepted with distraction. Sister Seraphina took a large sip of her tea, then her lips puckered, but her face seemed not to register anything except the secret worry she carried for Father Hernandez. Lieutenant Molina's closed-mouth attitude to the identity of the man apprehended next door did nothing to allay her anxiety.

Molina let her glass sit on a side table as she poised her pen over the notebook but wrote nothing down, which was rather unsettling.

Matt sipped his tea politely, then braced it on one slack-covered thigh. "So Temple nailed the bad guy. Personally."

"Yes," Molina said in her disconcerting tone that was half-bored, half-mocking. "Do tell us about it."

"He found me in the kitchen," Temple began. "I didn't know he was there. The lights were off when I came in, and I was trying to find a light switch that would work when he came up from the basement—I didn't even know there was one!—dragging a bag. At first I thought he was someone from the neighborhood, or a repairman or something. Then he dropped the bag and went for me. I didn't want to go upstairs, but I ran into the stairs and was forced up. I tried not to get cornered in a bedroom, but there was nowhere else to go. I managed to drag a trunk in front of the bedroom door, and then I saw the dresser on fire. I threw a table through the window—"

"Good thinking!" Matt said approvingly, sipping his tea absently.

Molina watched him, and did likewise.

Nobody batted an eye. Sister Seraphina sipped her tea frequently and nervously, her face reflecting worries other than the specifics of Temple's ordeal.

Actually, it felt more like an adventure in the telling. Temple warmed up to her tale, or perhaps to her tea. She took a throat-soothing sip. "Well. There I was, caught between the devil and the deep blue sea." Here she glared at Molina. "He looked like a demon, all in black with a burlap mask over his face, only his eyeless eyeholes staring at me."

" 'His eyeless eyeholes'?" Molina queried, her pen skipping over the lined notepad.

"You know what I mean! And then, while I was fighting the fire with a rag rug—"

"A rag rug," Molina repeated in a tone of utter disbelief, her pen moving. She buttressed herself with a long slug of tea.

"—he got me from behind with a chloroform-soaked cloth."

"A chloroform-soaked cloth," Sister Rose repeated in awe, nodding and sipping tea with a broad smile. "You are a brave girl."

"I was smothering, and I knew that if I passed out . . . so I gave him his ground—" she looked at Matt, who nodded approval "—and it surprised him, just like it was supposed to. The cloth lifted enough for me to twist away and slug his upper torso with my tote bag while I jammed a heel into his kneecap."

"Sounds . . . quite athletic," Sister Seraphina commented, guzzling more tea.

Temple refreshed herself as well.

"Then . . . ." she hadn't had as rapt an audience in years ". . . I picked up a table leg and when he charged me again, I hit him hard on the carotid artery."

"Carotid artery?" Sister Rose repeated the phrase as if it were Latin. "Is that something nice girls should do?"

"Definitely not," Temple said. "He went down for the count of—say, six. That was long enough for me to get out of the bedroom and down the stairs. He tried to follow, but then the door opened and this huge, helmeted figure blocked the exit and the whole Las Vegas Fire Department came in—my knights in shining slickers bearing battle-axes—and saved me and snagged him and even gave Midnight Louie the breath of life."

After a pause, Molina said, "You realize that none of this makes sense."

"No," Temple agreed demurely, "but it's a hell of a tea-party story."

In the silence, Sister Rose giggled. "Poor Midnight Louie. Poor kitty. He should have some restorative tea." She poured part of her remaining half-glass into a huge glass ashtray—no doubt kept for the bishop's cigar if and when he came—and placed it on the floor before the cat, who was grooming himself within an ounce of his overweight.

"Cats don't drink tea, Rose," Sister Seraphina advised her.

Louie stopped his compulsive licking and tapped a paw in the dark amber liquid. He jerked his paw back and licked it experimentally. He cleaned his long, white whiskers of every last trace. Then he lowered his head and trailed his long, red tongue in the substance. He slowly settled into his haunches and began lapping rapidly at the tea, glancing up once at Temple but never pausing in his imbibing.

Everyone laughed, even Molina. In fact, Molina was looking a lot more mellow. Then she flipped her notebook shut and regarded them.

"This comedy of errors will prove to be more terror than error by tomorrow, I think. You all should know that the person I have in custody is someone who is intimately connected with this parish and has been for some time. You all will be shocked by the suspect's identity. I can't say exactly what's been going on here—I have a feeling some of you could say more, but won't. I can say I know the suspect's identity only because I am a member of this parish. Perhaps I suffer from conflict of interest on this case, but so do the entire lot of you."

She stood up. "I've got work to do. I suggest you all go home and examine your collective consciences. I'll be in touch. Count on it."

After Molina left the room, they were silent for a few seconds, staring at the floor and clinging to their damp-sided glasses of brandy-laced tea.

"Sister," Seraphina ordered, her voice grim but stalwart. "Get some more tea."

Sister Rose leaped up, ever ready to serve.

"No!" Temple's voice croaked like a thirsty frog's. "No more . . . tea."

"Don't worry," Sister Rose chirped. "I would never waste the bishop's tea."

With that, she poured the rest of her almost-empty glass into Midnight Louie's ashtray, which he eagerly dispatched to the last, strong, delicious drop.

Chapter 35

White Elephant

"Do you think Molina would arrest us if you drove me home?" Temple asked.

She stood by the Storm, barefoot—or rather, in tattered hose. Her reclaimed tote bag and shoes drooped from her right hand, her key ring hung over her left wrist. Matt stood beside her, Midnight Louie drooping over *his* right arm.

"I think she'd arrest us if I *did*n't drive you home," Matt said. "You had a lot more of the bishop's tea than I did."

"So did Molina. She's much nicer when she's high."

"She was not high, and neither are you, really. You're just exhausted."

"I'm certainly not as high I used to be," Temple said, swaying into Matt and Louie, her head coming only to his armpit—Matt's, that is.

He straightened her, put the tote bag and the limp Louie into the Storm's backseat and baby-walked Temple around to the passenger side.

When she was installed in the seat, Temple stared through the windshield and counted stars. Actually, she couldn't see stars, just dusty water drops, but they glimmered almost like stars as the streetlights swept overhead in a soothing rhythm of light and dark. Sometimes it was nice not to have to drive.

"Speaking of Lieutenant Molina again," Temple finally said, "do you suppose that mean woman is ever going to tell us what really happened?"

"I think she's going to ask us what happened when our tea has had time to wear off."

"It's too bad that you weren't able to find Father Hernandez in time for our little powwow with the police," Temple added uneasily. She didn't want to say what she thought—what everyone undoubtedly thought. Father Hernandez had finally gone around the bend. But why? What had driven him to such sick extremes? And why wasn't Molina flaunting her shocking suspect? Was there more to the story, more that she wanted to tease out of some of them?

"Yes, it is too bad that I couldn't find him." Matt frowned as he thought about the priest. "Father Rafe is facing a lot of pressure." Matt shrugged off an invisible blanket of worry. "Maybe he was called out on an emergency anointing. I can't believe that he would do what happened tonight."

Temple wasn't buying it. "You know more about these people than you're saying, just like Molina said."

"So do you."

"Yes."

"Lieutenant Molina is not as dumb as you'd like to think."

"Not dumb . . . just different. I can't figure her out." Temple counted stardust drops in the windshield. She really was rather tired, and more than a little scared, in retrospect. "She found some minor information about Max and acted like she had the Holy Grail."

"What information?"

But that was about Max, and this was Matt. "Nothing important." One had to keep one's loyalties separate, sacred. All one's loyalties. Hadn't Sister Seraphina been trying to do just that? And maybe Father Hernandez, too, if the truth be known; the truth that Matt knew and would not tell, because he couldn't. And where were Peggy's loyalties now?

"I'm tired," Temple said.

"You should be."

"Will you put me to bed?"

"Electra will."

"What about Louie?"

"I'll put him to bed."

Temple awoke to the sun inserting needles of bright white pain under the nails of her miniblinds, hurting everywhere, but especially in her head.

She lay there, lazy and darn well entitled to be, contemplating the ragged Aruba Red ends of three broken fingernails. If Temple had good anything, it was fingernails. They practically had to be chopped off with a hedge-trimmer, and only the strongest metal files could dent their tenacious surface.

She did not look forward to repairing the damage to her handsome, homemade manicure.

So she lay there running the previous night's events through her mind, distressed to find that she was somewhat fuzzy on the details. Was it stress—or Sister Rose's tea?

She hadn't even looked at the bedside clock yet, although the level of light through the blinds suggested that it was later than she thought.

She still didn't move, lost in that delicious stage of waking when thoughts play ring-around-the-rosie, and sleep is a fluffy, pure-white cloud just waiting to sink down and waft her away again.

A sudden, sharp hissing from the living room had Temple upright in bed in an instant, her head throbbing just above the nape of her neck.

Hissing! She hissed back in irritation as she jumped out of bed faster than she wanted to. A cat fight was in progress, and it was up to her to bust up the combatants. They sounded like Donald Duck spitting thumbtacks. Matt must have let Caviar out of quarantine last night—oh, no! She froze for a second, suddenly grateful for the feuding felines. *Holy cats! Now* she knew who was the obscene phone-caller, and maybe the parish trick-player and amateur arsonist, and probably the cat crucifier. Meanwhile, she had animal-husbandry duties to perform and scrambled into the other room.

Two black cats in such full, furry bristle that their tails resembled radiator brushes faced off on the sofa. Louie looked as large as a Chow Chow, but Caviar had managed to puff her smaller self up to the size of a blow-dried Pomeranian with a static-electricity problem. Obviously, no feline mating rituals were likely to transpire here.

Temple clapped her hands. "Now, now, kitties. Polite fur persons get along."

Neither spared her a glance. Temple sped over to clasp Caviar gingerly around the middle and lift her down to the floor.

Caviar stalked away in a sideways, hunched posture, keeping her eyes on Louie and her awesomely amplified tail presented.

Louie yawned, stretched out so he occupied most of the sofa length, and regarded Temple with a smug expression. *My* sofa, it seemed to say; *my* place; *my* person.

Temple fixed herself a cup of instant coffee in the kitchen, checked the time told inside the pink-neon ring of the wall clock and scurried back into the bedroom.

High noon. Electra should be up.

In fifteen minutes Temple was two floors higher, at the landlady's door, ringing the doorbell that may not work.

"Hi, hon," Electra greeted her when the penthouse door opened.

Temple winced. Electra was wearing neon-lime leggings topped by a glitzy neon oversized T-shirt. Her white hair was accented with lime-green spray.

"Matt told me you'd had another unfortunate encounter

with a felon, only he said that this time you won. But you look a bit bedraggled, if you don't mind my saying so."

Temple glanced down at her well-bruised bare legs, and winced.

"I would say you should see the other guy, but none of us has seen him. Molina is being mum about the identity of the cat-hating, nun-baiting creep who tried to burn down Blandina Tyler's house."

"I'm lost," Electra confessed, "not having been in on the case. I still say you look as if someone frazzled your fringes."

"Actually, most of the damage done to me last night was accomplished by a little old nun."

"You've got to watch us senior citizens," Electra agreed with a chortle.

"Listen, Electra, can you do me a big favor?"

"Anything, dear girl—what is it? Another undercover gig? Maybe as a nun this time? With a habit and everything?" Electra was getting enthused. "That would be a piquant change of pace from stripper Moll Philander. I could be . . . Sister Merry Maybelline."

"No, Electra, nothing like that. I need a home for a sweet, lovely little cat who was headed for the gas chamber. Her name is Caviar and she's—"

"Oh, no, dear. I absolutely could not."

"But she's wonderful. I'll pay for her spaying. Louie doesn't seem too fond of interlopers, and—"

"No, cats generally aren't."

"Have you been talking to Matt about that, too?" Temple asked suspiciously.

"No. This I know. I can't take your cat. Absolutely not." Electra's tones indicated that the sky would fall in such a circumstance. "I don't care if you have two, but no, I can't have it."

"Louie cares, apparently. And why not, Electra? You've got room. You like Louie."

"I'm, um, allergic to cats." Electra did not quite look Temple in the eye. "Can't breathe around them too long. Sorry, Temple, but it's out of the question."

Temple had superb instincts. She could tell when she was being subjected to a verbal song-and-dance, and this was one of those tap-dancing occasions. Whatever Electra's real reasons for changing from the world's most accommodating landlady into a firm non-cat fancier, Temple knew she had not heard them.

Temple pondered. "Maybe Matt—"

"Yes. Ask Matt." Electra hushed her huge door shut, leaving Temple staring at the coffered mahogany panels.

Noon. The poor man should be up by now. At least he hadn't had to go back to work. Temple trudged down the back stairs to the lower floor, regretting that she'd worn her sequined tennis shoes. She didn't relish feeling short today, but was too tired yet to get up on her usual high horse.

Matt opened the door to her ring, wearing his gi, and broke into a sunny-day grin. "Here she is, Taekwando Tessie. You look as if you could use some caffeine straight up."

Temple nodded, encouraged by his greeting. "Given all the job and sleep disruption you've had lately—mostly my fault—I'm surprised that you're mobile."

"No *mea culpa*'s," he said. When Temple looked puzzled, he beat a loose fist thrice on his chest. " '*Mea culpa, mea culpa, mea maxima culpa.*' Catholic talk. Latin for 'my fault, my fault, my most grievous fault.' We used to get guilt in great big gulps in the church, but it's eased up lately. No sense in your clinging to the same outmoded behavior."

"Guilt has no denomination," Temple said, sitting on a seat of piled boxes and accepting the mug Matt offered her. "And it never goes out of style."

She sipped, then lifted her eyebrows with the coy surprise of a lady in a coffee commercial. "This is good."

"The real stuff. I had some before I went down to the pool and did my tai chi. Figure that: Western wired and Eastern tranquilized."

"Contradiction doesn't go out of style, either." Temple smiled. "Say, Matt, I've been thinking. Your place could use a few homey touches."

"Amen. Do you decorate, too?"

"No . . . but I matchmake."

This time *he* sipped and raised noncommittal blond eyebrows at her, like a man in a coffee commercial. My, they were good at being arch.

"How would you like an undemanding companion?"

He looked leery. "How undemanding, and what kind of companion?"

"Caviar," she said sheepishly.

"Louie isn't having any of it, huh?"

"She's so much smaller; it's not fair to leave her to duke it out with that big lug."

Matt, smiling, shook his head. "Didn't you get proof positive last night that size doesn't always matter in a set-to? It's spirit—and, in a way, say the Eastern masters, spirituality."

"With cats, its claws out, and spirituality is just so much spit and hiss. Besides, I don't know the actual size of my attacker. Lieutenant C.R.—Can't Relate—Molina wouldn't tell us who he was."

"We have no official need to know." Matt also looked like he didn't *want* to know.

"*I* do!" Temple said. "Louie was nearly turned into a tacked-up poster boy by that creep. Not to mention that he set fire to a truly fine, vintage dressing table."

"I don't think Molina has a reasonable motive yet—and she doesn't know if Miss Tyler was murdered or not, and if so, by her suspect, who may be . . . insane and unprosecutable."

"Despite this grim scenario, and our unspoken suspicions, you seem fairly cheerful this morning."

His answering smile was warm. "Why not? My prize—and only—pupil has come through a field test with flying colors." Matt glanced at her fingers wrapped around the mug. "Except for some nicks in her manicure. And . . . the mission that Sister Seraphina called me to is over, no matter how unhappily. I doubt that Sister Mary Monica will get any more unintelligible, obscene phone calls."

"Well, then," said Temple, "if everything is hunky-dory

except for the usual human tragedies, how about celebrating by taking a nice new friend into your life?"

"I've already got a nice new friend in my life."

The import of that statement almost derailed Temple from her mission to place a homeless cat. She smiled over her coffee mug and said nothing for a full five seconds.

"You should share your good fortune with the less fortunate," she said gently.

"Guilt again?"

"Always." Temple shrugged. "It works."

But they still smiled at each other.

The phone rang, and they jumped, guiltily.

Matt went to pick up the white receiver from the kitchen counter.

Temple let her eyes inventory the apartment. No color scheme yet. Caviar would fit in elegantly no matter what Matt did.

Matt turned with the phone pressed against his face like a compress, his expression serious.

"Two o'clock," he said. "Downtown."

Temple assumed a questioning expression.

"No . . . she's here."

Another pause. Who was calling? Electra?

"I'm sure she'll come." A pause. "Right. Good-bye."

He hung up, then eyed Temple.

"Two o'clock. Downtown. The police station. I think Lieutenant Molina is going to spill her guts, or at least try to get us to."

"Downtown!" Temple was thrilled. It sounded so official. "You? And me? Why us?"

"I doubt it's only us. I suspect it's the whole Our Lady of Guadalupe crew. Molina was very cryptic, very Charlie Chan. I think this is 'the suspects gathered in the parlor' routine."

"But we're not suspects. She's got the perp."

"Maybe."

Temple sipped the last of her truly well-brewed coffee and

stood up. "What did Molina say when you told her I was here?"

"Nothing. For about ten seconds." Matt grinned. "Now that she knows about my past, I can hear her wheels turning. You're right; it's kind of fun to mystify Lieutenant Molina. Especially when she's wrong."

"Well, I better get ready for my official grilling. We might as well go together. Can I drop a cat off here on my way out?"

"I'll pick you up on the way down," he said firmly. "And why don't you give Midnight Louie a chance to warm up to Caviar?"

"I'm all in favor of warming up," Temple said, slipping out the door and kicking up a sequined foot as a parting gesture in the true burlesque style. All she was missing was the drumroll.

Chapter 36

Louie Dodges the Bullet

I owe a lot to this little dish of Caviar.

She provides a quiet and admiring audience when I make my triumphant return from the House of Wax and Wayward Kitties, although she has a mysterious, smug expression painted on her piquant little mug that much reminds me of the officious Karma.

I tell her that she shows promise.

"And one thing I do promise," says she, as fast as you can say Jackie Robinson. "Nobody has any say over where I go, what I do, or what condition I am in."

"All right, all right," I say. "I will let your foul bowl of Free-to-be-Feline rest beside mine in perpetuity in honor of your acts on my behalf, but that is the end of it. This place is mine, from the pink maribou slippers in the bedroom closet to the French doors and patio to the disgusting litter box in the second bathroom to the escape hatch at the top of said bathroom, and I lay down the rules."

"You lay down about twenty pounds," says she with the agile stretch of a cool cat, "but face it, your time has come and gone, Fatso. You are outdated. You are not with it. You are a dinosaur."

"Listen," say I, "dinosaurs are a very hot item nowadays."

"Jurassic jitterbug," she jeers. "I admit," she goes on, "that I do not like old dudes in any condition being nailed up anywhere—with the exception of my unesteemed, absconding father, may his whiskers rot wherever he is—but do not get the impression that I have any sympathy for such benighted dudes as you. You are an anachronism."

"Listen," I hiss back, stung to defending my tomhood, "I am not now and never have been a relative to an arachnid."

"I mean that you are out of time and place, seriously out of date. The only way I would give you the time of day was if I were a water-clock!"

"Now, now Caviar," I say. "Such a nice, genteel name for a little dame. Surely your esteemed mother reared you to be more of a lady."

"Ladies get stomped. And, speaking of names, what is yours?"

Here I hesitate. "I have been called a lot of things."

"I do not doubt it," says she with a dainty sniff.

"Friday, once. Sergeant Friday."

"You do look like an unlucky dude, not to mention *passé.*"

"And . . . Blackie."

"Boston Blackie, no doubt," this little doll sneers.

She is arrogant, uppity, ignorant and downright insulting, but she is kin. I hold my temper, which is getting most temperamental at such restraint.

"And . . . Thirteen."

"Must be your age."

"Not . . . quite," I say, quashing a desire to cuff her halfway to the French doors.

I am always the gentleman, except when it occurs to me that the parents of this little doll could have exercised a tad of tough love. Since I am one of the said parents, it is sad to realize that she has passed beyond the reins of paternal discipline. No doubt my intervention now would be termed abuse. So I return to territorial rights.

"This is my place. I was here first. Miss Temple Barr is my person. No matter who you are, or what you did in the preservation department, which I admit showed promise, I am not giving up my present circumstances to make up for your past."

"We shall see," says Miss Caviar with admirable cool.

But she has forgotten entirely the issue of my given name. I was not born yesterday, and sometimes that is a strategic advantage.

Chapter 37

Resolution and Absolution

Matt wasn't surprised to find Sister Seraphina waiting in the office at the downtown police station. He was startled to find Peggy Wilhelm there, and so was Temple, he noticed.

He and Temple must be thinking the same thing: Peggy Wilhelm was tangential to the entire case—to the will, her aunt's death, even to the cat-show atrocity, if shaving a cat could be considered an atrocity by anyone other than a cat fancier.

Neither of them was surprised to find Father Hernandez absent, as he had been all of last night. Why was Lieutenant Molina drawing out the ugly inevitable, playing cat-and-mouse with all their fears? Had she found new evidence at the rectory? Did she need Matt's testimony on the blackmail letters to make the case? Perhaps that was the issue she would illuminate today.

Matt watched her with interest. She sat behind a big,

cluttered desk in this large but cluttered office that was clearly not hers; the family photos on the long table behind the desk showed rows of smiling black faces. The office must belong to some superior who had been apprised of this meeting, had approved and then vanished to leave the details to Lieutenant Molina—which indicated that her superiors respected her enough to allow the occasional offbeat approach.

But the lieutenant was nervous, Matt decided, watching her fidget with folders on the desktop and avoid the gathering eyes. She displayed the brusque efficiency of someone who did not like what she was about to do, but saw no other way out.

Matt braced himself. So far, Lieutenant Molina had shown a talent for unearthing embarrassing facts—lacks—about himself. She had also recently confronted Temple with some unappetizing information about her missing significant other, Max Kinsella. What? Matt wondered. Temple was usually so honest and open, but about Max Kinsella she was a locked-room mystery. The room that occurred to Matt was a bedroom, so his speculations veered quickly away from that unknown territory.

Lieutenant Molina cleared her throat and tapped a manila folder on the glass-topped desk, a teacher rapping for order and attention.

They hadn't been talking to each other, idly buzzing back and forth; they needed no formal convening. Maybe Lieutenant Molina did. What did C.R. stand for, anyway? Was that *her* lack, her secret?

"This is irregular," she confessed, almost hesitant.

She didn't like this closed circle, Matt saw, this mystery that was sure to explode like a fragmentation grenade and strike somebody—an entire congregation of shocked and sorrowful somebodies—any more than he did.

"I am confronted in this case with a number of inexplicable, seemingly unrelated events." Her vivid blue gaze touched every listening face. "Of course they are not unrelated at all. There are also . . . elements that do not seem to make sense. They do. I should warn you that I am not seeking a solution here; I know it. I am hoping that some unclear areas will resolve themselves. As a start, I will report on the solution to the hissing and obscene phone calls to Miss Tyler and the convent, to the attack on the cat Peter, to the shaving of the cat Minuet at the cat show. These, we know, were all interconnected, but the logic linking them was . . . distorted.

"Before I begin, does anyone here have anything to say?"

They eyed each other, each looking sheepish and guilty, for each was probably concealing something. Matt knew Temple bore the burden of more knowledge of another person than she felt comfortable carrying—but who was her confessee? He shared the same burden of Father Hernandez's blackmail letters. Did Molina know of those; would he be better off admitting their existence now?

Sister Seraphina had concealed Father Hernandez's flaw—his sudden dependence on a liquor bottle. Did she hide more?

And Peggy Wilhelm, was she hiding knowledge of her aunt's affairs that would make the elderly woman's death—her possible murder—understandable?

"We think Blandina Tyler was murdered," Lieutenant Molina said. "Her murderer has not confessed, but this was a simple case, in that respect. Whether the suspect is sane or not, a jury will have to decide."

"Who?" Temple asked, brushing a frivolity of red curls back from her forehead. "If the case is that clear-cut, we deserve to know who."

Molina's sad, forbearing smile said that she knew, as a priest does, that clear-cut answers are always the most ambiguous at heart.

"I told you all last night," she went on, "that we held someone you knew and trusted, someone whose name would shock you. Perhaps I shouldn't even be telling you this."

"Telling us what?" someone asked from the doorway, someone who had arrived unnoticed.

Sister Seraphina stood. "Father Hernandez! You're not—"

"I'm not what?" he asked rather testily. "What is everyone else doing here? And why was I waylaid by Sister Saint Rose of Lima as soon as I returned to the rectory and sent here?"

"You weren't at the rectory last night," Matt said, dismayed by his unintended, but unmistakably accusing tone.

Father Hernandez turned to him, then ran a hand through his sleek silver hair. He wore full priestly garb: black slacks and the white notch of a Roman collar at the neck of his black, short-sleeved shirt. Add a black suitcoat and he could play the organ for any memorial service Electra might want to hold, just as Matt had once. Father Hernandez did not look like a murderer. He looked gaunt and weary, but otherwise elegant.

His brief descent into the hell of a tequila bottle had not harmed him beyond the obvious. The real hell had come through the mail in the neat, damning lines of laser-printed lies. Or were they lies? Denial was the bottom line of most serious human failings. Did Lieutenant Molina even know of the blackmail? Did she know of Matt's concealed knowledge of it?

"No, I wasn't at the rectory," the priest said, his tone sharp. "Am I supposed to always be at the rectory? I was . . . in the church."

"The church, at that time of night?" Sister Seraphina inquired. "All night?"

"The church is for every time—night or day—though we are forced to keep it locked against vandals at night in these terrible times. Didn't any of you even look there? Can't a priest be in a church? What is the matter with you people?"

Molina smiled. "Are you on the wagon, Father Rafe?"

He flashed her a look full of thunder that swiftly became a nervous throat clearing. "I hope so."

His glance crossed Matt's; they smiled, briefly brothers, no matter what.

Matt felt momentarily absolved. Absolved of the recent

confidence he had borne so unwillingly, absolved of his ambiguous status: ex-priest. He never escaped the word and what it meant. Priest. There are no ex-priests, just as They say there are no ex-Catholics. The Force is always with you, Luke Skywalker, even when you walk—run—away. So are They. So Father Hernandez was not guilty of Blandina Tyler's death at least. Who was?

Molina finally took mercy on them and ended the suspense. "The person who killed Miss Tyler was apprehended last night, Father Hernandez. Yes, sit down; you'll need to. We have in custody Peter Burns, church attorney. I understand your shock. I've shared a pew with him at Our Lady of Guadalupe more than once myself."

Gasps greeted this announcement.

"He has been a member of the parish for . . . over ten years," Father Hernandez objected even as he sank down obediently on an empty chair. "He has volunteered his services in the church's behalf. There must be a mistake—"

"Indeed," said Lieutenant Molina. "The matter of Blandina Tyler's will is foremost among these 'mistakes.' We have found, after searching the Tyler house, which, thanks to Miss Barr did not burn down"—Temple nearly fainted at this fulsome praise—"seventeen wills dated at various times. That's why Burns continued to haunt the house, as it were, after Miss Tyler's death; he knew she stockpiled everything, and other wills might surface to cloud the legitimacy of his quite illegitimate will. That's why he finally decided to burn the house down. Now we have the wills he feared. The will Mr. Burns presented to Father Hernandez as the latest is clearly a forgery based on the previous wills and no doubt commissioned by Miss Tyler, but altered in its terms, particularly as to the disinheriting of the cats. Mr. Burns had a vendetta against cats, among other things."

"Then *he* shaved my Minuet!" Peggy Wilhelm said. "But why? I was miles away from my aunt's house, at the Cashman Center."

"Maybe—" Temple, thinking hard, hit bingo "—that was the idea."

"Not bad," Lieutenant Molina noted. "With her show cat attacked, Miss Wilhelm would spend the weekend at the Cashman Center guarding against further mischief, rather than visiting her aunt's house twice a day to help out with the cats."

They all mulled that over.

"He *wanted* Miss Tyler alone for the weekend?" Temple asked.

Despite her protests that Lieutenant Molina intimidated her, Matt noticed that Temple was the only one willing to speculate in the face of what Molina might know. Matt wondered if that was because she was the one with the least to hide.

"Miss Tyler and her cats." Lieutenant Molina savored those factors. "He did not count on his action at the cat show ensuring that the terminally curious Miss Barr would be sent to the house to feed the cats instead, or that Sister Seraphina—disturbed by the accelerating obscene phone calls to Sister Mary Monica, and finding Father Hernandez . . . removed from parish affairs—would call on her ex-student Matt Devine for aid. Instead of getting rid of one inconvenient niece, Burns ensured the presence of two peripherally involved strangers." Lieutenant Molina regarded Matt and Temple in turn. "I have always found peripherally involved strangers to be a pain in the neck. I believe that Mr. Burns is now of the same opinion. Shaving the Burmese cat was his first mistake, although he was not detected at the time."

"Birman," Temple put in scrupulously. "The cat was a Birman."

Peggy Wilhelm, in a sort of daze, gratefully nodded her curly head. "They were sacred temple cats in Burma hundreds of years ago. Most . . . prescient, intelligent animals, Birmans, and very sensitive."

"Burmese, Birman," Lieutenant Molina went on with a trace of annoyance. "The point was not the breed, but the threat. Some of you should have seen from the beginning the significance of the shaved pattern."

Everyone looked politely mystified.

"Down the back and around the middle," Matt heard himself saying. "A cross. Father Hernandez had commented on that."

"A cross." Lieutenant Molina beamed approval at Matt as if he were a prize pupil.

He felt himself flush at the attention—or perhaps at the approval—and dropped his eyes. This wasn't a classroom exercise. The harassment had turned a number of lives upside down, least of which, his. He didn't want good grades, he wanted an answer, *the* answer. He had always wanted the one, true answer that was never quite clear. *Mea culpa, mea culpa, mea maxima culpa.*

"Under interrogation, Mr. Burns proved to be somewhat obsessive about the topic of religion," Molina said. "Also about old ladies and cats. There's no doubt that he intended to crucify another animal. The black cat, Midnight Louie, would have been found nailed to the church door before Miss Tyler's funeral."

"Ahhh!" Temple clasped her fists to her chest and looked appalled. "Did he mean to imply satanism?"

"Possibly. Certainly he meant to abuse an animal. Was your cat on the Tyler premises for some reason, or did Mr. Burns take him from your apartment?"

Temple obviously had not considered this question. "I don't know. How would this guy even know I had a cat? He didn't know me from Adam Ant. No, Louie . . . Louie's just a man-about-town. He's always wandered, and he must have stumbled into this guy's path."

"Hmm." Molina was not impressed. "I don't buy it, but since the alternative is that your Louie put himself into Mr. Burns's path for some reason, I'll go along with it. Let's say that Midnight Louie happened to be visiting lady friends in Miss Tyler's house when Mr. Burns came looking for a big, juicy cat that no one could miss seeing stapled to Our Lady of Guadalupe's doors."

"Mr. Burns is Catholic," Sister Seraphina piped up.

"On the surface, yes. Why do you mention it?" the lieutenant wanted to know.

"Tacking a cat to the church doors—it's a sacreligious version of Martin Luther nailing his 'Ninety-five Theses' to the Wittenberg Cathedral door and starting the whole Reformation."

"Perhaps. Mr. Burns's attitude toward Catholicism seems to be highly antagonistic, given the statement we have recorded."

"But why?" Father Hernandez demanded. "This young man has been a member of the parish for over ten years. He has volunteered his legal services, both to the church and Miss Tyler. Why would he pose as a loyal parish member for so long? Why?"

"Four hundred and fifty-seven thousand dollars," Lieutenant Molina announced briskly. "The will was fraudulent. The monies he represented as comprising Miss Tyler's estate are grossly underestimated. The church would have gotten its pittance; the cats would have been homeless, and Peter Burns would have been immeasurably richer. Our fraud unit is still tracing accounts. He handled her financial affairs for the past decade, you see. She was a typical, modest, close-mouthed old lady. No one would suspect how much her money had appreciated with shrewd investments, not even Miss Tyler."

"Except—" Sister Seraphina stopped speaking suddenly.

All eyes turned to Peggy Wilhelm, who was shaking her moplike head.

"No, not me. Aunt Blandina was of a generation that believed that her age, her financial position and the state of her soul were equally sacred. She said nothing about any of them to me. I was still a child to her. Her forever-childish niece; useful, but untrustworthy, except with the cats. I was good enough to take care of her cats, but not her financial affairs, not anything else."

Temple winced at the self-disgust buried in Peggy Wilhelm's bitter words. Matt wondered again who had cast

Temple in the role of confidante. Like Molina, he had his suspect:

"Mr. Devine."

The lieutenant's voice made Matt jump as if he had been fingered in a crime. He liked being the observer, the judge, the confessor. He didn't like being the subject, the focus.

"You were the wild card," she said. "Sister Seraphina drew you from the deck; you were a student of hers in Chicago—" he nodded "—and you came onto the scene with a kind of unholy innocence. What forced her to turn to you? The obscene phone calls?"

He nodded again.

"Why not Father Hernandez? The drinking?"

He nodded yet again, not looking at anyone.

Molina smiled grimly, satisfied. "So we have Sister Seraphina and Mr. Devine trying to protect Sister Mary Monica, and Father Hernandez by default."

Father Hernandez pressed his lips together, tempted to defend himself and his sudden alcoholic turn. *No,* Matt willed him. *The rest of it may not have to be revealed. Let her suppose, and we will dispose . . . we priests, who serve the greater good, which sometimes is not served by full disclosure.* Their glances clashed and slid away.

"And we have Miss Temple Barr," Molina said, "who is trying to protect cats."

Temple, too, controlled herself, remaining silent while Lieutenant Molina went on.

"Mr. Peter Burns had not planned on these interlopers. He had planned on Miss Wilhelm being absent. The crucified cat was meant to distress Miss Tyler, and did. It was not meant to have other witnesses than she. Essentially, we believe, and Burns has indicated, he intended to weaken and harass Miss Tyler into a grave illness. He was tired of waiting; he wanted her dead. He wanted her money. He wanted the cats killed, one way or another—by his own hand, or by being cast out undefended into an unwelcoming world."

They listened to Molina and shook their heads. Peter

Burns, whom they had hardly known, seemed mindlessly demented.

"But why?" Sister Seraphina's astute eyes were unsatisfied. "Money doesn't motivate the acts of mischief and terror he performed."

"He had a motive beyond greed," Molina conceded. "Retribution. Mr. Devine?"

Matt looked up again. He was beginning to resent being called "Mr. Devine." Was Molina taunting him for the absence of the old honorific, "Father?" Father Devine. Father Matt.

"You suggested that I investigate the background of everyone in the case," Molina went on. "You knew how thorough I could be, from your own experience."

He nodded.

"I did as you said. And I found . . ." Molina sighed as if exhausted. "Miss Wilhelm, would you care to tell us about it?"

"About what?" Her voice was stiff, ungiving.

"About what happened at Our Lady of Guadalupe thirty-six years ago."

Peggy Wilhelm's eyes stabbed toward Temple.

"No," Temple said. "I never did. Honestly."

Peggy Wilhelm's hands became helpless fists on her knees, her stubby, middle-aged knees covered by a cotton culotte. Finally, Peggy Wilhelm spoke.

"Thirty-six years ago. You think I'd forget? You'd think everyone else *would* forget—why can't they? I lived here for a while, in this parish. At my aunt's house. None of you were here then. None of you would know. Lieutenant . . . !"

"It's the key." Molina's tone was not uncompassionate. "You must know, and they must know."

"Why? It's been such a secret all these years!"

"Because *he* knows."

"He?" Peggy Wilhelm seemed utterly confused. "But he never knew, the father. That was the whole point. We all . . . conspired to make sure that he never knew. It was our business. Family business. My fault. My sin. Not his. He was irrelevant. But not me. My heart magnified the Lord, and so did my body. They kept telling us what the Virgin Mary was like, so young, so pure. I was fifteen and I hardly knew how it happened.

"They told us so little then, it was still the fifties! Do you know how long ago that was? I used to read the New Testament, after the angel told Mary she would bear the Christ child, when she visited her cousin Elizabeth, who knew already and said, 'Hail, Mary, full of grace. Blessed art thou among women and blessed is the fruit of thy womb.' I used to have to say the rosary over and over, those 'Hail, Mary' words, but the fruit of my womb was sin. They kept using those words in church on Sunday, they even gave them a name, the Magnificat, Mary's rejoicing in her miraculous motherhood—'My soul magnifies the Lord, and my spirit rejoices in God my savior.'

"She said 'His mercy is from generation unto generation,' but I read the words and heard the words and felt only shame. There was no mercy for me and my child—not from the church or my family or any of you now who will be so quick to judge."

Peggy Wilhelm's troubled face searched their features and then lowered. She wiped her fingers across the corners of her eyes, which were dry. Her voice as she continued was even dryer, almost dead of expression.

"I was sent to stay with Aunt Blandina until it was over. Not even to a 'home.' Too public. A midwife was more discreet than a doctor, and whatever came, would be whisked away. I hardly remember. I wasn't supposed to. Nobody was unkind, they were just so shamed. We never spoke of it in the family afterward. Never. I was sent out of state to finish high school, and then to college. I grew up, I tried to forget, like I was ordered to.

"When my parents died, of broken hearts, I suppose, I moved to Las Vegas, I don't know why. To be near my only living relative. My aunt. She had started keeping cats by then, and I did, too. Beautiful, loving cats, who could not know. That's what I wanted, cats. I didn't want . . . men. I didn't want . . . children. And I didn't want strays. I wanted planned, beautiful purebred cats, all my own. I fed Aunt Blandina's creatures. No room, no time, no memory for me and mine. But cats everywhere. I love them, and sometimes I hate them."

"What about the money?" Molina prodded.

"Money? I don't need their money. They paid money to him to go away. Money to the midwife. Money to the people who took my baby. They never gave money to me." Peggy eyed Father Hernandez and Sister Seraphina with dull, judging eyes. "The church said money should go only to the good. I was bad. The church would get all the money, from my parents, from my aunt." Peggy frowned and rubbed her chunky hands over her forehead. "Except, the old will that Temple found. Once upon a time, my aunt remembered me, and that was written after . . . everything. I don't understand."

Everyone looked on, appalled and speechless. Except Molina.

"We're still trying to trace the last, legitimate will. From the versions we've found so far, we believe that your aunt left her estate equally: to the church, to the cats and to you."

Peggy Wilhelm started sobbing into the hands that covered her face. Defiantly, Temple rose and went to stand behind her, her hands on her shoulders.

Sister Seraphina glanced from Lieutenant Molina to Father Hernandez, then crouched beside the sobbing woman to take hold of her hands.

Matt found himself staring at Molina, demanding silent justification for this public revelation.

"Did you ever try to find that lost child?" Molina asked.

"No!" Peggy almost retched between sobs. "It had to be forgotten. Everyone wanted it forgotten. I had to forget it. I couldn't, but I had to."

"And no one tried to contact you?" Molina was cool, an interrogative machine.

Even distraught, Peggy Wilhelm responded to that authority as she had always responded to authority throughout her fifty-one years.

"No," she said. "Who would? The family was Catholic, infertile and delighted to take my . . . sin."

"What about your son?"

"Son?" Peggy looked up from her hands. She had never even known the sex.

"He searched for you when he grew up," Molina said. "He went to college and got a degree. He did very well for himself. And then he did a birth-parent search. Of course no one would contact you without your consent. And no one did, because he withdrew his request, but not before he had used his special knowledge to get the information he craved: your location. He was a lawyer by now, he knew who you were, and he knew you had lived with Blandina Tyler during your pregnancy. He discovered how rich Blandina Tyler was, and he came to hate her church and her cats and her money that wasn't coming to him. He deserved it, and he came to the parish years ago, intending to get it."

"He . . . never wanted to see me?" Peggy asked through her tears.

Molina shook her head. "He was obsessed with his own losses, not yours."

"That's why he called Sister Mary Monica!" Temple said. "She reminded him of his great-aunt, her age and her *cane!* That also clouded the harassment of his aunt. And he attacked the cats because they had usurped his inheritance, and because they made everything seem madness without a method. But he honestly would have cheated his own mother out of her aunt's money?"

"From what I can determine," Molina said, "he was roughly reared. His adoptive parents always reminded him that he was the product of sin. He found only obligation, not love, in his new family. He found them and the church harsh and unforgiving, and he became so himself. In a way," she added, eyeing Father Hernandez, "I agree with him.

"We've traced what records there are; we've found his parent search request. But it wasn't a parent he wanted; it was revenge and restitution. He is responsible for every bit of harassment that has plagued this parish, and he spent ten years worming himself into everybody's trust to do it.

"I'm sorry," she told Peggy Wilhelm. "It will all have to come out at the trial. I believe that your aunt's friends at Our Lady of Guadalupe can help you to deal with it. Truth is cleansing, at least I think so. If you have any questions, or need to know anything more, just call me."

Peggy nodded, her head still bowed.

"Would you like to see him?" Molina asked.

"I don't know. In all those years, I never met him. I no longer went to church; I certainly didn't attend Our Lady of Guadalupe."

"After today, you will be seeing his picture and reading about him in the newspapers. After today, the news circus will put him in the center ring." Molina was silent for a few seconds. "You could do worse than to confront the past with friends present; everyone here was his target, in a sense, because they stood between him and his deepest desire."

Peggy looked around at those who had met her son; some had known him—or thought they did—for years. Some, like Temple and Matt, had just met him, and thought nothing of him at all. She nodded and lowered her head again as Sister Seraphina rose on stiff knees and resumed her chair.

The office was crowded now, Matt thought; could it absorb the added force of such an explosively angry personality?

Molina used an intercom to instruct that "the prisoner" be brought in.

He came in handcuffs, wearing a set of City Jail Clark County jailhouse baggies and escorted by a blue-uniformed corrections officer. His round, plastic-framed glasses and short yuppie haircut gave him the look of a vintage prisoner—an escapee from a forties' crime movie.

Molina indicated the last empty chair. "Sit down."

He did so awkwardly, perching forward on the seat so that his manacled hands weren't jammed against the back of the chair.

Peggy peeked at him like a shy child, from between the fingers fanned over her eyes. He regarded her impassively.

"I . . . I don't see a resemblance," she said. "Do you know who I am?"

"Good!" he answered. "I don't want any relatives. They sent me away. And, yeah, I looked you up when I got to town. I know where you live. I know you coddle those stupid, fancy cats, just like your aunt was looney over her army of lousy strays. You people should have had cats instead of children."

Peggy winced at his derisive tone. "Maybe we were trying to make up for our loss, in some way."

"You would have made up for it in spades if I had managed to have my way."

"Peter." Sister Seraphina spoke soberly but not unkindly. "You did much good for the church. You helped the elderly widows with their financial affairs, you donated all your legal work for the church . . . was that only a sham?"

"Yes." His eyes narrowed. "You sent me away to that horrible house. It probably was no worse than what I would have had if I hadn't been bundled off like dirty laundry. Always the same lousy litany, 'the church says this' and 'the church says that,' and my mother was a whore and my father worthless."

"I wasn't here at the time," Sister Seraphina reminded him.

"You were. Or someone like you. You were all alike, you holier-than-thou types, whether you wore black habits and white collars or sat at home under paintings of the Sacred Heart and mumbled endless rosaries."

"That was a long time ago," Father Hernandez said. "I was reared under the same strict standards. Yes, they were intolerant and unforgiving, but the times and the church and the people in the church have changed, Peter. Why can't you change, too?"

"Because I don't want to, Father." He spat out the honorary address like an obscenity. "I don't have a father. I don't have one listed on any birth certificate and I don't have a

Holy Father in Rome and I don't have you. You're just a freak, a freakin' drunk, and you think I didn't enjoy watching you all flounder and fall to pieces? I was in control. I pulled strings and you danced, even the old bag in the convent. I know what hypocrites you all are; she didn't hurry to hang up on my naughty phone calls, did she?"

"She's nearly deaf," Sister Seraphina pointed out.

That seemed to shock him, the notion that someone he had persecuted was unreachable because of a physical failing. While his face was slack and surprised, Molina pounced.

"Why were the canes such a trigger? You hated Blandina's, even broke it after her death. And you called the only nun in the convent who used a cane."

"Canes." His face hardened with an old, hurtful memory. "There was a grandmother in my adopted family. She used to jab her rotten cane at me, easier than saying my name. 'You, there.' And they used to hit me with it when I'd been bad. I was bad a lot—but I made something of myself anyway. Good grades in school, law school on my own; I even had to fix my rotten teeth myself. I may look good, but I'm still bad, only now other people are paying for it."

"No." Sister Seraphina shook her head. "You're paying for it, only you don't see it."

"What about—" Temple had been thinking again "—what about the hissing phone calls to Peggy and Miss Tyler? I *thought* he did it, because I realized he had the right equipment. Did he?"

Molina's melancholy face lit up like a contestant's on a game show. "That was ingenious. Yes, Mr. Burns made those calls, and here's how." She pulled a manila envelope across the desk. "We had to confiscate this; prisoners are allowed very little in the county jail; anything might be turned into a weapon."

Molina pulled a piece of pale, translucent plastic from the envelope and exhibited it on the palm of her hand like a shell. A thin silver wire glinted at its front.

"He had braces," Temple remembered, "and I realized

they would make it easier to whistle when he talked, if he wasn't careful."

"You only met him—?"

"A couple of times," Temple said.

"Very observant, Watson." Molina's smile was almost mischievous. "But not braces. What you saw was the front portion of a dental appliance used to keep teeth that have had braces in line after the procedure." She eyed the sculpted hump of plastic shell sitting on her hand. "It's familiarly known as a 'turtle' because it's made from a mold of the wearer's upper palate, which is shell-shaped. If Mr. Burns let his turtle slip slightly out of position and spoke, he produced strange whistling, hissing sounds. A perfect way to disguise a voice. I know about turtles because I have a preteen daughter who may soon require such costly objects."

Molina returned her exhibit to the envelope. "Anything else you wish to say, Mr. Burns?"

"Your murder case is built on a shell of circumstantial evidence, Lieutenant." He relished his own taunts. "The prosecutor will have a cat when he finds the evidence so thin. Who is to say she didn't fall, even if I was on the premises that night? Only God, and He isn't talking. I plan to defend myself, and I will blow your case to smithereens!"

"Maybe." Molina nodded to the officer, who assisted Burns to his feet. "But the prosecutor is used to winning her cases."

As the handcuffed man left, Peggy Wilhelm spoke with some wonder. "He's an angry stranger. I don't know him. What happened all those years ago hurt me, and him, but separately. Sometimes I'm angry about it, but not that angry."

"You need to heal," Sister Seraphina urged. "What was done to you was wrong, but it was done by people who meant to do the best they could, according to their lights. You need to resolve the fact that good people can do terrible things to those they purport to love."

"You need to go to group," Temple said briskly. "I do, too. We can go to group together."

Peggy blinked at Temple. "What do you need to go to group for?"

"Oh, this and that." She leaned forward with mock confidentiality. "You'd be surprised who in this room needs to go to group."

Peggy bit. "Who?"

"Everybody," Temple pronounced triumphantly, and had the last, and only uncontested, word of the afternoon.

After leaving police headquarters, they all returned, by unspoken agreement and in separate cars, to Our Lady of Guadalupe.

They disembarked together in front of the convent and stared at Blandina Tyler's house, seeing it for the prison it had been almost forty years ago for a frightened, confused young girl. In a sense, the happenings at the house had kept several people prisoner for much too long.

"I wonder if Sister Rose has any more bishop's tea?" Sister Seraphina inquired.

"Regular tea will do fine," Father Hernandez said sternly. "There are no bishops in this parish."

Peggy Wilhelm hardly heard them. She regarded the house as if hypnotized. "Aunt Blandina remembered me in that old will. Do you think she was sorry?"

"I'm sure of it," Sister Seraphina reassured her with a quick hug. "Why don't I go see to that tea and you can all come in and have some."

"Better yet—" Temple flourished a key from the morass in her tote bag "—I still have a key to the house. I wouldn't give you two centavos for Lieutenant Molina and crew's search tactics. What say we hunt through the house for the latest version of the will?"

"I'll go," Peggy said quickly. "I want to check on the cats anyway."

Matt smiled to watch Temple entice Peggy into a treasure hunt for her own past. She was a pied piper of sorts, Temple, luring people from their heartsick ruts into a brave new world of her own imaginative construction. Who said Max Kinsella was the only magician around?

Sister Seraphina headed for the convent kitchen, where she would no doubt keep a sharp eye on Sister Rose's tea preparations.

That left himself and Father Hernandez standing together on the sidewalk, basking in the hot, healing sun, feeling free of a terrible revelation. Almost.

"I would guess," Matt said slowly, "that Peter Burns was the author of those threatening letters."

"That's likely, but you can't trust Lieutenant Molina," Father Hernandez said abruptly. "She could have found some evidence among Burns' things."

"Would she quash an investigation?"

"No."

"Then he covered his tracks. You're safe."

"A priest is never safe."

"Unless you are guilty of the crimes accused."

Father Hernandez's black, Spanish-olive eyes met Matt's cautious glance head-on, sharp and salty. "I swear to God, no."

Matt looked away. "I swore to God once."

"You did not swear; you promised church authorities to abide by certain behaviors—poverty, chastity and obedience. If the church finds the circumstances under which you made these promises questionable, who am I to feel superior because I have so far managed to honor them? The older I get, the less prone I am to judge, even Peter Burns. For all the ill he's done, he was a victim of an unforgiving time."

The sun was already swelling and heading for the western horizon. It baked down upon the church tower, turning it into a blazing white finger pointing at heaven. It painted false fire on the red-tile roof of Blandina Tyler's house. Matt squinted against the late-afternoon glare.

"If you are deceiving yourself, Father," he said carefully, "if you are a victim of denial so deep that it disguises itself as innocence even to you, I am carrying a terrible burden and taking a worse risk."

Father Hernandez nodded. "I can only swear by all I believe in that I am not the man those letters accused."

"It's not only your problem now."

"You're a good priest, Matthias." Father Hernandez put his hand on Matt's shoulder. "I will not let you down."

Chapter 38

Slow Dance on the Sands of Time

"I owe you dinner," Matt said over the phone.

"For what?" Temple returned quickly, pooh-poohing any sense of obligation.

"For the chauffeur service to Our Lady of Guadalupe, for the risk to life and limb."

"You already taught me how to preserve life and limb pretty well. I owe *you* dinner."

"Let me make the first move in this mutual-obligation society. Dinner. My treat. Someplace really nice."

"You can't go to dinner, you work those hours."

"Not tomorrow night. I'm off."

"Tomorrow! That's awfully soon."

"Why, do you have to fast three days before dinner out?"

"Well, I should . . . but okay, it's a date. What time?"

"Why not seven? I'm used to going to work then anyway."

"Fine. I'll meet you at the Storm in the parking lot."

Temple hung up with a smile. Matt was so serious about his obligations. Wait'll he found out what her idea of dinner out was beginning to be. Still, he hadn't given her much time.

Daylight was still rampant at seven o'clock of a Las Vegas September evening. Temple couldn't disguise her entrance under dark of night.

Matt was already by the car when she sashayed up—and she did sashay up in her purple-taffeta cocktail dress, a silver crocodile-pattern tote bag hung over her shoulder. He saw her from a distance—how could he miss?—and looked instantly worried.

Temple had never been one to let how she looked to someone else bother her. "Hi!" she greeted him in approved P.R. perky style.

Matt smiled uneasily. "I didn't wear a tie."

"Great!" she said, surveying his beige slacks and sport coat, the white shirt open at the neck.

"You look . . . great," he replied, unconsciously echoing her.

Temple smiled. She had checked herself out in the mirror, and concurred. Her dress was a halter-style purple-taffeta number that was modest around the Victorian-high collar, but that bared shoulders and back and clung to her torso to the hips, where it blossomed into a full, gathered skirt that ended above the knees. Matching strappy purple-satin high heels had been bought at a madly cheap Wild Pair shoe store in the local mall.

"Thanks," she said modestly.

Matt flashed a plastic card at her, as if eager to direct attention to other matters. "I got my Nevada driver's license in the mail today."

She took and studied it, even reading the statistics. "Height: 5′ 10″. Weight: 170. Eyes: brn. Hair: bld." Uh huh.

"Good! Gosh, you even take a gorgeous driver's license photo! Remind me not to show you mine." She returned the license and dug in her tote bag for her key ring, then tossed the keys in a jingling arc over the Storm's low, aqua roof. "You drive."

Matt caught the keys to his chest, looking surprised and surreptitiously pleased. He came around to open the passenger door. Temple waltzed in, settling into the purple petals of her crackling skirt.

Matt went around and slipped into the driver's seat.

Temple slung the silver tote bag onto the backseat and smiled dazzlingly. "Drive," she ordered. "Drive me someplace dark."

"It's not dark yet."

"It will be."

"I've got reservations."

"You always have reservations. Luckily, I don't. Drive me someplace dark," she instructed in a Lauren Bacall contralto that came quite naturally when she was feeling playful, "and you won't be sorry."

He drove, looking worried.

Las Vegas spun by, the Strip beginning to light up for the night against a sky still tinted dusky purple and gold and scarlet.

The mountains and clouds came closer; the lights skimmed into the distance. Traffic thinned as the Storm followed Highway 95 north to nowhere.

Temple sat contentedly in the passenger seat, enjoying the rush of motion, letting the city sink behind her and the night open up like a Purple-Passion-colored peony of desert and sky and sunset and mountain and distance.

She began to delve in her tote bag while speaking huskily, like a voice on the car radio, which was not turned on. Yet.

Matt watched the road, not knowing quite where he was going.

She watched his unrevealing profile, knowing exactly where she wanted to go.

"This," she said, "is my prom dress. I never throw out a good dress. It's also a time machine of sorts. Tonight is June third in nineteen seventy-eight and we are going to the senior prom. I bought this dress especially, and you have brought me a lovely gardenia corsage."

She pulled a white florist's box from the tote bag. "Oh, how great, I can pin it anywhere. It won't work on my dress—" she eyed the halter top that bared her shoulders "—but it'll pin perfectly to my headband."

Temple plucked off the purple and silver satin band and affixed the gardenia blooms to its right side. "There." She redonned the band and tilted her head at Matt, who glanced over and nodded dazed agreement.

"You are wearing," she said, staring forward into the distance that was darkening on cue, "a simple white evening jacket, so appropriate. Here's your boutonniere. Nothing garish. I hate tastelessly tinted flowers and so do you."

She leaned across the bucket seat to pin a red carnation to Matt's lapel. He was beginning to look alarmed as well as mystified.

Temple sighed happily and settled back into her seat. "I cannot tell you how wonderful it is to be going to the prom in a decent car. With a decent driver."

"Isn't this prom a little deserted?" he asked tentatively.

She smiled at the expression. Empty desert stretched on each side of the car, with a far, faint twinkle of Las Vegas lights in the rear-view mirror the only civilization. Darkness rang down on the desert with the speed of a black-velvet stage curtain.

"How far do I go?" he asked.

We shall see, thought Temple. "Stop wherever meets my specifications: dark and private."

Despite the emptiness of the land, it was all claimed and every off-road ended in a visible glitter of ownership. Matt finally pulled the Storm up a dirt road, then drove a few feet onto the desert floor before he stopped.

"Temple—"

She held up an imperious hand, like a conductor. This was her Lost Symphony and this time it would be played right.

"They usually hold senior proms nowadays in fancy downtown hotels, where it costs a fortune and everybody is trying to act so cool and so sophisticated. But we attend this tiny high school in a small town and we only have the school gym, all strung with crepe paper and a corny silver-mirrored ball—look, there it is!"

She ducked her head and leaned into the windshield. Matt did too. A full moon obligingly swung into view, tinted blue by the shaded top of the windshield. *Bluooo moo-oon.* Temple had checked in the paper that morning. Perfect timing. O *sole mio.*

Temple pulled a tape cassette from the bottomless maw of her tote bag and popped it into the tape player without pushing it all the way in. "Maybe we should check out the auditorium."

Matt got the cue and came around to open the passenger door.

"Thank you," Temple simpered in sixteen-year-old bliss. Such a polite young lady.

She brought the tote bag with her as she got out and went around to the driver's side of the car. She opened the driver's door so the interior car light came on, then pulled on the headlights Matt had extinguished.

"Oh, the decorating committee did a beautiful job," she raved, stretching her arms up to the star-sprinkled sky.

The sunset was a memory, a last welter of red haloing the mountains' jagged profile. The Storm was an oasis of light in the desert, its headlights beaming into the blue-velvet dark like those huge, sky-sweeping spotlights used at grand openings everywhere.

"Temple. The lights will wear the battery down."

"Not as much as the tape player." She plopped into the Storm's front seat to lean over and push in the tape. She turned up the volume, and music began filling the empty desert air.

When she exited the car, she picked up the tote bag, set it atop the Storm's hood and pulled out a thermos bottle.

"Of course we've got that tacky prom-committee magenta-colored punch that's far too sweet, probably made with Hawaiian Punch, but between you and me, that awful punk

Boots Battista spiked it with vodka, so it tastes a little better."

Temple poured the punch—it was indeed a lurid, red-pink shade—into two plastic cups and offered Matt one.

"Temple," he said, "you're creative and wonderfully crazy, but—"

"Shhh. This is our prom night. The one you never had, and the one I had but shouldn't have. We don't get many second chances. Listen to that music."

"I don't recognize it."

"You will. I specially recorded my all-time favorites. Maybe some of them are a little chronologically off, but, hey, they're classics."

Bob Seger's "We've Got Tonight" was unwinding slowly.

Temple held out her arms. "Let's dance."

Matt stood paralyzed, an untasted cup of Teen Time punch in his hand. "I . . . I don't dance."

"Right. You do martial arts. And the martial arts are designed to keep people at a distance. Dancing isn't." Temple stepped closer, took his plastic cup and put it on the car hood. "Do you . . . shuffle?"

He looked down at their feet, at a dimly visible desert floor hard and sandy, just like a hardwood floor sprinkled with cornmeal for no-slip dancing. Perfect, Temple thought. If only I can bring it off. She put her left hand on his right shoulder. Then you do the hokey-pokey and you turn yourself about. She extended her right hand, elbow crooked, wrist cocked, palm up, like a magician or an emcee presenting something. *Voila!*

"It isn't hard if you try," she softly quoted her current martial-arts instructor.

"Temple—"

We've got tonight, the Bob Seger classic promised, who needs tomorrow? Matt took her hand. The center of his palm was only slightly damp. Better than dweeby Curtis Dixstrom already.

Temple led. For a man who could dance over a poolside mat in dazzling defensive moves, he was a statue on the dance floor, or the desert floor. She had expected herself to lead all the way.

She made sure her shiny purple shoes carefully bracketed his shuffling feet without puncturing toes and listened to the music, moved to the music.

The beat quickened into John Mellencamp's rhythmic teenage anthem. All right, hold tight. Who ever knows if they're doing it right? Amen. Forever and ever amen, as in a country song. No country music unwound on Temple's tape, just soft-rock classics, just distilled teenage angst and ecstasy, just hope pure and simple.

"Stand by Me" segued into "Sometimes When We Touch," with all of its impassioned lyrics and instrumentalization. Temple loved her setting, her lights, action, camera, but she was beginning to feel a teensy bit foolish, despite her determined intention not to. Here she was, dancing with a handsome cigar-store Indian, playing with fire and ice, interfering in something she hardly understood. . . .

Matt's hand suddenly moved to the back of her waist, which he had avoided so far.

Temple held her breath.

He caught her to him, crushed her to him. As embraces went, it was convulsive and awkward, and it took her breath away.

She dared not move. The singer sang, the tape ran on, the moon shone at the same steady rate, her heart beat well above her aerobic target zone, her face was forced sideways into his shoulder, her fragile gardenias were getting bruised by his chin; she could smell their battered fragrance flying free to perfume the whole damn desert. . . .

He stepped back, away from her. She felt like a fool. A failure. Tears stung her eyes. You can't go back, and you can't take anyone with you, not even for their own good. Other people's "own good" often destroyed them, and you as well. She was sorry, so sorry. . . .

Matt looked down at her, as if he had never seen her before. He wasn't touching her anywhere at all now, and the gulf between them was more than a few years and different sexes and different parts of the country and different cultures, different backgrounds . . . it was endless, depthless.

He looked down at her, the moon burnished his blond head, he leaned down

And Temple saw, realized

Temple was back there where innocence began

He was going to kiss her

She knew it

It was probably his first kiss

It was hers

And the moment was perfectly innocent and scary and sweet and she had forgotten everything adult she ever knew; she was just amazed and grateful

And it happened

It went on forever and for not long enough

Their lips touched and that was all

And nobody expected anything beyond the instant

And it was magic.

Again.

Chapter 39

Aftermatt

"Dinner was great," Temple said primly in front of her apartment door. "The restaurant was very understanding about our car breaking down in the desert, and we weren't that late."

Matt nodded agreement, still disoriented by the unexpected evening and trying not to show it. He had been trying not to show anything all night, though the moment of the kiss had slid almost naturally into another song, another shuffle, and then Temple had gathered up her memory-lane props and suggested they try the restaurant.

"I had a wonderful time."

She was saying the stock teenage line as if she meant it, smiling up at him with the gardenias moon-white against her flagrant hair. He would never forget the scent of those gardenias against his chin, storming his nostrils with their heady, honeyed scent. Had she planned even that when she pinned them to her headband? He was beginning to recognize that Temple was a peerless organizer of special events, from public-relations campaigns and murder investigations to ambushed emotions.

"It was the Perfect Prom, Matt. Trust me; I'm an expert on imperfect proms. Perfect. And they almost never are."

"It was a little late."

She shrugged. "I'd better get in, or my folks will be blinking the porch light. They do that kind of thing."

He glanced at the eternally lit carriage lamp beside the door, wondering if he should kiss her again, kiss her good-night. He didn't want to, not on the brink of this threshold so identical to his own, in these familiar surroundings, under the glaring light. . . .

Matt took her shoulders—bare, a foreign surface, an intimacy—and bent down and kissed the top of her head. It was his Perfect Prom, too.

Temple smiled that smile women have sometimes, the one that is accepting and undemanding, and slipped inside her already unlocked door.

He was surprised a few moments later to find himself standing by the elevator, dumbly waiting. Usually he walked a single flight; tonight he moved in a numb cocoon. Father Hernandez flashed into his mind. He would have to keep in touch with him; he was responsible now for the secrets that he knew and kept, not only for Father Rafe's sobriety, but for his innocence.

He walked off the elevator without remembering being on it and let himself into his unit.

"What the—?"

An island of items sat in the middle of his bare floor, as if a visiting child had piled some toys there: an ivory plastic tray filled with grayish sand and a slotted spatula. A set of stainless-steel dishes, one filled with water, one with a mound of noxious-looking green pellets. A plastic jug with a label reading "Pretty Paws." A box labeled "Free-to-be-Feline." He looked around.

A lean little black cat reclined on his Goodwill sofa like a pagan idol, front paws stretched long before it, golden eyes regarding him with the aloof interest typical of the breed.

Matt bent to retrieve the white envelope atop the Free-to-be-Feline and read the note inside.

"Electra managed the transfer while we were out dancing. Give this nice kitty a chance! Cats are quiet and clean, cheap, and make great companions—and Louie is major miffed about another set of paws around the place. Her name is Caviar, but you can call her anything you like. Pretty please! Temple."

Matt looked back at the cat, who suddenly leaped off the couch and approached him with mincing, silent steps. She walked like a runway fashion model, each long leg slightly crossing the other with every step.

The envelope also contained a coupon for spaying at the "veterinarian of your choice."

Matt sighed as the animal massaged his calves, leaving short black hairs on his slacks. He gave it a cursory pet and it began purring. It had spent some time with Temple, all right.

He checked his watch—almost eleven. He wasn't used to winding down at this early hour, but the television in the bedroom didn't attract him. Maybe getting the cat settled would distract him, not that it meant that he would keep it. Her.

She followed him into the kitchen as he moved the food, and leaped atop the countertop with a happy chirrup.

"I hope you're not a spy, Caviar," he told her. "I don't need any turncoats reporting back to Temple; she's nosy enough already."

His voice echoed strangely in the rooms bare of rugs and furniture. He realized that he never had anybody visit him here, that he was always utterly alone in his home and as silent as a monk in his cell.

Matt wasn't sure that having a cat to talk to was much improvement in his private life. He went into the bedroom, where the futon was perpetually unrolled on the floor, where the small color TV sat on a secondhand brass stand, where two cheap particle-board bookcases formed the biggest solid front of furniture in the place.

He turned on the television without checking the channel or the program schedule from the Sunday paper. Was this room that much different from the cell Peter Burns was occupying at this moment? Was he himself as imprisoned by his lifelong past with the church as poor, crazed Peter, whose obsession with what he hated about the church had directed his entire life?

Matt sat on the lone kitchen chair that served as an informal clothes tree and took off his shoes—black wing-tips left over from parish priest days and still so suitable for more formal civilian occasions. And socks, also black.

He threw them across the room. They silently hit the wall and fell to the floor, looking like dead bats.

Temple was crazy! Out of her mind to mess with his life that had already been messed up so thoroughly by other people. By family, such as it was. She didn't know, even with her investigative instincts, what she was getting involved in. He had wanted to hit her with the ugly reality, to shout it out. The church's dirty laundry was coming out in the wash with a vengeance these days, and the statistics, although vague guesstimates shrouded in secrecy, weren't pretty, given the traditional noble concept of the priesthood: up to fifty percent of priests were not celibate; as many as thirty-five to forty percent were gay. Most priests, however sincere their vocation and their spirituality, had found a home in the church precisely because their families had failed them in some way. Some families had failed so spectacularly that young seminarians were unconscious of the hidden booby traps in their own psyches. Now, in public, idols were falling on all sides, all answering to the name of "Father."

Not him. Not anymore. And he had made none of the traditional missteps, had nothing sinful to hide. Perhaps that was his biggest failing. He had been too successfully inhuman.

Matt shut his eyes in the bright room. He knew his own history like a longterm shrink. He knew the whens, the whats, the whys. The only thing he didn't know was how to escape it, overcome it, resolve it, integrate—in psychobabble jargon—the past with present and future.

His sexual future was the least of his worries, and now Temple had confronted that in her own inimitable way. He was surprised to find himself smiling in the middle of his sober thoughts. He knew no one—no woman—who could have confronted the issue in that innovative, intuitive way and pulled it off.

She had literally taken him back in time to a point from which he could now consider a different path. And she'd done it with such a brilliant, whimsical and determined piece of role-playing that to disappoint her and not play along would be like taking a Baby Ruth bar from Shirley Temple. Despite her small size, her youth, her fey good looks that she always felt held her back, Temple was implacably supportive and a very wise old soul in her way.

For the first time, Matt's eternal, invisible force field of restraint, of distance, of sexual repression, had cracked all at the same instant, and the breakthrough had seemed so natural, so innocent for the fractured seconds of the high-school kiss.

After Eden came the flaming sword. He winced as he metaphorically peered into the closet in his soul and the emotions Temple had triggered that night peeked out. Some surprised him. Fear, and pride. Fear of acting like a fool, of being bad at something any man his age knew inside and out. Fondness and begrudging gratitude. But no guilt. It was a Perfect Prom for him, too, like the music she had provided that was neither too fast nor too slow, too little or too much, too cold or too hot—a swift trip to the past, with no more pressure than he could handle at the moment.

Emotions he could control; he had been doing it all his life. Where emotion and instinct and hormones intersect, though, is a true battleground. He still had hormones, Matt was discovering now that he was alone, despite his long and mostly successful attempts to disown them. The instant they raised their imperative heads, he summoned conscience to beat them back.

Temple had recently been deserted by a man who had meant a great deal to her, he reminded himself. She was vulnerable; perhaps she was attracted to him precisely because he was certain not to rush her into more than she could handle now. And there was the challenge: women couldn't resist the kind of challenge he represented. And the more they tested him, the more he resisted, as if his life depended on remaining unmanipulated, uncontrolled.

And then there was that teenage self of his, who longed for love and understanding, who had sacrificed sex in order to be something better than he thought he was and who now, disillusioned to his sensitive, randy soul, was perfectly capable of being just what Temple wanted, because the closet door could burst open now that Father Matt was no longer there to guard it and so much time had been lost, and she was a sweet, mostly safe human being and he could think about taking advantage of her, using her to ease his own way into the real world he had never been part of.

That realization made him understand the priests who had failed, made him understand that he could still very easily become one of them, despite having left the priesthood.

Matt opened his eyes to the empty, dazzling-white walls, then went to the bathroom. He knew what he should do now: the seminary cold-shower trick that they all had joked about. "The needles of death."

He stripped off his clothes quickly, as if disowning them, but he was not quick enough to avoid glimpsing his bare body in the long slit of mirror on the bathroom door.

He avoided seeing himself in mirrors, dressed or undressed. Being a stranger to himself was part of being a mentor to everybody else. But for a split second, he saw himself as someone else, a true stranger, and he glimpsed for the first time what others might find attractive in his face and body, what a woman might be drawn to.

The insight scalded him with unwanted intimacy with himself. He was used to thinking of himself as the edited outline of a man, like the male figure sent into space by NASA, genitals diplomatically erased like evidence of an unfortunate malformation, as in so many images of modern men. Today's vaunted sexual frankness built its bawdy-house on the same foundation of nineteenth-century prudery and shame upon which the church had erected its sexual orthodoxy.

He stepped into the deep white bathtub and reached for the shower knob, an old-fashioned porcelain ship's-wheel shape with the word "COLD" printed at its center—cold water like a dash of reality, shriveling, almost painful. But he wasn't in the seminary anymore. He reached instead for the knob marked "HOT" and turned it slowly.

It came out cold at first anyway. As it warmed, he fed in some cold until hot, flaming swords of water flogged him and steam rose and hissed all around him, fogging the long mirror on the door and the square mirror on the medicine chest.

When he picked up the bar of soap from the built-in holder, he could have sworn that for a moment he smelled gardenias.

Chapter 40

Louie Dines on Crow

At last I have the old place to myself again, and can look forward to having my delightful roommate to myself, too. A gentleman needs the presence of a person of the female persuasion, especially if she is unrelated to him.

Miss Temple Barr has been gadding about a bit of late with Mr. Matt Devine, and although I am pleased at the absence of the troublesome Caviar, I am more than somewhat miffed when Miss Temple Barr comes home wearing a particularly sumptuous gown, whose full skirt would make a most pleasing bed, and rushes right past me without a word.

She does not even check the Free-to-be-Feline bowl, and I have been gracious enough to show my approval of my exclusive residency by actually gumming a few of the pellets down!

I repair to the bedroom to find her sitting on the bed. I

would leap joyfully into that inviting lap, but Miss Temple Barr has her hands on her lap, which normally would not stop me—she can move them—but they are holding some sort of hair collar and affixed to it are two pale floral blooms that broadcast the most revolting odor I have ever encountered.

Miss Temple Barr shows no inclination to change her position or throw away the reeking growths. In fact, her olfactory faculties must have hit a down day, for she sits there smiling and actually raises the abominations to her nose.

I do understand that persons of her species are sadly lacking in nasal abilities, but this is ridiculous. To further add to my impression that she has become completely unhinged, she then gets up and goes into the kitchen.

I follow quickly, expecting some tender treat from the meat drawer in the refrigerator.

Apparently her eyes have also been affected by this strange malady, for she opens the refrigerator and puts the foul flowers inside. Then she closes it *without selecting a tidbit for me.*

I have not witnessed such irresponsible behavior in years. I am forced to express myself, at which she looks down at me with a fond smile.

"Louie," she says, as if seeing me for the first time, as if I have not always been there but jumped out of the refrigerator or something. "Are you happy now with Caviar gone?"

I would be happier with some caviar in front of me.

Miss Temple moves to the opposite counter and fusses with something. My hopes perk up.

She turns while emptying a thermos container into a tumbler. A dark, bloodlike liquid crests in the glass before she stops. Then she picks up the small box that plays music and returns to the bedroom—all the while without feeding me anything.

After a slow, shocked start, I race after her.

Miss Temple Barr is bending over the bedroom stereo

machine, which she has not used since my arrival, although I see a dusty stack of Vangelis cassettes piled beside it that I suspect are among the last traces of the vanished Mystifying Max.

Instantly a blast of loud, rhythmic so-called music is pouring into the room. I am not against music, but I lean to improvisational jazz in an outdoor setting; indoors, I prefer something smooth and classic that aids the digestion, like harp solos.

This is not either. How is a dude to sleep with such a racket going on?

I can see that this is not Miss Temple Barr's worry. She is busy removing her garments, without bothering to remove herself from my presence, which is once again forgotten.

I turn my back, which courtesy she overlooks.

When I next see her, she is not wearing the usual Garfield T-shirt, which I abhor (that could be *my* kisser on every chest in America!). Perhaps she wishes to make amends, and I must say that this filmy garment will go far to accomplishing exactly that, and I am not of the same species even.

Miss Temple Barr sings along to the tape while she performs her evening ablutions in the bathroom. I never like to witness humans at the act of cleaning themselves. They make such a mess of it and use so many unnecessary implements when a good, long lick would do as well and is always available in every circumstance.

On occasion I attempt to demonstrate my methods to Miss Temple Barr, but she mistakes my grooming lesson for affection.

She turns off the lights and occupies the bed.

Under the cover of darkness, I leap up and decide to investigate what might have driven her slightly mad. Cautiously, I sniff along her arm and discern the lingering scent of the awful flowers.

I am not against greenery, being a connoisseur of the

catnip variety, but these stinky pale flowers are dangerous.

I had hoped to hear a word or two dropped about the case, but will obviously hear no more than these lovesick wailings on the stereo. I am beginning to think that my, er, purported relative is right in the belief that a simple operation can remove many of the compulsions of the single life.

So I am left to muse on my own affairs, which recently included a visit and report to the landlady's companion, Karma.

I tell Her Sacredness that her predictions do not have much relevance. When I tell her the name and profession of the criminal, she interrupts me with an imperious mew.

"A lawyer, you say? It was in the Tarot."

"You mentioned all sorts of high-toned occupations: Empress, and this here Hierophant, but no lawyers."

"But I told you that Libra was a key. Do you not see? Libra's symbol is the scales."

"I like fish myself."

"No, that is Pisces, you fool."

"I thought the Fool was one of your fancy cards."

"It is. The scales that represent Libra is that metal instrument used to weigh goods—"

"Aw, why did you not say so in the first place? I have seen the like in several meat shops."

"And," she adds with a triumphant little tail shake that I do not find at all alluring, but then, she is not my type, which is unusual as I am a pretty liberal dude usually in such matters. "And . . . the scales are used as the symbol of justice. So there is your lawyer predicted by the cards, if you were intelligent enough to see it."

"Your cards always predict what has already happened," I grumble. "What else do you claim?"

"Your account is full of Father Hernandez. I told you the Hierophant would be a key figure."

"He did not do that much, except hide out a lot and indulge in unpriestly behaviors, like drinking."

"Also the card of Temperance showed up. It is astonishing how much the cards tried to tell. They cannot be blamed if the recipient is deficient. Or simply deaf to the spiritual."

"The Tarot cards did not mention anything about me being bagged by a dude who wanted to turn me into a decorative door hanging."

"The cards spoke. You did not listen."

Apparently, Karma is not too strong in the listening department, either.

I shake my head and slink off. I must admit, however, that I have been instrumental in resolving the fate of dozens of cats, as duly predicted. Had I not been sniffing around Mr. Matt Devine and the Tyler house, had I not been nabbed, who is to say that the murderer of Miss Tyler might have gone undetected and the money might not have finally come to its rightful inheritors—cats and Catholics?

As I work my way down two floors to my own abode, where I anticipate a fond reunion with Miss Temple Barr, I reflect on some disturbing words from my departing, er, alleged offspring.

Although I am much relieved to see the industrious Miss Electra Lark gathering Caviar's belongings into a pile preparatory to moving out the whole kit and kaboodle, my joy is short-lived.

Just before she is swooped up by Miss Electra Lark and borne elsewhere, I care not where, she manages to whisper a parting phrase in my shell-like inner ear.

"It is a good thing," she says, "that I left a message about your whereabouts for Miss Temple Barr while you were being detained by a burlap bag."

"You? You left a message? How?"

"Some sleight of paw with a newspaper and the Free-to-be-Feline. You really should eat that stuff. Not only is it excellent nutritionally speaking, but it literally saved your hide."

"Naw," I say. "You have not got the street smarts to

start manipulating people in this shameless manner. It takes years to develop the skill."

"Maybe," she says in an ignorantly cruel parting shot, "it runs in the feline family."

Happy as I am to see the last of her tail, I am equally morose to remain alone to await Miss Temple, while I contemplate the fact that the lady sometimes known as Midnight Louise may be righter than she knows. She might indeed be kin.

Even now as I lie on my own bed and relive my humiliating recent conversations of the cat kind, I am jerked out of my reverie when Miss Temple Barr rolls over on me like a petite ton of bricks. She is exceedingly restless tonight.

Her hand clutches my belly fur, then tickles me.

"Perfect," she murmurs in a sleepy, sappy voice.

At least she has finally given me my due. I am at last able to slip off to Lullabye Land, where it is no surprise to find myself dreaming of carp, caviar, catnip and crime.

Midnight Louie Objects

I am nit one to complane, since I am well aware that this iz knot a becoming posture. But I have knot been treeted in a flattering manner in this pease of outwright fixshun.

Number one, I waz left languizhing in the literal bag at the clymaxx, when I actua!!y had the situashun well under controll and waz about to spring a surprize exit on the perpatraitor and leed a lejion of catz to Miss Temple's resque. If she had not taken matterz into her own pretty little feet and made like Nansi Ninja, I cud have performed my custamary rezcue operashun with my usua! elan, instead of being depicted as gooffy and foggy and in kneed of artifishial oxygen. This iz the true fixshun!

Franklee, I have been ill-treeted by the females of all speeshees in this book.

First, Miss Temple Barr showz unpressadented indifferens to my wants, kneeds and even my whereabowts until the very end. I do not thing that her obsesshun with Mr. Matt Devine bodes well for eether of them, or for my well-being.

Second, I am subjeckted to the metafizzical mewlings of the know-it-a!! (espesheally after eventz have unwownd) Karma, Miss Electra Lark's undercover psykkic lady Birman.

Third, I am confronted with the pateete but hostil Caviar, aka Midnight Louise, tresspessing on my own turff and on my own name, which has a sertin cashay in thiz town and a sertin fame (well-dezerved) far beyond it.

Besidez espousing some noxsheous notions, this Midnight Louise individual showz dizturbing signz of hanging arownd. Do I sniff spin-off here? I can only hope that she wi!! distrackt Mr. Matt Devine long enuff to keep him aweigh from Miss Temple, or vice versa, but I am not sangwine (espesialee after my forced blood-doner duty).

Even my blue-ribban performance at the cat show has been made lite of!

I am az mad az he!! and I will not ~~take~~ take it anymore.

Midnight Louie, his mark
(not made in ink this time! You figyure it out}

Carole Nelson Douglas Rejects

Louie, Louie, Louie. . . .

Often, in the heat of finishing a book, I inadvertently leave the computer on overnight.

When I do, I return in the morning expecting the pleasure of printing out my full opus, only to find that Midnight Louie has lived up to his name and has left what an acerbic friend of mine calls a "love note."

It pains me to reveal that Louie uses a somewhat heavy paw when tripping over the keyboard. I usually "clean up" his typographical errors, not to mention his many misspellings. Despite his innate intelligence and formidable vocabulary (even his grammatical airs, I could say), his education was strictly on the street. This time, given the nature of his complaints, I have reproduced his endeavors uncensored.

You can see why I am named as sole author of these

exercises: printed unedited, Louie's portions would be incomprehensible except to fanatical cipher-solvers.

As for the throng of his complaints, only one deserves comment: at one time—in fact, at most times in the history of the world—the male of every species won applause for propagational performance. But times have changed. Not only are modern minds aware of the horrors of overpopulation, but modern female minds are all too aware that their assigned role in this scheme of things was exploitive of them.

The mathematical chances of a gentleman of the old school—like Louie—encountering one of his many unacknowledged offspring are staggering, as are the numbers of offspring one tomcat can sire in even a short lifetime. We are talking thousands here.

So he is lucky that his encounter with Midnight Louise, or the like, did not occur years earlier. Perhaps he has heard of the phrase, "sins of the fathers"? Nor should he be surprised that a female of any species is less likely in these enlightened days to be seduced into the former view of her place in the world: prone.

In fact, Louie should be proud that at least one of his offspring has demonstrated the ability to adapt to a modern world where responsibility for one's actions and offspring—and indeed, for the good of the species—is more prized than the old swaggering machismo of promiscuous propagation.

I don't like to stand on soapboxes, but Louie has aggravated me one time too many. He had better watch out, or I might find the keyboard taking steps of a neutering nature toward him at some future time.

It is nit nice to make fun ov the mannue!!y cha!!enged. Wait till next tome! Lllouie

Oops, left it on again!